Pivot Line

Pivot Line

rebel farris

THE
FALLING SMALL
DUET, PART TWO

Cover Illustration by **Javier Chavarria of MaelDesign.com**
Cover Design by **Regina Wamba of MaelDesign.com**
Interior Graphics from **Depositphoto.com**
Edited by **Sandra Depukat of One Love Editing**
Proofread by **Jenn Wood of All About The Edits**
Formatted by **Erik Gevers**
Poetry of Michael E. Reid used by permission of **Michael E. Reid**

For every boy or man I loved and lost throughout my life.

*Thank you for teaching me what it means to love and be loved.
Though we may not have had the real thing—your role in my life
taught me valuable lessons, and sometimes the most painful
lessons are the ones we really needed to learn.*

Dear Woman

Sometimes

You'll just be too much woman.

Too smart,

Too beautiful,

Too strong.

Too much of something

That makes a man feel like less of a man,

Which will start making you feel like you have to be less of a

woman.

The biggest mistake you can make

Is removing jewels from your crown

To make it easier for a man to carry.

When this happens, I need you to understand,

You do not need a smaller crown—

You need a man with bigger hands.

—Michael E Reid
Dear Woman, 2015

Chapter One

Now

I killed Jared. I can't believe the words ever came out of my mouth again. How many times did they tell me talking like that would get me nowhere? Bridget would be livid if she heard those words again. My hands are shaking. The room seems to spin. I gasp for breath before a sob forces its way out.

The cab of the truck is silent except for the muted sounds of navigating the streets of Austin. I drop my phone into my lap and look at Asher. His brow is furrowed and his jaw ticks. He's angry. But there's a tinge of sadness in his eyes like he knows that this is the end of the tour. The end of our band. And I can't stop the flood of guilt—I'm the cause of that.

The fog is thick, settled over the city like a heavy blanket. It feels foreboding, but I'm sure it's just the situation. The reason we are in this truck to begin with.

He pulls the truck into the parking lot of the recording studio, and I can feel immediately that something is off. Even before I open the door— the fog swirling with the movement—and hear the piercing wail of the building's alarm, I feel it. Shutting the truck door, I take a deep breath, steeling myself for the reckoning that is about to happen. The moist air fills my lungs. It feels heavy like my heart, my stomach. How did we get to this point?

I can't see more than a couple of feet in front of my face, but the flashing red lights of the alarm color the fog between me and the building, showing the way. Asher joins me once we reach the sidewalk leading to the building, but stays silent. Step by step on shaky legs, I move closer. Closer to the love of my life. Closer to facing the consequence of my decisions. Shattered glass crunches under my borrowed shoes as I reach the front door that is nothing more than a metal frame now.

Blinking, I clear the memories. That's not a path I need to go down. Not now.

Dex is sitting next to me, holding me across his lap. He pulls back and brushes the hair away from my face before running his thumb over my cheek to chase away the tears. He believes me. I can see it in his eyes. It's not pity; it's heartbreak. His eyes say he knows I'm responsible and he doesn't want me to have to live with it. He gathers me in his arms and sighs. I'm not exactly sure what he's thinking, but his gun is still sitting on the floor in front of me, and he's not telling me that I'm under arrest. Nor is he trying to placate me with words about how I'm not at fault. That's a bit of a relief.

"What am I going to do with you?" His voice breaks through the quiet patter of raindrops on the office windows.

His brows are drawn together as I lean back to look at him. "That's it?"

His shoulders tense. "What do you want me to say?"

"I don't know. You're under arrest... or something? Isn't that what you wanted? A confession? I'm so tired of fighting this. If you're gonna arrest me, just do it." My arms hang limply at my sides as he lets me go.

His hands move to frame my face, his sea-green eyes locking onto mine. "No. That's not what I want. It never has been. I'm not lying to you, Mads. I've seen the evidence. I know you didn't do it and I'm going to prove it. I've been looking for another angle, something that Martinez hasn't considered, but I haven't even found a place to start. I'm gonna end this for you. I promise. I want you to tell me everything about that night when you're ready." His eyes close and his lips brush over mine tenderly. "But I think we should call it a day and head home right now. I'll go next door and tell Nate that we're leaving. Will the receptionist cancel your appointments?" He sighs again, leaning his forehead against mine.

I nod, speechless and a bit dazed.

"I'll go talk to her, too. Just gather your stuff to leave. When we get home, we'll deal with all of this. Together."

I reach out and skim my thumb over his bottom lip. A shiver runs throughout his body, and I feel it when it reaches his hands that still bracket my face. The corner of my mouth tugs upward slightly. I like that I seem to have the same effect on him. He half-heartedly smiles back at me and places a quick kiss on my lips before standing up. He silently picks up his gun and puts it back in the holster.

My eyes are glued to him as he walks with an athletic grace toward the door. He stops and looks back at me once more.

"Be right back," he says. There's a hint of exhaustion in his voice, like he just fought a battle.

And perhaps we did because I feel it, too.

Sitting there for a minute, I stare at the door. I don't want to get anywhere near that video again. There's a feeling creeping up my spine, like even coming close to the computer will make it start playing. Releasing a breath through my nose, I steel myself. I grab my computer case from the closet, then walk to the desk, pushing the laptop shut and disconnecting the power cord.

With that taken care of, I gather my purse and look around for anything else. The sight of Evan's phone on my coffee table sends a pang through me. I scoop it up and clutch it to my chest. That's it. I take a deep breath and turn to the door. Dex is there, waiting for me. He holds out his hand, and I take it.

Minutes later, I'm sitting in the passenger seat of my car, heading home. My mind is replaying everything that has happened today from the time I woke up, but it all comes to a screeching halt when I remember one thing he said.

"What did you mean by *we need to talk?*" I ask.

"Yeah," he says absently. "That reminds me—"

"You do understand that those words are like the international lead-in to a breakup, right?" I interrupt him.

"What?" His face scrunches as he briefly takes his eyes off the road to glance at me. "That's not what I meant. I wanted to run through possible suspects with you and get your thoughts on them."

"What do you mean?"

"It's likely the stalker's someone you know."

"It took you the last almost two months to come to that conclusion? Because Martinez was saying that years ago, but it never helped because everyone checked out, had alibis and such."

"You don't think there's a way they could get around something like that?" His lips tip down into a half frown. "I'm just thinking about all the evidence, and there seems to be a protective vibe, you know? That tells me that the motivation isn't sexual, it's caring. Twisted, but still good intentioned. And it stands to reason, with all these people surrounding you, who care for you, one of them might be the suspect."

"That's ridiculous. None of my friends are stalking me. They know what all this has done to me and that it hurts more than helps, so I don't buy that at all."

"What about Nic? He hasn't been around much, and he has access to your house—"

"I trust Nic more than most people in my life. No. He wouldn't do that."

"What about that guy Asher?" he asks.

"Asher has been in Atlanta for weeks. On a commercial flight when the stalker was at the mall."

"What about—"

"Dex, just don't. It's not a great way to start a relationship, accusing my friends of shit they wouldn't do, and making me pissed off at you in the process."

"We're in a relationship?" he asks, threading his fingers

through mine and raising my hand to his lips. He kisses the back of my hand and smiles.

"I didn't—" My mouth opens and closes as I flounder for the words.

"I get it. I had a nice long conversation with someone who knows you far better than me, so I understand. I'm in it for the long haul. I have a feeling that when you realize what this means to you, I'm gonna be a lucky man."

He kisses my hand again as we pull into the garage at my house. I take a deep breath, not knowing what to say, so I say nothing. I don't understand what I feel for him. I haven't had time to think about it. Police, paparazzi, stalkers, FBI, US Marshals, Chloe and Evan leaving... it's all too much. Last night feels like so long ago when I think of all that's happened since we left the park.

"Let's get you inside," he says, turning off the car.

Then

"I'm moving into the house," Jared said as he sat on the couch next to me.

We'd finally gotten the girls to sleep after several hours of coaxing and assuring them that everything was going to be okay. It took several hours, giving statements to the police, handing over the flowers as evidence, being treated for shock by the EMTs out of the back of an ambulance, and then finally walking home.

I started to reply, but he halted my words when he spoke again.

"I don't like that he's been in this house. Especially because he's taken an interest in the girls, but also because I'm worried about you, Maddie. I don't like that I could be thirty feet away from the house if something were to happen. I know how you feel about me right now, but this changes things. I can take one of the rooms upstairs, and if anything happens, I'm here."

"Okay," I answered quietly.

"Okay?"

"Okay, I get it." My voice rose in defense. "Frankly, I don't want to be here alone right now anyway."

"Really? You're not going to fight me on this?" he asked, looking dumbfounded.

"You act like I'm irrational. Since when have I ever defied common sense?" I stood up and started to pace. "Someone has broken into my home, has been watching me for God knows how long. I can protect myself, but I'm not stupid enough to turn down help. I don't care who it comes from." I choked back a sob that was threatening to come out. "Jared, he was with our girls. He could've taken them. I'm not going to take any chances, not with them."

"Okay. I'm also going to call a security company and have a security system installed tomorrow. You okay with that too?"

"Yeah, sounds good," I said absently.

My mind kept running through my entire life, searching for clues to who it could be. What did I do that could've invited such behavior? It had to be something around the time we went to Germany, but I was drawing a blank as to what that might be. I couldn't think of anyone suspicious hanging around.

"Hey, I'm sorry about this." Jared stopped my pacing, grasping my shoulders and blocking my path.

"It's not your fault," I sighed. "I just feel so stupid. I had to've done something to invite this, but honestly, the only thing I can think of is the band. Maybe it's a deranged fan, pissed about the band breaking up. Though, even that doesn't make much sense—we were never that popular. That's the only thing I can think of at the moment. I can't even fathom another scenario."

"Does it matter? Who knows why they're doing it? You can't always explain crazy. The only thing that matters is that we stay safe and that the police catch him." He tipped my chin up to meet his eyes.

The guilt forced me to look away, and I broke from his hold to continue pacing. "Did Officer Martinez tell you when they expect to have the results of the testing they're doing on the flowers?"

"Yeah, he said he'd probably stop by tomorrow once the report gets processed. He told me you might need to meet with a detective. If they decide to investigate."

I stopped in my tracks. "What do you mean, *if* they decide to investigate? There's even a chance that they won't look into it?" I turned back to face him.

"Maddie, there isn't much to go on." He sighed, running a hand over his head. "Just your word that you had flowers show up in your room and a guy giving our girls a flower at the park. It isn't exactly a violent crime."

I felt the sudden urge to throw something well up in me. All the frustration, fear, and anger needing an outlet, a release. I reached for the first object within reach without thinking.

"That's bullshit! Someone broke into my dorm and now my house to leave those flowers. That's fucking creepy. Do you have any idea what that feels like?" I looked down at my hands and realized I was holding onto a clay bowl that Cora made at school. She'd be devastated if I broke it. The thought grounded me as I set it back down.

"Of course I do." He was in front of me as I straightened. "I feel that way, too. I don't like it either. Because I love you and the girls, Maddie. I care about what happens to you as if it were happening to me, too." He reaches out to touch my cheek.

"You've gotta stop fucking saying that." I slapped his hand away. "I've got enough to deal with at the moment."

"No," he said.

"What the fuck do you mean, no?"

"I mean no, I will not stop telling you that I love you. I will not stop fighting for you. I'm never going to leave your side, and if you want to keep pushing me away, that's fine. Push all you want, but I'm not going to leave you alone ever again. You wouldn't be fighting this so hard if you didn't care.

7

Deep down, I know you feel this. This—you and me. What we have. Something like that doesn't go away."

"What if I'm fighting it because I'm still in love with him—you ever think about that?" I spat the words at him.

"Fuck it," he said and took the step to close the distance between us.

His hand dove into my hair, and he pulled my face to his. Faster than I could blink, his mouth descended on mine. It felt like we were moving in slow motion. At the first contact, tingles spread over my lips. My heart raced, and goose bumps chased a shiver that echoed throughout my whole body. I wanted to fight it, but the sensations he was causing were stunning me into inaction. I'd forgotten that indescribable magic pull he held over me. I opened for him, and his tongue drove in, twisting with mine. I lost all coherent thought as the familiar taste and smell of him filled my senses, sending my brain into overload. He pressed his body flush against mine, and I surrendered to him.

Moments later, he pulled back, resting his forehead on mine. "You feel that? People die for that feeling. They start wars and conquer impossible odds for that," he whispered between heaving breaths. "That's real, and I'm not walking away from it."

He pushed a loose strand of hair behind my ear as his eyes searched mine. I remembered the same look on his face just before he told me we were through. Coming to my senses then, I pushed him away. I wasn't doing this with him.

"You can't love two people. And I know I love him. So, you can take your little demonstrative kisses and shove them up your ass. We—we are not doing this. Ever. Again."

Turning, I ran to my room, away from him. Ashamed of my traitorous body and the stupid way he made me feel. All I could think about was how shitty it felt when he left, and I knew I never want to travel down that road again. Not with him. We had no epic romance. Fairy tales did not involve the prince up and leaving the princess for years to find herself, before they could have their happily ever after. That wasn't the way it worked. There was no such thing as true love. What I felt for Law was proof of that. Jared could try to convince me until the day we died that we had something epic, but I'd never risk my heart with him again.

Chapter Two

Now

I open the back door, and the alarm starts its warning beeps. I toss the laptop bag, my purse, and keys on the kitchen counter and hurry over to the panel. Once the beeping stops, the quiet of the house becomes evident.

Everyone is gone. The girls are at school, Nic's at his place, and Evan left with Chloe. Nic doesn't live here full-time. He has a room here that he uses when the loneliness of his lifestyle becomes too much for him. Here, he has family and love.

I know the feeling all too well, myself. It's the quiet moments that everything becomes too much to bear. When the sound of silence is so deafening, you can't think beyond it. It echoes in your ear, forcing your darkest thoughts to repeat in your mind on a loop.

The snick of the door shutting behind me reminds me that I'm not alone. The realization settles in my mind that this is the first time Dex and I've been truly alone. Well, if you don't count our failed romp in the car.

I take a deep breath and turn to face him. "Looks like we have the place to our—"

I'm cut off as his lips descend on mine.

A shiver runs down my spine at the contact. My heart

races double time. Dex sweeps his fingertips down the side of my arms, leaving a trail of goose bumps in their wake. He curls his hand around the back of my neck while his thumb teases over the pulse point in my neck. An involuntary moan escapes me, and I gasp as I pull away.

"What do you want, Maddie?" he murmurs as he lets go of my neck to smooth his hand down my back.

"I don't know." I search his face. "I mean, I do know. I just don't know how to tell you. I've never had to do this before. I just—I don't think I'm ready."

"What if you're never ready? You willing to pass up a good thing because you're too afraid to leap?"

I close my eyes. Dex's thumb traces my lower lip. I shudder, spurred by the heightened sensation of the contact. His touch feels almost electric. I open my eyes to find him watching me, not missing a thing.

"Everything that's been happening scares me, but it all pales in comparison to the way you scare me, Dex."

"I don't know how to get you past whatever is holding you back," he says, shaking his head slowly. "I've never been so sure about something in my whole life."

I break away and walk back to my bedroom to do something other than this.

"You can't say that about someone you don't know. And you don't know me—the other half. The part that only close friends and lovers know is so different from the person I am every day. What happens to me when you see that side and decide it's not for you? I can't go through that. I can't open myself up to something like that right now."

"We all have our secrets. Everyone is hiding something. Sometimes we just have to trust that when we're ready to share the heavy stuff, love will be enough to overlook our faults. Just let it go and let me decide. I'm never gonna do anything to hurt you on purpose."

I stop in the middle of my bedroom and close my eyes, considering his words. No one can guarantee they won't hurt another person. I know that better than most.

"Some lose all mind and become soul, insane," Dex quotes. *"Some lose all soul and become mind, intellectual."*

"Some lose both and become accepted," I finish for him, cocking my head to the side. "I didn't take you for a hipster." I raise an eyebrow at him for quoting Charles Bukowski to me.

He shrugs. "I'm an artist. And it's the best way to get my point across." He shifts a bit, looking uncomfortable. "We're all some mixture of mind and soul. My theory's always been that when you meet that person you're willing to work for, it's because their level matches your own. Maybe not in the same way, or for the same reasons, but enough for them to accept you as you are."

"How do you know?" I take a step toward him. "How do you know I'm at your level? You don't even know me."

"It's hard not to recognize when you're staring at a piece of yourself. I told you about my mom and my past and you didn't even bat an eyelash. Instead, what I got was just a taste. An hour of what it feels like to have your trust. I've watched you since the moment I met you. You embrace life in the little moments. You're compassionate. Hell, in the short time I've been shadowing you, I've met at least fifty people who rely on your kindness in some way. You're not just talented, but smart, and successful beyond most people our age. You're strong because most people would've buckled under this situation and run or hide. But there's also a darkness to you, and in some ways you're broken. I get that. What I don't get is, why don't you see it?"

"See what?"

"All of that. Everything that makes you, you. And all the reasons I've fallen in love with you."

I draw in a breath and hold it. I freeze because I just don't know what to say. Dex crosses the space between us in two short strides and cups my face. His eyes search mine.

"Don't. Don't freeze up. I don't expect you to say it back. I don't expect you even to know how you feel. You haven't had time to breathe yet. I just can't keep it in anymore. I love you. That's not going to change, no matter what you're hiding."

He kisses me. It starts out slow, lingering. A gentle exploration. He slides his hand to the back of my head, while his other arm wraps around my waist, pulling me to him.

"Just breathe, Maddie," he whispers.

"I can't," I say, pushing away from him. "I think we did this all wrong. If I'd met you some other way, if you knew the other stuff first, then I could believe you and this would work. But you've inserted yourself into my life. I can't just think about the fallout of my secrets in terms of myself. And that's always going to be a problem."

"You're saying that if we can't make a go of a relationship, we can't be friends?"

"No," I say. "I'm not—I don't know." I shake my head, rubbing my temples.

"I'm not saying this because I think it's necessary, but if you need reassurances, I'll still be around if things don't work out. I love your girls almost as much as I love you. And Audra loves you, too."

"I don't know." I sigh. "I don't know how to do this. Any of it."

"Just let go."

His breath caresses my shoulder one second before he presses his lips to my skin. A fine shiver courses through me, and I can't deny one thing—I want him. I don't know why. It defies all my rational thoughts. *Fuck it.* I turn and grasp his face, pulling him down to me. I kiss him. I'm not gentle or loving. I'm ravenous. Turning off every nagging thought in my head, I let go. Every doubt and worry fall away as his hands cup my thighs and he lifts me in an effortless motion. I wrap my legs around his waist.

Wetness pools between my legs at the feel of him. His strength, his size, the hardness pressing against me. It's almost too much. I don't even feel us moving, but he lets go of me, and I've a second of panic before I bounce on the bed. The shock must be written all over my face because he watches me with a smirk before leaning over me.

The bed dips down as his hands press into the mattress next to my head. "We do this, you're mine. You get me?"

I nod, running my hands up his arms, feeling his shoulders flex as he dips down.

"Are you sure?"

"Yes," I reply. "I want you."

His head tilts to the side as he regards me. "I'll take it."

"How gracious of you," I say with a smirk.

He hooks his arm under my waist and tosses me farther toward the center of the bed. "You're gonna get it."

"I certainly hope so." I laugh out the words.

His eyes darken as he pulls his gun out of his waist holster and sets it on my nightstand before kicking off his shoes. He moves with a slow, predatory-like grace. My skin prickles in anticipation of his touch. My phone rings from my purse in the kitchen. He pauses.

"Ignore it," I say, reaching over to tug him onto the bed.

He moves above me just as the phone stops. I pull at his shirt, and he leans back, pulling it over his head by the collar. My hands are already on him, smoothing over the hard planes of muscle before my mind catches up. Beautiful.

The phone starts ringing again.

"You should probably get that," he whispers.

I groan, pouting. "It's not on my list of priorities at the moment."

He leans forward and catches my puckered lower lip with his teeth. My body arches up toward him, and he takes advantage, pulling me over him as he rolls onto his back.

"The sooner you find out what they want, the sooner you can get back here," he says, slapping the side of my thigh.

Sitting back, I decide to be naughty, trailing my tongue down his chest. I caress his hard length through his jeans, keeping my eyes trained on his. I'm satisfied when his eyes roll back into his head with a groan as I nip him just before standing up. The phone stops, and before I can decide to ignore it, it starts up again. With a frustrated sigh, I leave the room. I choose to cut through the dining room, in a hurry to grab my phone from my purse before the voicemail picks up, when I halt in my tracks.

"Dex!"

I can hear the panic in my voice, so it's not too shocking when he comes running around the corner shirtless and holding his gun. He lowers his weapon and takes in the scene.

Seven dead hummingbirds are scattered across the dining room table, with a message spray painted in sloppy blue letters on the wall. The paint, still wet and dripping in streaks, spell out the words:

One by one, they all must fall.

Then

"We really ought to work on furnishing these bedrooms," Jared said as we set boxes down in the empty bedroom he'd chosen.

He picked the bedroom farthest away from the Jack and Jill-style rooms the girls occupied. More privacy for him. Due to the state of our individual finances, though, the other two rooms were still bare and unfurnished.

"That's all I have for now. Nic's coming over later to help me move the furniture." He offered me a strained smile and turned away. "Thanks for helping me."

I felt dismissed, and I didn't know what to say. I'd woken up from a restless sleep to the doorbell and found Jared on the porch next to a stack of boxes. We'd carried the boxes upstairs in silence. That was the first thing he'd said to me all morning. I walked back down to my room and went into the bathroom. Catching sight of myself, I cringed. My hair was sticking out in all directions. A huge rat's nest of tangles on one side and the makeup I forgot to wash off was running down my face.

Yuck. I wouldn't want to look at me either. I showered quickly, then dressed and went to the kitchen to grab a Coke. I halted in the doorway at the sight before me. Jared was on his hands and knees. Cat was hanging underneath him, her little arms and legs wrapped tightly around him. Cora was sitting on his back, holding on to his shoulders. Giggles echoed around the room.

"Do it again, Daddy," Cat demanded.

"Again," Cora echoed.

"You ready? Hold on tight," Jared said, and then his hands came off the ground, and he gave a growly bear-like roar.

The girls squealed with glee. I didn't want to interrupt, so I leaned on the doorframe and watched them play together. He bucked and crawled around for their amusement. I smiled. He really was good with them. The longer he was around, the more they adored him. Maybe I was too hard on him. I decided then that I'd at least stop yelling at him, but I still needed to keep my distance and set clear boundaries.

The doorbell rang again. Jared twisted and spotted me.

"I'll get it," I said, pushing off the doorframe and heading for the door.

I peered out the vertical window that framed the door and saw a van with a security company logo. There was a man in a uniform and baseball cap standing on the front porch. I opened the door.

"Hi, I'm here for the install—Maddie?"

I squinted my eyes to make out his face. The bright light of day behind him kept his face in shadow. I leaned forward a little.

"Blake?"

"Funny, I keep running into you. Small world, huh? Though, I did see Jared's name on the work order this morning. Chose this one to see what kind of place he lived in. I'd no idea you guys were still together," he said, smiling. His eyes roamed over the space, taking in the house. "Didn't you have his kid right before graduation?"

"Kids," I corrected. "Twins. A few days after graduation."

"Oh, cool. That makes sense."

I frowned, not understanding what he was saying.

"I haven't seen you back at the gym. It's pretty cool now,

isn't it? All the new equipment they're getting."

"I wouldn't know. I don't go there anymore."

"Really? Oh." His shoulders dropped. "Well, you want me to come in and get this system set up for you?"

"Yeah. Come in."

I stepped aside, and he followed me into the foyer, putting those paper booties over his shoes.

"I'm going to start with the attic. A lot of times these old houses've had previous systems in them at one point, and there might be existing wiring. That'll save you some money if I have less wall drops to complete the install. You want to show me where the attic access is?"

"Sure. It's upstairs. This way." I led him up the stairs to the door and pulled it down from the ceiling, unfolding the built-in ladder.

Blake started climbing up to the attic.

"Do you need anything else, right now?" I asked. "A flashlight? I don't think the lightbulb up there works."

"Nope. Got one right here." The sound of ripping Velcro was loud as he opened a pocket on his uniform pants and pulled out a tiny flashlight.

"Okay, I'll be down in the kitchen if you need me. Jared's around, too."

"Okay. Thanks, Maddie," he said and disappeared into the dark space above the house.

I walked back down the stairs. Just as my bare feet touched the cool tile floor of the kitchen, the doorbell rang again.

"What is this, Grand Central Station?" I complained to no one.

I spied Jared and the girls out in the backyard, digging in the garden that ran along the concrete patio. I internally sighed as I made my way back to the door. This time when I glanced out the window, there was a squad car parked behind the security van, and Officer Martinez was standing on the porch. I opened the door and gave him a polite smile. It was a lot like trying to smile at people at a funeral. It felt awkward

to do it, but manners dictated that you smile anyway.

"Miss Dobransky. You're looking much better today." He returned my awkward smile.

I assumed he was referring to the fact that I was pale, clammy, and on the verge of passing out last time I saw him. I nodded.

"Please, come in." I stepped aside and opened the door wider for him.

I led him to the living room and started to sit on the couch but remembered again that I was thirsty. He sat across from me on the chair.

"Can I get you something to drink? A coke or some bottled water?"

"Do you have Dr. Pepper?"

"Sure do. Lemme get you one."

I retrieved his drink and sat down on the sofa.

"I assume you have some news regarding my case?"

He dug into his pocket and pulled out his wallet. Flipping it open, he pulled out a small square of paper and slid it across the coffee table between us. It was a picture. A girl, probably a few years younger than me. Her hair was reddish brown like mine, and she had warm brown eyes. My face twisted in puzzlement as I looked back to the officer.

"That's—" He cleared his throat. "That's my sister. She's been missing for a little over four years now."

"I'm sorry," I said, furrowing my brow. "But does this have something to do with my case?"

"They decided not to assign your case to a detective."

"Can I ask why?" I asked. "I'm not making this up."

"I believe you. There's just not enough evidence, and even if there were, we're still very limited in how we can handle stalking cases."

"I'm not following."

"We can't just arrest people for being near you or giving your kids flowers. You can file a restraining order, once we find out who he is. But even then, we have to catch him in the vicinity or have evidence of breaking and entering before

we can press charges."

I cursed internally before asking, "And your sister?" I was failing to understand the connection.

"Before she disappeared, she said that weird stuff was happening to her. Things moved in her room like someone had been in there. She swore someone was after her. No one believed her. We thought she was being dramatic, just looking for attention. Then one day, she was gone. She wouldn't have run away. She loved her family, and we loved her. There were other things, too. It never added up. That's why I became a cop. They wouldn't investigate. They wouldn't look for her. She was eighteen, an adult, so they said she probably left. There was no evidence to suggest otherwise." He sighed. "Look, I know this is probably just the consolation prize, but I believe you. The guys at the station, not so much. So I'm going to look into this for you when I can. They keep us pretty busy, but I'll make time."

"Thank you." I didn't know what else to say. "I appreciate it."

I saw movement out of the corner of my eye and found Blake standing there.

"I've gotta get some equipment from the van. I just wanted to let you know that I'll be right back. Is it okay if I let myself back in?"

"Yeah sure, that's fine," I answered and then turned back to the officer. "They didn't find any fingerprints or DNA on the flowers?"

"No. The only thing we have is your statement and the vague description your daughters gave. That's not enough to go on. But here—" He opened his wallet and slid another rectangle of paper across the coffee table. "That's my card. If you have another incident or notice anything else suspicious, give me a call. That's my cell listed."

He stood, and I followed him to the door.

"Though I'd like to not hear from you again. You know?" He smiled. "I hope nothing else happens."

"Yeah, one can hope that this is all over. Thank you again

for your help. And for believing me."

"Have a good rest of your day." He smiled again and turned, then halted. "Are you installing a camera-capable system?"

"I have no clue. Jared set this all up."

"Well, if you do, remember to save the recordings after any event. Those systems self-purge after a preset length of time. We'll need all the evidence you can get."

"I'll keep that in mind. Thanks. You have a good day, too." I waved and closed the door.

Chapter Three

Now

"I need to call Diana and John," I say, racing across the dining room to the kitchen.

"Who?" Dex asks.

"Cora and Cat's grandparents," I explain. "They're retired. I'm going to send the girls with them, on vacation, somewhere far away. Out of the country or something. I can't have them around this. This is too much. In all the years of stalking, whoever this is hasn't made a threat like that before."

I make it to my purse and pull out my phone, searching the contact list. My heart is racing, and I'm struggling for breath.

"Hey," Dex says, placing his hand over the phone. "Slow down. Let's think this through."

"Think this through!" I yell and then struggle to drag in air. I brace my hands on my knees to control my breathing and calm down while I finish. "Listen, Dex. We don't know each other that well. You asked me the other day why I was training. This. This is why I've been training. I'm not going to sit around like some delicate flower, waiting to see what the bad man will do to me."

"That's not what I—"

23

"I know, but what you don't know is that I've plans in place. I'm not going to sit quietly by and let my life get torn apart again. I'm not going to wait and see if one of those dead birds symbolizes my girls. He made the mistake of leaving me alone for three years. I've had time to think about everything. Time to realize what I did wrong. Time to put plans in place to make sure it doesn't happen again." I don't know if it's the words or just the act of talking, but as I finish that spiel, I catch my breath, and the anxiety attack passes.

"I'm just saying that you need to calm down," Dex says. "Just talk to me, Maddie. Tell me where your head's at."

"This is worse." I start pacing the floor in front of the kitchen counter. "The last time he started escalating, it was nothing like this. And you were right in the car. Nothing he has ever said has seemed malicious, but this—that's not caring. That's…"

Dex takes a seat at one of the barstools. "It's not good."

"Yeah," I say, still pacing. My hands are shaking, my words spilling out faster than normal. "First things first. I'm getting the girls out of here, and Hope, too. Audra can go with them. If you're okay with sending her away? I mean, if you want to stay around for this. I don't blame you if this is too much. But if you are, I think you should separate her from me."

"You've gotta stop this, Maddie. I understand the impulse—believe me. Though I wish I handled things like you. You have this knack for pushing everyone else out of the way so you can face problems alone. I get it. But you need to understand that it's not always what's best for you or them. Your strength is the fact that you have all these people who love you and are willing to stand by you."

"They're just kids, Dex," I shout. "They aren't going to help in this situation, and I won't leave them in harm's way."

"I'm not asking you to," he shouts back, matching my tone. "I'm just saying that we should wait until we know what this even is. What if it's a prank? This doesn't match your stalker's MO. It could be anything. Flying off the handle and pulling the kids from their school could end up being an unnecessary disruption to their lives. So why don't we call Martinez and get the investigation started on this, and then decide what we're doing? Okay?"

Dammit. I don't like it, but Dex's right. We don't know what this is.

"Okay." I nod. "I'm calling Bridget, so she can get here before the police." I check the time on my phone. It's only one in the afternoon. "After that, I'm going to call the security guys and have them take the girls to the Mad House after school. I don't want them coming home to this and a swarm of police in their home. Then we can call Martinez. You good with that?"

"Sounds like a plan," Dex says and then tugs my elbow, standing and pulling me to him.

His arms come around me, and he kisses my forehead.

"You probably should get a shirt on," I remind him when I become all too aware that he's still shirtless.

"Yes, ma'am," he says as he grins down at me. "I love it when you get bossy with me."

I snort and shake my head. That's exactly what makes me nervous about him. My phone rings. I jump, and it falls out of my hands, tumbling to the ground. I move out of Dex's arms, reaching down to pick it up but kick it across the room instead. *What am I? One of the Three Stooges?* I cross the kitchen and finally get a grip on the phone. Bridget's face is on the screen.

"Bridget?" I answer, a little freaked out that she's calling when I just decided to call her.

"Finally," Bridget says. "I've been trying to call you. I have some news. Is Holly around?"

I walk over to the window in the kitchen that overlooks the driveway. "I don't see her car, but Marcus's Honda is parked in front of her garage door, so I assume she's there. It's only one. She doesn't leave for work for another few hours."

"Good, I'm coming over," she replies. "I'll get her and

meet over at your place."

"Okay? I was just fixin' to call you anyway because I need to call the police. There's something at my house that you gotta see."

"Shit, another flower?"

"No, this is worse. You have to see it. I'm not sure what to make of it."

"All right, I'm on my way," she says, and the line cuts off.

I turn back, but Dex is already gone. I search through my contacts. *One phone call down, two to go.*

Then

It had been three months, and there were no break-ins, no strange men lurking around the corner. Life had returned to normal. All that meant, though, was I had time. Lots of time to sit around and think about what I'd lost. Aside from derby and work, which was something. But compared to my schedule for the last few years, it felt like I was sitting still. I sighed, missing the band more and more every day. Staring at the wall, I mindlessly stirred the pan filled with pasta sauce.

"What's that about?" Jared asked over my shoulder.

I shrieked and spun around, flinging a trail of tomato sauce across the counters. "Holy crap, you scared me."

"I wasn't even quiet." He grinned. "You were just off in your own little world, staring at the wall, making little noises."

"I wasn't making noises," I grumped.

"You were, but the question is… what are you thinking about?"

"The band," I confessed and turned away to clean up the mess.

"What about them?"

"I miss it. Being onstage. Performing. Even just sitting around and writing music, rearranging covers. I don't get to spend a lot of time doing that. Don't get me wrong—I love working at the studio, and I'm learning a lot. I just spend more time filing or getting coffee than I do working on actual music."

"I see."

"Do you?" I teased.

"I do. And I think I might have something that interests you."

"I'm listening."

"I know a guy—"

"You know a guy? You know that's the way guys where I'm from tell you about some shady handyman who can fix just about anything. I'm not sure you want a handyman working on me," I said with a playfully sinister expression.

He pulled the kitchen towel from my hands slowly, the smile on his face growing. "You're going to get it for that." He held opposing corners of the towel and started swinging it so it twisted up.

I yelped and tried to dodge him, but he blocked my exit. The first snap of the towel missed completely, but that didn't stop me from yelling out and laughing. I grabbed the pot lid off the counter to use as a shield. We were apparently loud in our play because the girls dashed around the corner.

"We want to play, too," Cat said.

The pasta water started boiling over. I dashed to the stove to stop the mess, turning down the flame and stirring the noodles.

"Sorry, baby. We can't play anymore. Mommy's gotta finish dinner."

"Tell you what," Jared said. "Why don't you go pick out the movie for after dinner?"

"Cora, come on." She grabbed her sister's hand with a grin. "Daddy says we get to pick the movie." They both ran from the room, giggling.

Jared leaned against the counter next to me, crossing his arms over his chest. He leaned back a bit until he caught my eye.

"I met this guy at work. He's another instructor. Can play anything, but he prefers drums. We've been playing around on the instruments after hours a few times. He said he's interested in joining a band. I told him about you. He wants to meet you. If you're interested."

"What kind of music?" I asked.

He shrugged. "Pretty much anything."

"He any good?"

"Yeah, the best I've seen in a while. I think you should meet him. Swing by the school after my class."

"I don't know. You know, that was the thing about punk; I may have loved it, but I don't think I ever fit. Punk is born out of huge amounts of emotions that are hindered by limited technique." I sighed, remembering all the times I frustrated the hell out of Spence. "When I joined them, I had more technique than necessary. Spence and I worked on finding a middle ground because I wanted a clean sound and complexity of notes; he wanted simplicity and raw sounds. I had the emotions…"

Realizing that my anger toward him was what fueled a lot of that passion, I shifted my focus away from him. He didn't need to read that on my face. I turned off the flame underneath the pots. Tears pooled in my eyes as the enormity of what I lost sank in, but I refused to let them fall, squeezing my eyes shut.

"It wasn't about getting famous or making money. We did it because we loved the process of transforming those emotions into sound. Punk isn't just music. It's a culture. Actually, it's many cultures. Everything from the Aggro Hardcore to the Art-schooled. I've a hard time believing that I'll ever find that again."

"Then don't. Find a new journey. Create a new sound that is all you. Merge your blues and punk roots, find your current emotions, and make music that comes from where you're at right now."

I pressed my hands into the counter and bit my lip, afraid to turn and look at him. I didn't want him to see my heart breaking with the realization that I'd have to move on.

It wasn't just the music. Law hadn't called me back. I'd

broken up with him, but I'd hoped that he would see reason. That he would come by to find Jared at his apartment, me in the house, and realize that things weren't the way he imagined them. But with Jared living inside the house, due to the stalker, he might not see things that way. And maybe that was why he wasn't calling. Maybe Sloane had told him, and he'd decided to move on. Either way, it was around the thirtieth unanswered message that I decided to stop calling him.

I just needed to wake up and accept that he'd moved on. The band was over. I needed to move on, too.

"Okay," I agreed.

"Okay?" he asked skeptically.

"Yes, okay. Is there some reason why you never believe me when I say okay to you?"

"Nope," he said with an innocent look on his face. "Just making sure."

"Whatever. Drain the pasta, will ya," I said, handing him the potholders.

Now

The doorbell rings. I check the clock on my phone and realize that it's only been fifteen minutes since I hung up with Bridget—the downside to living close to work.

I round the corner into the foyer just as Dex is letting Bridget, Marcus, and Holly enter.

Bridget's eyes meet mine before she nods to her right. "We should go into your office and talk about the news I have before the police get here and we move on to the rest of it."

I nod in reply and follow them. Holly and Bridget sit in the chairs across from the desk. Dex and Marcus remain standing, and I take the seat in my office chair. Bridget looks to Holly. "Are you okay with them being in here?" She looks to Dex and Marcus. "Because I have news about Roz."

That name has both Holly and me stiffening, but Holly's

eyes take on a faraway, lost look. Roz is Holly's ex-boyfriend, and to say they had a volatile relationship is putting it mildly. She shakes her head. "No, it's okay. Just say what you've gotta say," she says, but her voice comes out rough and timid.

I can admit that hearing Holly like that puts me on edge, more than I already was.

"About thirty minutes after Chloe and Maddie left this morning, I got a call from the DA," Bridget says to Holly. "Roz's parole hearing was moved up. Due to *good behavior*, he'll meet with the parole board in December."

"How the fuck is that possible?" Holly asks, her brows drawing together as anger takes over her voice.

"I don't know," Bridget says. "But you're going to need to speak before the parole board."

I rise from my seat. Concerned for my friend, I kneel down in front of her.

"We'll do it again," I say, grasping her hands. "Together. Same way we did last time. He won't get to you, and he sure as fuck won't get to Hope. I promise."

I look at Bridget to make sure I'm not talking out my ass. I want it to be true, but I'm not confident we can pull it off. Bridget nods, but the look on her face isn't as reassuring as I hoped it would be. Holly shakes her head as tears streak down her freckled cheeks. She pulls her hands from mine and wipes her face. Standing awkwardly, I lean over to hug her. I hate seeing her like this. She's always so strong.

"I'm gonna talk to Jerry," Holly says, her voice muffled by my hair as she squeezes me back. "This is why I work for him. He promised to protect us, you know?"

I nod and lean back.

"That's bullshit, Holls," Marcus blurts. "You don't fucking need him. I told you, you don't need to be connected to that shit. Dex and I got your back."

She told him. I'm floored as I watch them curiously. Guilt seeps in that I haven't been around enough to know that they were becoming that close; Roz is a subject Holly keeps locked down.

"I already told you no," Holly snaps. "The motherfucking cops' idea of protection is a goddamn piece of paper. And that shit means nothing to him. You've gotta fight fire with fire."

I lean back against the desk as Holly stands, her face turning red with anger. That's the Holly I know. Her hands clench into fists as she faces down Marcus. They have a silent standoff as they stare at each other.

"Fuck this shit," Marcus mutters as he turns and leaves, slamming the door behind him.

"He'll get over it." Holly shrugs, waving his exit off with nonchalance. "I gotta get ready for work. The nanny got here just before we came over. I'll let you know what Jerry says."

I grab her hand and squeeze it because I know she's putting on a brave face right now. She has to be scared shitless—I am.

"Let me know if you need anything," I say. "I'll get security for Hope if it comes to that. You know I'll do anything. Money is not, and will never be, an issue."

Holly nods, but I know she's holding back. The damn stubborn woman has trouble taking help from anyone. She hugs Bridget and me, and with a nod to Dex, she leaves too.

"Well, where's this other shit?" Bridget asks after Holly closes the door. "I swear, I need a raise," she mumbles.

"Done," I say with a shrug.

She rolls her eyes at me. "I'm not serious."

"It's in the dining room," I say, moving back to my desk chair and opening my personal laptop. "Detective Martinez and the CSI unit should be here any minute. Just make sure not to touch anything."

I leave her to it as she walks out of the room, then work on pulling up the connection to the security server. I know that'll be one of the first things they ask. Dex sits across from me, steepling his fingers at his chin.

"Hey, will you go grab my purse and work computer from the kitchen counter and put them in my car?" I ask Dex. "I don't want them becoming part of the crime scene. I've an

31

idea brewing."

"Sure. You care to enlighten me?" Dex asks.

"Later," I add, looking at my phone. "We don't have much time."

He nods and leaves the room. I pull up the security feed just as the doorbell rings. Crossing the room, I check the window next to the door just to be sure. Martinez stands there with several people behind him, his face marred by a frown. I open the door wide.

"It's in the dining room," I say without preamble. "I already pulled up the security feed server on my computer."

Detective Martinez enters and walks back to the dining room as four crime scene techs follow him in without comment. The last one halts in front of me.

"Can you point me in the direction of your computer?" she says. She's a petite woman with mousy brown hair who looks to be around my age, if not younger.

I close the door behind her and motion to her to follow me.

Chapter Four

Now

Sitting in the corner of the L-shaped sectional sofa in my living room, I'm bored out of my mind. They've been at it for hours. First pictures, then dusting everything for fingerprints. *That shit's gonna take forever to clean up.* I answered all the detective's questions, and he disappeared outside with the other cops who had arrived. Voices carry through the open front door as the media shouts questions that'll go unanswered for now.

Dex sits next to me and pulls me to his side, running his hand over my hair and kissing the top of my head.

"Are they ever gonna get done?" I ask, meeting Dex's eyes. He shrugs. "You're a cop. Don't you know about this stuff enough to say if they're getting close to finishing up?"

"Hush," he says, putting his finger over my mouth and looking around. "That's not common knowledge to everyone on the force, you know? I have very little to do with these CSI guys." He cuts his eyes to Bridget, who looks as bored as I feel with her chin propped in her hand in the chair across from me.

"Sorry," I mumble as one of the CSI guys walks by, turning his head to look at us as he passes. "But Bridge already knows." He opens his mouth to say something, and I hold up a hand to stop him. "For the record, I didn't tell her. She found out on her own." He doesn't say anything back, just looks at Bridget. "I just... we got stuff we need to do before we have to get the girls from the Mad House. We can't be at this forever."

"Soon," he says as he leans down and brushes his lips over mine.

A throat clears on the other side of Dex. I pull back and peek over his shoulder. Detective Martinez is standing there, lips pinched, eyes wandering everywhere but in our direction. Bridget raises an eyebrow at me. Dex turns to face him.

"What's up, Joe?" Dex asks.

Joe? I feel a bit ridiculous that I've known him for years and have never once asked for his first name.

"We found something on the video footage that I want you to see," Martinez says.

We all follow him back into the office where Martinez—*Joe*—directs the CSI tech to hit Play. The computer screen displays the view from the camera in the dining room. You can see Dex and me through the archway that leads into the kitchen, but we're far enough away that you can only see our feet, facing each other. Joe does a little hand signal to speed it up, and the tech fast-forwards. It hits me at that point that there were no birds on the table when we got home. We weren't that distracted.

A chill runs through me at the thought that he was in here while we were home.

From this view, you can see my purse and laptop sitting on the counter, and I've a sick feeling that the stalker may have foiled my plans, but soon a male, wearing a hoodie and a backpack, enters the frame. Joe signals the tech to slow the replay back to normal. The intruder pauses for a moment, then squats and opens the backpack. It's clear that he knows where the camera is by the way he moves around the room, yet never turns enough to catch a glimpse of his face or even a profile.

He pulls out a can of spray paint and a plastic bag,

dumping the dead birds on the table. All of it happens over a few minutes. He paints the words on the back wall, then picks up the plastic bag and paint can, stuffing them back in his bag. He exits through the kitchen, and my mind gets stuck on the fact that he didn't pause or even look at my work laptop. I was sure he would've gone for it, and I let out a tiny breath of relief.

Martinez puts his hand on the tech's shoulder, and she pauses the recording, just as I walk into the dining room on the video. I'm relieved because I know what happens next.

"That's enough," Joe says. "If you got what you need, you can leave us, Julie."

She pulls a little thumb drive from the side of my computer and shuts the laptop. When she clears the arch, Joe speaks.

"You were in here the whole time and neither of you heard anything?"

"No," I answer.

"What were you doing?"

"We were... busy," Dex supplies.

Martinez takes a step and sits on the edge of my desk, clasping his hands together in front of him. "I have to say, I find it odd that you guys didn't hear anything. What I find more disconcerting... is that there was video footage of the incident on your security system. Up until this point, he was always careful enough to erase all evidence of his presence." Martinez's brows dip low as his lips press together. His eyes lock onto me.

"I'm not sure what you're getting at," I say.

"Come on, Joe," Dex says. "You can't be thinking that she staged this? I was here with her the whole time. I've been with her for months."

"You don't think you've been compromised? We watched the rest of that footage, and honestly, I find it hard to believe you're able to remain objective in this case."

My stomach drops as I realize what we almost did. Dex could lose his job. It was so stupid.

Dex leans against the wall, arms crossed in front of him, looking decidedly unaffected by Martinez's words.

"I'm taking this to the chief. I'm going to recommend you be removed from this case. It's clear that your interests no longer align with the department."

"And what interests are those?" I ask. "That you're trying to build a case against me?"

Martinez looks away but doesn't deny it.

"Unbelievable," I mutter as I pin the detective with my gaze. "We've known each other for years. When did you stop believing me?" The answer to that is rather obvious, so I'm not sure why I asked.

"That's enough, Maddie," Bridget intervenes, then directs a steely gaze at the detective. "I'm going to need you to leave. If you'd like to come back with a warrant, we'll cooperate at that time. But I'm advising my client to remove you from the premises, now."

I fall into the chair across from my desk while Bridget rounds everyone up and shows them to the door. Burying my face in my hands, I can't help but wonder how I got here. Every step I take turns out to be a misstep that threatens everything I've worked for. And Dex. God, Dex could lose his job.

"What are you thinking?" Dex asks, tugging my hands away from my face. He's kneeled down in front of me, so I see the concern marring his features.

I laugh without humor. "I think it's clear that once again the cops are leaving me on my own to deal with this freak." I shake my head. "I should've known that trusting them to take care of it while I try to carry on with my normal routine was a mistake."

Bridget comes back into the room. "Well, they're out of the house. What's the plan?"

"I'm thinking we take this to Dawn," I say, and Bridget pulls a skeptical face. "There's a video I didn't tell the cops about."

"When did you get a video?" she asks.

"When I came into the office this morning. Just before the FBI and US Marshal arrived."

"What? Why am I just now hearing about this?"

"Because we were distracted, discussing other things. You know?" I shifted my head to the side in Dex's direction.

"Fine," she relents. "What is it?"

"Just a collection of mine and Dex's greatest moments with a warning to look deeper into his motivations."

She raises an eyebrow at me, her gaze darting to Dex and back. Dex looks unaffected by the turn in conversation.

"Yeah, I know," I sigh. "He knows. We talked about it. He's good, I swear."

Her jaw drops. "Well, if you trust him, I will." Bridget's lips pinch together as she stares Dex down. "Just know, if you hurt her, I'll make your life a living hell and bury you in lawsuits until you can't breathe. And that's not a threat. It's a promise."

Dex shrugs. "It doesn't matter because I have no intentions of doing that. I love her. She worked her way into that number one spot next to Audra. I'm here to protect her and help her with anything she needs. You feel me?"

The corner of Bridget's mouth tips up into the hint of a smile, and she nods.

"Anyway. I'm going to take the video to Dawn and see if she can identify any digital footprint that might help figure out who this is." I sigh again. "I just need to clean up this mess first. I'm not leaving it for the girls to come home to."

"That... I can help with," Bridget says. "You'll have to pay for it"—she grins—"but I'll have a cleaning crew and painters here in no time. You don't have to worry about it or even look at it again."

I muster up a smile for her. Even if worry tinges all of my emotions at the moment, I'm still grateful to have such a great friend.

Then

It was late, and the girls had fallen asleep during the middle of the repeat performance of the latest Disney movie they'd chosen as after-dinner entertainment. Wide-awake myself, I took in their sweet little cherub faces. They were curled up on the couch between Jared and me. As my gaze traveled up, I met Jared's eyes. He smiled at me. He seemed so happy and content. My heart melted a little.

"You want to risk it and carry them upstairs?" I asked quietly.

"But I was enjoying the movie. I want to see how it ends," he deadpanned.

I smiled and rolled my eyes at him. "I'm itching to get into the music room and play right now. Plus, my foot's asleep."

"Sounds good."

He cradled Cora in his arms. She curled into his chest and sighed contentedly. Cat and I followed them up the stairs. A few moments later, we met in the hall after tucking them into their respective beds. I turned to head back down the stairs, but Jared grasped my hand, halting me.

"Thank you." His voice was near my ear, body close enough that I could feel the heat through my thin nightgown and robe, but not touching.

"For what?" I asked, turning to him. I had to drop my head back to look up at his face.

"For everything. Having the girls, living here, all of it. I'm happy, Mads. You make me a very happy man." He smiled genuinely and walked past me down the stairs.

I stood there, stunned motionless for a moment before heading down the stairs, too. When I got to the bottom, I could hear the soft strains of the piano as he plucked notes from his mind and played with abandon.

I loved when he did this. For a moment, I leaned against the frame of the archway, listening. Jared was so talented—joining the military was truly a waste of a beautiful mind. He did it to follow in his father's footsteps, a sense of duty to make his father proud, but music owned his heart. Memories of sitting with him while he played, the day he gave me my first guitar, flitted through my mind. I'd promised to write his music for him. Crossing the room, I grabbed my journal off the shelf and dug into my bag for a pencil. I sat on the bench next to him. I'm not even sure if he was conscious of the fact that he always left a space for me. Closing my eyes, I listened to the music until I started seeing the notes in my head. I started frantically scribbling down each one as fast as I could to keep up.

When he came to a stop, I'd over ten pages of music written down.

His attention shifted to me and a tender expression overtook his face. "You wrote it down?"

I glanced away with a shrug. "I told you I would, one day."

He stared at me for a moment and then sighed, looking out the window in silence. The bright moonlight from a full moon outside was the only source of light in the room. Shadows played across his face with the movement.

"I was going to wait to do this. I've been thinking a lot about us," he said as he rose and pulled something out of his pocket. "I think the only thing keeping you from me now is fear. Fear that I'll leave you. That I would ever do something to hurt you again."

I stared at him, having no idea where he was going with this. He hadn't bothered me with talk of "us" since shortly after he moved into the house. A creaking sound broke the silence as he set an open velvet box on top of the piano in a strip of moonlight. Inside glittered a diamond ring.

"I bought this for you while I was still in training. I used to pull it out every night and think about the day I got to put it on your finger. I carried it with me every tour. Every time shit felt hopeless, I'd take out this ring and think about that perfect day I had to look forward to. It got me through a lot of rough shit. You got me through it."

Anger surged through me. "You decided to break up with me and avoid me for four years—"

"I know," Jared interrupted, his voice laced with regret. "I

39

thought I was doing the right thing, Maddie. I thought it was the only way to give you the freedom to chase your dreams." He squeezed his eyes shut. "There's not a day that has gone by that I haven't regretted that decision. I'm so sorry... for everything."

"I get that, but why would you tell me this now?"

"I think you're afraid that I'll leave again. The only thing that's holding us back is that possibility. But you should know just how unlikely that is. I want to put this ring on your finger, right now. I'll do anything to prove to you that I'll never hurt you again. For as long as I live, you have me. You'll have me whether you say yes or no. Because you're it for me, Maddie." He pushed his hand through his hair and with his other hand pressed a key on the piano, letting the haunting sound echo around us in the quiet room. "Nobody can see into my soul the way you do. No one makes me smile or gets me as angry or can keep me on my toes like you do. No one listens to what I say when I'm not talking or is content with just being in a room with me, listening to me play the piano. Just you. Always you. Only you. Will you marry me, Madelaine Rose Dobransky?"

Tears ran down my face, falling silently into my lap. I felt like I couldn't breathe. It was surreal and very real all at the same time. He brushed the tears off my face with his thumb. It had been nine months since Law and I broke up. Law had never called, nothing, just left town. I'd gone through a whole phase of worry about what I was doing that made it so easy for the men in my life to just walk away from me without a backward glance. I realized, in that moment, that I'd just been refusing to listen to what Jared was telling me. He never walked away; he was trying to do the right thing. Misguided, but still frustratingly noble. I couldn't deny that my heart still belonged to him. He'd taken away my last good excuse.

"You going to say something, Maddie? I'm dying here." I peered into his pleading blue eyes, so bright and familiar to me.

I nodded, incapable of voicing my response at that

moment.

"Yes?"

I gasped for breath I didn't realize I was holding. "Yes, Jared. I'll marry you," I choked out.

He cupped my cheeks in his hands and pulled my face toward his. His lips brushed against mine, gentle and sweet.

"I love you," he said, relief thick in his voice.

"I love you, too, Jared."

His lips crashed into mine, and he kissed me with the same abandon he usually reserved for the piano. I stroked my tongue against his, inviting him in. Part of my mind knew that I was jumping back into treacherous waters without a life raft. He could crush me this time, and I'd never recover. But he had more than proven his intentions over the last nine months. There was no reason to doubt him anymore. That didn't make it any less scary.

He pulled me up to stand between his legs, pushing me back into the piano. The discordant notes sounded as my butt bumped into the keys. He rested his forehead on my belly, gripping my hips with both hands, trembling.

"Please tell me I'm not dreaming."

"This isn't a dream, Jared." I ran my fingers through his hair to soothe him.

He reached behind me and pulled the ring out of the box. As it slid onto my finger, a smile grew on his face. Jared stood from the bench. His body pressed into mine, his eyes growing heated as he slowly undid the belt of my robe, exposing the lace-and-satin nightgown beneath. Grasping my waist, he picked me up, placing me on top of the piano. More dissonant notes floated throughout the room as I rested my feet on the keys. He ran his hands down the outside of my thighs to hook behind my knees. With a quick tug, he pulled me to him so our bodies were pressed together and aligned perfectly. I could feel his excitement between my legs. I felt him pulse. Unable to help myself, I moaned at the hardness of him.

My surroundings faded as I wrapped an arm around his

shoulders and ran my tongue up the side of his neck. I whispered, "I love you," as my tongue traced the shell of his ear.

A tremor ran through his body as he pushed me down, laying me back on the piano. He ground himself into me. He pushed the skirt of my nightgown up to my waist and ran his palm from my neck down my body to the edge of my panties, making my back arch off the hard surface. His thumb rolled over the sensitive bundle of nerves, and I gasped.

"Perfect," he exhaled. "I'm going to taste you and touch you until I've had my fill. Then I'm going to make love to you. Are you okay with that? Because once I start, we're going to be here all night."

"Yes," I hissed as he dragged my underwear down my legs.

Goose bumps broke out across my skin at the gentle tease of his grazing fingers. He sat back down on the piano bench, hooking my knees onto his shoulders and pulled me toward him until my lower body was supported only by him. He then set about fulfilling his promise.

# Chapter Five

Now

My stomach twists in knots as I navigate the streets of Downtown Austin. It hit me, the second we got in the car, the enormity of what I'm walking Dex into. Nervous is an understatement. I haven't let anyone into this part of my life who wasn't around before.

What will he think of me after this?

The question repeats in my brain like a loop of audio until I pull into the underground parking beneath the black skyscraper in the heart of downtown. Dex has been silent the whole short ride, looking out the window and tapping his fingers on his leg. The low volume of the radio and street noise are the only things breaking the silence between us.

For my part, I know it's the nervous tension filling me to the brim, but I'd give anything to know where his mind is at right now.

I park the car and pick up my phone, dialing the number. It rings once.

"Yello," Nic answers.

"We're here. Did you get everything set up?" I ask.

"I sent Parker down to meet you in the lobby," Nic says. "He'll go through the guest process with Dex."

"You're sure you're okay with this?" I ask, my voice

hitching.

"If you're comfortable bringing him here, then I'm happy for you, Ned," Nic replies. "You know me. This place is only a secret for everyone else's benefit."

I snort. "You've got a point."

"I'll try and make it down to see you while you're here, but I've a few things on my plate at the moment. Dawn is waiting for you, though."

"Okay, see you soon, Lucky," I say. "Love you."

"Love you, too," he says.

I hang up the phone and take a deep breath to steel myself. Dex is watching me intently.

"Your friend Nic has something to do with this place?" Dex asks with a raised brow.

I nod. "He owns the building."

Dex blinks.

I give him a hint of a smirk. "Yeah, that doesn't surprise me. A lot of people underestimate Lucky. They see him as a dumb man-whore or porn star or whatever. The guy does have a brain. He just lacks inhibition or insecurity. This place is his baby. He created a place for people to be more like him in that regard. You ready?"

We walk through the sliding glass doors that are only a few feet away from my reserved parking space. Two security guards stand off to either side but straighten when they see me.

"Miss Dobransky," Kyle says with a nod.

I stop, then turn and slowly walk backward. "Hey, guys. How's Kim holding up?" I ask Noah.

"She's great," Noah replies. "Getting restless, now that the baby's due next month."

"Good to hear. Yeah, the last month is a beast, but it's worth it." I turn my attention to Kyle. "Did Bobby do well in his tournament?"

"He did," Kyle replies, a grin only a father could sport taking over his features. "They're going to state finals."

"Awesome." I smile back. "Gotta run. Take care, guys." I

wave with my fingertips and grab Dex's hand, leading him toward the lobby.

We walk past the elevator and staircase that takes non-members up to the first floor, then we approach the doors that lead to the members-only part of the building and where the true lobby lies. A third security guard pulls the door open for me.

"Miss Dobransky." He nods in greeting.

"Thank you, Colin," I say with a smile. He's a relatively new addition to the team here, and I don't know him that well yet.

"What is this place?" Dex murmurs as he looks around, taking in the gleaming black marble floors and white walls sparsely decorated with modern accents. "Those security guards were armed. I get the feeling that if you weren't holding my hand, I wouldn't be standing here."

"You wouldn't," I reply, but my attention is quickly diverted.

Parker spots us and shouts my name, making his way over at a brisk pace with a huge grin on his face. He grasps my face. His eyes shine with mischief and joy, and then he kisses both my cheeks.

"There you are," Parker says, releasing me. His eyes roam over Dex from head to toe with a leer, lips pursed as he nods in approval. "You've been away too long, but now that I see what's been keeping you, I approve." He grins and fusses with my hair, then turns back to Dex. "Welcome to the Black Building, Mr. McClellan. I'm Parker, Mr. Gallo's executive assistant."

Dex raises an eyebrow at me as he shakes Parker's proffered hand. "Nice to meet you."

Parker tugs my hand and looks to Dex, nodding his head as an indication to follow. Dex has an uneasy look on his face as he walks with us, and I get distracted by Parker's chatter. Parker leads us to his office just off the lobby. Dex and I sit in the chairs across the desk from Parker, and Parker shoves papers in front of Dex.

"Just sign these and you can get going." Parker's smile softens the demand.

Dex looks to me with pinched brows. "What are these, and what is this place?" His gaze wanders the room as if he can see through the walls.

"We can't tell you until you sign that." I motion to the papers. "It's just a standard NDA, saying you won't disclose anything that you see or find out about this place, and a liability waiver. Nothing here is illegal. It's just that privacy is the cornerstone of this business." I wave my hand, indicating the whole building.

"And I hafta sign this just to go with you upstairs to talk to your friend?"

I nod slowly and tilt my head. "There are other reasons to know what goes on here. Reasons that have much more to do with me." I swallow roughly. Nervous butterflies dance in my stomach like they're in a nightclub. I've a horrible sense that he'll hate me and walk away after this.

His eyes never stray from me. "If I sign this and we go up there, you'll tell me everything?"

I give him a nod in reply.

The look on his face is intense, but he grabs the pen off the desk and signs without even looking at the papers. My jaw drops, because I've never seen someone come through here and not read the contracts before signing. I can't take my eyes off him as Parker takes the pen and notarizes everything. Dex signs Parker's notary book when prompted. He sits back in the chair, looking relaxed, as his hand reaches over and takes hold of mine.

"I meant every word I've said to you," he murmurs.

I snap my mouth shut. Dex kisses my hand.

"That's it," Parker says. "We're all done here."

We stand and leave, heading across the lobby to the bank of elevators in the middle of the building. The U-shaped alcove has three silver elevators doors, three black, and two red ones against the shorter wall. We walk over to the red elevators, and I place my hand on the black screen in the middle of the two doors. A green light passes over my palm as it scans.

"This place has biometric security?" Dex asks.

"These doors do, but this is employee-only access and leads to the offices. And like I said, privacy is cornerstone to this place. Anyone that gets on these elevators has been fully vetted, background checked, and preapproved."

Dex's brows inch up. "You work here, too?"

"Not really. I'm part owner. I sit on the board, but I don't have any daily duties. It's enough to get me access, but I don't have an office here or anything."

"But I've been vetted?" he asks.

"Yeah, Nic does that. He probably had you checked out the night you guys met. If you think I'm hard to earn trust from, you haven't gotten acquainted with the king of trust issues. He has people on the payroll whose only job is to vet anyone who walks through the doors—both the public and the private side of the building."

I look around the lobby as we wait for the elevator to arrive, trying to see it with new eyes to understand what Dex must be thinking. There isn't another soul around right now, but it's late afternoon, which means we're in between the lunch rush and the night guests. I know I'm avoiding telling him about this place, but the truth is that I'm scared. I decide to start with the easy stuff.

"See those silver doors? Those will take you to floors one to ten. That's the public side of the building. The first two floors have restaurants, a nightclub, spa, a lounge bar, and a few boutiques for shopping. Floors three to ten are a hotel," I explain.

"And those?" Dex points to the black doors.

"Those are members-only residences, but not many people live there. Private rooms. And the club levels."

"Members of what?"

My heart rate picks up, and I look away. "The Black Mask Society," I mutter. Taking a deep breath to steel myself, I force myself to meet his eyes. "It's a place where secret desires come to life. It's not all sexual, but a good portion of it is. And because I know it will come up sooner or later... Nic built this place for me."

I stare at the security panel in front of me. My mind races through the various reactions he could be having at the moment, but I'm too scared to look. The elevator dings and the doors to the elevator on the left slide open silently. Distance. I need distance. It feels harder to breathe. I dart inside and wait for Dex to follow. My heart rate increases with every millisecond he hesitates.

Then

I was keeping pace with the pack on the inside curve of the track. Feeling a hand tap the side of my hip, Holly—our jammer—was right behind me, searching for an opening. I skated closer to the outside track, forcing the girl next to me to move just a tiny bit. Reaching back with my left arm, I waited for her to grasp my hand for the whip assist.

A girl from the other team caught on and tried to move in for the block. I shoulder checked her and got Holly to the front, scoring a point for our team. The jam ended seconds before the buzzer went off, signaling the end of the bout.

Putting my hands on my knees, I let my wheels roll me around the track as I tried to catch my breath.

"Mah bitch!" Holly shouted as she skated up next to me. "Fuck, yeah, that was awesome. Nice move."

She slapped my ass and flung an arm over my shoulder as we skated off track to the area next to the bleachers where our team had left their bags. I grabbed my water bottle and started chugging as more teammates gave me props for the final point. Reaching into my bag, I felt around for the little velvet box. I'd taken the ring off for the game, but I was about to put it back on, now that we were done for the day.

I slid it on my finger, admiring it. It wasn't a huge diamond or flashy. Just a single stone in a plain gold band. It was perfect for me, though. I wasn't all that girly, and I didn't wear jewelry often.

"What in the motherfuck is that?" Sloane asked, grabbing my hand. "No! Get out. You got engaged?"

"Yes!" I beamed. "He proposed last night."

"That must've been one hell of a proposal," Sloane said. "I thought you'd sworn off him—for life?"

"Why do you have that shit-eating grin on your face?" Holly asked as she plopped down next to me.

"Jared's making an honest woman out of her," Sloane said as she jerked my arm nearly out of its socket, showing my ring to Holly.

"No shit? You're like legit back together now?"

"You have to tell us all the details—no holding back on this, woman," Sloane demanded. "We need everything."

I told them all I could remember, which was nearly all of it, except for the more private physical aspects of our reunion. I felt like I could burst from happiness, which was a far cry from my modus operandi of late.

"Holy fuck. Does he have a brother? I want one, too," Sloane whined.

I laughed. "No. He's an only child, like me. Besides, you have Max."

"Does who have a brother?"

I froze at the sound of Law's voice behind me. Of all the days to make a reappearance. I turned slowly and took him in. He was bigger, more cut than he'd ever been when we were together. He was wearing a plain tee and jeans. Gone was the nerdy punk rocker, and in his place was a sexy-as-hell fighter. *Holy shit!* My mind went blank. I'd no clue what he just said. My mouth watered and I swallowed hard.

"What're you doing here?" I asked, coming to my senses.

"I needed to talk to you."

"No, I meant—why are you here in Austin? I thought you left to do the fight circuit?"

He gave me that same crooked smile with one dimple I'd always been a sucker for, and it felt like the floor had fallen out from under me. *Fuck. Fuck. Fuck. Fuck. Fuck*, I chanted in my mind. I shouldn't feel this way about someone who was not my fiancé.

"Keeping tabs on me?" he asked.

"Yes—no—Sloane mentioned it." I struggled for purchase.

"Can we talk?" His hand went to the back of his neck, making the colorful skin on his tattooed arm bulge.

"Sure," I replied absently, not moving.

"Can we step outside? The lobby?" he asked, looking around us.

I noticed then that the whole team had stopped and were looking back and forth between us like we were playing a Ping-Pong match. *Shit.*

"Yeah." I finally went into motion and skated to the nearest exit door. When the door shut behind us, the sounds of the game and the crowd hushed into the silence of the empty lobby. People walked by on the sidewalk beyond the glass wall of the convention center, but we were essentially alone. The table they used for ticket sales sat vacated, so I skated over to it and half sat on it.

"What's up?" I asked, trying to be casual.

"I've been fighting." His hand went to his neck. I was mesmerized by the motion of his contracting muscles as he kneaded it.

"Yeah, I know." Looking away from him, I watched the cars drive by on the street outside. "Like I said, your sister mentioned it."

"I did it because I was angry at you, at myself. It felt good to beat the shit out of people. My dad asked about you. I finally told him about what happened, and he kicked my ass. He said that you were doing the right thing and I was a little shit about it. He's right. I wanted to tell you I'm sorry."

"Now?" My eyes snapped back to him. "It's been almost a year since I last laid eyes on you."

"Fuck, Laine. I know. I was fucking stupid. I don't know the first thing about kids or being a parent. I miss you. Every goddamn day."

I was thankful I was sitting down as the room started to spin around me. Unbidden tears tracked down my cheeks. It felt like I was being torn in two. I was cursed; shit like this didn't happen to normal people. *You can't be in love with two people*, I told myself. I made my decision, hadn't I?

"I'm engaged," I said, looking down at my hand and twisting the ring on my finger.

"That's it? It doesn't matter what I do or say, he wins."

"It's not a competition. But yeah, you left, so what was I supposed to think, Law?"

"You were supposed to fight for me. Or was I never that important to you? Was it always him?"

"Fuck you, Law. Fuck you. I called. I left messages. What did you think would happen? That I'd drop everything to chase you around the country? You don't get to come back and start this shit. Not now. I'm finally in a place where I'm happy again. You fucking wrecked me. And he was there, fighting for me. Unlike you. You walked away."

"There's that fire." He smirked. "You know what that is?"

"This is me, telling you to fuck off."

"That's you feeling frustrated because you still feel this—" He motioned between us. "But you're fighting it. And that's perfect. That's my in."

"I'm done here," I said, standing up.

He grabbed my arm to stop me and pressed his body against my back.

"Does he know how much pleasure you get from being tied up? How you detonate like an atomic bomb when I stick my finger up your ass and play with your clit while you ride my dick?"

A shiver ran down my spine from his words. "Fuck you."

"You know you want to." He traced his finger down my bare shoulder.

I ripped my arm from his grasp and skated toward the door, back to where the games were still being played.

I used a turn stop to halt my motion as my eyes landed on

Jared. He stood in the doorway. A white-knuckled grip on the door and the look on his face let me know he wasn't happy with the situation. He was glaring in Law's direction. He took a few long strides toward me and grabbed my waist, lifting me off the floor in a crushing kiss. I closed my eyes and let him have this. Jared deserved better than me, but if I was what he wanted, he was getting everything I had.

"You ready to go? The girls want to get ice cream on the way home. They're with the team right now. Bonnie said you were done for the day and could leave if you want."

"Yeah," I said. "Let's get outta here."

Chapter Six

Then

I walked in the door after a long day at the studio. It took me a moment to realize that I couldn't see through the glass doors to the office any longer; something gray pressed against the panes of glass. Curious, I walked over to the doors, but before I got there, I noticed that everything from the music room was gone. *What the hell?*

I continued to the office door and twisted the knob. It opened with ease, but the loud sounds of drums assaulted me. I pushed open the door to find Asher sitting at a drum kit set up in what appeared to be our music room, but not. He stopped playing as soon as he spotted me. Gray soundproofing tiles covered the walls, windows, and even the ceiling of the entire room. As I took in the room, looking over the space, my gaze landed on Jared, who was standing there with a huge grin on his face.

"You're home," he said, walking over to me.

"I think so," I answered absently.

All of our musical instruments were set up on racks, and the piano sat in the middle of the room.

"How did you do all this?" I asked.

"You like it?" Jared wrapped an arm around my waist, pulling me to him.

"Yeah, I guess."

"Well, we need a space that won't get the cops called while we write and practice our music, and this room was just sitting here empty." He shrugged and gave me a chaste kiss.

So that was it. We were really doing it. After meeting with Jared's friend and coworker, Asher Cross, we decided to give it a go and start a new band. Asher was beyond talented on the drums, but the fact that he could play other instruments increased his understanding of the different variables of music and made him a valuable asset to the writing process.

But this—turning the office into a practice space—was a surprise. We didn't have a name for the band yet, but we were finally going to start writing some music. Nervous excitement warmed me from the inside.

"Well, it works," I said. "I'd no idea anyone was here until I opened the door."

"Cool," Jared said, his face lighting up with a proud smile.

His light blue eyes sparkled with delight, and his thick waves of black hair were coated with white drywall dust. My gaze fell on Cora and Cat, sitting in an area behind the door, set up with a shelf of toys and books to keep them occupied. I smiled at that because he always thought of the girls.

"What're we doing for dinner?" I asked, setting my purse down on the armchair in the corner of the room.

"I ordered pizza, so you don't have to cook."

"Could you be any more perfect?" I asked, happy with his answer. I looped my arms around his neck.

"I'm only perfect for you," he said and kissed my nose.

"I'm going to have to get used to this, aren't I?" Asher asked, still sitting at his drum kit next to us.

"Totally, dude," I said and stuck my tongue out at him.

We hadn't known each other for a long time, only a few weeks, but Asher and I clicked. We enjoyed teasing each other.

"I need a beer," Asher complained, rising to his feet. "Either of you two saps want one?"

"Yes," Jared said.

"Sounds good," I replied at the same time.

"You ready to get some work done tonight?" Jared asked once Asher was gone.

"Absolutely, but first, I'm going to go change into something with a stretchy waistband."

"Okay, hurry back. I'll set your guitar up for you."

"Thank you. I love you."

"I love you, too," he said, and then kissed me properly. "Now get your butt in gear."

He slapped my ass, and my thoughts grew heated. It must have been written all over my face. He gave me a quick kiss, a heated look of his own darkening his eyes, and said, "Later."

Now

It's only a handful of seconds, but it feels like an eternity before Dex comes around the corner. He doesn't stop. The determined look on his face grabs my undivided attention. His body collides with mine and pushes me into the mirrored elevator wall behind me as his lips descend. He pins my arms out next to my head and presses his body against me. The laptop bag and my purse slip off my shoulder and sag down to my elbow. He lets go of that hand and pulls them off, placing them on the floor, not stopping his assault on my lips.

With my hand free, I reach for him, but he catches it in midair. The doors slide closed and we ascend. He twists both of my arms behind my back and clamps my wrists down with one of his. I moan into his mouth. His other hand threads into the back of my hair and tugs, breaking the kiss. I pant for breath and open my eyes.

He tilts his head as he studies me. I try to look away, but his grip tightens in my hair, forcing me to look at him.

"Why? Why do you keep running away from me?" he asks.

I can't answer that question. Even if I wanted to, I wouldn't have the words to voice everything that's constructed the wall between us. I bite my lip and avert my gaze, focusing on his chin. He spins me around to face the mirrored wall behind me and pulls me back to his chest.

"Can you see what I see, Maddie?"

I meet his eyes in the mirror.

"That's fear, but what I know of you is that if you didn't want this…" He tightens his grip on my hair even further, and my eyes roll back in my head. A breathy moan escapes my lips. "You could get out of this hold in seconds. You could fight me off and tell me to go away. But you like this. You desire this. You want me to be the one who does it, but you're fighting me at every step. Why?"

I meet his eyes in the mirror. "You like this? Does it turn you on?"

"You turn me on," he whispers in my ear and presses himself into my hands—proof that he means what he says. "You could grocery shop and I'd get hard watching you."

A smirk tugs at my lips but quickly dies when I think about what he's asking.

"What's your breaking point?" I ask. "What could I do to make you turn away? Because everyone has one. And once you see inside, do you think you'll still love me when I push you past that point?" He doesn't respond, so I push on. "You say you love me so easily, but it's not that easy. I'm dead inside. I've been that way for years. And this—this is where I come to feel. Nic's the one who gave that to me… Does that bother you?"

"Do you fuck him?"

"No," I answer without hesitation. "Never have, never will. But you might not be okay with what we do here either way. Evan doesn't even know about it because he wouldn't be okay with it." I level a stare at him.

Dex nods, his brows pinching together. "Will you let me in?"

"Honestly, I'm having trouble understanding why you even want in." I pull my hands from his grip and turn to face him. "Why chase after someone with so much baggage? Is it really worth the trouble?"

"I think it is," he says gruffly. "Show me, tell me—either way, it doesn't matter. I'll be honest with you if any of it bothers me, but I also might surprise you."

"I want to believe that." I look up into his eyes, which have softened. "I do. I've never done this before and it... Letting someone in is hard. Letting someone see the things I've worked hard to keep secret. You know?"

"I get it, more than you know," Dex says and tugs me to his chest.

His distinct, woodsy smell fills my senses, relaxing me. I finally put my finger on it. His cologne or body wash has a definite undertone of cedar to it. It's comforting. I listen to his heartbeat under my ear and feel my body relax into him. He makes me feel safe and that in itself is enough to put me on edge. It's getting easier to trust him the harder he fights to break down my defenses. I'm just not sure that's the safest place for me.

The elevator dings to signal our arrival at floor twenty-five. We step out, and I lead Dex to the door at the end of the short hall. There are only two doors in this hallway. One leads to the emergency staircase and the other into the office suites. I swipe my card and place my thumb on the scanner. After a few seconds, the door buzzes and I pull it open. Dex takes the door and motions for me to go in front of him.

Loud shouts and gunshots echo around the room. The boom of an explosion shakes the floor as we walk around the corner. A first-person shooter game takes up the entire ten-foot-tall wall, in wide-screen glory, across from a sectional sofa. Dawn's head of green hair, pulled up into a messy bun, is visible over the couch.

"Take that, bitch!" Dawn shouts into the headset. "I just owned your ass."

She spots us as we round the corner of the couch. Silence fills the room as she pauses the game.

"Ruby, I gotta go. Mads is here. Yeah," Dawn laughs. "I'll let you know."

"Working hard, I see." I raise a brow and cross my arms in

front of me.

"Eh, slow day. Plus, Ruby's been on my ass to try out that new demo she got her hands on. Honestly, it's not bad. There're a few graphical glitches near the edges of the playing field, but it's some of the most responsive FPS play I've had."

I just stare at her because half of that went straight over my head. She unfurls herself from the couch and stands before me. She's a little shorter than me and curvier, like Bridget, but her cut-up black *Resist* tee and leather miniskirt display the badass that she is. She's barefoot as she walks around the couch. I've known Dawn since I joined the derby team and introduced her to Nic. Back in the day, she was a crazy rebel hacker. She presides over anything and everything that has to do with tech in this business.

"Dex, this is Dawn." I motion between them. "Dawn is Nic's chief tech officer. Dawn, meet Dex, my boyfriend."

Dex's head jerks to face me before a smile graces his face. I take a deep breath because that's the first time that title felt real for him. They shake hands and exchange pleasantries.

"Come on," she says, motioning to us. "Follow me to my domain."

We walk behind her down the long hall, past office doors. Most are open, so I'm not surprised when I hear the voices within.

"You cost me five dollars, Mads," Vic says, leaning his blond head out the doorway.

I smirk at him and shrug. "Should mind your own business."

Vic and Cole man the security desk this time of day. There are cameras everywhere in this building, and definitely one on the elevator. Cole appears behind Vic. His white teeth contrast with his dark skin as he smiles at me.

"You knew we'd be betting," Cole says. "It's the first time you've brought a man here that you'd let touch you."

"Come on," Dawn says to Vic. "You *had* to know that was a dumb bet—he's only been here five minutes."

"I'm Cole, by the way." He offers his hand to Dex.

"Dex," he says as he shakes Cole's hand, then Vic's as Vic introduces himself.

Dex glances at me curiously but doesn't comment on the fact that I knew we were being watched and failed to tell him. I'd like to think I would've thought to tell him if he'd tried to take it much further.

"Now that you satisfied your curiosity about him," I say, raising a brow, "I suggest one of you needs to be watching that feed."

"On it, boss lady," Vic singsongs as he turns back into the dark room.

"I'm not your boss," I correct. "Just the voice of reason."

Cole grins again before following Vic back into the dark room. "Boss's mistress done put you in your place, son."

I roll my eyes. They were forever calling me that around here because I'm the only person they've ever seen tell Nic what to do—and he actually does it. But I've had to endure a lifetime of him for that privilege.

"She did the same to you, shut up," came Vic's reply.

I snort as we continue to Dawn's office. We only make it two steps before we're stopped again, this time by the background-check guys. I lean back into Dex.

"You should get used to this," I whisper to him. "Everyone here is going to be curious about you."

"We weren't expecting you until tomorrow," Keith says. "We've already got a pool going for Third Thursday."

I hold up my hand to stop him. "Quiet. Don't tell me about it because then I hafta tell Nic, and he'll shut that shit down."

"You're still on for tomorrow?" he asks.

At my nod, his eyes light up, and he ducks back into his office. The other guy, Richard, introduces himself.

"Nice to finally meet you," Rich says to Dex. "I was wondering if you'd put in an appearance. I did your background check months ago."

"That's not awkward," Dawn says. "Back to work, Rich. We have business to attend to."

She places a hand on his face and shoves him back into his office, rolling her eyes. Another head pokes out, and Dawn cuts them off before a word is uttered, clearing the path for us. We finally reach her office, and she ushers us in, shutting and locking the door behind us.

"Sorry about that, Dex," Dawn says, taking the seat behind her desk. "We don't get many visitors up here. Plus, these guys have been with us since we started. We operate more like a family here than a business, most of the time."

Dex takes a chair as I set my bag on the edge of Dawn's desk and pull out my laptop.

"I'm not sure if this video has a self-destruct on it or any of those other hidden tricks. I didn't turn it off, just shut the lid. I want you to see if you can find anything that might help us identify this creep. Something that might be embedded in the video?"

"I won't even turn it on," Dawn replies. "I'll quarantine the hard drive and scan it, then download the files. If anything is there, I'll let you know."

"There's something else I want you to look into." I look back at Dex, unsure of how he'll take this. "I'm sure you heard about Chloe?"

"Yeah, Ruby was telling me about it while we were playing earlier," Dawn says. "Bridget called her."

"Well, I didn't want to talk about it over the phone, but I want you to investigate the hack into the WitSec database. See if there's any sort of digital trail there too."

Dawn nods. "You think it's related?" I nod and release a long breath. "Got it. Is he trustworthy?" Her eyes dart to Dex.

"Yeah," I reply.

"I hope so, since you just asked me to commit a felony in his presence. And I know he's a cop."

"I'm her boyfriend first, cop second," Dex says, leaning forward in his seat. "You guys have a hard time keeping secrets." He pins me with his gaze.

"She didn't tell me." Dawn shrugs. "No one did, but I

make it my business to know everything about my friends. Especially this one, since she's a magnet for trouble."

I sigh as they watch each other, having some sort of silent battle of wills.

"Just know that if you hurt her, I can erase your identity and have you deported," Dawn says, leaning forward and propping her elbows on her desk.

Dex smirks. "Is this before or after I'm buried in lawsuits?"

Dawn laughs. "Of course Bridget got to you first. We'll probably rock-paper-scissor it out."

They both chuckle, and I've the sudden urge to kiss him. I relax a little, knowing that he gets along with my friends.

"Right, well, we'll get out of your hair," I say. "I'm going to give Dex the grand tour. Just call me when you have something."

"Can do, Cap'n," Dawn says in a silly voice, raising her hand in a salute.

I huff a chuckle myself as I grab Dex's hand and tug him out of his seat.

Chapter Seven

Now

We slip out of the office quickly and quietly to avoid getting caught in more conversations. When we reach the lounge room at the front of the office suite, I turn back to Dex. Going up on my toes, I kiss the corner of his mouth.

"Thank you," I say, smiling softly.

He gives me a lopsided smile, revealing one dimple. I reach out and trace it with my thumb. A tremor runs through his body, and he closes his eyes.

"For what?" he asks, his voice a rough whisper as he opens his eyes.

I shrug. "For putting up with me and the threats from my overprotective friends. It means a lot to me that you mesh well with them. They're important to me."

His eyes light up. I realize with a start what I'm really saying—he's becoming important to me. It feels like the floor dropped out from under me. *How could I have let him worm his way inside, knowing that he could walk away?* He might just yet. I turn back to the door and lead him to the elevator with renewed purpose. *By the end of this tour, he'll know the real me, and whether he sticks around after will be up to him.*

The trip down to floor twelve is fairly quick. Both of us are quiet, the nervous energy radiating off me, filling up the small space. We step out into the hallway. The wall of solid glass opposite us exposes the downtown landscape beyond. This floor of the building only has one room, and the hall circles around it, closing it off from outside view. The beige carpeting and plain white walls only serve to highlight the view.

I tug Dex's hand so he'll follow me to the nearest door. The door opens to reveal the pitch-black space within. I dig my phone out of my purse, then switch on the flashlight app and lead him down a few steps before urging him to sit in a seat.

"Wait here," I whisper to avoid the echo of my voice. "I'll go to the control room and turn on some lights."

The control room sits on this level, just behind the elevator shaft. My heels clack on the concrete floor, echoing around the expansive space. I dig my keys out of my purse and unlock the control room with the master key Nic gave me long ago. I hit the master switch for the lights, and the click echoes loudly as the spotlights turn on, highlighting the stage area below. The black walls and seats absorb most of the light, but there's still enough that I can see Dex looking around the room from the seat where I left him.

The room consists of a stage, with stadium seating on all four sides. It takes up both the eleventh and twelfth floor of the club and is the main area for shows that attract a lot of members.

I walk out of the control booth and approach him cautiously, building the courage to say what I need to with every step. *Inhale, summoning strength and courage to move forward. Exhale, releasing my fears and reservations.* My finger twists in the rubber band at my wrist in anticipation.

"We call this the arena," I say, my voice a little rougher than I hoped it would be. I clear my throat. "They do all sorts of shows here. But only one that I'm involved in."

I hear the snap of the rubber band as I let go of it, but I don't feel it. Dex looks at my wrist. His brows draw together as he reaches out and gently takes it into his hands. He turns my hand over, inspecting my wrist.

"Why do you wear this?" he asks.

I hesitate before answering. It's hard to put into words the things that I've never had the urge to explain before.

"It's supposed to remind me that I can feel something. That I'm alive. It's not always effective, but it helps sometimes."

He tugs on my hand until I sit down on his lap. His fingers brush aside hair from my face as he looks me over. "I assume that this isn't music-related. So what kind of show do you do here?"

"You asked me before about why I train, and I said it was to prepare for all this mess, but it's not entirely true. They host cage fights here, every third Thursday. I fight here. Men, women, it doesn't matter. There are a particular set of people who get off on watching fights or being in them. To do it in a place like this, where there are no rules..."

"Is that your thing?" he asks.

"Not the way you're thinking. I do it to feel something— it's not sexual. It's an acceptable outlet for my urges." I take a deep breath to steel myself. "After... after, Jared..." *Fuck, this is harder than I thought it would be.* My heart races as I struggle for breath. Dex nods and saves me from explaining more. Tears well in my eyes, blurring my vision. I breathe deep to stop them as I pull his hand down so I can turn away from him. "God, I don't want to talk about this." I drop my head back, speaking to the ceiling.

"You don't have to—" Dex starts.

I shake my head adamantly, cutting him off. "No, you need to know *why* I do this. Why this place exists. Nic, he gave me this place. Granted, he already had the connections to set it up, from a group he ran in college. So it wasn't a big leap to give it a permanent location. But I never put money into it. I'm only part owner because he wanted me to know it was for me. I was in a dark place back then." I snort a petulant laugh. "Still am, if I'm honest. I haven't always accepted who I am, what I like. He wanted to prove to me that I wasn't as twisted and sick as I believed myself to be. This place is a sort of therapy. With a flourish only Nic could provide."

"I don't think you're any of those things. I happen to love everything I've learned about you," Dex says, sliding his hand up my thigh and pushing my skirt up with it. "It means a lot to me that you're willing to show me all this. I know it's hard to open up sometimes."

I nod. My skin tingles in the wake of his touch, and I close my eyes, just feeling it. "You have no idea."

"Probably more than you think," he mutters.

I open my eyes. "How so?" I ask.

"When I was younger, I was angry at the world. I hurt people. I pushed everyone away. Physically, emotionally. Even with Marcus, I was a dick, but he didn't care. He would be a dick right back and shrug it off. But that's only because he understood where it all came from. Even when I wasn't willing to admit it to myself." It's his turn to look away as he swallows heavily. "Audra's mom. She was my half-brother's fiancée. I knew she had a thing for me, and when he pissed me off, I texted him from her phone, telling him to meet her. And I made sure we were fucking when he got there."

"Whoa," I say, a little more than appalled by that.

He gives me a wilted smile and continues. "At the time, I couldn't care less. I lied to her and used her as a means to an end. Made her believe I was in love. That was the only time I ever touched her, but the fact that she got pregnant left little room for my brother to forgive her. It wasn't until Audra came to me that any of that changed. Before she came into my life, I had only a fraction of a soul. All I did was work, eat, fuck, and my art. I was weak. Because pushing people away and being alone is the easy thing to do. Staying around, depending on someone and having them depend on you, that's the hard stuff. You make me want to work for this, Maddie. You're the only woman I've met that's made me want to try and stick it out."

"But you don't even know all of it," I argued. "What

happens when you don't agree with—"

"I don't need to know everything to know you're worth whatever work I hafta put into it. Did the story I just told you change how you view me?"

I think about it for a second, but the answer is pretty simple. "No, that's not who you are now."

"Exactly," he says a little smugly. He slides his hands up from my hips, cradling the sides of my face. "The past is the past. It molds us into who we are, but it doesn't define us."

I might just make you eat those words, I think. But I don't have the heart to say them out loud. I just shake my head. He needs to see the rest of it.

"Come on," I say and tug him from his seat. "There's lots more to see."

Then

After a month of writing sessions with Asher and Jared, we had come up with twenty-three songs for a possible album. Using my laptop and a microphone, we recorded a demo CD of our top five songs. Jared and I both sang the songs together. My bluesy guitar playing, a little punk inspiration, and our harmonic vocals made something I was so proud of. We had a distinctive sound.

I was on top of the world, especially after giving my boss, Nate, our CD, and his offer to produce an album for us. I was going to get firsthand knowledge on the production side of music, which was a dream come true. I was practically skipping my way through work as the time grew closer. Jared was taking the girls to stay at his parents' house for a few days. We had our studio time scheduled, starting at noon. It was only half past ten, but soon Asher and Jared would arrive, and we could get to work. It was going to be the longest four days of my life.

I set my Coke down on the desk and moved the desk chair in front of the filing cabinet, then got to work filing the contracts and other various papers Nate had handed me when I walked in. No sooner did I sit than the phone rang. I scooted over and grabbed the receiver and answered. The rest of the guys were in the recording booth, wrapping up with the current rental.

"Barton Creek Recording, this is Maddie speaking. How can I help you?"

And nothing. Just some heavy breathing or sawing on the other end. I tried again.

"Hello?"

I checked the phone. The mute wasn't on, and the line was in use. Weird. I hung up. It didn't ring again, so I went back to filing. I lost track of time. Next thing I knew, hands were covering my eyes and familiar lips landed on mine. I kissed him back. When he broke contact, I grinned.

"Who is this?" I asked.

"You better know who it is to kiss him like that," Jared whispered in my ear.

"Oh, it's you." I tried to feign disappointment.

"That's how we're going to play this?"

He spun my office chair around to face him. My smile grew bigger when my gaze landed on him. I'd never tire of looking at him. His gorgeous black hair had grown out again to the tops of his ears, even though the sides and back were still kept neat and short. His black stubble was already beginning to show in a five-o'clock shadow. Delicious.

"As long as you're ready to play? I'm down for anything you got. Bring. It. On." I licked my lips.

"You're impossible, woman." He grabbed my hand, plucking me from the chair. "We've got work to do."

"You're the one who came into my work looking all dead sexy, kissing me senseless, when we have zero alone time for the next eighty-four hours," I pouted.

"I *will* make it up to you," he said slowly, emphasizing each word with a step as he walked me backward toward the door.

"You better."

I turned down the hallway and into the large room outside the recording booth. Barton Creek Recording was not a big operation by any stretch of the imagination. We had one recording booth. The studio was built in a beautiful stone-sided building that used to be a small church before the church moved to a larger location. All the outer windows were stained glass with various religious scenes inlaid. The raised dais that once set the stage for a pulpit was walled in to create the recording booth with a large plate glass window facing the large room we were standing in. The small hallway we had come from had several rooms, the tiny kitchen, a couple of offices, a storage room, bathrooms, and the crash pad. The crash pad was just a tiny room with blackout curtains and several cots lining the wall to crash on during long recording sessions.

We mostly rented and produced local bands wanting to record demos. Lately, Nate had been toying with the idea of starting a record label for the ones he actually got in there with and produced, like he was working with us. We were getting star treatment, and I took that to mean good things were headed our way.

I rolled a chair over in front of the three huge panels that made up the soundboard. The walls on either side of us were lined with shelves stacked with various tuners and other things I was only beginning to get a handle on. The manual on this shit was a longer read than the Bible.

I watched Nate in fascination as he switched things on and adjusted dials.

"Do you need me to get anything? Are we all set up?" I nodded to the recording booth where Asher was setting up his drum kit.

"Yeah, here." He reached into the front pocket of his button-down shirt and pulled out the little notepad he kept there. He ripped out a page and held it out to me. "It's all on the list."

That was the way Nate operated, or we operated. He went around and made notes of what he needed and shoved a list at me when he had a moment; I fetched.

After getting everything set up, we played through the twenty-eight songs and voted them down to a final thirteen that would make the cut for the album. Twenty-eight hours in and functioning on two hours of sleep, we were in the process of cleaning up a track and recording the drums. I was sitting next to Nate, listening intently to the beat through the headphones.

"He's good," Nate said, picking up one side of my earphones.

"I know," I replied. "I'm not sure why he wasn't already picked up by someone. You should hear him let loose—fucking John Bonham, Jr. there."

Nate nodded and adjusted a dial. Hitting the intercom button, he spoke to Asher. "Take it back three bars. I think I had some interference. You're doing good, kid."

Asher nodded, then started again, doing exactly what was asked of him. He was shirtless and sweaty. It wasn't hot in the recording booth, but drums were hard work. He had a tattoo on the left side of his chest, over his heart, that I hadn't even known was there before. It looked like crossed drumsticks with a name and date above them. It made me curious as to the story behind that.

I sprang from my seat when Nic walked in with dinner. This was probably the most excited I'd ever been to see him. Plus, I was a little delusional and a lot giddy on endorphins from the lack of sleep. I somehow managed to retrieve the bag of tacos from Nic without chewing his arm off, which was exactly how hungry I was.

"Nic, I love you."

"I know." He winked. "It's why I do what I do."

"Nate, heads up." I tossed him a taco. "Tell Asher to take five and come eat."

He nodded and complied while I laid out the rest of the food on the coffee table. Then I got up and went to the door of the crash pad. I opened it quietly and stepped in. Jared was asleep with his back to the door. I shook him.

"Hey, wake up. It's been two hours, and the food's here."

He hooked an arm around me and pulled me down onto the cot with him. We were lying face-to-face.

"You should sleep with me." He snuggled into my neck and took a deep breath.

"I wish we could, Jare, but the tracks don't record themselves. Let me up." I squirmed to get out of his grasp, but he squeezed me tighter. "Come on. If you keep me here any longer, I'm going to fall asleep, and there's Torchy's waiting on us."

His eyes flew open, and I laughed. Not many could resist the call of a Torchy's taco. My mouth watered thinking about the barbacoa taco with my name on it out there. I rolled over him, and halfway up, I froze. I could make out the dark shape of a small object on the cot perpendicular to the one Jared and I were on.

"Jared, do you see that?" I asked, pushing off him so he could turn over and look.

I turned on the light and was blinded for a moment before my eyes adjusted, and sure enough, there on the cot was a single red calla lily.

"Shit," Jared cursed.

"Was that there when you came in here?" I asked.

"I don't know. I was a fucking zombie when I walked in here."

"I'll call Officer Martinez. You go eat."

"There's a piece of paper under it."

"Don't touch it. Leave it. Officer Martinez will know how to handle it. I want to get out of here and go back in there with the others."

"Okay." He sat up in the bed, scrubbing a hand over his face.

Perhaps because I was exhausted, perhaps because the girls were safely away at Jared's parents' house, but I didn't freak out like I normally did. I went to my purse, dug out Officer Martinez's card, and called him. When he was on his way, I sat down and ate my food.

Chapter Eight

Now

Dex and I find ourselves arriving on the twenty-second floor at the entrance to the main club. It's a long hallway lined with colored mood lighting and a waterfall that spans the wall opposite the windows that overlook the city below. The sun is still setting, so it isn't quite as impressive as it is at night.

Just before the doors leading into the club, there's a counter. Sitting behind it, Nikki—the hostess—is playing on her phone. My heels click loudly on the black marble floors as I approach, and she looks up. A smile breaks out on her beautiful face. Her dark skin is flawless, but her wild, natural curls with their honey-colored highlights make her seem more down-to-earth and approachable.

"I was wondering how long it would take you to get here," Nikki says. "Cole texted and told me you were showing a guest around." She grins, leaning her elbows on the counter and looking Dex over without a hint of shame. "Mmm mmm mmm, tasty. If he doesn't work out with you, you could always send him our way." She winks at Dex. "Come here, girl. It's been too long." She hugs me over the counter and cradles my face, giving me a quick kiss on the lips.

"Nikki, this is Dex. Dex, meet Nikki. She's the club's lead hostess, and Cole, the security guy you met upstairs, is her

73

husband."

Dex's cheeks tint a pale pink. That's the only hint that he caught what she was offering. His face otherwise remains impassive as his eyes dart to me. I smile at him, wondering how long it will take him to say something about this place or the people who frequent the club.

"Do you want to explain to him how this works, or should I?" I ask Nikki, changing the subject.

"It would be my pleasure," she says with a smirk. She reaches under the counter and pulls out containers of paint, some paintbrushes, and a mask. "Come here, honey." She waves Dex over to her.

He hesitates, and I give him a little nudge forward.

"Everyone who comes in here gets painted by me," Nikki says, peeking up through her long lashes at Dex before taking his arm and running her long fingernail up to his shoulder. "Well, I've never gotten to paint your girl here, but I'm hoping your presence here'll change that."

Dex looks back at me, a small smile tipping up the corner of his mouth.

Nikki continues. "On your left arm, you get a white stripe if you're open to participate or red if you're part of a couple or group looking for others. If you're just here to watch or be watched, we leave it bare. Your right gets one of these." She gestures to the remaining paints and switches her hold to his right arm. "Pink means you're open to women, blue for men, yellow for both, and green means you're open to everything. And again, bare if you're just here to watch or be watched."

Dropping his arm, she picks up the mask. "Everyone who comes in here wears one of these. Most of the members have their own, but there are a few back here for guest use, like this one. Some people still like the anonymity of the mask, so it isn't optional. But anything goes in here aside from that. You can take it downstairs to one of the private rooms or upstairs to an exhibition room."

"The mask is required in all the members-only areas," I add. "Even the private rooms, which are monitored. The only reason we aren't wearing them now is that it's not technically open."

"Yeah, you guys still got about an hour." Nikki holds out the mask to Dex. "Here, keep this one. I'm sure you'll need it soon enough."

"Thanks," Dex says as he takes the mask.

"No problem," she replies. "Hope to see you around." She looks at me with a sly smile. "I gotta head to the back and restock the paints for tonight. You're still on for tomorrow, right?"

"Yeah."

"Okay," Nikki says, replacing the paint under the counter. "Enjoy the rest of your tour, Dex. Later, Mads." With a wave, she disappears through the door behind her, leaving Dex and me alone.

"Sooo—" I draw out the word. "You want to see the inside?" I nod in the direction of the curtained entrance to the club.

"I do," Dex drawls as he loops his arms around me. "But I also really want to get you alone right now."

He walks me backward until my shoulders press against the window. My heart skips a beat, and in that moment his lips are on mine. My breath, and any words I may have thought of, evaporates. The kiss goes on until I find my brain thoroughly scrambled. When he finally breaks away, we both struggle for breath. He presses his forehead against mine.

"You really have no clue," he murmurs. "You're like a nugget of gold trying to convince everyone else you're just an ordinary rock."

I shake my head. "You really should reserve that judgment until after you've seen it all."

He raises his scarred eyebrow. "There's more?"

"Yeah, there is." I take a deep breath.

I get lost in his eyes as he studies me. My phone dings and I jolt. Dex steps back, and I dig the offending object out of my purse. A new text message from Nic is there.

> Where you at? Want me to meet you?

> We're at the club. I'm thinking... Maybe we should just show him?

> Don't think that would go over well. But whatever you want. It's your ball game.

I snort a laugh as I type. Dex looks at me with pinched brows and a small smile, before turning away and wandering into the club.

> Yeah. I'm not sure I've the words to explain it. I never thought I'd ever have to.

> You know I'm happy to help you. And if it doesn't work out, that's OK.

> I don't know. Chances are, he won't be on board.

> Don't do that. You won't know until you try. *Diana Ross voice* You will survive.

> *LOL, you're a dork, but I <3 you.*

I glance at the time at the top of the screen and gasp.

> *Umm... maybe tomorrow, Lucky. We gotta get the girls soon.*

> *KK Let me know*

I'm just about to stuff my phone back in my purse when it dings again. This time, it's a four-word text from Dawn.

> *I'm ready for you.*

> *Be right there.*

I walk into the club, searching for Dex. The red walls are lined with alcoves filled with black booths and benches, framed with black curtains that can be drawn for privacy. Cages hang from the ceiling for dancers and adventurous patrons. Catwalks frame the room from above and lead to glass-floored rooms. It all seems fairly benign when empty like this.

I spot Dex chatting with a bartender, Seth. They laugh. Seth stocks the shelves with liquor, prepping for the night's business. Dex's back is to me as I approach, but Seth freezes when he sees me, and his eyebrows climb up.

"He's with you?" Seth asks.

Dex turns around and his eyes light up for me.

"I really wish people would stop acting so surprised about that," I say.

The corner of Dex's mouth twitches. "I don't know. I

kind of like it."

"Of course you would." I laugh silently. "What're you two up to?"

"Oh," Seth says. "He was asking about what it costs to be a member here."

I nod. I know the answer. There's no set price. Membership is built on monthly donations based on what the member can afford to pay, and all donations are kept private. Nic didn't want to create a world where only the rich elite were allowed to participate, so he relied on some rather extreme vetting with interviews and background checks. The whole process is rather invasive, but worth it if this kind of place can help the applicant. We have members that range from college students and schoolteachers to celebrities and politicians.

"I take it you filled him in?" I ask, and Seth nods. I turn to Dex. "Dawn's ready for us. We should head upstairs."

Dex pulls me to his side and kisses my forehead. "Thanks, man," he says to Seth, reaching out and shaking his hand.

"No problem, bud. It was nice to meet you."

"Same here," Dex replies as he starts toward the door.

We retreat to the elevator. Since there are only a few floors between the offices and the club, it's only a few minutes before we find ourselves standing in Dawn's office again.

"You should sit," she says.

I frown and sit in the chair across from her desk. Dex sits too.

"It's not the same person," Dawn says. "The video you gave me wasn't encrypted very well. It took me less than a minute to break it. I was able to find the mobile IP address from its creation, but since they're assigned randomly and change frequently, it doesn't really help. It tells me that the person who made this is in Austin, but that's obvious because they had to be near you to take the video. That's not to say the person isn't somewhat skilled. They did wipe any other identification from the video, but the fact that they missed this makes me think they're not as thorough."

"I'll take your word for it," I mutter.

"On the other hand, the hack into WitSec was done by someone with some impressive skills. Aside from the obvious, that they could get inside in the first place..." Dawn laughs. "I followed the digital trail, if you will, and it was forwarded through so many foreign servers that I thought I wasn't going to find anything. But you have to look at this." She waved us over to her computer.

Her screen is filled with zeroes and ones, which are moving in some sort of pattern. Dex is chewing on his lower lip with a furrowed brow, but I don't see any signs that he understands what we're looking for.

"You're gonna have to help me out here," I say. "What is this?"

"Unfocus your eyes," Dawn instructs.

I cross my eyes and then try to stare through the computer. I start growing impatient. It's like one of those annoying magic-eye pictures at the mall. I finally see it, and my stomach drops. My hand flies up to my mouth as I back away. Dex glances at me but turns back to the computer with a determined look.

"It's him," I say as I drop back into my seat. My head feels like I just did a stint on the Tilt-A-Whirl.

"It can't be." Dawn turns back to me. "People like me... we don't dumb ourselves down. It's an ego thing. The guy that made this bread crumb did not make that video. I can promise you that. But it's not outside of the realm of possibility that your creeper hired someone to get that information."

"But..." I dig my phone out of my purse. "Here. Look at this."

I open the photo app to the picture of the scene from my dining room earlier today and hand it to her.

"Oh," Dawn says and swallows heavily. She looks back to the hummingbird flapping its wings in binary code on her computer and then to me. "Well, it's shaping up to be a signature. But what's the deal with hummingbirds? I thought your guy's thing was your favorite flower?"

"It is. It was. I mean—he changed the background screen on my laptop to a calla lily when he left that video, and that was just this morning."

It was just this morning, but I already feel like I'd lived through months over the last few hours. I rub my forehead in frustration. I'm exhausted, too.

"I noticed," Dawn mutters.

A frown mars her features as she studies the picture on my phone. Dex sits on the edge of her desk.

"The only thing left to figure out is, why are there seven birds?" Dex asks. "I think Dawn's right."

Dawn holds up her fist, and his shoulders jump in a silent laugh. He bumps her fist before he continues.

"I don't think these are the same person. And maybe this"—he points to my phone—"was a message for Chloe, not you. But with her being in custody, whoever is after her thought you were the best conduit to get to her."

"Fucking great," I sighed. "I can't deal with this. Like I needed another person breaking into my house."

Then

It had been a long day at the studio, then roller derby practice. We had put the final cuts for the music on our album after weeks of adjustments. The process was way more complicated than I thought it was going to be, but I was thrilled to have gone through the experience. Nate had assigned me to work with him on our new clients, instead of just coffee and filing, and that was thrilling, too.

Officer Martinez said they hadn't been able to lift any fingerprints from the evidence he picked up, but the good news was with that added to my case file, they were more likely to begin an investigation. I hadn't heard anything back, though, and that was troubling. I was choosing to push it to the back of my mind because everything else was moving in the right direction.

The house was dark when I walked in. "Hello?" I called, my voice almost echoing in the empty dark space.

The hair on my arms stood on end. *Where are Jared and the girls?* I walked back to the kitchen to set my purse on the counter and grab a Coke. Jared was sitting at the dining room table in the dark, motionless. I frowned.

"What're you doing? Where are the girls?" My voice seemed hollow in the stillness surrounding us.

"I took off from work early today, drove the girls out to my parents' place," Jared replied. "We need some alone time."

"Can't argue with that," I said, sitting in the chair next to him, trying to shake off the uneasy feeling I had. "That doesn't explain why you're sitting here in the dark."

"We need to talk," he sighed, scrubbing his hands over his face and leaning his elbows on the table. My whole body went on high alert. "I got called today. My unit's being deployed to Afghanistan."

"What?" I jumped from my chair, the urge to pace taking over my body. "How is that possible? You're out of the Army."

"I'm not out of the Army." He grasped my arm, halting my movement. "My contract was for six years' active duty and two years of reserves. I still have nine months of reserve duty. It's why I report to Camp Mabry once a month."

"I thought that was some veterans' thing." I rubbed my forehead with my free hand. "How long?"

"Nine months." His voice was void of emotion, and no further explanation came.

My mind was overwhelmed with thoughts, but I chose to focus on the least painful thing to quell my panic.

"This is horrible timing. We're done with the edits. The album releases next Tuesday. Not that I expect any sales. We haven't played any gigs. I was hoping to talk to you about setting up a show. Ruby wants us to play our first gig at her bar."

"I know," he said solemnly, looking out the window. "I'm not worried about that. I'm worried about you. You have a stalker, Maddie. This means I'm leaving you and the girls here alone."

That was the last thing I wanted to think about at that moment.

"I know," I echoed, crawling into his lap. "I'm trying not to think about that because it honestly doesn't do any good. We can't live our lives in fear of this creep."

He kissed my forehead and hugged me closer. "I don't like it."

"We don't have a choice. Do we?" My voice sounded timid and small. I hated the weakness it exposed.

He huffed out a breath, pushing my hair away from my face. "You could go stay with my parents?" His thumb brushed over my cheek.

"No. I can't," I argued, shaking my head. His hand fell away. "I've my job, the derby, the girls have school. We can't just up and leave everything behind."

"I had to try." He gave me a sad smile. "I talked to Nic about moving in. He agreed. He can stay in my old room upstairs, or out in the guest house. Your choice. You okay with that?"

"Yeah, that sounds great, actually." I picked imaginary lint from his shirt. "I don't want to be here alone."

"Good," he sighed, hugging me tighter.

"He can choose where he wants to stay," I muttered, snuggling closer. "I don't care either way."

"I'll let him know." Some of the tension left his body. "He'll be here on Sunday."

"So soon?" I asked. "When are you leaving?"

"I have to report to Camp Mabry on Monday."

"Oh," I replied for lack of anything better to say.

A tear tracked down my cheek, and he brushed it away.

"Don't cry. I can't handle it right now. Just try to look at it this way: it means we have two whole days to ourselves before I leave." He shifted me, so I was straddling his lap. "I spent the whole day with the girls. My parents are driving them back on Sunday evening. Forty-eight hours of me and you."

He kissed my collarbone and trailed kisses out to my shoulder, tugging my shirt aside.

"Whatever will we do with all that time," I said on a sigh, trying to let go of my worry and fear.

"I've got some ideas." His voice dropped low, making my belly clench.

I smirked. "Oh, really?"

"Yeah, I'm about to get creative." He waggled his eyebrows, a grin tugging one side of his full lips upward.

"Are you?" I laughed, then froze when his eyes pinned me in place with a heated look. "I love you," I whispered.

"I'm about to show you how much I love you right now," he said, pulling my shirt over my head.

Chapter Nine

Now

We're walking in the back door, after picking up the girls, when it hits me like a ton of bricks. Today has been the longest day of my existence. We ate dinner with the kids at the Mad House, so it's nearly ten when we finally make it home. I feel ragged to the bone and dead tired. My shoulders slump and my eyelids grow heavy as a yawn forces its way out of me.

The smell of wet paint permeates the air, though Bridget and her workers cleared out of here over an hour ago. Passing all the paparazzi outside the gate when we got home, it dawned on me that it has been less than twenty-four hours since the media was stirred up by that video and the more graphic version showed up on my laptop. I woke up this morning not trusting Dex and finished the day introducing him to the world that encompasses my deepest darkest secrets. And Chloe and Evan are gone.

It's only been a handful of hours, but it feels like it's been years. I wish I could sit down with Evan and just talk to him, which is funny, I know. Normally he'd have to pry it out of me, but now that he's not here, I just want to tell him everything that has happened.

I press my hands on the counter, gripping it tight so the

squared bottom edge bites into my skin. I can hear the girls talking about their day, but none of it's registering.

"Ugh, what is that smell?" Cat asks, walking past me to the entrance of the dining area.

Cora and Audra follow in her wake, but they all freeze at the doorway. I've a momentary panic attack, thinking that the vandalism is still there. I eat up the distance in a few short strides.

"Holy shit, that is awesome!" Audra exclaims.

"Whoa, when did you decide to redecorate?" Cora asks.

I stare at my newly painted dining room in shock and maybe a little awe. *Leave it to Bridget to take creative license with my house.* I take in the freshly painted wall covered in bright graffiti art. There are guitars, skates, music notes... It's all very... me.

My shoulders heave in silent laughter. I'm rendered wordless, unable to articulate a reaction. My brain's just too tired to process any thought or feeling I might have about it. Dex massages my shoulders as another yawn cracks my jaw.

He leans down to my ear. "You should go to bed. I'll get the girls down for the night and join you in a few minutes."

I stiffen at that but then force myself to relax. He didn't say anything inappropriate. It's just a force of habit to keep that part of my life away from the girls. I know they heard it by the look of shock on their faces as they turn to me. I nod and turn to Dex, going up on my toes to kiss his cheek.

"Thank you," I murmur. "I'm beat."

I turn to the girls and hug each one, including Audra, kissing them on the cheek and telling them good night. I hear Dex telling them that we decided the dining room needed a change this afternoon as he ushers them up the stairs. I head to my room. I strip off my clothes while brushing my teeth. I'm too tired to be bothered with anything else.

My eyes close as soon as my head hits the pillow.

The loud screeching alarm rings in my ear long after it stops. I wander through the dark hallway, guided by the thin, pale strips of moonlight that fall across the floor through the windows of various rooms that line the hall. I hear a grunt and look up. He's standing there, highlighted by the moonlight, blood soaking his shirt from the shoulders down. His lifeless eyes pin me into place.

"You," he grates in a hoarse, raspy whisper that seems too loud in the quiet between us. "You did this to me."

Tears streak down my face. "I'm sorry," I plead.

"That's not good enough. You have to pay," he says as he moves toward me without taking a step. The moonlight follows him, so I see his face as it distorts into an angry mask. His hands wrap around my throat. I can't breathe. I claw at his hands, trying to scream, but the pressure on my throat is enough to keep my silence.

I sit up, gasping for breath and choking. I cough loudly, nearly gagging myself. Dex's hand rubs over my back, soothing.

"Shh, it's okay. You're okay," he coos.

A sob racks my body. "It's never gonna be enough. I can't ever make it right."

"Come here," he says, tugging me down and tucking me into his side.

My head rests on his shoulder as he pushes my hair back from my face with one hand while the other one traces a line from my shoulder down to my wrist and back up again.

"We can't ever make it right, but we can make better choices going forward," Dex says in a soothing voice. "Try to be the best version of ourselves and make it better. The past can never be rewritten, but we can learn from it and move forward."

"How?" I ask.

"You're already doing it. It floors me how you can't see the mark you leave on everything around you. So many people love you because you give so much of yourself to make them happy. You've made it my mission in life to make you see that and make you happy."

I spread my hand out on his bare chest and listen to the steady rhythm of his heart. "You only say that because you don't know what you don't know."

"You could tell me, but I'm gonna be honest with you."

His chest rises under my hand with a deep breath. "I think you take on too much responsibility with this. Sometimes, murders happen, and it's no one's fault but the one who committed the homicide."

I laugh darkly. "I almost forgot that you're a cop for a minute there."

"What does that mean?" he asks.

"You know that whole murder bit's bullshit? He wasn't murdered. I tried telling them that, but no one wants to believe me." I sit up, shaking my head. "No, they just want to make money off it. The news gets ratings, the police get a major case, paid interviews are offered... It was all for spectacle, and it still is. He killed himself because of what I did. It's really quite simple. And either way you look at it, he wouldn't have been there if it weren't for me."

"I did read your file, so I know that you feel that way. I just don't understand why," Dex says somberly.

"Why do you think it's murder?" I ask.

"Because the forensics—" Dex starts.

I interrupt. "Right, because someone told you. I was there, and I'm telling you something different. I studied their evidence. Bridget was allowed discovery when they were pressing charges against me, and that's the thing. There's no real evidence to suggest murder. His prints were the only ones on the gun. Ballistics put the shots at point-blank range. Even the angles... I may be grieving, but I'm not stupid. And this, the fact that I've gotta explain it to you... I'm trying hard to trust you. I want to believe you, but here, you're actin' like one of them.

"And it's clear that a line has been drawn. Someone wants me locked away. They wouldn't have inserted you into my life to find evidence otherwise. They just don't have anything to make it stick. But it's only a matter of time. If they can't find it, someone is going to make something up. Even Bridget's seen convictions built on shitty evidence. So, you're either on their side or mine."

He sits up again, clasping my cheeks, forcing me to look at

him. "I'm on your side."

I search his eyes. I see nothing but sincerity and love.

"I'm trying to give you the benefit of the doubt," I say. "Because, right now, everything inside of me is screaming to send the girls away. Someone is coming. Something is going to happen before all this is over, and I can't imagine that it's going to be a tea party. Bridget, Holly, Dawn, Ruby… they're all big girls and can choose to stick around, but it's my job to ensure the girls' safety—"

"I agree," Dex says.

My jaw drops. "What?"

"I was going to talk to you about it in the morning, but I think they should go to their grandparents' for a while."

"What made you change your mind?"

"When we were at your friend's office and she showed us the hummingbird she found in the binary code, it was bothering me because I felt like I'd seen it before. And I remembered this—" He gets up and crosses the room to where his clothes lay on a chair. He pulls out a piece of paper from his jeans pocket and hands it to me. "When we first met, this was sitting on the chair in my station, just before you showed up."

I unfold the paper, and my stomach drops like I swallowed a sack of lead weights. It's a sketch of a hummingbird. And now that I'm looking at it, I do remember him asking the other artists if it belonged to them. So it definitely has something to do with me. Not just Chloe. I take a deep breath because I just don't know what this all means.

"I had seen something like this before through work. When we were at the Mad House—you and Tina were finishing up dinner—I asked your friend Monk to use his computer, and we found it."

"Found what?"

"It's a symbol a few Mexican cartels use when going to war. Mostly ones in central Mexico that have a heavy Aztec influence. Do you have any connection to Mexican cartels?"

I raise a brow like that should even be a question. "No.

Why would I?"

"I don't know for sure if it's a connection—it's a bird. It could mean anything. I was going to ask if it was your favorite bird, but you already dealt with a lot of news yesterday. I just figured this could wait until morning."

"Well, you *figured* wrong. No, hummingbirds aren't my favorite bird. It really doesn't mean anything to me. And granted, the stalker's already twisted enough to use my favorite flower, but that doesn't explain the message. The fact that there were seven dead birds. Or that it was in Chloe's WitSec file hack… You should've told me. This isn't good. We don't know what we're up against and we need to get the girls out of here. Now."

"So you could do what, exactly? Ship the girls off to their grandparents' in the middle of the night—"

"Yes!"

"—causing them to stress and worry about the danger their mother may be in? They may still be kids, Maddie, but they're almost thirteen. You can't hide this from them completely. You have to think about how it's going to affect them."

He's right. But I don't want to admit it as I pace the floor. I want to slap him down for daring to tell me how to handle my kids. I stop to look at him. *What is it about him that triggers this fight-or-flight response in me?* I'm either running away from him or fighting him about everything. It had been like that since the moment I met him. Like he could see right through me, and it made me want to hide or kick his ass, but it was more than that. He scared me because the way he affected me was so different, so much more. *What does that say about everything that has happened?*

Not wanting to think about that, I shift my attention back to the current situation. I'm being unreasonable. Dex was trying to help, and I can't find fault in that. And with that thought, the fight leaves me. My shoulders drop, and I stop pacing.

A tiny smile plays at his lips. Not enough to seem like

gloating, but enough that I know he's happy with my response.

"Fine, whatever," I grumble. "How do you want to do this, then?"

He looks over at the alarm clock on my nightstand. "Well, seeing that it's three in the morning, we should go back to sleep." He pats the bed next to him with a yawn. "I don't think you realize what your naked pacing is doing to me."

I finally focus on myself, only now realizing in my tiredness earlier that I forgot to put on a nightgown. A smile tugs at the corner of my lips as he adjusts himself under the covers. I answer with a yawn as I crawl back in bed.

"I don't normally sleep naked," I add.

"I could get used to this," he says, pulling me to his side. His hand runs down my back, squeezing my ass. "I think I might insist that it be a regular habit when I'm here."

I propped my chin on his chest. He gives me a sleepy smile, flashing those adorable dimples. I lift up the blanket and peer at his flannel pants with a frown.

"What if I insist the same?" I ask.

His eyebrows rise. "I think that can be arranged because I do normally sleep naked. I just didn't want to freak you out if you weren't expecting me to be here when you woke up."

"How thoughtful of you," I huff a laugh. "But I really don't mind."

"Hush, woman. Go to sleep. Morning will come soon enough."

"How am I supposed to molest you in your sleep if you keep your chastity pants on?"

"Patience, Maddie. All good things come with time," he murmurs as his eyes drift shut.

I rest my head on his shoulder and listen to his heart beating steadily as his breathing evens out. I can't imagine that I'll be able to get back to sleep, but I close my eyes and think about what tomorrow will entail. There's already a lot on the agenda, but just thinking about getting back in the ring tomorrow night makes the muscles in my shoulders relax further.

Then

I was skating around the track as fast as my wheels would roll. We were doing qualifying tests for the upcoming season. Bonnie was timing us two at a time. I was currently in the lead against Bridget, but she was gaining on me, the rest of the team cheering us on. On the last lap, my eye caught on a guy in the visitor area, snapping pictures of us. I was distracted, and Bridget zoomed past me just as we crossed the finish line.

It wasn't a race, but I was pissed at myself for not winning. I put my hands on my knees and let my speed slow to cool down.

"I can't believe I caught you," Bridget said as I rolled up beside her.

"I was distracted by that," I said, motioning to the guy in the visitor area. Practices were closed—family and friends could drop by, but this guy I'd never seen before. "You know who he is?"

"No," Bridget answered. "Never seen him."

Bonnie, facing the other direction, had already started another set of girls. No one but Bridget and I had noticed him. Maybe because I had a stalker, his presence bothered me more than the others. Call it morbid curiosity, but I skated over to the visitor area.

"Are you here for someone?" I asked, tilting my head.

He lowered his camera to look at me. "Are you the one from the band Stateside, Laine Dobransky?"

"Yes," I answered and froze.

How did he know about Stateside? The album had been out for months, but our sales were abysmal, due to lack of promotion. I scrutinized him from head to toe. He was average-looking, wearing a button-down shirt and jeans. A slight gut, but not too prominent. He didn't look familiar at all.

"Is it true that you're engaged to your bandmate, Jared Wilson?"

"Yes, but—" I held up a hand in front of me as he snapped another picture.

"And that he's currently overseas in Afghanistan?"

"Listen, just who the fuck are you?" I demanded. "Why are you asking about this?"

"I'm sorry," he said as a blush stole over his cheeks. "I sometimes let the story get away with me. I'm Josh Banks from the *Austin Chronicle*." He offered his hand.

"Story?" My mouth opened and closed like a fish as I tried to grasp hold of the situation. "Why are you doing a story on me?"

His hand dropped as he realized I wasn't shaking it. "You don't know?"

"I've no clue what you're talking about. How do you know about my band?"

"Oh, two days ago, someone created an online video using your song 'Coming Home' with a montage of soldiers returning from the war. I figured you would know since they had to purchase the rights. It went viral. But it blew up on the global stage when someone found out that the singers are actually separated by deployment right now. Your song's a hit, but you and your fiancé are the bigger story. Do you mind answering some questions?"

"I'm sorry. She's not available for comment at this time. You're not allowed in here. I'm going to have to ask you to leave," Bridget said from my right, startling me.

She grabbed my shoulder and spun me around. Ruby, Sloane, Dawn, and Holly stood behind me but skated around to form a wall between the reporter and us.

"As your lawyer, I'm advising you not to talk to anyone." Her face was plastered with a huge grin.

"My lawyer?" I asked, my brows creasing in confusion.

She shrugged. "I think you're ready to hire me."

"But you're a criminal lawyer." My brain was fried from

the bombardment of news.

"Yeah," she sighed. "I went to school to do entertainment law, but it's surprisingly hard to break into—especially around here. Now, I have an in. And you're going to love having me working for you."

"I am?" I sort of laughed; I was trying hard not to cry.

"Of course you are," she cooed, patting my head.

"Okay," I said skeptically, "but I don't have any money to pay you."

"I bet you do. When was the last time you checked your album sales?"

"Not for weeks." I shook my head. "There hasn't been any activity on it."

"Well, you should check." She grabbed her bag off the floor from the center of the track and tossed her phone at me. "Go ahead. I have a feeling about this."

I logged into my account with our distribution company, and my wheels flew out from under me. I landed flat on my ass. The girls gathered around me, curious as to what was going on. I'd never seen so many digits in all my life. Well, not associated with my name. *Holy fuck. I'm rich.*

Bridget grabbed the phone from me. "Looks like I'm getting a raise." She laughed loudly.

"This is unreal. How could this happen?" I asked, still trying to wrap my mind around it.

The door slammed shut to the practice area. Asher and Nate were coming toward me, both wearing matching grim expressions.

"I see you already found out," Asher said as he approached. "I came to make sure you get home okay. Have you looked outside recently?"

"No," I answered.

"It's a circus out there," Nate said. "Word got out that you were here."

"Holy shit, you're famous," Holly said, gripping my hand. Sloane settled on my other side.

"That can't be true," I denied.

"Look." Ruby held up her phone, and the video the reporter mentioned was on her Facebook feed. She pushed Play, and our song started filling the space.

"Your picture is on the news, too," Carly, one of my other teammates, said, walking up beside me.

She was showing me a local news clip from her feed. The sound was off, but the local reporter was talking, and a picture of Jared and me from high school filled the space next to his head. *What in the actual fuck? This isn't how you* made it, *right?* We hadn't even toured or even played a gig.

Nate's voice pulled me from my reverie. "Maddie, I think we should head to your house. We have some calls to make. You need to arrange for a publicist and a lawyer—"

"She's got one of those," Bridget said with a grin. "Bonnie, I think we're going to cut out of here early to go handle some stuff. Cool?"

"Yeah, yeah," Bonnie said, looking as shocked as I felt.

"I'm coming with," Holly said. "Moral support."

"Me, too," Sloane added. "She needs her stylist and best friend." She grinned at me.

Asher reached down to help me off the floor. "You ready for this? There's a lot of people outside. We just gotta make it to your car. I'm with you through this. Okay?"

"How are you dealing with this? Did you see our numbers?" I asked.

"I'm fine." He tilted his head. "But I'm not the one they're after for a personal story. I get to enjoy the dough rolling in, but I don't get the shit that comes with it. Nobody's concerned about the drummer." He smiled.

"Yet," Bridget stated. "I wouldn't get too comfortable. Fame can turn on anyone."

I took my skates off and packed up my stuff. I walked toward the door, Bridget, Holly, Sloane, Asher, and Nate in tow. At the front door, I got my first look outside. They weren't kidding. There was a crowd of people with cameras and microphones, standing around waiting. It was surreal to think they were there for me.

"We're coming, too," Dawn said as she and Ruby rushed to join us. "We'll run interference."

Ruby pounded her fist into her hand. "Just another night for me." She grinned.

Bridget handed me a jacket. "Put this over your head and go straight to your car. Don't stop. Don't say anything."

"This is surreal," Holly said, echoing my thoughts.

"I wish Jared was here," I muttered, gripping my keys tightly. Then I opened the door to my new reality.

Chapter Ten

Now

When I enter my office, I close the door and the smile I plastered on my face all morning falls away. The tears that had been just below the surface gather until they hover on the edge of my lashes. I cross the room. The blinds covering the full-wall window that overlooks the creek below glide open. I take deep breaths to stop myself from outright crying.

Rain. It's still raining this morning. Two days in a row of rain, no matter how light, signal a weather event for this city. The land of eternal sunshine. I don't mind. I like the rain. It staves off the all-consuming heat and mutes the vibrant colors of the landscape into something more... bearable.

God, that sounds depressing. What can I say, though? I'm alone at work this morning as Dex takes my girls, Hope, and their security team to the airport to meet Diana and John. They'll be gone for a week, and when they get back, they'll stay with Carly—one of my teammates who has a few kids of her own—until this situation gets handled. Then he's taking Audra to her grandfather's house, here in Austin.

I sit on the floor behind the couch, facing the window and watching the rain streak down the glass. Alone. I'm only here because it's a public enough place that I should be safe while being alone. I'm not even sure what's on my schedule, with

Chloe gone and my laptop out of commission…

That last thought spurs me into action. Picking myself up off the floor, I cross the room to my desk. I dial the extension for our IT department, and it rings a few times before a voice answers.

"Maddie—I mean, Ms. Dobransky?" the male voice asks.

I'm not sure who I'm speaking to since these guys fall under Nate's management. I don't interact with them outside of company holiday parties and other functions.

"Yeah, hi," I say. "I need to get a new computer setup today, if possible."

"Is there something we can fix on your current computer?" he asks.

I bite my lip to come up with a good reason. "No, I had to—I took it off-site and lost it."

I want to smack my forehead. That was the lamest excuse in the history of excuses.

"We have a tracking app installed on it. Do you want me to see if I can locate it for you?"

"No!" *Fuck, calm down, Maddie. The worst they could find out is the address.* "No, sorry. I just need something to access my schedule and email from the server here. At least, for today. I'll look into finding my laptop this evening."

"Umm… okay? I can dig up one of the old laptops we have as backups. Will that work?"

"Yeah, that's fine. Thank you."

"No problem, it might take a while to find one that works. I'll bring it to you, though."

"Sounds good."

I place the phone back on the receiver and look around for something to do, other than twiddling my thumbs. My gaze runs around my room, past the guitars I've mounted on the wall, then reverse back to them. I can work on my music. I've a few songs I've worked on, but haven't given enough thought to write them down yet.

With a nod of my head, I veer back toward my desk and fish out an old journal I used to use for writing. I pull it out and freeze as the old doodles and stickers on the inside cover open the floodgate of memories. I press my temples and breathe, but I'm mildly shocked that the memories aren't as painful as they once were.

The spine creaks as I flip through the first pages of music notes. Chord diagrams and hand-drawn bars of music fill each page as I search for the first empty page. The journal is about three-quarters full and contains all the music I've written over my lifetime—which is sad that there isn't more at this point in my life.

I set that on the coffee table and walk over to the guitar. I brush my hand over the old Fender. I smile, thinking about the day I put it up in here.

"I want you to sign this," I said to Stevie.

His chin drew in, and his face smushed into a half smile, half frown. "You don't want me ruining that old beauty."

"Stop that," I chastised. "It's not ruining anything. It's already valuable because it's a classic, but it'll be priceless when the original owner—and badass blues musician—signs it." I grinned.

A grin stretches my face as my fingers trace over his signature. I pull it off the wall and pluck a string, cringing at the weak, out-of-tune wail it produces. I sit on the couch and begin the process of tuning, playing, and writing my music. I get lost in the process and only stop when my stomach growls. I check my phone and see it's already lunchtime.

I play the last song again while considering where to order lunch from when my door opens. I freeze. Asher strides in, dropping his bag by the door. He removes the guitar from my hands and pulls me from the couch to wrap me in a tight hug.

"Are you okay?" he asks.

I nod because I can't talk with my face smashed into his chest like this.

"Really?" he asks again, pulling me back by my shoulders.

A smile tips the corner of my mouth as I take in his tired face. "I am. What're you doing back? How did you even find out?"

"Unlike Holly, the rest of your friends happen to like me.

Both Dawn and Bridget called to give me an update. They were sure you would overlook it. Plus, they know you as well as I do." He grins.

I huff. "Whatever, it's been a day. I haven't slowed down..." I drift off as I realize I could've called him anytime in the last few hours. Jeez, I'm a bad friend.

His brows draw together, calling bullshit on that line. "That's not it. Why didn't you tell me about all the other stuff that happened before I left? He's back, isn't he?"

I break away and sit back down with my guitar, holding it like some kind of shield. "Maybe... maybe I didn't want to drag you back into this. Someone should have some peace after everything that happened. And if you can stay out of it, I was going to let you."

"You know a reporter found me in Atlanta? Started asking me about that night again..." he murmurs, looking out the window. "I had no clue why anyone would be interested in digging that up, and told him so, but now I know..." He turns back to face me, his eyes pinning me in place. "You can't keep anyone out of this, Mads."

I swallow heavily. Asher sits in a chair across from me, rubbing his face with both hands. His hands fall away and he looks exhausted. We both stare at each other for a drawn-out moment.

"I'm sorry," I say.

"Don't," he says, holding up a hand. "You don't have to be. I know you were trying to help, but you can't protect any of us from this. Like it or not, we're in this together."

I can't think of any valid argument to that, so I sit there, not knowing what to do.

"You're writing?" Asher leans forward to pick up the journal off the coffee table between us. He's silent as he flips through the last couple of pages. A smile tips his lips. "This is good stuff. Play this one for me."

He pushes the journal back across the table in front of me and gets his bag from the floor, pulling out drumsticks. It brings a smile to my face.

"You still carry sticks with you everywhere?"

"Of course." He glances at me with a wry twist to his lips. "I play every chance I get. Which isn't much these days, but it keeps my skills fresh."

Guilt floods me as I remember Chloe's comment yesterday about him wanting to do something more creative. I can't help but feel I've been letting him down in a way.

"Don't do that." His voice interrupts my reverie. He sits across from me, eyes astute. "That guilt is written all over your face, but you shouldn't feel that way. After what happened, well, it's completely understandable. I wasn't playing for a while either, but you knew him better than me... I just get it. That's all."

"I just feel a bit ridiculous, Ash," I say with a sigh, plucking a string on my guitar. "It's like I'm waking up and realizing I've been asleep for three years, while everyone else kept living. I just—I let you down—I let so many people down. Why do you—why would anyone still care?"

"Are you serious?" he asks, his brows drawing together.

I nod, wide-eyed.

"You may feel like you've been asleep or whatever. But you're still here for every one of us in your own way. Shit, you gave me this job. I love the travel and the music. It's an awesome job. You still treat everyone like family. Just because you aren't playing music doesn't mean you're letting us down. Is that really how you feel?"

"No—yes—I don't know. It's just that I keep finding out little things that I haven't paid attention to, like Chloe saying that you wanted to do something more creative."

He huffs. "I only told her that I missed performing. And that was at your birthday party after we were onstage. We were talking about you, actually."

My eyes narrow as I watch him cross over to my desk and empty out my pencil cup and grab a few other items. He sits a stack of files on the coffee table in front of him, turning over the pencil cup, and taps on each with his sticks. His head tilts to the side, listening for the tone. I watch him, debating with myself to question what they were saying or leave it alone.

"You gonna start?" he asks.

I stare at him for a few seconds before I decide to leave it. I nod and look down at my notes to see what he wanted me to play. It's one of the newest ones that I wrote this week. If I had to give it a word to describe it, it would be hopeful. Which just seems weird, that I'd write something like that in the midst of all this turmoil. I wish I could delve into the deep recesses of my mind to see how everything works because sometimes I don't even understand myself.

A smile fights to break free on my face, and I start playing. Asher drums out a beat along with me on his makeshift kit. I play on autopilot, just watching him with a bit of awe. He's talented. The beat not only complements the music I wrote but challenges it, too. I start hearing other instruments in my head as we play along. My smile grows, and we get lost, playing song after song.

Asher's eyes light up. I feel a pang in my chest as I realize how long it's been since I've seen him this happy. We laugh and play, and everything else melts into the background. He suggests a few adjustments, here and there. Asher's not just a drummer. I don't think there's an instrument he can't play, but drums are where his heart lies, like me and my guitar.

"We should get Nate," I say, feeling lighter after we wrap up another song.

The door pops open, and I shriek, jumping from my seat, almost dropping my guitar. "Goddammit, I think my heart just stopped."

"You're too easy." Nate shakes his head. "I've been standing here outside the door for the last ten minutes. This glass wall isn't exactly soundproof." He grins. "I was afraid to come in and break the spell."

"There's no spell to break," I say. "Come in. We want to get your feedback."

Nate crosses the room in a few quick strides and sits in the seat at the end of the coffee table to my right. He opens his mouth to speak, but before he has a chance, a soft knock at the door stops him.

"Come in," I call.

The door opens, and a man enters, carrying a laptop. "I'm just here to set up the computer. Don't mind me," he mutters as he darts to my desk.

There's something itching at the corner of my mind. A familiarity that keeps my eyes locked on him. He's a heavyset guy, wearing a baseball cap pulled low over his face, and he keeps his head turned down, so I can't see him. If it were any other time in my life, I wouldn't question it. With everything going on, my senses are on high alert.

"What's your name?" I ask.

"What?" he asks, still not looking up.

Nate's brows drop, and he turns to look at the newcomer. "That's Brad. He's our IT guy. Been with us since the expansion." Confusion is stamped on Nate's face as he looks back to me. "You haven't met him before?"

"Brad," I murmur, trying to place the name. *Why is that ringing a bell?* I gasp as he looks up and familiar brown eyes meet my own. *What in the ever-living fuck?* "Brad Boyd?"

Then

"You look beautiful," Sloane said, pulling back from doing the final touches on my makeup.

"You're not bad," Priscilla said to Sloane. "I was skeptical about you." She turns to face me. "You know hiring friends usually isn't a good idea in this business."

Priscilla, who we affectionately called *Press-zilla* when she wasn't around, was my publicist. She was a bitch, with very little redeeming qualities aside from being good at her job.

"You ready?" Asher asked.

He didn't seem much different than normal. Sloane had dressed him, but she had stuck with his usual grungy rocker look. Aside from the expensive price tag of his clothes and the fancy haircut we both were subjected to, he hadn't changed much. Me, on the other hand—my hair was short for probably the first time in my life. She had also dyed my hair to bring out the red tones in my natural color. I was officially a redhead.

"Yeah," I said.

We were sitting in the greenroom for a late-night talk show. We weren't performing, because Jared wasn't back yet from his tour. He was due to come back soon. I wasn't sure how he was going to handle all the changes. Our lives had done a one-eighty while he had been overseas. I mean, I was sitting in a greenroom for a national network talk show in New York City. This was only the second time I'd ever left the state of Texas.

"We've gone over your talking points already. You did okay in rehearsals. Just try to be charming. The world is rooting for you," Priscilla said to Asher and me. "Promote the album. Tease the tour you'll start when Jared returns. And get personal on the separation, how much you miss him. They eat that shit up."

"Okay." I nodded.

I caught Asher's eye and pretended to hang myself when she wasn't looking. He smiled and turned out the door. We walked down the hall to the side of the set. I could hear the murmur of the crowd, see the glaring stage lights.

"This is surreal," I whispered.

"I know." Asher grabbed my hand and squeezed it.

"Five minutes," a guy with a headset on whispered at us as he rushed by, doing whatever it was he did back here.

The talk show host started his monologue as the house band's song came to a close. The audience cheered and clapped, then finally quieted down. I'd watched this show from my home many times growing up; I never in a million years thought I'd end up on here as a guest. They interviewed famous people, and I was still having a hard time with the fact that people knew who I was. Strangers talked about me. I wasn't sure I'd ever wrap my head around it.

"Oh, shit. He's talking about us," I said, feeling light-headed as the talk show host started his bit to introduce us.

Asher squeezed my hand again before letting go. The dude with the headset popped up next to me from out of nowhere and motioned me to walk past the curtain. I swallowed the startled scream and plastered on a smile, striding out with Asher right behind me. The audience wasn't as large as they sounded, and I relaxed a little. This was just like performing with One Dollar Bet, but with talking and without the tiny skirts.

The crowd clapped and cheered. There were a few hoots and hollers before they quieted down, and we began to talk. It started with small talk, pleasantries, easier questions like how we found out that our song became a hit. I told him the story about finding out in derby practice. He asked about derby. It all kind of flowed and wasn't near as hard as I'd imagined it to be.

"But I think it's fair to say that everyone wants to know how you're holding up. Have you spoken to Jared recently?"

"Yeah, about a week after all this blew up, he called. It was an awkward conversation to tell someone that they were famous. I don't believe it myself most of the time."

"How does he feel about it?"

"I don't think he believes me. They don't get a lot of news out there, so I'm pretty sure he's convinced that this is just another practical joke."

"You guys do that a lot?"

"No. Yes." I laughed and scrunched my nose. "We've been known to pull one over on each other from time to time."

The audience laughed.

"You have to tell me about these practical jokes," he pleaded.

Priscilla had prepped me for this. We had decided to go with the story about the bikini and the girls' birth, and after telling it once already in rehearsals, it wasn't nearly as nerve-racking as I imagined. I got animated, and the audience was laughing. I relaxed even more. This wasn't bad at all.

"He gets back from overseas in a few months. Do you guys have any plans?"

"Other than starting our tour, no."

A few cheers rose up at that. *Whoa, people are excited about that?* That blew my mind. He talked to Asher some. We played a little game that the show was famous for, and then it was over.

"The tour starts in March, and from there you're making thirty-two more stops across the US?" he asked, and I nodded. "Their first show will be on March eighth in Houston, Texas. Be sure to check out Stateside's website for more tour info. Well, I wish you the best. I look forward to seeing your concert when you make it back to New York." He smiled.

"Thank you," I said.

Asher thanked him, too, shaking his hand.

"Asher Cross and Laine Dobransky of Stateside," he said, and the band started playing to commercial.

Chapter Eleven

Now

"I'm sorry, Maddie," Brad says. "I should've told you years ago. No. I should've talked to you before I accepted the position. But I needed the job, and you were leaving to go on tour. Then all that stuff happened to you. I didn't want to stir up anything. I'm sorry."

Asher and Nate's heads look back and forth between Brad and me. I'm rocked to the core, tongue-tied as a thousand thoughts fly through my mind. I can feel the blood drain from my face as the worst one of all occurs to me. *Could he be my stalker?*

Nate's brows inch toward his hairline. "You two know each other?"

"You could say that," I say, trying and failing to keep the bite out of my voice.

Asher leans forward, watching me. Brad looks down again but pulls the baseball cap off his head, rubbing his hand over his short hair. He wrings the cap in his hands. I honestly don't know what to do with this. I mean, it's not like I can just ask him if he's been stalking me. If he was, I doubt he'd just tell me.

"Why would you even take the job, knowing that this is my company?" I ask.

He takes a deep breath and looks back up at me. "Because I needed the job."

"Why wouldn't you just work for your dad?"

"He sold the company years ago," Brad says. "Right before I graduated high school. Lost all his money gambling."

Oh. I take a breath. I don't know what to do with that information. Normally, I'd feel sorry for someone in that situation, but I'm finding it hard to muster sympathy for Brad fucking Boyd. Even though I still feel responsible for my mom's death, a part of me would always blame him, too. Both him and Lisa. When they decided cheating was a better option than just being honest... I massage my forehead with my fingers as I stop that train of thought. I don't want to have to deal with an unwelcome blast from the past.

"I don't think I'm the only one wondering," Asher says, glancing to Nate. "How do you two know each other?"

"It doesn't matter," I say.

"We used to date," Brad says at the same time.

I roll my eyes to the heavens. Asher laughs, and I cut him a look. His face goes blank.

"We were preteens—it hardly counts. I sincerely hope you don't go around telling everyone that, considering what you—"

I stop myself. I don't want to talk about this. I don't need everyone in the room to know about it. And he knows full well what I'm talking about.

"Nah." His mouth twists into a wry grin. "Outside of people we went to school with, no one would believe me."

I hold back a snort as I look him over. *The years haven't been kind to him.* He has a stain on his shirt, one that's missing a button and has half come untucked. He looks tired. An awkward-as-fuck silence fills the room. Asher shifts positions in his seat, but no one speaks for what seems like an eternity.

"I'm surprised you didn't know this already, Maddie. He's been with us for, what? Four years?" Nate asks, turning to Brad.

"Yes, sir," Brad answers. "But to be fair, she doesn't come

near my office, and I've actively been avoiding her."

"Where is your office?" I ask.

"Back in the original building. I think it used to be the kitchen?"

Oh, well. That does explain a lot. That's right next to... I shake my head, trying to derail that train of thought. It's silent for a moment, but I don't think anyone has anything left to say about that situation. I don't. Brad walks back to my desk and resumes setting up my computer.

"Well, that brings me to what I was going to say," Nate says, breaking the silence. "What I heard of the songs you wrote is great. What are the odds of getting you into the studio to record them?"

"Uh, I hadn't thought that far into it. I just wanted to get this stuff in my head written down."

"We could always rent space from another studio here in town?" Asher suggests.

I shake my head. "That's not necessary. I can..."

I stop because I'm just not sure I can go into that part of the building. I haven't even attempted it in four years. I don't want to promise them that I will, when the possibility remains that I could let them down. Both men stare at me, expecting some kind of an answer. I squirm, avoiding their penetrating stares and looking everywhere but at them. *Has my office always been this small?* I try to draw in a breath that seems to lodge in my throat. The lights dim.

I see Asher and Nate in front of me, and I try to speak, but nothing comes out. Asher's face twists into a frown. He moves to get up, but the door behind him opens. He stops as a new person enters the room. All the sounds are muffled. I squeeze my eyes shut, trying to clear my vision. Familiar hands brush my hair back from my face. A subtle woodsy cologne tickles my nose. His hands cup my chin. I open my eyes finding his aquamarine gaze. Dex.

I wrap my arms around him and squeeze. Like finding my anchor, I hold on to him as the room returns to normal and my breathing evens out.

"You're back," I say, my voice muffled by his shirt.

He chuckles, and I hear the rumble deep in his chest. "Miss me?"

I nod. "I feel safer when you're here."

I pull back and look up at him. His smile takes my breath away but in the best way. His head dips and kisses the corner of my mouth.

"You okay?" Dex asks.

I nod. I turn to find Asher and Nate watching us. My cheeks heat up. I fight back the urge to hide in Dex's arms again.

"What did I miss?" Dex asks, breaking the awkward silence.

Another scent invades my senses. My eyes land on a large paper sack next to Dex's feet.

"Please tell me that's what I think it is?" I ask, my mouth watering.

"It is if you think it's Salt Lick barbecue," Dex replies.

His head tilts to the side. A grin kicks up one side of his mouth, exposing a sexy dimple. *Damn.* I lick my lips, and his eyes grow heated. I look away.

"My dad lives out in Driftwood, and I usually swing by there every time I'm out that way," Dex explains. "I didn't know what you would like, so I got a couple pounds of everything. There's enough to share."

"Thank God," Asher says, his shoulders sagging in relief. "I was contemplating diving across the table and running with it."

I laugh. "You wouldn't've made it far."

"I'd be counting on you taking him out, leaving it fair game for me to grab it and lock myself in my office," Nate says, his eyes locked on the bag.

A deep belly laugh erupts from me. I can't blame them. Texas barbecue will do that to people.

"Ash, you want to go grab some plates from the break room?" I ask.

"Yes. Yes, I do," Asher says, jumping over the back of the

couch. "I'm starving."

"I'll go get us some drinks," Nate says, standing. "Coke?"

"Sounds good," Dex replies.

"Yes, please," I say, leaning into Dex. I look up and catch him watching me. "Thank you."

His face softens. "I'll buy you barbecue every day for the rest of your life if it makes you smile like this."

My heart skips a beat, and I stare at him for a moment before I gather my wits. I wrinkle my nose. "Nah, it wouldn't be special if you could get it every day." I kiss his cheek. "But thank you, it's very thoughtful. I do appreciate it."

A throat clears, and I jump, startled. Brad stands near my desk, wringing his hat in his hands again.

"It's all set up," Brad says. "You can use the same login to get on this one." He gestures to the computer. "If you need anything else, just call my extension." He looks around a bit. "Anyhoo, I'll leave you two... I really am sorry, Maddie."

"Brad," I sigh. "I don't know what to say or how to deal with this."

"I promise you, I didn't mean anything by it. I didn't even know this was your place until I came in for the final interview with Mr. Thompson and saw your name on this office. He offered me the job on the spot, and I couldn't turn it down. Lisa—" He stops and swallows heavily.

A dark laugh bubbles up. "Lisa?"

"Yeah." Brad puts his hat back on and looks down at his feet. "She got pregnant senior year. We have a son, Dylan. We weren't ever together, but it doesn't stop her from calling about the child support." He sighs.

I press my lips together and nod. Okay, maybe I feel a little bad for him because I'm sure that whole situation is... unpleasant, knowing Lisa. The second he leaves the room, Dex speaks.

"Who was that?"

"It's the weirdest thing, but exactly what I wanted to talk to you about. That's my ex-boyfriend from junior high and part of high school. I just found out he's been working here for the last four years."

"How is that possible?"

"His office is in the old part of the building, and I haven't been in there since—you know. And he said he's just avoided me all these years. It's really weird, but I don't think it would be that hard. I'm only in the office sporadically and haven't had any tech issues. But here's what I'm thinking. He has access to my computer."

Dex's eyebrows raise. "You think he might be your stalker?"

"It's possible," I say, biting my lower lip and shrugging.

His gaze zeroed in on my mouth. "Is there a reason why you would think that, other than the fact that he's been hiding that he works for your company?"

"No. Not really. We didn't end well, but I never got the impression that it bothered him much."

"I'll check him out. I got some news for you, though. I had Marcus working on some stuff for me since he has some free time while Holly's at work. That cop who busted us at the park. He isn't a cop."

"What? You were looking into that?"

"Yeah, I made a mental note of his badge number," Dex says as he taps his temple. "I didn't want to worry you if it turned out to be nothing."

I blink, a bit stunned. "Okay. What does that mean, though?"

"Whoever that was did some impressive level impersonation of a peace officer. You didn't recognize him?"

"No, never seen him before in my life." I flop back on the couch, my mind officially scrambled. "It's like, the more I find out, the more I don't know what to think."

"What was that guy's name?" Dex asks, pulling his phone out of his pocket.

"Brad Boyd. He's from Canyon Lake, too, but I assume he lives in Austin now."

The door opens, and Asher strolls in with the plates and silverware.

"I'm going to step outside," Dex says. "Get Marcus to look into that tonight as well."

"Okay," I agree and watch him walk out the door.

"I gotta say," Asher says, "I was skeptical about him at first. But I've never seen anyone pull you out of a panic attack like that. He seems to be good for you. I take it things are going well?"

"Yeah, so far," I say, looking down at my hands.

"But...?"

"Have you been taking lessons from Evan?" I smirk.

He smiles. "No, it's just what friends do when they're worried about another."

"I took him to the club yesterday, before it was open, and explained it a bit. But he hasn't seen it—you know—when people are there. We're going there tonight. I've a fight, so we'll see. I just can't help but think this might be too much for him. That he'll walk away, you know?"

He laughs. I mean, he really laughs, and I can feel my face heat with anger. He catches sight of me and stops.

"Sorry." He clears his throat. "That's a bit ridiculous, though. No guy I know thinks, *my girl is into some kinky shit, how horrible.*"

"Not everyone is okay with that stuff, and he might be one of them. I don't know if I can go down that road again, but I'm trying."

"I think it'll be okay. I'll be at the club tonight. If you need backup, let me know." He grins. "It's good to be home."

I start pulling out the food and laying it on the table as Dex and Nate walk in, and conversation stalls as we all dig in.

Then

"Get dressed in this." Sloane tossed a dress at my head. "I've got shoes, too."

"What am I getting dressed for now?" I whined.

We had just returned to the hotel after the talk show. I

was exhausted.

Ruby bounced on the bed beside me. "We're in New York. And we've got a VIP—you. We can't not hit the hot clubs. Plus, you don't have the kids with you. You need to get out and live a little while you can."

"Exactly. You have your whole entourage of badass bitches to entertain. We love you, but there has to be perks, too," Bridget said, coming out of the bathroom.

"What do you mean, perks? You're getting paid. Sloane, too. Holly, Ruby, and Dawn are the only ones here out of free will alone."

"But we would've been stupid to pass up a free trip to New York." Ruby grinned.

"Truth," Holly said, bumping fists with Ruby.

"Fuck, yeah," Dawn agreed, popping her head over the back of the couch.

"Come on, get dressed so I can do your makeup and hair. We've got reservations to keep," Sloane said, pulling me off the bed. "If you don't hurry, I'll call Press-zilla to join us."

She grinned evilly. I booked it into the bathroom and could hear their laughter trailing me inside. I took a quick shower before getting dressed. An hour later we were all dressed and headed through the lobby to the waiting town car. Asher met us at the car.

"There's something I have to tell you before we get there," Sloane said, looking at her phone and sending another text message. "My brother is here for a fight, and when I mentioned we were going out, he said he was going to join us."

My head snapped in her direction. "What?"

"He's just going to be at the same club as us, not a big deal."

"It's a horrible idea," I protested. "Why would you even tell him where we're going?"

"I didn't think about it," Sloane said, looking sheepish. "I was just excited about being in New York…"

Everyone else remained quiet. The rest of the ride was

silent. We pulled up outside a nightclub, where paparazzi were scattered about, waiting to grab a picture of entering VIPs. Dread filled my body. I hadn't been "famous" long, but long enough to despise people roaming around with cameras and questions.

We shuffled a little getting out of the car, me being the last to exit. The girls gathered on each side of me to block me from the cameras. That plan failed miserably as soon as I heard his voice.

"Laine," Law said.

I turned to see him wearing a perfectly tailored suit. *Why does he have to look sexier every time I see him?* I closed my eyes, trying to erase the vision. When I opened them, he was right in front of me. *Fucking perfect.* Cameras flashed in my periphery as people shouted questions that I didn't even bother to hear.

"Why are you here?" I asked.

"I'm in town for a fight. Thought I'd come see you while we're in the same place."

"You know I'm still with him, right?"

"Have you walked down the aisle?"

"I'm not doing this." I turned to walk into the club, and he caught my hand.

"Doing what? I'm just here to hang out, catch up. I didn't ask anything from you."

"Yet." I tried to put on a brave face as I pulled my hand from his grasp.

"I like the hair and this dress," he whispered into my ear, his hands landing on my hips.

My elbow flew back to catch him in the stomach, but he was quicker than me and grasped it before it made contact. He grinned that lopsided, one-dimpled smirk at me.

"I got a hotel room. You can hurt me all you want there."

"Fuck you."

"That's what I'm offering."

Infuriating. I felt the hair on the back of my neck stand up. I was so pissed. I marched forward, trying to lose him.

115

Sloane cast me an apologetic look. I'm not sure how I ever convinced myself that I loved him. Nobody in the entire world could get under my skin the way he could. We got up to the VIP area, where I headed straight for the bar.

"I need three shots," I yelled to the bartender over the loud music.

"Of what?" the bartender, a blonde woman close to my age, shouted back.

"Whatever will get me drunk fastest."

"That kind of night, huh?" She smiled.

She lined up three glasses and poured three shots. She turned the bottle label toward me and grinned.

"Vodka. It's easier to shoot. If you were sipping, I'd go with whiskey." She shrugged and wiped down the counter. "Has tall, dark, and broody behind you got something to do with your urgency?"

"Everything," I said, tipping back the first shot. "My ex."

"Oh, rough." She made a face like she tasted something sour.

I threw back the other two shots and ordered a coke to wash it all down. She slid the coke across the bar.

"Good luck with that," she said with a smile, her eyes flicking to Law behind me.

I turned around to find him staring at my ass. His eyes heated in that way that I knew he was thinking up imaginative things he would do to me if given a chance. I rolled my eyes at him and walked over to the reserved table we had. The girls were already on the dance floor. Asher was warming the seat in the U-shaped booth. I sat next to him.

"You not going to get out there and dance?" I asked Asher.

He shrugged. "Not my style."

I laughed. "Okay, then."

Law showed up holding a bottle of water and started to sit next to me. I cut him a look that said he would meet an untimely end if he did, and he moved to the other side of the table. Asher's gaze bounced between Law and me.

"Asher," Asher said.

"Law," Law replied, shaking his offered hand.

"Oh, shit," Asher said. "You're Law Russo. Like, *the* Law Russo."

"The one and only, that I'm aware of."

"You two know each other?" Asher asked.

"Very well," Law insinuated with his tone.

I cut him a dirty look.

"I watched your fight last week out of Vegas. That was badass. The odds were on the other guy. You took him out in eight seconds. I bet your promoters were pissed."

I tuned them out as they talked about the fight. This was going to be a long night. I took another shot and then joined the girls on the dance floor. Countless songs later, I was breathless and thirsty. Sweat gathered on my hairline and the back of my neck.

My phone vibrated in my clutch that pressed against my thigh. I ignored it because we were trying to take a break from all the madness. When it buzzed again, I decided to look. It could've been Diana contacting me about the kids.

Two missed text messages. They were coming from an unknown number.

your finally getting the recognition you deserve. so proud of you

btw you look stunning in that black dress and i like the new hair

As I was reading these, a third one came through that knocked the wind out of me. A picture of a red calla lily with the inscription: **for you.**

I took a screen capture of my phone and pulled up Officer Martinez's cell number and sent it to him. It took a few minutes for a reply.

> Where are you?

>> In New York.

> I'll take this to the Captain. Maybe we can finally get a detective assigned.

>> I'm coming back to Austin tomorrow. I want to meet with your Captain.

> I'll see what I can do.

>> Thanks.

I put the phone back into my purse, but looking down at my hands was when it hit me. I wore a white blouse with black high-waist pants at the interview today. I was wearing the black dress at the club. My panicked gaze darted around.

"What's wrong?" Law asked, moving to sit next to me.

"He's here," I said absently.

"Who's here?"

"Him. Him. He's watching me now. He knows what I'm wearing right now."

"Laine, calm down. You're not making sense."

"Asher, go get the girls. We have to go." I dug the phone back out and pulled up the texts and tossed it to him.

He looked down at the phone and back at me, recognition blooming on his face. He nodded. "On it."

"Laine, explain to me what's going on."

"I've a stalker, okay? Why do you care? Just go back to your—whatever it is you do these days."

"Have I not been making myself clear?" He gripped my shoulders, forcing me to face him. "I still love you. Of course I care."

"You have a real funny way of showing it because as far as I'm concerned, if you love someone, you fight for them." I shrugged his hands off.

He laughed darkly. "You know, I told myself that exact same thing, trying to let you go."

"What the fuck is that supposed to mean?"

"It means, you're one to talk. Did it ever cross your mind to fight for me, Laine?"

I felt the rug get pulled out from under me as I realized he had a point. We both could've tried harder, but the thing about us was that we both sucked at communicating. I couldn't think about it anymore. What was done, was done. I was still engaged to Jared.

"I can't do this with you, Law. Not right now."

"Law, you should probably go," Sloane said from behind him.

He turned to her, and I could only guess what his face looked like.

"Look, you're my brother, and I love you, but this, with Laine, is a lost cause. And we have bigger things to deal with."

"Fuck that. If she's scared that someone is after her, I'm at least going to make sure you guys make it back to the hotel safe."

"Whatever," I grumped, shoving at him to move so I could get out of the booth.

When he didn't budge, I crawled over his lap. He halted my movement with firm hands on my bare thighs. I leaned toward him until my mouth was next to his ear.

"Cut it the fuck out," I whispered in my most deadly voice.

His stubble scraped my cheek as his head turn to mine.

"I think you forget how well I know you," he whispered in my ear. His lips teasing the shell scattered goose bumps across my flesh. "I trained you. If you didn't want me touching you, you would've stopped me before I had the chance, Bumpkin."

His hands drifted off my thighs, and I moved to finish climbing over him.

"Stop," he said in that low voice.

My body halted and my core clenched before my brain caught up to what he just did. I cut him a scathing look as I got out of the booth.

"I made the call," Bridget said. "Our car is out front."

"Let's go," I said, leading our group to the exit.

A shiver ran down my spine as we neared the door. Law looked over at me and took off his jacket.

"Here, put this on." He draped the suit coat over my shoulders.

My senses were flooded with his familiar smell as I tugged it around me to ward off the chill.

We rushed out to the car, but just as I was halfway there, a paparazzo darted in front of me, hounding me with questions I refused to hear. His camera flashed in my face. Law put an arm around my shoulder, tucking me into his side, and pushed the guy out of our way. He helped me in the car and then crawled in behind me. I waited as everyone else got in. When we got back to the hotel, Law started walking away without a word.

"Law," I called after him.

He turned back to me.

"You guys go on ahead," I said, looking at Bridget.

"We'll wait in the lobby," Asher said, eyeing Law.

"That's a better idea." I smiled at him.

I took off Law's jacket and handed it to him.

"Do me a favor, please?"

"Anything." He smiled.

I gave him a weak smile back. "Go get a girlfriend. Not just a groupie that you can sleep with for a night, but find someone you care about. *Train* someone new."

"See, that's the thing I don't get. You seem to think that I made you this way."

"I wasn't like this before I met you," I threw back.

His head tipped back with a sardonic laugh. "No? I seem to remember you following my commands from the first night I met you. Challenging me to assert control with that smart mouth of yours."

"Fuck yo——" I didn't finish because he moved faster than a snake striking, and his mouth was on mine. His tongue darted in and stroked mine. He didn't linger. It lasted just long enough for my lips to tingle. My hand rose up to my lips as I stared at him in shock. Tears filled my eyes, blurring my vision of him.

"Just move on," I pleaded. "It's been two years. I'm not breaking up with him. I *will* marry him."

"We'll see, Bumpkin," he said, his lips pressed together in a forced smile. "I think the day we have a civil conversation will be the day I know you're truly done with me. But now, it's just going to take time for you to remember who you belong to. You're always going to be mine." He turned away before I could respond. His shoulders slumped over as he walked away, disappearing into the crowded New York street.

Part of my heart cracked open, telling him to go. Part of me would always love him.

Chapter Twelve

Now

I drop my empty plate on the coffee table and lean back on the couch, fighting the urge to pat my belly in fully sated satisfaction. I sigh, wanting to let my eyelids drift shut and just take a nap. Dex sets his plate down and tugs me to his side. His lips press into my temple.

Asher smiles and my cheeks heat as I reciprocate. The color has returned to his face, and the dark circles under his eyes are a little less noticeable.

"That hit the spot," Nate says, interrupting the quiet. "Thank you, Mr. McClellan."

"Dex, please."

"Sure thing. Thank you, Dex." Nate smiles and claps his hands together, his eyes glimmering with excitement. "Now that we're running on all cylinders, you want to try this again?" His eyes meet mine.

"I'm serious, Mads." Asher clasps his hands together in a fist and props his chin on it. "This is great stuff, and I think we're ready. Just tell us what you need."

"I think planning to record might be getting a little ahead of ourselves," I say. "We should look into finding at least a bass and rhythm guitar player."

Nate nods. "You want to hold auditions? This town is

crawling with talent."

"Maybe." I shrug. "I might know someone, but I think it might be better if one of you feel him out. We didn't part on the best of terms." I flip to the back of my journal where there's a little pocket and pull out the yellowed scrap of paper. "I think the new stuff is good, but I think I might be losing my edge. Been out of the scene too long. He can help with that." I slide the paper across the desk and hope swells in my chest. I might be able to heal at least one old wound.

"I'll talk to him," Asher says, picking up the piece of paper. "Anything I should know?"

"He's a local, but last I heard, he'd been out on the west coast. We might have to fly him in, but I'll cover it if he's game. He's a good guy, Ash. I think you and him will get along just fine."

"What does he play?" Nate asks.

"Anything he wants to. We'll find someone for what's left."

My phone chooses that moment to go off, blaring Devo's "Whip It" from my purse. I rush to grab it.

"You better have a good reason for calling me during the middle of the workday, since you insist on making me keep that stupid ringtone," I say in greeting.

A chuckle kills the silence on the other end of the line. "It will never get old, Ned," Nic says.

"I'm in the middle of something—make it snappy," I retort.

"I want to make sure you get to the club early tonight," Nic clips out. "I'll be waiting in the penthouse. I need to talk to you before your fights tonight."

I freeze. Nic isn't usually vague, and there's only one reason he would be, but that can't be it. I look to Dex, thinking about the fact that he'll be with me.

"I wasn't coming alone," I breathe out.

"He needs to be here, too." Nic pauses.

Confusion wraps its way around my thoughts, but I know I can't ask for clarification. There are too many ears in the room to have a private conversation. I just have go along with it and see how it plays out. He doesn't sound tense, but there's a caution in his words that lets me know something is up.

The clock on the wall reads a quarter past four. "I can be there in about an hour."

"I wouldn't push it further than that," Nic says.

"Okay," I sigh. "See you soon, Lucky. Love you."

I school my face as I tuck my phone back in my purse, turning back to face the others.

"Something just came up. I've got somewhere to be." I smile. "Family stuff." I wave it off. "I think we have somewhere to start with this music, though."

Nate and Asher stand. Dex follows, but his eyes never stray from me. He's alert and has a curious yet guarded expression. I ignore him, for now.

"Yeah," Asher says. "I'll contact your guy. Let you know how it goes."

"Sounds good," I turn to Dex as they leave. "Do you have a suit?"

"At my place," he replies.

His intense stare has pressure to it, as if he's attempting to read my mind through sheer force of will. I look away.

"Good, we'll swing by there. I can change there, too."

I walk to my closet, grabbing the garment bag off the rack. Laying it on my desk, I return to grab a duffel bag from the floor.

"You ready?" I ask.

Dex nods. "When you are."

He takes the bags from my hands and gestures me ahead of him. In the back of my mind, I think the move is sweet but I'm too distracted by what Nic could possibly want to give it credence. He wouldn't just call and demand me to meet with him out of the blue. He usually just waits until I'm around because he knows we'll see each other soon enough. It must be important. I just have no clue what that might be.

Then

Sloane clapped her hands together and tucked them under her chin with a huge grin. "I can't wait to get there. This is going to be so amazing," she gushed.

I leaned back into the plush leather seat of the limo. We navigated the streets of Manhattan toward Greenwich Village, where a small photo studio with a world-famous photographer awaited.

"It's fucking dope that you'll be on the cover of *Rolling Stone*," Holly said.

"It's pretty badass," Dawn added. "I want to see what Miss Bubbly, here, cooked up for you. She keeps going on and on about how great it's going to be, but ask her what they have planned and she shuts the fuck up real quick."

"She won't even tell me," I grumped.

Bridget glanced up from her phone. "Or me."

"That's because I want it to be a surprise," Sloane said. "And if I told any of you, Maddie would find out. 'Cause you bitches can't keep secrets."

"We can keep secrets," Ruby defended. "Just not from each other." She shrugged, looking out the window.

Holly's phone vibrated in her pocket next to me. She dug it out, and her face lit up as she read the text. Curious, I leaned toward her to check it out and immediately jerked back.

"Why in the world would you be smiling over a dick pic?" I asked.

She turned to me with her wide smile still intact. "You'd be smiling too if that was the dick being sent to you." She waved the phone in my face, and I looked away.

"Lemme see," Dawn said as she grabbed the phone away from Holly.

Her and Ruby's heads bent together as they both look at the phone.

"That's pretty impressive," Ruby said. "But there's no way

he's a grower."

"Oh, it grows, bitch," Holly smirked.

The phone passed again, as Sloane and Bridget satisfied their curiosity.

"How the fuck do you take that?" Sloane gasped.

We all burst out laughing.

"I guess Max isn't genetically blessed," Ruby teased.

"It's not about size, it's how they use it," Sloane defended. "Plus, that is some next-level shit right there. I wouldn't even describe it as large."

I shrugged. "She's got a point. He might have a cock the size of a donkey, but if all he does is come before you and fall asleep, well, it doesn't do anyone any favors."

Ruby snorted. "Says the only two who're in a relationship."

"Exactly why dick pics are pointless," Dawn grumped.

"I can honestly say I've never gotten a dick pic, ever," I said.

Ruby's jaw dropped. "Seriously?"

"Not even one of your guys ever sent you one?" Bridget asked.

"No," I responded. "What's the point? I already know what it looks like."

"Okay, stop," Sloane said. "See, why do you have to do this? Anytime she opens her mouth about sex, all I can see is her with my brother and I want to gouge my eyes out."

Part of me wanted to expand on the finer points of her brother's dick, just to torture her some more. But that was not where my mind needed to be wandering, especially after him showing up last night. And I'd zero desire to expound on Jared's body parts or any part of our intimate moments.

Ruby ignored her. "There isn't a point, but that doesn't stop guys from sending them anyway."

"Which is why I prefer pussy over dick, any day," Bridget said.

"Girls are definitely better at eating muff, but I gotta have the dick, you know," Holly added.

"Fuck all that noise," Dawn exclaimed. "I'm perfectly happy in my relationship with my Magic Wand. I don't have time for all that drama."

"What's a Magic Wand?" Sloane asked.

"Only the best vibrator ever," Bridget said, while still intensely tapping away at her phone. "God bless the Japanese." She made the sign of the cross like some devout Catholic in prayer.

I couldn't stop the laugh that bubbled up from me at the utter seriousness on her face. Bitch took her vibrators seriously. It wasn't long before it caught on and we dissolved into laughter.

The limo stopped outside a redbrick building. We stumbled out of it, still laughing as more dick jokes were made. But I tuned it all out at the sight of the building in front of me and the task I knew awaited me. The place had huge black-framed windows that spanned the height of the multi-storied building.

A petite woman with black hair styled in one of those edgy androgynous haircuts greeted us. She ushered us inside to an open loft space filled with white walls, soaring ceilings, lots of light from the massive windows, various photography equipment, and a small seating area.

The photographer greeted each of us with dual cheek kisses. His accented voice gave away his European lineage if his greeting habits left any doubt. I couldn't quite place the accent, though. Sloane grabbed my hand and led me to an area allocated for dressing, where she yammered on to a hair-and-makeup artist about her vision. I tuned it out and let my mind wander.

"Here, change into this." Sloane directed me to a curtained area to change clothes, handing me a black robe.

I changed quickly. Dawn, Holly, and Ruby chattered away from a nearby couch, while Bridget hunched over her laptop with the phone pressed against her ear, working. I could hear the quiet snick of the hangers as Sloane shuffled clothing around on the racks on the other side of the curtain. I said a silent prayer of thanks that Press-zilla trusted Sloane enough to let her take charge of the shoot today.

After what felt like an eternity later, the makeup artist nudged me. I oohed and ahhed over her work enough to be polite. I hoped my smile came across as genuine, but I was quickly discovering that playing dress-up, the beauty regimen, and the focus on my outer self just didn't do it for me. I never really thought about it before, but now that it was being shoveled to me with the ferocity of a snowblower, I was quickly learning to despise it.

Sloane was chatting with the photographer, and they were both laughing and gesturing with their hands. Sloane was glowing, living her dream and surrounded by her element. I was thankful I was able to play a part in that. It didn't matter if it felt like torture to me; seeing her happy eased the sting. I tapped Sloane on the shoulder. She smiled as she turned to me.

"Where are the clothes you want me to change into?" I asked.

The grin never left her face, but it definitely left her eyes.

"You'll be wearing this for your first look." She looked down at her hands.

My eyes followed hers. "That's an American flag, not an article of clothing."

"I had a feeling you wouldn't be enthusiastic about any of this, so I wanted to start with the more risqué stuff," Sloane said quickly. "I've plenty of other outfits." I fought back an eye roll. "Just humor me. This probably won't even make it to print."

"No," I said with finality.

It was rare that I protested anything she did, and I saw the hurt flash across her face before she schooled her features. Sloane was used to people bending to her will with little or no effort.

She grabbed my elbow, leading me toward the couch where the girls sat. "Just hear me out. This is *Rolling Stone*, not *Playboy*. It's going to be tasteful. And if you're worried about the fact that the photographer is a guy, well, don't be. He's gay. And the makeup artist just went downstairs with the rest of the crew, so it's just us here. And I know you aren't shy. We've all seen enough in the locker room. So just... humor me, okay?"

"Uh, oh," Dawn singsonged. "What are you trying to make her do?"

"She wants me to wear this." I grabbed the flag from her hands. "Only this."

"It's not only that," Sloane defended. "We have these combat boots, too. And you'll have your guitar."

"Oooo, that's hot," Ruby said.

"Holly, help me out here," Sloane pleaded.

"I don't see the big deal." Holly shrugged. "I'd do it."

"Really?" I asked. "It doesn't seem too much to you? I want to be known for my music, not my body."

Holly rolled her eyes. "But you have the body, so why not use it? You won't have it forever."

"If they asked you to pose in only an apron for some cooking magazine, you'd do it?" I asked Holly.

Her mouth twisted in thought, and she shrugged. "Hell, yeah." She grinned.

"You won't be showing anything that you haven't already," Ruby added. "I went to your concerts. And really, are you surprised? Sloane's been dressing you for years."

"I'm kinda surprised you have a problem with it," Bridget says, looking up from her laptop. "You always seemed so comfortable with your body. I always thought you were a badass feminist bitch."

Am I? I don't know. Maybe. I didn't know at that moment why it was bothering me. I wasn't expecting it, though I should've. I was comfortable with my body. I never had any complaints, but I also didn't dwell on it either. It had been a while since I was onstage in those skimpy outfits I wore in One Dollar Bet's concerts. I remember being hesitant at first, but not caring after. The more I thought on it, the more I felt kind of stupid for protesting.

"Give me the damn boots," I said, holding out my hand with a sigh.

Sloane's eyes lit up. "You're going to do it?"

I shoved my feet in the boots, not bothering with the laces, and plodded over to the white backdrop that curled across the floor in front of the camera. I held the flag in front of me as I pulled the tie of the robe and shrugged my shoulders until it hit the ground. Sloane rushed over with my guitar and scooped the robe off the ground. I spared a tiny thread of thought for the windows facing the street but decided that protesting further would only delay the inevitable. Best to just go along and get it done.

I wasn't happy, but the photographer never asked me to smile. It went a long way in making me feel more comfortable. In fact, he never asked me to do anything, just barked orders, and my body went on autopilot to obey. I tried not to think about where that malleability came from, but looking at his sister's eerily similar face, and with his departure only hours before, memories assailed me. Thoughts I knew I'd regret, but I was powerless to stop their onslaught.

My hand drifted to my mouth as my lips tingled like an echo from the kiss he left me with the night before. *Maybe he's right. Part of me will always belong to him.* Steely resolve settled over me. It didn't matter what we were, or what he turned me into. I was my own person. I could choose, and my mind was made up. I was always going to choose Jared.

Chapter Thirteen

Now

We pull into a dirt parking lot outside a little, rundown warehouse in East Austin. I glance over at Dex. I'm not sure where we are, but this can't be his home. He puts the car in park and cuts the engine.

"You live here?" I ask.

He nods absently. "Home, sweet home." He smiles, his dimples peeking through. "Impressed?"

"I'm reserving judgment." I grin. "I thought you lived near me. Audra goes to the girls' school."

"She's part of the magnet program," he says, opening his door.

He takes a few long strides around the car to get my door and offers his hand. I take his hand and step out.

"That's impressive. Those programs are fairly competitive, aren't they?"

He smiles sheepishly. "Yeah, she's a good kid. Can't take any credit for it. She's done it mostly on her own." His brows furrow. "Though I'm trying to change that."

He leans around me into the car and grabs my bags.

"I can get that," I say, reaching for the bags in his hands.

"It's my pleasure." His tone is firm but not defensive.

I sigh, giving up. "You're doing a great job from what I

can tell." His head jerks back in confusion. "With Audra—the father thing. Though you're okay at the bag-carrying gig, too." I smirk.

"Just okay?" He laughs and shakes his head at me.

"My bad—you're one fine specimen of bag-carrying glory," I deadpan.

"Better," he murmurs as he tugs me to his side and kisses my temple. "Follow me." He sweeps his free hand out in front of us, and I follow him down the well-worn path from the parking lot to the door.

The sun is still out, though it's already well past the tree line. The dingy beige paint on the corrugated tin siding is highlighted by the fading sunlight. There are a few weeds scattered about, but no grass or any other vegetation. Only one small window covered by security bars faces the street. It doesn't feel very homey. I get to the front door and wait as Dex enters a code on the keypad lock. I'm expecting it to be dark inside but am taken aback when I walk in. The entire wall opposite the entry is glass and overlooks the river at the bottom of a small cliff.

I walk through the short, wide hallway and find that the glass wall spans the entire building. My heels click across the rust-color-stained concrete floor as I'm drawn to the view like a magnet. The other side of the river is steeper, showcasing one of my favorite features of Austin, the striated limestone cliffs. It's gorgeous.

"It's a beautiful view, isn't it?" Dex asks, startling me.

"Unexpected," I say, turning to him. "How did you find something like this?"

He shrugs, setting my bags down on a cream-colored leather sectional I didn't even see until now. "I could never see myself as one of those guys that end up in a suburb with a white picket fence. I just asked the realtor to look into something commercial that didn't have zoning restrictions. He found this place. Just got lucky."

"Very lucky," I murmur, looking around.

The space is open and sparsely furnished; one large room

that holds a living area and kitchen. The ceiling is two-stories high, and the windows—that aren't windows but three glass garage doors—span the height. There's a loft space toward the front of the building that seems to be divided in two by a solid wall and cut off from the downstairs by plate glass walls. It's kind of amazing.

"You want the tour?" he asks.

I nod.

"Those doors lead to a bathroom and a storage room that's empty. I thought one day I might add a bed and make it a guest room. It's the only room that has a window that faces the front. Those stairs there lead up to Audra's room." He points to a very modern set of metal stairs with wood steps and industrial pipe railing on the far wall of the living area. "And that door past the kitchen leads to my studio and the access to my room. Which way do you want to go?"

"You have a studio?"

His cheeks tinge pink, and a shy smile lights his face as he turns away. "Yeah, one of the bays on the garage was cut off from the rest, so I decided to set up space in there for my art."

"You do more than sketching and tattoos?"

"I dabble in other mediums, I guess." He shrugs.

"You sound entirely too modest about that. I'm betting that's a treasure trove of Dex insight. I wanna see it."

"After you." He gestures me toward the only door off the kitchen area.

The clicking of my heels echoes in the mostly empty space as I make my way to the door. I open it tentatively and peer in. It's much like the rest of the building. No need for lights due to the giant glass garage door. Canvases line the walls, most turned away so I can only see the backs. The only furniture is a long wooden table, an industrial rolling ladder, some shelves, and a stool. A couple of really large canvases that wouldn't fit into a normal space lean against the wall covered with a drop cloth. My fingers itch to yank it off, but I'm captivated by a painting of Audra that is left uncovered.

She's standing in a field of bluebonnets, looking close to her current age, and laughing. It's a large canvas, and as I move closer, I can see that his style uses short brushstrokes that give movement to the varied colors. The reds of her hair contrast the blues of the flowers. I reach out, drawn to it, but stop short.

"May I?" I ask.

Dex is watching me as he nods.

"This is amazing. It's easy to forget who you really are when I almost never see you in this environment. How do you do this? You can tell it's one stroke by the texture, but the color isn't solid—all these variations make it look like real hair." I take a deep breath and turn to him. "What do you do with these? Do you sell them? Show them in galleries?"

He shakes his head. "The painting I do mostly for myself. I find it relaxing, and it helps me work through my thoughts. That one there I painted around the time she moved in with me. I was struggling to figure out who I needed to be for her, and I just knew I wanted her to smile like that every day."

Holy shit. That is unbelievably sexy. My lips curve up as I think about that for a moment. I'm definitely in uncharted territory when I find it hot that a guy wants to make his daughter happy. I try to distract myself from my urge to jump him by turning to the other canvases. There are a few paintings of objects and urban landscapes. My eyes are pulled to the covered ones with the ladder in front of it. If I had to guess, those are bigger issues for him to work through, and it has me insanely curious.

"Can I see that one?" I nod my head in its direction.

"It's not finished, and I want to say no, but it would be highly hypocritical of me to demand that you open up to me and keep things like that from you." He doesn't move but tips his head in that direction. "Go ahead—just pull on the drop cloth. It'll fall pretty easily."

I walk over to it. My fingers curl around the edges, and I look back to him to make sure he's okay with this. He looks unbelievably vulnerable, yet confident, as he stands there. His arms are relaxed at his sides, his head held high, but worry tinges his eyes.

I give the cloth a tiny yank and step back as it falls to the floor with a whoosh of air. My hair billows around my face, and I pull it away from my eyes before I register that I see myself. The painting is of me. I'm not looking in the viewer's direction—my face is in profile—but I recognize the color of my hair, the clothes.

"This is from the day we met up at the coffeehouse," I murmur.

"I started painting it that day," he says from behind me. "I didn't know what I was feeling at the time. Why I chose that moment. But it took me almost this whole painting to put it together. I think that was the moment I fell for you."

In the painting, I'm looking at his drawings of my tattoo design. My fingers rest on the page in a loving caress. Strands of hair have fallen out of the twist that they were styled into that day, and I'm biting my lower lip. I run my hand over the canvas in front of me. It has the same texture of tiny strokes. My mind boggles at the hours of work he had to have put into it. Awestruck. That's all I'm feeling. It looks like a picture of that moment has been printed on the canvas.

"You must have a photographic memory," I whisper.

"I do," he says softly next to my ear. I hadn't even heard him move. "How do you feel about it?"

"I think you're more talented with a canvas or a piece of paper than I'll ever be with a guitar. I hate to sound like a broken record, but it's amazing. I can't think of any other word for it."

He turns me to face him. "You're not creeped out by it? I mean I have a twenty-foot-tall painting of you in my studio."

"No," I say, entranced by his eyes. "Why would I?"

"I was worried it would bother you because it could be taken as a little stalkerish." He takes a deep breath. "And with everything that's been going on…"

"It's not like it's a painting of me in a private moment with someone else. This was a moment in your life. Your memory.

It's a gift to me to see myself through your eyes."

A dimple appears with his hesitant smile. "I love you."

Leaning forward, he brushes his lips over my forehead before squeezing me in a tight hug. My arms wrap around his waist. We stand there like that for a good bit. He feels so right, so solid in my arms. He steps away, clearing his throat.

"We should get ready to go. I'm pretty sure you said we would be there in about thirty minutes from now. And if we don't get out of here, I'm going to throw you on that table over there." He lets out a shaky laugh.

I shrug. "I'm not opposed to that, but you're right. We need to be on time."

"You can use the guest bathroom to get ready," he says, backing away and holding up his hands as if to ward me off. "It's the door next to the entry hall."

I fight a smile unsuccessfully. "Aye, aye, Captain." I salute him and head toward the door.

He starts climbing the circular staircase to the second floor, watching me as I go. I can't blame him. I'm having a hard time taking my eyes off him, too.

Then

The front door slammed shut. I cringed. I wasn't sure who was there—if they were coming or going—but I continued working on the song I was writing. This would be the first I'd ever written alone. I had to get these feelings out.

Jared's homecoming had not been what I was hoping it would be. He was distant and withdrawn. He didn't play with the girls anymore. I didn't know what to make of any of it because he wouldn't talk to anyone about it. We had all tried. We were scheduled to go on tour the next week, and I wasn't sure how that would work out. So, I buried my pain in the notes and lyrics of this song I was writing.

The door to the music room creaked a little as someone opened it. I recognized Asher's blond head, sneaking in. My lips tipped up in an amused expression.

"What're you up to, all stealth-like?"

He shut the door quietly behind him. "I came to talk to you about a problem."

"Okay, shoot," I said, setting my guitar down.

"I found this when I stopped at a gas station yesterday." He held out a magazine.

Tabloid was a more accurate word for it. I took it from Asher's hands. The cover was two pictures of Law and me, superimposed next to each other from last month when I was in New York. One was of us going into the nightclub; I was smiling and holding his hand as we walked in the door. The other was me curled into his side wearing his jacket, with his arm around me. We looked like a couple out for a night on the town. My stomach turned as I read the caption.

Boxing's bad boy, and notorious loner, takes a rare night on the town with America's military sweetheart. Does this spell the end of her wedding plans? (More on pg. 8)

"This is such bullshit!" I said, tossing the tabloid to the ground. "Why would they wait over a month to print that garbage?"

"His return date wasn't a state secret," he replied, his eyes flicking to the door.

"That's some bullshit, too. This isn't even partly true."

"I know. I was there," Asher assured. "I just thought you should be prepared in case Jared sees it."

"In case Jared sees what?" Jared's biting voice filled the room.

I froze as dread filled me. Jared and I were on shaky ground since his return. This was honestly the last thing we needed. He approached. I didn't move. Trying to cover it up would imply guilt. I wasn't guilty of anything, but I wasn't eager to shove it in his face either. He leaned down to pick up the tabloid from the ground. I closed my eyes.

"When was this?" His voice was deadly quiet.

"Last month, in New York," I answered.

"You took him to New York with you?"

"No." My eyes flew open. "It isn't what it looks like. He was there for a fight and found out through Sloane where we were. I didn't invite him *or* have much to do with him."

"Bullshit," Jared snarled. "You're holding his hand and smiling. And this... this one, you two look pretty cozy, getting into a car together. I think it's exactly how it looks."

"I was there, man. She hardly even talked to him," Asher defended. "The only reason he left with us was because the stalker fuck showed up. He was helping me get the girls back to the hotel."

"What?" Jared asked. "You trying to get in her pants now, too?"

"You know what? Fuck you, Jared. You want to be a dick to me for whatever reason you won't talk about? Fine. But you're not dragging other people into this. That's just a sleazy tabloid—do you expect anything they report to be true? I suppose you believed the alien babies story, too? Nothing happened—I said it, he said it. You can believe it. But I'm not going to stand by and watch you tear everyone down. We've got a tour set to start next week, so you need to get over this shit, real quick."

"I knew this would happen the second I left," Jared said, throwing the tabloid in my direction. "He's been looking for his opening to get you back, and you're so blinded by your cock lust for him you can't see the truth."

"Hey, man," Asher interrupted. "You might want to take a break before you say some shit you can't take back."

"I'm not taking a break," Jared yelled. "I've got something to say, and I'm going to say it. I'm fucking sick of this shit."

I raised my voice over him. "What the fuck are you talking about? This is one fucking tabloid and a made-up fucking story about something that never happened."

"Do you have any idea what it's like to be with someone that everyone wants to fuck? Guys constantly jerking off to thoughts of you. It's sick."

"What the fuck are you talking about?"

"That picture you did for the cover of *Rolling Stone*? Yeah, they shipped those out there to us. Every guy in our unit was jerking off to *my fucking fiancée*, naked and wrapped in an American flag. Fuck!" He pulled his hair and turned away.

"Hey—" Asher put his hand on my arm. "I'm going to let y'all work this out. You going to be okay?" His eyes darted to Jared.

Jared turned and at the sight of Asher's hand on my arm reacted like a bull seeing red. He charged at Asher, knocking him into the wall. I stumbled back from the force. Jared raised his fist to hit Asher, and I reacted like I was trained. Sliding onto the floor, I put one leg between his, locked my ankles together, and twisted my hips, knocking him off his feet.

"Asher, just go," I said, my breath labored. "I'll take care of this."

Asher nodded and walked out the door. Jared lay on the ground, breathing heavily. I crawled over to him. Silent tears made tracks down my face, stubbornly clinging to my chin before falling away.

"Please stop this," I pleaded. "Just talk to me."

"You want me to talk to you like he does?" He said glaring at me. "I heard him that day at your roller derby game. What he said and how you reacted. Want to be a little slut? Ride my cock while I finger your ass?"

My ass fell back to my feet as I sat there, stunned. I didn't know what to say to that. That deep-seated part of myself that I'd never been ashamed of until that moment reacted to his words. He hadn't touched me beyond a chaste kiss and a brief hug in the two days he had been back. He saw it, too, because he moved in like a tiger prowling and gripped the back of my hair.

"Is that what it takes to keep you?" His hands tightened, and my eyes rolled back in my head. "There it is. Who are you? Laine or Maddie?"

"Yours," I replied. "Call me whatever you want, but I'll always be yours, Jared."

"Is that right?" he asked, pulling my head back. He ran his

nose up my neck, licking my pulse point. I shivered in response. "I can call you a slut and you'd still be mine?"

I tried not to react, but the low, breathy moan escaped me anyway. I was starving for his touch. This wasn't what he wanted, but it was him, prodding my secret desires.

"And you like it. Who knew my sweet, innocent Maddie had a twisted dark side?" He exhaled next to my ear. "He knows, doesn't he."

"Jared, stop," I pleaded. "I only want you."

"Do you want me, or do you want this?"

He stood, still holding my hair and keeping my face eye level with his dick.

"Go ahead, take it out."

I knew this could only end badly, but I wanted him so much. I stopped thinking as I scrambled to pull open his pants. His cock sprang forward, bumping my lips. I gripped it and gave it a few pumps before wrapping my lips around the head and swirling my tongue. His cock twitched in my mouth. I closed my eyes and sucked it in, pulling on his hips until it hit the back of my throat.

"Jesus." His grip tightened in my hair. "Open your eyes. He may have taught you this, but you'll know whose dick is in your mouth now."

I wish I could've stopped the flood of wetness between my thighs. I loved the way he was talking to me, but not the why. I tried to pull back, but he pushed his hips forward, keeping my head in place with the grip on my hair. My eyes watered, but I couldn't tell if they were tears or lack of oxygen. He continued until his movements became jerky and his balls tightened at my chin. He released my hair and pulled out.

"Enough of that. Take off your clothes," Jared commanded.

I got up and did as he said. I was torn. Everything about this felt like a dream, my wildest fantasy, but with a sinister undertone I wished wasn't there. I didn't want to do it, but I didn't want to stop. I watched him as I pulled my shirt over my head and he did the same. I didn't know how to fix this. I pulled my pants off.

"Good. Now bend over the piano."

"Jared, please," I pleaded again. "Make love to me."

His hand pushed between my shoulder blades, bending me over the piano. He stood behind me, so I couldn't see him anymore. His tongue trailing up my seam shocked me, and I gasped. His fingers pumped into me, working me until I came. Before I could process the sensations, his cock slammed into my pussy.

"God, you're so fucking wet. This is how you like it?"

He slammed into me harder and faster. My hip bones rubbed on the edge of the piano. I couldn't find a grip to hold off the bruising thrusts. He pulled my head back by my hair, eliciting a moan.

"Answer me."

"Yes," I hissed out. "Are you happy now?"

He released my hair and grabbed hold of my breast, pinching my nipple, hard. At the same time, his fingers trailed in the wetness surrounding his cock and trailed it up to my ass. I came in waves, building on top of the other until it became so intense I screamed for release, the sound absorbed by the soundproof room. My muscles shut down communication with my brain. I twitched and convulsed violently for him. He followed me, finding his release until he sagged against my back.

"Holy shit," he breathed. "I can see the attraction."

"Fuck you," I said, pushing him off me and gathering my clothes to leave the room.

I walked straight to our bedroom and collapsed on the bed, as tears flooded my eyes.

Chapter Fourteen

Now

Dex's hand rests on my lower back, guiding me as we cross the basement lobby of the Black Building. It's a good thing too because I'm not watching where I'm going. I can't take my eyes off him. He kept the short beard, and it only adds to the sexiness of the perfectly tailored suit. It's a nice suit, but I think it's more about the man inside it that's getting to me.

He hasn't stopped touching me since we left his place either. I'm a little nervous about what this could mean. This is odd behavior for Nic, and I can only take it to mean that something bad is about to come at me. But there's nothing to be done but go up there and find out. All I can do is steel my nerves and hope for the best. Dex is serving as a good distraction from all those thoughts at the moment.

We stop in front of the red elevator. I place my hand on the scanner, tapping my toe with barely constrained impatience until the green light indicates the elevator is on the way.

"You wanna tell me why we're in a rush to get here?"

"I've no clue why he wants to meet with us." *Especially considering what you do for a living*, I think but don't add out loud. "Nic wanted us here early to talk about something, and it sounded serious, but he wasn't specific."

"You look beautiful," he murmurs, kissing my cheek.

A lopsided smile spreads across my face. "I believed you the first three times you told me."

"I still think this dress would look better on my floor." He backs me into the wall next to the elevator door, crowding me in the most delicious way.

I laugh. I'm not sure what about this dress he likes so much. It's a simple red Furstenberg pencil dress that Sloane picked out for me years ago. It only gets worn when I come here to the club. Its hemline hits just above my knees, and the neckline is a modest boatneck. The back is a little lower cut, and it's sleeveless, but nothing risqué enough to cause the reaction he's having to it.

His lips brush over mine lightly just as the elevator dings. He pulls me to him and walks me backward into the elevator without breaking lip contact. My pulse races as I cling to his biceps. His hands drop to my hips and smooth up the sides of my rib cage. I moan into his mouth as I lean into him, pressing myself against him.

He breaks the kiss, and I take a step back, leaning against the wall for support. My knees are weak. Our breathing is labored as we stare heatedly at each other. I close my eyes to calm myself. When I open them, I realize he's doing the same. His blue-green eyes meet mine as he stuffs his hands in his pocket and leans against the opposite wall. The air in the elevator feels too thin to breathe but thick enough that you could cut the sexual tension with a knife.

"I think all the interruptions are getting to us," I say when I collect myself.

A smile tips up one side of his mouth. "I'm just going to stay over here, for now."

"Good idea," I agree.

The elevator comes to a stop, and I move to the door to exit. The doors slide open with a quiet snick and lead directly into Nic's penthouse apartment. I step out into the foyer, and Dex follows.

"Hello?" I shout, hoping for an answer.

"In here," Nic replies, his voice coming from the direction of his living room.

We walk the short hall and turn the corner into the open space that is the living room and kitchen area of the penthouse. There are two full walls of glass pocket doors that retreat into the walls and open the area to the rooftop deck, complete with a pool, hot tub, and covered bar area, where he hosts quite a few parties. But for the moment, the doors are shut, and he's alone in one of his typical custom suits, sitting on the couch and sipping a golden liquid from a rocks glass.

He tilts his head in indication that we should sit.

"I need to tell you something, Ned. Something I've been keeping from you, and it has to do with him. That's why I wanted him here."

My eyes lock on to Dex as he sits back on the couch, not an ounce of emotion on his face to betray what he thinks about this news.

"Maddie, you know who my grandfather is and what I do for him."

I nod because I don't think he needs a verbal affirmation. His grandfather is *the* notorious mob boss who runs pretty much everything in Las Vegas. And I know that Nic has been working with him for years, being groomed to take over the family business one day. But I've no clue why he would even dare to bring this up in front of Dex. I told Nic who Dex was—an undercover cop in the organized crime division— the first night he got back from LA. It's why he's steered clear of us for the most part. Or so I thought.

Nic faces Dex, resting his elbows on his knees. "My grandfather is Lorenzo Beneventi."

He pauses, and I see the recognition flit across Dex's face. His eyes narrow and his jaw ticks for a fleeting moment before he resumes his neutral mask. The cursory look of anger is so brief, I think I might have imagined it.

"He told me about his arrangement with you," Nic continues, talking to Dex. "That you worked for him before taking the deal to become a cop. And that he was the one who encouraged you to take the deal. I also know you still work for him. Even if you've been given this temporary reprieve to come to Austin to raise your daughter."

Dex nods, still stoic. "He gave me five years. Long enough for Audra to get into college."

What in the actual fuck? This explains why Nic didn't seem bothered about bringing up his connection to his grandfather in front of Dex. So many questions race through my head, it almost makes me dizzy. I want to know why he didn't tell me, though I suppose that's kind of an awkward subject to bring up. Yet, he could've told me at the diner, when he was explaining his past and his connections to organized crime. He had let me believe they were former connections. But one question stands out above the rest.

"What exactly do you do for Nonno—I mean, Lorenzo?" I ask.

Dex's lips pinch, and he looks down at his hands. After a moment, he pins me with a blank look. "You don't want to know the answer to that."

Yes. Yes, I believe I do want to know. I'm so fucking tired of all the secrets and surprise revelations. I can't trust someone who's willing to lie by omission, and especially from him. We're already on shaky ground after I found out that he was assigned to investigate me and not identify the stalker, as I was led to believe.

"He's a cleaner," Nic says. Dex cuts a glare to him. "She's a big girl, Dex. She can handle the truth, and I think you've already figured out that if you want her to trust you, you need to trust her."

"Was a cleaner," Dex says with a biting tone. "I'm retired, for now—five years. We agreed to five years."

Holy shit. My mind tries to wrap around that bit of information. I've been around Nic long enough to know that *cleaners* are the guys they send in to "take care" of a problem. They are deadly and smart enough to know how to kill someone and make it look like an accident—sometimes even making it look like the person never existed in the first place.

I blink. I don't know how I feel about that information.

Nic's lips flatten into a firm line, and he breathes through his nose, clearly striving for patience. "Yeah, well, he wanted you to know that the terms of your agreement have changed."

"That's not gonna happen." Dex stands—to leave, to fight, I can't tell. "I'm not bringing that life anywhere near Audra."

"I really don't think you'll have an issue with the change," Nic says, raising his hands in a placating manner. He cuts his gaze to me before returning his attention to Dex. "I think we both know how you feel about her and what kind of lengths you'll go to—to take care of this problem."

Dex stills, watching Nic with narrowed eyes, his body all tense lines, like a tight coil ready to spring.

"My grandfather arranged for you to be introduced to Maddie." He nods in my direction. "He knows about her situation, but he can't get involved without making things worse for her. Because no one can know of her or my connection to him. You being here worked in our favor. I wanted you to protect her, and because I know your reputation, you would see to it that this will no longer be a problem for her in the future." Nic pins me in place with a pointed stare. "But because of your... developing relationship, I wanted her to know what kind of man you are."

I ignore that last comment for the moment because I don't really know what to say to it, but I do have questions about the whole situation.

"You arranged for me to meet him? How?"

"Nonno called in a favor to get Dex's name put in Holly's ear. When I told him you were looking for a tattoo artist, he thought it was the perfect opportunity. But when that wasn't enough, we used our inside contacts to get him assigned to you through more official channels."

"But the stalker wasn't around when I met him," I defend. "I don't understand."

"You and I both knew it was only a matter of time before he came back, Ned," Nic answers. "We had to take the opening while we had it." He shrugs. "I approached Nonno about it back when you decided to get rid of your security detail. It just took a while for the pieces to fall into place."

My mouth opens and closes like a fish out of water as I try to think of what to say to that. Six months. It took them six months to concoct this plan to fuck with my life—actually, less than that. I'd let my security team go six months before I met Dex, but that tattoo had been scheduled for several months before. Nic knows that if he forced someone on me that I'd have fought it. I thought the stalker was done with me. And I'm not too proud to admit that I can be quite stubborn.

"You knew about this?" I ask Dex, looking up to him where he still stands, like this whole conversation makes him unable to relax.

"No," Dex says, looking at the ground. "I do know Lorenzo is capable of stuff like that, but this is the first I'm hearing of him being behind all this."

"You didn't tell me that you were still involved in all that. You said you'd told me everything, but obviously that's not the case."

Dex doesn't respond, still looking at the ground with his hands in his pockets. Nic remains laid back, sipping his drink like he didn't just drop a bomb in my life. It pisses me off.

They lied to me. Both of them. Dex said that he was trusting me with his story to get me to trust him, but he only gave me half of the truth. And Nic... Nic knew this the whole time and never told me. I can feel the numbness setting in. *Fuck. Fuck them.*

I don't know how to feel about Dex's secret occupation. I only feel the anger of betrayal and the sting of lies, lying just below that numbing void of emotional repression that seems to be my natural survival instinct. I do what I always do—build a wall and leave it to deal with another day. I'm sure somewhere deep down I've an opinion on this, other than the anger—I'm just not sure in this moment what that feeling is.

This is all too much. I catch the time on the giant clock that hangs on the wall in front of me, and I realize that I need to be downstairs soon. Which is great, because I need some time to process this, but also, I'm looking forward to venting some pent-up aggression.

"Well, this's been lovely," I say, raising my voice a little too loud. I cringe at it. "But I've gotta get ready for my fight. I'm sure I'll see you around later."

I get up and walk away without a backward glance and leave them to sort out whatever they need to. I need to be alone right now. And I *really* need to punch something.

Then

I walked toward the tour bus, exhausted. We were on our third tour stop, in New Orleans. I'd just come from the backstage area, talking with fans and a few press members about the tour. This shit was insane. I cherished the moments on the bus when we were driving. I could just get lost with my guitar, surrounded by people I love.

My feet practically drug across the pavement, but I still had enough energy to open the door and hoist myself up the steps. I came to a halt immediately at the vision in front of me: Two people, tangled limbs, dry humping on the couch. The familiar voice, flooding the room with moans.

"What the fuck?" I asked.

The two scrambled apart with panic-stricken faces.

"When did this happen?" I asked.

"Today," Holly said meekly, which was so not her style. Yet, she made no move to cover her bare breasts from me, which was definitely a Holly thing to do.

"She was waiting here for you," Asher said, fixing his clothes before turning to me. "And one thing led to another." His fair cheeks were splotchy with embarrassment as he studied the floor.

"One thing led to another?" I asked, fighting to keep the smile from my face unsuccessfully. Laughter roared out of me. "I can honestly say, I never saw this coming."

They were sitting on the couch next to each other when I fell across their laps, still overtaken with giggles but too exhausted to stand anymore. I rolled over, looking at the ceiling.

"Put your shirt on, bitch," I said, smacking Holly's shoulder. "I need to talk to you, and it feels like I've a tit microphone right now."

She laughed and pulled her shirt over her head, shoving me out of the way to pull it all the way down. I rolled back in place on her lap.

"That shit wouldn't be a problem if you didn't plop your ass down across us," she said.

"I can't fucking stand any longer," I whined. "And the couch is the only place to lay down. Unless I was game for the kitchen table." I shrugged. "You know I love both of you, so we're fixin' to talk. And this way I can ensure that you listen, too."

"Whatever, bitch." She leaned down and kissed me on the lips, with a smirk to soften her words.

Asher groaned and leaned his elbows on my hips, squirming beneath me. I could feel his arousal where I lay across his lap. My whole body started bouncing in silent laughter.

"You two need to stop that," he said.

Holly and I laughed together this time. When our laughter finally quieted down, I got serious.

"What about Roz?" I asked Holly.

"We broke up." She shrugged. "Found out he had more than a few side hoes."

"When?"

"A few weeks ago," she murmured.

"Why didn't you tell me?"

She frowned. "You'd more important shit to worry about than some fuck boy that didn't deserve my attention."

"And this?" I asked, my gaze darting between the two of them. "You did give thought to all the complications this could create if this goes south? Holly, you're my best bitch, and Asher is my best guy friend. And he's the drummer for my band. We work together, live together. You're both family. And you know what family means to me."

"We can adult that shit, but I don't see it goin' sideways," Holly said.

Asher nodded. "It's not like that, Mads. We've given some thought to it."

"Yeah, I'm sure. In the whole hour you've been off stage?"

"It started back in Houston, but we stopped it because we weren't sure. So it has gotten more than an hour's thought," Asher added. "I think we have something real here."

Holly smiled and leaned into him. He pulled her to his side, kissing her forehead. He cupped her chin and tilted her to face him and brushed the lightest kiss across her lips. They stared at each other, both filled with longing and hope. It was such an odd match, but apparently it was working for them. And if they were happy, it made me happy for them.

I sighed. "Y'all are adults. I just expect that you know enough not to drag me into it. I got enough drama on my plate as it is."

"About that..." Holly shifted to look down at me. "Where's your fiancé?"

"He went back to the hotel suite that Nate booked for the girls and us," I explained. "He doesn't do the backstage stuff."

I knew where this conversation was going and didn't want to talk about it, so I shifted my attention to anything else.

"What is that smell?" I asked. "It smells amazing in here."

"She made us dinner," Asher answered. "Five fucking courses. She just finished. It's still hot, but also why you didn't get more than an eyeful."

I snorted a laugh. Holly tapped my shoulder, and I sat up, giving her space to move out from under me. I shifted over so I was leaning against Asher, as she set out plates and dishes of food on the table. I didn't want to move, but my stomach gave a loud grumble.

Asher scooped me up and carried me to the table, sitting me down on the edge of the booth-style bench. I scooted in as he sat across from me, and Holly took the place next to him.

"Just because y'need to eat this shit I made for you doesn't mean I'm gonna drop it. Evan's taught me some tricks, and I'm gonna get some answers." She chewed thoughtfully for a moment. "Asher's told me about most of it, but I wanna hear it from you."

I grabbed a bread roll out of a bowl and pulled my knees to my chest. "I don't know what you want me to say. I don't have any answers. He won't talk to me about it."

"I'm not worried about him," she said, pinning me with her gaze. "I'm worried about you. And the girls."

"I've got it under control," I snapped. "I'm not letting anything affect my girls."

"Hey," she soothed. "Nobody's sayin' you're not doin' right by those babies, but shit's gotta be takin' its toll on you."

"I just gotta convince him to get help, Holls. That's it. It's just hard with the tour to make time for it, and I get that. I don't know, but Asher's seen it. He'll be fine one second, and the next, he's raging against everyone. And the crowds don't help. Nate's had to come up with an alternate exit for him to avoid the VIPs and backstage ticket holders at every stop. It wasn't that bad in Houston or here, but Dallas was a shitstorm."

"I saw some of it on TV. Fuck, to see Press-zilla's face when that shit went down. She's had to hustle, for sure."

"It was priceless."

We both broke out laughing, and it felt good to laugh about it. I missed my friends and home. It hadn't even been a month. Asher had been my saving grace these last few weeks. He kept me sane when the shit hit the fan. I knew it was horrible to laugh about poor Priscilla's overtime, trying to smooth over Jared's very public freak-out, but if I didn't laugh about it, I was going to cry about it. And laughing just felt better.

"She took it out on a trash can in one of the dressing rooms," I added on a gasp. "It was Worldstar, trash can edition."

Holly wiped at her eyes. "I bet the trash can almost took her out with those pencil-skirt suits and heels."

"It so did," I wheezed out. "Her heel stabbed through it and she was hopping around on one leg, trying to shake it off."

"You're shittin' me!"

"No," Asher chuckled. "It happened."

"You guys need a personal chef," Holly said. "I gotta be around for this shit."

I sobered a bit at that. "You know I'd do it in a heartbeat, but we really can't fit another person on this bus."

"I'm just talkin' out my ass, bitch," Holly responded. "I haven't even finished culinary school yet. And the team wouldn't know what to do without both of us." She smiled.

"True," I agreed.

"Now eat," she demanded. "Fuel up, 'cause we're gonna take on New Orleans. I know 'bout this blues place on the other side of the river. And if that shit doesn't sound like a Maddie thing to do, nothin' does."

I perked up at that. I'd completely forgotten where I was, with everything going on. I hadn't had a chance to hang around a group of old-school blues musicians. It would be good to take a break from everything and remember my roots. And once again, I was reminded what awesome friends I had. They kept me grounded, reminding me who I was. I'd never stop being thankful for them.

Chapter Fifteen

Now

I grab the jump rope off the wall and walk to the center of the warm-up room. I changed upstairs in my room at Nic's penthouse before sneaking out the back way and heading down here. I left Dex upstairs with Nic—maybe that was a bitch move, but I can't be bothered to care at the moment.

I count my skips as I hop on the balls of my toes over the fast-moving wire. I can feel the sweat starting to build up on the back of my neck, and I stop, moving to the heavy bag to warm up my arms. The thumps of my fists fill the void of silence.

The door to this room squeaks when it's closing, and that's the only thing that gives him away. When I look up into the mirrored wall ahead, Dex is leaning against the wall behind me, one leg crossed over the other, hands in his pockets. He looks relaxed, but his eyes hold a tinge of apprehension.

"Nic brought you down?" I ask. *Thump. Thump thump.*

He nods. "Do you want me to leave?"

"No." Thumpthumpthump. "Why would I want that?"

"Because I'm not just a cop, which is already a sin in your book," he huffs, "but a dirty cop. And a killer. Why would you want anything to do with me?"

"As if I'm the shining example of purity and all that is decent in the world?" I pause for a moment from throwing punches to belt a dark laugh. *Thumpthump. Thump.* "You should know enough by now to know that can't be further from the truth."

"Why did you leave, then?"

I sigh and stop to catch my breath enough to speak, resting my hands on my knees. "Because it was too much. And not all that is you, Dex. Yes, I'm frustrated that you didn't trust me enough to tell me, but I understand why you'd be reluctant. It'd be highly hypocritical of me to hold it against you. But you're not the only one who kept shit from me." I stand back up. *Thumpthump, thump. Thwack.* The bag swings wildly as I deliver a powerful kick.

Dex remains motionless, watching me. "You doing okay?"

"I don't know, to be perfectly honest." *Thumpthumpthump.* "I don't know how to feel about it. On the one hand, he's right—I wouldn't have agreed to you protecting me otherwise, but on the other, I wish people would stop trying to manipulate me, you know?" *Thwack, thwack, thump.* "First, Martinez's story that you're working to find the stalker, now, Nic's hand in setting it all up. I just—"

His lips flatten out to a straight line as he bobs his head in agreement.

"Can I tell you something?" I ask. *Thump. Thump.* "I don't want you to take it the wrong way."

"You can tell me anything, Maddie."

I lean forward to brace my hands on my knees and catch my breath. "I wish you'd stayed up there," I murmur. "Not because I don't want you to know about this, but everyone who knows me... it's hard to watch. Nic won't even come down here for my fights. Not after the first time. He lets me do it because he knows why I feel the need to, but he doesn't approve."

"I've seen you fight before. I know you can handle yourself."

"It's not that, Dex." I grab my water bottle and take a

deep pull. "This is a fetish club. The first fight, I'm usually paired off with another woman. That's something akin to mud wrestling. Two sexy women, fighting each other." I shrug. "It's easy. But when I fight a guy, that—" I release a breath through my nose. "It's rape fantasy, Dex. The guy will try to grope me at some point. I'll make him pay for everything he does, but you need to be prepared that you're not going to like it. You can't step in. No matter what it looks like, I'm in control. We have safe words to stop if things get out of hand."

"Why?" he asks.

It's a loaded question with such a complicated answer. I shrug.

"For them, it's fantasy fulfillment. For me, it's penance."

He doesn't say anything. His nostrils flare and the muscle in his jaw twitches, but he remains motionless, his face impassive. A knock at the door interrupts us, and I turn to find Parker at the door.

"You're up," he says.

"You have that mask Nikki gave you earlier?" I ask Dex, crossing the room to gather my stuff.

"Yeah," he answers.

"You need to put it on now. I can tie it for you," I offer.

He reaches in his inner coat pocket and pulls out the silky black mask, handing it to me.

"You're gonna have to squat or go down on a knee." I smile at him.

He obliges, and I make quick work of tying it with a loose flat knot. When I'm done, I tie mine around my ponytail to make sure it's secure and follow Parker out the door. Parker holds open my black satin robe, and I slip my arms into it. I can feel Dex behind me, but he doesn't comment. I'm beginning to recognize this as his observer mode.

We walk to the entrance of the arena. There's quite a crowd out there tonight. The lights are down, and music is playing as the announcer introduces my opponent. A spotlight follows her as she walks in from the opposite entrance. I missed the name, so I've no clue who I'm fighting tonight.

The spotlight swings my way. "Please welcome the one and only undefeated champion of the Black Society..."

I tune it out as I search Dex's face for any kind of emotion. I want to know what he's thinking more than anything.

"Phoeeeeeeeenixxxxxxx!"

That's my cue, the stupid fight name that Nic gave me. *You'll rise again, Neddie*, he told me.

Catching Dex's hand, I start walking. About halfway there, I can see Vixen standing on the far side of the cage. She's weak but a masochist, so the pain only spurs her on. I can feel the adrenaline flood my system in anticipation.

I start to hop up to the edge of the platform but stop and twist around, pulling Dex by his lapels.

"You gonna wish me luck?" I smirk.

"You don't need it. Just make me proud."

He kisses me slow and unhurried before letting me go. The crowd cheers as he lifts me up and sets me on the edge of the stage. I shrug off the robe, and Parker takes it from me. The referee shuts the chain-link gate behind me, separating me from Dex. Dex turns to Parker to say something.

I face my opponent, feeling the fight surge within me, the need for violence a siren's call to the darkness in my soul.

The referee rambles on about the rules. I tune him out because I've heard it all before. I shake out my arms and legs, bouncing on the balls of my feet. I shake hands with Vixen when the ref tells us to. She offers me a smile. Fights here aren't competitive. It's more for show, so we keep it pretty friendly. I stretch my neck, keeping a straight face. I'm not in the mood for niceties.

The bell rings, and she rushes at me. I stand there, relaxed, and step to the side, turning on my toes to follow her movement. I catch the back of her neck and shove her into the fence. She can't slow her momentum, and the cage gives a satisfying rattle. The crowd responds.

She recovers quickly and moves toward me, more cautiously this time. We circle each other, looking for an opening.

"Rough month, Phoenix?" she taunts.

"Could be worse." I shrug. "I could be fixin' to get my ass kicked."

"It's going to be that kind of night?" Her eyes gleam in anticipation. "Sounds good. Bring it."

While she's talking, I take the opportunity to inch closer, closing the distance between us. I keep my guard up high, so the right hook I throw comes easy. The smack of skin meeting skin is muffled by the sounds of the crowd as I connect my fist to her lower jaw. She stumbles to the side a bit, but a satisfied grin takes over her face. I'm watching her eyes, so I fail to see the tell. Her leg sweeps out, catching me behind the ankles and knocking me flat on my back.

Shit. I'm not even fully on the ground before Vixen's on me. She pulls her arm back to return my punch, but I see it coming this time and close the distance between us. I wrap my arms around her shoulders, pulling her to my chest. She bucks and pulls, but my left fist is secure in my right hand. I'm locked on. Her only move is to use her lower body. I'm counting on that as my opening.

When she moves, as expected, I push my hip up with her, knocking her off balance. It's just enough to draw my knee up and get my leg wrapped around her waist. I pull her using all my weight until we roll over. She's been practicing and breaks my hold. Her fist connects with my stomach. I lean forward, pushing my weight on her to manage her range of motion.

We grapple for a bit, while I try to contain her hands. I finally get a grip and rear back, nailing her with a three-punch combo. *One, five, three.* She laughs. Her cheeks, turning pink and puffy, are going to bruise.

She screams in frustration and goes wild, bucking and clawing, her composure and training out the window. I let loose and just start throwing punches. My vision narrows. Darkness closes in until the only thing I see are the spots where my fists connect to her body.

Someone comes at me from behind. I don't think. I can't think. I throw back my elbow and turn to launch myself at the newcomer. Next thing I know, I'm being pinned to the ground by three men.

One sits on my legs, another has my left arm, and the referee has his knees digging into my right while holding a rag over his bleeding nose. The crowd is going insane. Their cheers and chants are at near-deafening levels.

"I'm okay," I say to the guy on my left. "You can let go."

"You sure?" he asks.

"Yes, let me up," I yell over the music and crowd noise.

They watch me as they reluctantly let go. I stand up and find that Vixen's partner, husband, boyfriend—I don't know, but he's always with her—is helping her up off the ground.

I walk over to her and gently grab her face. "You all right?" I ask.

She nods. "It was a good night. You got me." She smiles.

"I'm sorry. I think, maybe I shouldn't've fought tonight."

"Don't be." She leans on her partner. "I'm so turned on right now. We are about to get our fuck on. If I were halfway interested in girls, I'd ask you to join. It's just not my thing. He just doesn't like to hurt me, and I need the pain every once in a while, so this is our outlet. Thank you."

The ref grabs our hands as the announcer's voice booms over the loudspeakers.

"The winner... by submission—Phoenix!"

The referee holds my hand in the air.

The only thing I can think is that I didn't see her tap out. That's dangerous. I feel off tonight. I think missing the last fight has led to a buildup, or maybe it's just a perfect storm of everything going on. The guilt feels heavy in my gut, but I channel that into energy for the next fight. Vixen kisses her guy deeply, and he picks her up, carrying her from the cage. My eyes search the audience, but I don't see Dex anywhere.

There are several spotlights trained on the cage, but the audience is in the dark. I can't see past the first two rows.

"You good to go?" the referee asks.

I nod. The announcer, who turns out was the guy holding my left arm, raises his mic. It's hard to recognize anyone here. Everyone, even the fighters, wears masks. His deep voice reverberates through the room as he calls out my next challenger. I lean against the cage, mopping my face with a towel and drinking the water that is handed to me. A medic comes over and starts fussing over the state of my hands, but I can't feel it. I'm more annoyed with his presence as I shoo him off.

"Ladies and gentlemen, this is the main event of the evening. Iiiiiiiiiittttttttttt'ssss tiiiiiiiiiimmmmmmmmmmeeeee! This fight is three rounds of extreme cage fighting in the Black Society Third Thursday competition. In the blue corner, our current reigning, undisputed champion with forty-nine wins and zero losses, trained in American boxing, Krav Maga, and Brazilian jujitsu. Weighing in at one hundred and thirty-five pounds at five feet eight inches tall— Phhhooooeeeeeeeeennnnixxxx!"

He stops to let the audience cheer and whistle. There are a few boos thrown out as well. I'm not well-liked in the mixed-gender fighting. I've seen other fights, and they usually end up fucking. I'm just not here for that. It's not the reason I fight, so I disappoint this crowd. Every. Damn. Time.

"And introducing our challenger, weighing in at two hundred and five pounds, standing six feet and two inches tall, Dieeeeeesseeellll!"

I toss my empty water bottle and towel to a guy nearby. Mixed-gender matches don't allow face hits. Or hitting in general. It's more about grappling, holds, and submission.

Diesel enters the cage. His eyes roam over my body with a leer. He turns to the crowd, throwing his hands up with a yell and pounding his bare chest. Thick ropes of a tribal tattoo run across each arm, crossing at his chest. I've seen enough tattoos in my lifetime that these are not impressive at all.

163

Images of pistols and half-curled fists flash through my mind, tattoos with personality and stories behind them. I bet there's a story behind Dex's dragon. Diesel's are just a showpiece. *Look at me, I'm a badass with tattoos.*

I'm not gonna lie, though. The rest of him is hot as hell. Dark hair, tall, and muscular. His loose gym shorts hang low on his hips, exposing a deep V of muscle. I've fought Diesel quite a few times, and I always had the suspicion that Nic picked him because he hits all the checkboxes for my type. Except for the personality. I like the deep ones: intelligent, broody, with the weight of responsibility on his shoulders an almost visible strain.

Law didn't seem that way at first. He was fun. But the second I met his dad, I knew. He had his hooks in me deep. This cage is the only time I allow myself to think of him because Diesel isn't standing in front of me anymore. I don't see crappy tribal tattoos as I shake his hand.

The fact that we wear masks helps with this illusion. My mind settles, my focus narrows on my opponent, and the same words repeat in my head like a mantra: *I will not give in. You do not own me.*

"You ready for this, sweetheart?" Diesel asks, gesturing at his dick.

My eyes narrow. "Try shutting your mouth before you ruin this for me. You know I don't like it when you talk."

"I gotta keep you talking somehow." He shrugs. "It keeps my dick hard when you say this shit to me." He grabs himself and adjusts its position.

"Quit playing with your pencil dick, and let's get to it. I don't have all night. There's a schedule to keep."

He groans. "Goddamn, that smart mouth of yours does it for me." His eyes flash with a smirk.

I close my eyes as those words hit me. When I open them, I charge. *Fuck waiting around for him to come at me.*

Then

"...a real New Orleans adventure," Holly said, as we hopped onto one of the red trolleys that travel the network of wires that hover over the streets.

I was so taken by the sights as we passed through the French Quarter that I forgot she had started talking again. That city had a pulse, a rhythm. Like the city itself was constructed of music, and it bled through every pore in the concrete roads. Holly tugged on my sleeve, and I pulled my gaze away from the window.

"Are you even hearing me?" she asked, tapping her foot and standing in the aisle. "This next stop is where we get off."

"I'm distracted by the city." I waved her off and stood. "It's my first time here, you know."

"You'll fucking love it. This isn't touristy New Orleans, this is authentic." She winked.

We made our way toward the front of the trolley and jumped off just before it started moving again. I froze in place. Just ten steps ahead of me, Jared was standing under a sign that read Canal Street Ferry Terminal, looking handsome as ever. He smiled and walked toward us.

"Took you guys long enough," he said, wrapping his arms around me.

I pulled back to see his face. "You came."

"Of course. I wouldn't miss your first trip to a real blues club. It'll be just like old times, yeah?"

I leaned in and took a deep breath. Jared's familiar scent surrounded me, comforting. It was such a change from the way he had been acting. I was going to embrace every moment I had him back.

"We're taking the ferry?" I asked.

Holly nodded. "Yeah, it's a few blocks from the ferry terminal on the other side to where we need to go."

"Wouldn't it be faster just to drive there?" Asher questioned.

"And miss the boat ride across the Mississippi?" Holly

asked. "Fuck that—we gonna do it right."

I tipped my head back and laughed. "Holly, I think your Cajun is showing."

Asher's head whipped toward her. "You're from around here?"

"Holy Cross, born and raised." She tipped her head. "It's over that way, on this side of the river. Shit, I couldn't miss a chance to return home." Her eyes tracked back to me with a grin. "And catch up with my best bitch."

"Huh," Asher grunted, looking thoughtful.

"It only took one time of hearing her ask for mayonnaise for me to figure it out." I laughed.

"How do you say it?" Asher asked.

"It's not may-o-nays, or man-ays like Mads says, it's my-nez," Holly grumbled. "It's not even weird. You fuckers are weird."

"I think it's adorable." I pressed my hands, palms together, underneath my tilted head with a smirk.

"It's why I love me some Maddie," Holly said, ignoring me. She tugged me to her side by the bottom edge of my jacket. "She's like a slice of home for me. It's why I had to introduce you two. Maddie, meet Nawlins. Look out, NOLA, you 'bout to find out just who Maddie is," she shouted loudly toward the water, as the ferry rocked loose from the dock.

I hugged her hard, shushing her as I tried to hide from the attention she just called to us. Some people farther down the railing on the ferry glanced in our direction, but for the most part, we were largely ignored.

"This explains so much about you," Jared said, shaking his head with a smile.

"Yep." Holly shrugged. "Now you know what put the hood in this hood rat. Come on." She pulled Asher and me toward the back of the boat. "We got shit we need to do."

Jared followed behind us. We stood at the railing near the raised ramp. The water churned in frothy white mounds below.

"My Papère taught me this. Here." She shoved her hand

into her pocket and pulled out some change. She handed me a penny and gave one to Asher and Jared too. "We have to pay the ferryman, and he'll grant us a wish."

My brows drew together. "Didn't we already do that when we bought our tickets?"

"Not that ferryman, da Ferryman. Papère said he lives at the bottom of the Mississippi and he grants wishes to those who believe. Shit, I know it's stupid, but just humor me. I've never crossed the river without doing it." She shrugged.

A slow grin spread across my face. "That's incredibly cute, you know?"

"Bitch, please," she protested, but I swear a blush colored her cheeks in the dim light of the ferry. "Just rest it on your finger and thumb, like this, and think of your wish. Then just flick your thumb."

The muddy water below churned angrily. The hair on the back of my neck pricked up. I had the overwhelming feeling that someone was watching us and the sudden urge to run welled up within me. I didn't normally believe in superstitions, but there was something about that river. The wind whipped my hair in every direction, making it slap over my face and tangle in my mouth. I closed my eyes and thought of what I'd wish for. Jared's arm brushed against mine as he flicked his penny into the water, and I knew what I wanted.

Please let us find an end to whatever is wrong with Jared.

I flicked my penny and watched it disappear into the muddy waters of the Mississippi. Turning to face the wind, I found Jared looking at me. A tiny smile played at the corner of his lips.

"You're the most beautiful thing I've ever seen," he said, his voice rough with emotions.

My muscles relaxed as I stepped into his arms. "You're not too shabby yourself, handsome." I kissed his cheek. "Thank you."

"For what?" he asked.

"For the compliment. For coming out with me tonight.

It's nice having you here." I sighed, resting my ear on his chest and listening to his heartbeat compete with the hum of the ferry's engine.

The boat rocked as it came into contact with the dock. With a loud clang, it connected. Jared's body jerked under my ear, his heart racing. His arms tensed around me, squeezing me. I pulled back to see his eyes, flat, emotionless, staring into the distance.

"Hey," I spoke softly, brushing his cheek with my fingers.

He didn't move for a moment, and then his eyes narrowed. His gaze slowly tracked down to me.

"Jared?" Dread swamped my gut.

He was looking at me, but I wasn't sure he was seeing me. Then his brow smoothed out. His eyes cleared. "Did you say something?"

"We're here." I nodded in the direction of the dock. I realized then that we would have to walk to the other side to get off.

Asher and Holly were already heading that way. Holly's laugh rang out as Asher leaned down with his mouth near her ear. I couldn't deny they were cute together, but Asher was so not her type. I couldn't help but feel that this wouldn't end well. For any of us.

Jared took my hand and led me to the exit as I shook the thoughts of Holly and Asher off. They were adult enough to handle it. It wasn't my place or my business anyway. They looked happy enough at the moment.

"When did that happen?" Jared asked, watching the two as they waited for us on the street corner.

I suppose *waiting* for us wasn't the word for it. They were making out. "In Houston, apparently. Though it didn't become a thing until tonight, I suppose. We didn't get too in-depth about it. I walked in on them dry humping on the tour bus."

Jared snorted a laugh. I cleared my throat as we sidled up to the two lovebirds. They broke apart and looked over at us.

"It's this way," Holly said as she turned and started down

the sidewalk.

The walk was short, and soon we were standing outside what looked like a large two-story house that had been converted into a dive bar. It was dark, but I could still see that the once-white siding was dingy and gray. It sat on the street corner like a wizened old man, knowing it owned its spot in the world. The signs proclaimed it to be *Old Point Bar—Air Conditioned* like it was the biggest selling point. Bluesy guitar strains carried out the open front door. People talked loudly on plastic chairs around plastic tables under a porch that looked like a hard wind would knock it down. I was instantly in love. Holly was right. This wasn't a tourist trap. This was an authentic New Orleans bar.

We walked in, and the woman behind the bar froze. Her salt-and-pepper gray hair had fallen out of its ponytail, framing her weathered face. She was slim and petite, but her stance behind the bar gave off the vibe that she was not one to mess with. The glass she held in her hand shattered as it hit the floor.

"Holly?" the older woman asked, squinting her eyes as if she wasn't seeing clearly.

"Aunt Mae," Holly said as she walked to the end of the bar and rounded the corner to embrace the woman.

"Holy fuck, child. Mais, give a vielle a heart attack. I thought you'd never come back after my defan brother..."

The smile on Holly's face dropped, and the old woman patted her cheek.

"Where y'at, cher?" Aunt Mae asked, a sad, sympathetic smile warming her face.

"My friends are in town." Holly looked back to me and motioned me over. "This is Maddie, her fiancé, Jared, and my boo, Asher. Y'all, meet Aunt Mae."

"Go to bed! Dis one yours?" Aunt Mae descended on Asher faster than a rattlesnake striking, squishing his cheeks as she tsked at him. "You be taking care of my Holly?"

"Yes, ma'am," Asher said, trying to smile, but his lips only curled up.

I covered my mouth with my hand to hide my laugh.

"Let him alone, Mae." She stepped in between her aunt and Asher. "Shit's new, so don't go scaring him off. I didn't bring him here to make introductions like that."

"Don't boude." Aunt Mae pinned her with a bland look. "Doesn't hurt to axe, cher."

Holly shook her head. "I need to get Maddie's ass onstage tonight. Is Ol' Gus around?"

"Up dere now." Mae nodded to the stage, set back farther into the building. "When he takes a break, you tell him what you want. Want sum'in to drink? You ahnvee?"

"No," Holly answered. "I already cooked for us."

"Still puttin' to use what your mama and I taught you?" Aunt Mae asked with a gleam of pride in her eyes.

"Yep." Holly nodded. "Still have a little over a year left of school, but I'll be a chef in no time."

"Good. It'd make your daddy proud." Someone down the bar called for Mae. "Shoo, shoo. Go vay ya. I'll bring your drinks, 'kay?"

I only understood half of what Holly's aunt Mae was saying, but I caught the dismissal in her tone and started looking for a place to sit. I spotted a table near the stage and tugged Holly's arm.

"We can sit over there?" I pointed to the empty table.

Holly smiled. "Perfect."

Chapter Sixteen

Now

My feet only get two steps into my charge before the bell rings out and the referee steps into my path. I skid to a stop as the ref's hands meet my shoulders. He gives me a weak smile, but my attention is diverted. Murmurs spread through the arena as the announcer steps into the cage. I step back, a sinking feeling in the pit of my stomach. The announcer approaches Diesel, and they speak for a brief moment before the announcer turns on his mic to address the crowd.

"Ladies and gentlemen. There's been a change in our schedule for tonight's events. Diesel will return to the cage in another fight this evening. We have a new challenger coming to the stage. Standing at six feet five inches tall, weighing in at two hundred and thirty-five pounds..." More murmurs fill the arena. "Please welcome to the stage, Draaaaaagooooooonnn."

I snort a laugh at the stupid name. The spotlight swings over to the arena entrance I entered from earlier, and the sight before me pulls the rug out from under my feet. I sway a little and reach out, grasping the chain-link wall of the cage. *No.* Why would they do this? *No.* I blink, hoping the vision would will away. It doesn't change as the loud, ominous strains of the song "Conform" by Siege boom out over the loudspeakers. The floors and the links of chain beneath my fingers vibrate with each pluck of the grinding bass.

Nic doesn't just walk but swaggers beside my new opponent, wearing the same tailored suit he was in earlier. Loud chatter sweeps the room because everyone here knows who he is, but they also know he doesn't come to the fights. When they get to the edge of the platform, my opponent hops up with a lethal grace and turns to give Nic a hand. His muscles ripple under the spotlights, giving movement to the massive dragon tattoo on his back, only covered from the waist down by black cotton gym shorts. My heart rate increases as I meet Nic's eyes.

Nic smirks. *Asshole.* He leans in close so only I can hear. "It's a shame this wasn't my idea. That look on your face is priceless."

I straighten from the cage wall, and he backs away, holding his hands out in front of him to ward me off. The anger flows just under my skin, making my heart slow like it's pumping thickened lava through my veins. The slow thud of each beat echoes in my ears, shushing out the din of the crowd. The announcer hands Nic the mic.

"Boy, do we have a special treat for you," he says, playing up the accent that we grew up with but have long since lost, for the most part.

You can almost hear the collective sigh from the females in the room. I suppose this is how people close to Matthew McConaughey feel when he speaks to a group of fans. It's amusing, but not enough to distract me from my frustration. I realize with a start that I missed whatever he said, lost in my thoughts, as Nic turns to wink at me before exiting the cage and taking a seat in the front row.

I catch the ref's hands moving out of the corner of my eye as he explains the rules to my new opponent.

I can see it now. Well, I suppose the truth was that I could always see it. It was in the curves of his muscular shoulders. The way his arms were always slightly bent as if to help bear the weight. His feet always apart. I hesitate to drag my gaze up, but when they meet the turquoise eyes behind the mask, I suck in a breath. That same look I see in my eyes every morning that I look into a mirror is there, a dark hollow void hidden in their depths. A kindred spirit. My heart thunders like a stampede caught in my chest. That's the scariest thing about him—he's my match.

My mind whirls as I try to grasp for a solution. Because I know right then, he's everything I ever wanted. Someone who wouldn't offer to bear the weight of my burdens, but walk beside me in companionship. And I know. With my track record, I'll fuck it up. All I see before me is a choice, and fuck if it doesn't feel like I'm being ripped down the middle. *Run.*

"Phoenix, you good to go?" the ref asks.

I nod. He backs away, slicing his hand through the air. The bell rings.

"You really do look like a firebird right now. The way the lights pick up those red tones in your hair. You're beautiful," Dex says, moving toward me.

"What the fuck are you doing?" I grind out from clenched teeth. *Run.*

"This." He lifts one leg and stomps his foot on the cage floor, deliberately. My eyes are narrowed to slits as I focus on him. "You asked me to make it clear what I don't like, and this is it. I'm not going to stop you. You want to fight, fight me."

"I don't want to hurt you," I say, but it comes out as more of a growl. *Run.*

He tips his head back to laugh, and red colors my vision. *Fight.* I strike. Sweeping my leg out and under him, I throw my shoulder into his chest. I realize my mistake almost as soon as I make it. I don't know one thing about how Dex fights. I've never seen him come even close to aggression in our time together, and I forget to read him before I make my move. Big mistake. His big arms wrap around my shoulders and pull me down with him. I'm so stunned by his quick reflexes that I'm pinned underneath him faster than I can blink.

Shocked, I don't even fight back. I gasp for the breath that was knocked out of me. I don't even know what I want. I've been running since the day I met him, and I don't think I'm strong enough to fight him anymore. Because this fight is all in my head and my heart—that shriveled-up black thing that somehow still beats in my chest.

"Did you mean it?" he asks.

My eyes find him, and he's looking through me again. I don't like it. No one is supposed to be in here but me. *Fight.*

I growl, "What the fuck are you talking about?"

"That my past, who I am, it doesn't bother you," he explains.

The crowd starts booing. We've been motionless too long. He's not even holding me. That's all it takes for my mind to flip. I become aware of his body pressing me into the mat with his weight. That's all it takes for that lust to come roaring to the surface. The warmth of his flesh seeps into me. His woodsy smell invades my senses. He's watching me so intensely that he sees the change. The left corner of his mouth twitches. I wonder if he knows that he always leads a smile with the left. *Why do I even know that?* I bite my lip, and my brows draw together. His left dimple flickers as the twitch becomes a smirk.

He leans on one elbow, running the other hand down my side, hooking it behind my thigh and pulling it to wrap around his hip. A trail of fire is what it feels like. I squeeze my eyes shut and take a breath. The crowd rumbles in approval, and it slams me back into reality.

"No," I grind out as I use the imbalance of his position and the advantage he just gave me to take back control of the situation.

I'm on top of him now, and as I look down to him, he's grinning. "Liar," he accuses.

Darkness crowds my vision. *Challenge.* No. No one can see me here. No one can join me here. *Pain.* It radiates from the core of me. I want to hurt him. I want to scare him away. He can't be here. The dark is for me alone. This is my penance—my just desserts.

My fist snaps through the air toward him. He's faster. He grabs my wrist, stopping me just inches away from his cheek. That left corner of his mouth twitches again. *Asshole.* I roll off him, away, breaking his hold on my wrist. I rise to my feet at the same time he does. My body remains crouched, on alert, as I circle him, looking for my opening. He doesn't seem bothered by it. He stands, back straight, tracking me as I circle him.

"You shouldn't be here," I say.

He shakes his head. "That's where you're wrong. I was here before we ever met. I'm not scared to go there with you."

I tilt my head.

His head shakes again. "I don't mean this cage, Maddie. You know what I'm talking about, just as I know what you're talking about."

The dark. *Fuck you.* I move in and strike, landing my fist in his gut before he spins me around, holding me. My back presses to his chest. My arms are trapped beneath his bulky arms. His breath puffs out next to my ear.

"Holy shit, you have some fire in that arm," he wheezes out, his voice drawing closer to me. His tongue trails the side of my neck to the space just below my ear. I shudder in his hold. "I don't understand all of this, but fuck if I'm not curious." His forearm, covered in the small tattoos, moves until his hand cups my breast. "All I know is that I want you. But it's more than that. I want to own you. Possess you. I want this to be mine." He trails his thumb over my nipple, and my body jerks in his hold. A tiny moan escapes me. "I've never met someone filled with so much darkness that still managed to shine so bright. Like a moth to a flame, Firebird. I'm yours."

I turn my head to look at him, to respond in some way, but his lips are on mine before I can blink. All thoughts flee from my mind. My lips part on a sigh, and his tongue strokes against mine. The fight leaves me. I go limp in his arms. His hold loosens, and I turn into his embrace. He leans into me just enough to lift me, and then I'm wrapped around him as I pull his bottom lip into my teeth. My back slams into the cage. The cool metal links press into me. The crowd is louder now, but it's not boos or cheers; it's a cacophony of moans and screams. Pleasure. A thrill runs through me.

Dex breaks away, wedging his thigh underneath me to support my weight. I search his face for something as he grabs my wrists and pushes my arms up against the cage.

"Hold," he grunts.

All I see in his eyes is hunger. The ravenous look of a starving man, staring at the last piece of food. My fingers lace into the chain links. His eyes return to mine. His hands move to the collar of my tank top, the straps digging into my shoulders as he pulls. The tearing fabric echoes in my ears as I suck in a breath. As the shirt tatters fall to my sides, his fingers find the zipper at the front of my sports bra. He yanks and I'm exposed, in more ways than the obvious. His hands grasp my ribs, his fingers pressing into my skin.

"You're not stopping me," he growls.

"No, I'm not," I respond, as my eyes roll back in my head and my back arches.

His mouth is on me again, biting and sucking his way from my neck to my breasts. I moan. Opening my eyes, I find Nic in the front row, watching. Despite the woman writhing on his lap, sucking his neck, his focus on me never wavers. A small smirk plays at the corner of his lips. His eyes hold his triumph in plain view. He nods.

Touch her, I mouth to him.

Nic pushes her legs open, his hand exposing her core to me. He pushes his fingers into her, and her head drops back on his shoulder. I squirm and pull Dex in tighter with my legs. His mouth detaches from my nipple with an audible pop, and he looks at me and tracks my gaze behind him. His hand wraps around my ponytail, and he yanks my head back, swallowing my cry with his kiss.

"Mine," he gasps.

"Yes, yours." I hum with pleasure as I release the cage wall to grip his shoulders. My nails dig into his skin. A rumble of pleasure reverberates in his chest. I smile at that.

"Why do I feel like the fly that just landed on a spider's web," he pants, pulling back to search my face.

"Perhaps because you are." I shrug.

"I'm a selfish man, Maddie." His grip tightens in my hair. "I don't want to share you."

"All right. Then don't," I say with another shrug. "You're in charge."

His eyes dilate, and my heart flips. *What is happening?* I don't have time to ponder it because he pulls me close and turns. With a few quick strides, we are out the cage door. He walks like a man on a mission as he carries me up the stairs and out of the arena to the bank of elevators we came from the first time I brought him here. I wiggle in his hold to get down, but he only grips me tighter. He's not asking as he puts my hand on the biometric scanner and operates the elevators on his own. I stop shifting and hold on, waiting for his attention.

He doesn't speak. He doesn't set me down, just keeps his hold on me. When we get to the penthouse, he speaks. "You went this way earlier. Where did you go?"

"My room. It's over there, down that hall." I point off to the right, and he moves in that direction. "Second door on the left."

He opens the door, and his hand reaches out, feeling the wall for a light switch. I chuckle to myself.

"Penny, lights at fifty percent, windows open," I say.

The lights come on, and the panels that cover the full wall of windows opposite us retreat into the walls, revealing the city lights below. Dex sets me on the ground and takes in the room. Directly in front of us, with its headboard against the wall to the left, is a king-sized canopy bed. It's flanked by two full-size chests of drawers, and on either side of those are two doors, one leading to the closet and one to the en suite bathroom. To the right is a large open space with only two pieces of furniture, a chaise and an armchair. In the center of the room, chains hang from the ceiling off a metal grid. His eyes linger on it.

"Welcome home, Mistress," the female computer voice intones. "I trust your fights went well tonight? Would you like me to start the shower at your preferred settings or run a bath?"

Dex's head whips in my direction.

"It's Maddie, Penny. And no, we'd just like some privacy," I answer.

"Very well," Penny replies.

"Your friend has a pretty fancy smart home setup," Dex states.

"I am not a mere smart home, sir. I am an intelligent digital construct. Penthouse. Penny is my given name," Penny drones. Though there was definitely a pout in there, if computer voices could sound pouty.

"Penny, I said privacy," I interrupt. "You're not supposed to address guests anyway."

"Who are you people?" Dex asks. "What the fuck is an intelligent digital construct?"

"Penny is just Dawn's brainchild." I wave it off. "Artificial intelligence. She's kept on a private server and given full run of the penthouse, but she's harmless. Though, it's a little creepy at times."

I shut the door behind us. Dropping the tattered remains of my shirt on the floor, I move toward the bed. Glancing back over my shoulder, I find Dex watching me.

"What do you know about Dominant-submissive relationships, Dex?" I lie on my side on the bed.

He shrugs. "Not much, to be honest. Just the chatter that happened after those movies came out."

I rolled my eyes. "How about power dynamics?" I pat the bed next to me in invitation, but he doesn't move. "Ever given any thought to who holds power, in any situation where control is given to an individual?"

"No, I haven't given it much thought." He crosses his arms over his chest and stands there, watching me, but it's clear that he's not getting any closer at the moment.

I sit up, zipping my sports bra closed. "Okay, let's take the president. He gets elected, people vote for him. Who holds the power?"

"I don't understand what this—"

"Just answer the question," I sigh.

"The president does." He shifts his weight to one foot and frowns.

"He just gets in office and does whatever he wants because he has the power? What happens if the people who voted him in are unhappy?"

"Then he doesn't get reelected," he drolls. His lips become a flat line as he pins me with a stare.

I nod. "He has to bend to their will. Do things that make them happy. So, who holds the power?"

"The voters who put him there, I guess."

"Exactly. Control that is given can be just as easily taken away. Therefore, the giver is the one with the real power."

"Makes sense."

"It took me years to understand all of it. What I am. Why I do it." I stand and cross the room to him. "I'm a sexual submissive, Dex. It doesn't make me weak. It doesn't mean I'm helpless or some sick, twisted freak. I don't necessarily need it. I've had regular sex quite a bit, and I didn't dislike it. I just—"

I start to pace as I glance at him. He's not giving anything away, and normally I like that about him, but right now it's just frustrating. "I'm a giver. I like to do things for other people, and sex, for me, can become... confusing. I give everything to my partner and take nothing. Most people, normal people, are a balance of both give and take. What a Dom does for me—it takes away my choice in the moment. Gets my head out of its focus on my partner and allows me to just feel. No thoughts, no worries, no guilt. Just pleasure given and received. And I'm not telling you that you have to be a certain way or accept some position to be with me. You just need to know this is who I am and why I'm this way."

"Stop," he says, and I freeze midstep. "As adorable as your pacing is, it's very distracting. It makes sense, but I don't get what has you so anxious about it."

"Because I've never had to do this before. I've never had to explain this."

He raises an eyebrow at me in question.

"I'm serious. I've only ever had one top, and that was years ago. We both kind of fell into it without giving it a name. It took years of therapy to understand all this. Because it wasn't until after that relationship ended that I found out how hard it would be to live without it, or to be with someone who couldn't understand it."

"Come here," he says, holding out a hand to me. He pulls me to him and wraps his arms around me. "I understand it." His fingers trace along my jaw. "I just have one question."

I nod.

"Where does your friend Nic fit into all this?" he asks.

"Sounds like I'm right on cue," Nic says, standing in the now open doorway.

Then

"This is just some place you heard of?" I asked, pinning Holly with narrowed eyes.

She shrugged. "Aunt Mae's worked here longer than I've been alive, but it's not like she owns the place."

I gave her the side eye and took a deep breath.

Turning my focus to the stage, I studied the weathered old man up there. The lighting onstage wasn't very powerful, and his dark skin blended with his dark clothes and the dark wood paneling of the wall behind him. Only his instrument, a pearl-white Gibson ES-335 guitar, was truly visible. I'd a feeling that was his goal. He played a bluesy, twangy melody as his fingers plucked the strings and his other hand slid back and forth over the frets. It was hypnotic.

By the third bar, I recognized the song as "I Can't Quit You Baby" by Otis Rush. I closed my eyes and swayed in my seat, just absorbing the musician's soulful voice. The tinkling piano keys and slow brush rhythm accompaniment was also lost in the dark behind him. It gave the tune a haunting feel, and I was captivated.

"Earth to Maddie," Holly said, snapping her fingers next to my ears.

I opened my eyes. Everyone at the table was looking at me expectantly.

"Sorry," I murmured with an apologetic smile.

Jared leaned forward and captured my hand, pulling it to his mouth. "She does that with the blues. Gets lost."

"You could say that," Asher laughed.

"I was just sayin'—you gonna get on the stage?" Holly asked. "Gus will be off the stage after this song."

"Can I do that?"

"Of course—it's fuckin' open mic night, bitch." She grinned deviously. "You think I'd bring you to a place you couldn't feel at home? And I know you're at home on the stage. I got you." She winked.

My heart raced at the thought of getting to play something different than our regular tour set. I grinned widely at her. I couldn't ask for a better friend.

"I wanna go up there with you," Asher added. "You know what you want to play?"

"The possibilities are endless," I answered.

"Brothers Osborne?" Asher suggested.

"Definitely fits the vibe here." I nodded. "What songs do you know?"

"All of them," he said with a shy smile. "They're one of my favorites."

"We could do 'Love the Lonely Out of You.' Since it's just two guitars."

"Sounds like a plan." Asher nodded once and turned back to the stage.

It didn't take long before the song was over and Holly was dragging us to the stage. House instruments were shoved in our hands, and we took our places on the dark stage, Asher with an acoustic guitar, me with an electric and a microphone.

It felt anonymous on the dark stage. I allowed myself to get lost in the words and the notes I plucked on my guitar. When Asher joined me with his guitar, my heart soared.

The song was a soulful surrender to a lover, sexy and heartfelt. My eyes were trained on Jared as the words fled my mouth. When a gorgeous blonde in a denim miniskirt approached him with a tap on the shoulder, I fought hard not to falter. He patted her back as she hugged his neck and took my seat next to him.

I wasn't sure who she was, but as she leaned in to whisper in his ear, my vision tinted green. It was obvious that they knew each other as they talked through my performance. Jealousy filled my heart, making it feel dark and nasty. I'd never been one to get jealous. I'd never been in a relationship where I didn't feel secure about the other's commitment to me until that moment. And that hurt.

When the song was over, I turned to Asher, placing my hand on the mic. "You know any of the songs from my old band?"

"I thought you'd never ask," he answered with a wicked grin.

I whispered in his ear the song I wanted to play. He laughed loudly and got up to put the guitar away and move to the drum kit behind us. I stood and moved the chair I was sitting on to the side. Adjusting the mic, I told the crowd we were about to shake things up.

Asher led the song, setting a rhythm, and I followed with the fast-paced grungy guitar licks. Then I opened my mouth to sing the song that Spencer wrote for me all those years ago. It was written as a joke after he walked into the kitchen one night while Law and I were discussing some rather intimate suggestions for our alone time. The thing was—it was good. It had a catchy tune and quickly became our most popular song.

It felt weird not hearing Spaz's bass or Spencer's guitar join us. But I shut out that pang of loss that echoed in me. It was time to take my revenge.

I may look like a saint, but I'm a sinner.
I'm the girl that brings you to your knees.
All you have to do to please me...
is spank me like a bad girl.

I knew once the words were out of my mouth, I'd have his attention. His head snapped in my direction from the bubbly blonde. His face became a hardened mask. Narrowed eyes watched me as I put on my show.

Tie me up, touch me, tease me
Make my body your new religion
I'll beg until you lose control
And you spank me, I'm your bad girl.

I was working the crowd, playing up the sex appeal like I used to. A crowd began to form in front of the stage. I felt powerful again at that moment, weaving a spell over the crowd as I captivated their attention.

I realized then I'd been suppressing myself, trying not to garner too much attention for fear that it would set Jared off. But that just pissed me off. We could've grown together, but he forced us to grow apart and then decided he didn't like who I'd become. *Fuck him.*

I stopped watching him then, turned my attention to the crowd and played for them, letting my hands slide over the guitar seductively. *How had I let myself become so powerless?* We were tearing each other down. I watched as the audience became enthralled, watching me intently, hypnotized by my music, my voice. *This is me, this is my strength. I'm a siren.* I'd been hiding it out of fear. *No more.* We would be who we were meant to be, and if it didn't work out, then it didn't work.

The song ended, and people cheered. I made my way back to the table, getting stopped every few feet by someone who wanted to ask about where the song came from or if they could buy the CD. I didn't know the answer to that. Spencer had controlled most of the group business, and even though we never recorded in a studio, he had made a demo from one of our garage practices and sold copies at gigs. Whether or not they were still out there was beyond me.

When I got back to the table, Blondie was nowhere to be found. Instead, Jared had tossed aside the pretense of a glass and was drinking straight from the bottle. I could see the unfocused quality to his eyes as he pinned me on the spot with narrowed eyes.

"Thanks for rent," Holly said, glancing up from her phone. "I've already gotten over ten thousand hits on this video."

"You posted that?"

"Why not?" She shrugs. "I'm sure someone else is gonna, too. That was some real shit. Just figured you'd be happier knowing that a friend was receiving the payoff rather than some tool."

"True."

"I think whores usually like to get paid themselves," Jared muttered before taking another swig.

I'd like to say I was shocked, but by now I was becoming used to his violent mood swings and sudden shifts in temper. I should've known that this night would end this way. We hadn't had a nice night out since before he was deployed. Plus, I couldn't fully blame him because I chose to poke the bear.

"We should probably get back to the hotel. Asher, would you give me a hand?" I gave Asher a pointed look and jerked my head in Jared's direction. Hopefully, he would get that I needed to get the drunk out of the bar without making a scene that would end up on tabloid websites. I'd no desire to listen to Press-zilla bitch at me.

I pulled out my phone, searching for a local cab company number. Asher offered a hand to Jared, and when he didn't take it, Asher moved to pull him up by his arm. As soon as he made contact, Jared kicked out, scooting his chair across the floor. The result was a loud grating sound and a lot of angry looks since the next act was already playing onstage. I gripped the phone tight in my hand and grabbed Jared's other arm to drag him outside. As we were walking toward the front door, I went back to my task on the phone, only an active call was already in progress. Shit. I must have accidentally dialed it.

I put the phone to my ear. "Hello? Is this the cab company?" I asked, not knowing which one I'd accidentally dialed.

There was a click, and a male voice came through the line. "Yes, did you need a ride?"

"Yeah. We're at the Old Point Bar on the corner of..." I drifted off to search for street signs. "Patterson and Olivier."

"We have someone nearby. They'll be there in five minutes."

"Awesome, thanks." I hung up.

I turned back to find that Asher had Jared propped up against the wall by the door. Holly was still inside, and they seemed to be having a heated exchange. I hung back, reluctant to wade into the fray of Jared's bad mood. My back was to the street when a car pulled up behind me. I turned to find a black sedan. The window rolled down.

"You order a cab?" the voice from inside asked.

My brows scrunched in confusion. *Shouldn't a cab look like a cab?* Maybe I'd called some uber-fancy discreet cab company. I shook it off, waving Asher and Jared over with a shout. The way Jared yanked his arm away from Asher and swayed on his feet told me this was gonna be a fun ride. Holly came out just in time to say good night. I made plans to meet her for breakfast at our hotel before she drove back to Austin and we moved on to Chicago.

After I assured Asher that I'd be fine getting us back to

the hotel, I climbed into the back seat and told the driver the name of our hotel. He set off, and I watched Holly and Asher go back inside the bar.

"You know, I'm a big boy. I can get myself home," Jared said, breaking the silence.

I turned away from the window. "You're drunk, Jared." I sighed. "And I don't want to fight with you tonight."

"I'm good, Mads. My fiancée just got up on a stage and announced that she's a kinky freak, attracting a bunch of dudes to come hit on her. I'm peachy."

"Nobody hit on me. What the hell are you talking about?"

He snorted in response but stayed quiet. I scoffed.

"Those people were just asking about where they could find the song. And you're one to talk, having some bimbo hanging on you while I'm up on the stage."

"She was not some bimbo. She was a soldier, stationed over in Iraq when I was there."

"In other words, someone you fucked back when we weren't together?"

He didn't respond, and I knew I was right. *Fucking hypocrite.* I was done with this conversation. I was tired of him making me feel like I needed to walk on eggshells and pretend to be someone I'm not.

"At least it was normal sex, with a normal girl."

Anger and hurt warred with each other inside me. I knew that I wasn't normal, but I always thought that he loved me despite it. Now it felt like he despised me because of it. And it hurt because it was true. What Law turned me into wasn't *normal*, but it was me. My gut wrenched. *How did I get so fucked up?*

The cab pulled up to the hotel, and Jared got out. I pulled a fifty out of my wallet and handed it to the driver and scooted out myself. I was about to take a step toward the hotel when I heard a voice. I spun back, and the cabbie had his window down.

"Your change." He waved money in the air.

I approached the window and waved it off. "You can keep

the change."

I leaned down, and for the first time, really looked at the driver. He was wearing a green hoodie with the hood pulled up, his face lost in shadow.

"You know," he said, "tryin' to force things to live when they should be left to die never works."

His voice seemed familiar, but I couldn't quite place it. My mouth opened and closed as I tried to think of a response, but as his window rolled back up and he put the car in gear, my focus dropped to the passenger seat.

There was a single red calla lily sitting there. I gasped, and my voice caught in my throat with an intensity that stole my breath, choking me. The ground rocked beneath me.

He pulled away from the curb, and I chased after him, banging on the window. I had to know who it was. He didn't stop or look at me, and soon, I couldn't keep up with the car. I stood in the street, watching as he took a right a block later.

It only hit me after he had vanished that I should've gotten the license plate number, but it was too late.

Chapter Seventeen

Now

Nic struts inside, no hesitation. Dex's eyes track him, but he doesn't say a thing. He hasn't said much in the last two days, and that bothers me. I can't figure him out. He's very good at keeping his emotions in check, keeping that carefully constructed, neutral facade. It both worries and excites me.

Nic's arm hooks my waist and pulls me to him, away from Dex. I'm so focused on Dex that I don't give it much thought until I see his eyes narrow and the lines of his body tense.

"You left too soon," Nic says, squeezing me as he kisses the side of my head. "We were just fixin' to get our girl off."

"Lucky," I sigh, exasperated. "Cut it out." I push his hands off me and step away.

"I don't share," Dex growls.

The deep, possessive tone travels down my spine. Goose bumps prickle my skin as my thighs tense. I like that. I like that a lot. A smile tips the corner of my mouth as I peek up at him through my lashes.

"Say it again," I say, but it comes out all breathy.

Dex's eyes snap to me. His features don't soften but take on a carnal quality. I feel it. That magnetic pull. Like a cord, he's tugging with the dilation of his eyes. I want him to own me. He has no idea.

"I. Don't. Share."

My feet are moving before my brain registers it, but my progress is halted by a hand on my arm. I follow the hand with my eyes, up an arm to meet Lucky's eyes. He looks worried.

"Slow your roll, lovebirds," Nic says, his eyes on Dex. "*You* need to know what you're up against."

"Lucky—"

"No," Nic says firmly. "You two need to talk."

Dex is watching the exchange, his eyes tracking every movement. The tense lines in his stance and his clenched fists are the only things giving away the fact that he's holding himself back. And I think that is the sexiest thing about him. The amount of self-control he displays on a daily basis is mind-blowing. It's a rare talent.

"He's right. Submission isn't my only kink. And you need to know all of it. You don't have to like it or participate, but you do have to accept it—accept me."

"Yeah, your girl here is a bit of an exhibitionist, with some voyeuristic tendencies, too."

I cut a scathing look to Nic. "What he means is that I like to watch people—fuck, foreplay, it really doesn't matter. It turns me on. But I also like to be watched. And out there, what you were doing… it was amplified by the fact that we had an audience."

"And I helped her out with a little show," Nic adds. "I know I've a habit of crossing boundaries, being inappropriate, but you should know I love this girl. Just… not in a romantic way. When she was born, our parents sat us down, Evan and me, and let us hold her. They told us she was ours to protect. She was our little sister in all but blood. And I'll continue to protect her to the day I die."

Nic's look holds so many layers of meaning as he holds Dex's attention. Nic finally breaks away, turning and walking to the dresser. Dex's shoulders relax. It's a subtle change. I don't think anyone would notice unless they were studying him as thoroughly as me. Nic opens the top drawer, and I know what he's doing. I turn away to stop myself from stopping him.

"You want to know what I do for her. What we do here. It's this."

I hear the thunk, and I can't help it when my eyes are drawn by the sound. I glimpse the whip and cuffs on the floor before I turn away, numbing tingles sweeping my body. I look at Dex, but his eyes are focused on Nic.

"Maddie's not like other women. She was a normal child, but... something happened. She stopped processing physical pain the way a normal person does. No one knows why. But if you can imagine not ever feeling pain, you'll understand why sometimes she feels the need to chase it. Like she's hoping one day she'll feel it, if she tries hard enough or often enough."

"Nic, please..." I whisper as tears well in my eyes. I don't know whether that's a plea to stop or to keep talking. It feels like being flayed open and laid bare. Nic and Evan are the only ones who know this about me, aside from our parents. It's not a genetic disorder, but it's an extremely rare psychological condition related to trauma. Unfortunately, I don't remember what caused it. I don't even like to think about it, much less tell anyone. So, in the back of my mind, I'm sort of thankful that he's doing the talking for me. I don't know if I ever could bring myself to do it.

"I think she processes emotional pain more strongly because of it," Nic continues. "When her emotions run too high, she seeks out ways to try and inflict pain on herself. She also happens to be attracted to a certain type who has a tendency toward—" Nic pauses like he's thinking of a way to say it kindly. "—rougher handling."

I can't bring myself to look at Dex. I don't want to know what he thinks of me. My whole body is clenched. I'm terrified because I know this is it. The moment he runs. Who would want something so damaged? Who would want a fucked-up deviant monster like me?

"After... after Jared..." I take a deep breath and try and

steel myself to tell him the worst part. "I wasn't dealing with it real well, and Evan found me... I was..." I look away, blinking furiously to stop the tears. "I was cutting myself. They took everything sharp out of the house until I agreed to therapy. I just wanted to feel something. I needed to feel something."

Tears burn cooling tracks on my heated skin. I take my wrist wraps off to give myself an excuse not to look at Dex. I can see from my periphery that he's not moving. It hurts as much as it relieves. And it really hits me that I want him to know. I want Dex to know me. My feelings for him are much stronger than I'm willing to admit to myself.

"I spent six months in a treatment program. And for the most part, I'm better now. I've tools to help with it, like the rubber bands..." I can't bring myself to finish. Thankfully, I don't have to because Nic is here for me.

"This is one of her coping mechanisms for that," Nic adds, motioning to the whip and cuffs on the floor, "so she doesn't injure herself chasing what she can't have. That, and the fighting, both of which I monitor closely to ensure she doesn't get seriously injured. We have on-site medical staff, just in case. But you need to know, even if it looks sexual, it's not, for her. At least not with me. We joke, but we've never been like that. She's not that way in that ring either. At least, not until tonight."

Silence settles between us, broken only by my sniffles as I wipe away the last of my tears. My heart feels like it will beat through my chest with my ever-increasing nerves. No one speaks, no one moves. But it doesn't feel awkward—it's just heavy. The arduous thud of my racing heart seems to echo around me. Dense with the weight of anticipation. All my fear and worry bubble to the surface, masking that small thread of hope holding me together.

Nic breaks the silence with a sigh and picks up the stuff from the ground, returning it to the dresser. He stops in front of me on his way out. His lips press into my forehead as he tugs me toward him.

"It'll be okay. No matter what," Nic mutters, and with another sigh, leaves us alone.

Silence reigns again after the click of the door closing. I wish to God that Dex would speak. Move. Something. Anything. This is it. This is the pivot line. He either accepts me or he walks away. The tension is burning a hole right through me until I finally break, my eyes seeking his.

Then

I felt electric, alive, as we played our fourth concert of the tour. We were in Chicago. There was a sea of people at the end of the stage. Literally, thousands had come to hear us play; a fact that seemed surreal, despite seeing the number of people before me beyond the stage lights.

The other reason it was so thrilling was that Jared seemed like himself again when he was onstage. I would've liked to say we recovered. That he finally had that moment of clarity and talked to me about what was going on with him, but that didn't happen. He had dropped the sex hang-up and his fascination with Law, but that didn't mean that he was happy.

Something had happened to him on this last deployment. Anytime I tried to talk with him, he shut me down and left the room. Each day was some new adventure in what he would get pissed about. And then there was the drinking. I'm not sure if he knew we had found his stash of empty and half-full bottles of alcohol on the bus. He was discreet enough about it that it went unnoticed, for a while.

Without Asher, I'm not sure I would've made it this far. He had become my rock in a sea of grief, mourning what I'd lost. He stepped up with the girls when Jared would push them away, playing with them and distracting them from their disappointment, though their tutor and nanny, Kim, kept them busy enough that they weren't too aware of it. Kim was a godsend, in her late thirties, with an Ivy League Ph.D. in child psychology and education; she was the best money could buy. I still missed my friends, I missed derby, and I missed home, more and more with every mile that took us farther away.

When we were onstage, though, it was just us and the music. The old light returned to his eyes, and I had him back, if only for fleeting moments.

The song we were playing, our last of the set for the evening, was coming to a close. Dread filled me as I wondered what new adventure of shit we were going to embark on this time.

"Thank you, Chicago!" I yelled into the mic as the last strains of the guitar faded out.

The fans cheered and screamed, and my heart filled to bursting. There was nothing quite like that overwhelming feeling of acceptance that came with this type of popularity. It was easy not to let it go to my head. The second we stepped off the stage I'd be greeted with the reality of my life, so I let myself enjoy the moment while it lasted.

Nate was waiting for us backstage. He stepped up and became our manager for this tour. Before we made it all the way offstage, the crowd began to chant, "Encore, encore…" We'd never done an encore because we played every song we ever wrote for them at every concert. *Though, that's not entirely true.* An idea popped into my head at that moment.

"Hey, get someone to bring me a stool and my acoustic," I said to Nate. I fixed my gaze on Jared, searching his eyes with pleading hope. "Stick around for this, will ya?"

A little line formed between Jared's brows as they pulled together, but he dipped his head in agreement.

I chugged the bottle of water I was handed and used the towel to wipe my face off, then turned back to the stage.

As soon as I was visible again, the crowd lost it. I smiled and walked up to the microphone.

"You're in luck, Chicago." The crowd went wild, and I laughed, waiting for them to quiet again. "We've never played an encore before, but I've something I'd like to share with you. I've never played this before, for anyone." I glanced over to make sure Jared was still there. "We'll see how it goes. This is something I wrote by myself. I usually don't write by myself, so this is a lot of firsts for me. And it's all for you, Chicago."

A roadie brought out a stool and my acoustic electric guitar. My hands shook as I adjusted the microphone, so I could sit and sing. I'd never been this nervous before, but I'd also never put my heart out for public consumption like this either. The lovely part of playing shows of this size was that the road crew would've pretuned this guitar for me, so I began to play the song I'd been writing since Jared's return from overseas.

"This song is called 'The End of What I Knew,'" I said into the microphone.

A hush fell over the crowd as the words of the first verse fell from my mouth, the music spilling from my soul.

Is this the end,
of what I knew?
Is this the end,
of what we used to be?
Is this the start,
of something new?
Or is it just the amount
of all we're ever gonna be.

When I find myself all alone,
this distance between us,
causing all this silence.
I think—I think of your smile,
the one with love in your eyes,
Pride in your sigh.

I took a breath as I built up the song to the chorus. Strumming the guitar with my eyes closed. Imagining he was the one in front of me.

If we are meant to be.
Why won't you talk to me?
Open your heart for me.
I'm dying for you, can't you see.

I sang three more verses and repeated the chorus several times. When I hit the last note and let it fade, I was met with absolute silence. Tears built up in my eyes, and I started to stand. The crowd went wild, cheering and screaming. I thought it was loud, but then it heightened to a deafening roar. I looked behind me, and Jared was walking toward me. He didn't say a word, just grasped my cheeks and kissed me. The guitar fell from my hands and clattered to the ground, producing feedback as I kissed him back. I couldn't think beyond the relief that he heard me.

I could taste the alcohol in his mouth, and I knew he had already started drinking. When he broke the kiss, he rested his forehead on mine, wiping the tears from my face.

"I do love you," he said, taking a ragged breath.

"I love you, too. More than you'll ever know."

He tucked me into his side as we walked offstage together, waving to the crowd as we made our exit.

"What the fuck was that?" Asher asked with a grin as soon as we neared him.

"Where did that come from?" Nate asked. "I didn't know you'd written any new material?"

"That was fucking magic, Maddie," Asher said excitedly. "You had them enthralled. So fucking awesome."

Asher held up his fist to bump, and I met his with my own. I gave him a tired smile. I felt exhausted.

"I'm going to make a few calls. We need to get you in a studio to record before we leave for the next city. Release it as a single. It's going to top the charts, guaranteed," Nate said.

"Okay," I replied, yawning.

"Hey, let's get you back on the bus," Jared said, squeezing me to him.

I nodded, and we started to move toward the back of the building. When we neared the back door, two security guards waited to escort us to the bus.

"It's pretty crazy out there. You have a lot of people with backstage passes tonight," one of them said, then opened the door.

There were barricades in place, but the screaming was loud as excited fans caught sight of us. I plastered on a smile and prepared myself to sign autographs. This was pretty standard after show business. I gripped Jared's hand and followed Asher out the door.

We had maybe made it about ten feet when I noticed out of the corner of my eye that Jared wasn't signing autographs. His face had drained of color, and he was breathing rapidly. One excited fan hoisted herself up on the barricade and attempted to grab at him. His pupils dilated, and I watched in slow motion as he knocked her hand away and grabbed her by the collar of her shirt. I rushed over and grabbed his face, forcing him to look at me.

"Let her go, Jared. It's me. I got you, Jared. Just let her go," I coaxed.

He blinked and pulled his head from my hands.

"Don't ever touch me again," he sneered at the girl as he let go. He turned, storming away from the crowd.

"I'm sorry." I gave her an apologetic smile and then turned to chase after him.

When I got to the bus, he was already inside, yelling.

"Why are there always fucking toys on the floor. How many times do you need to be told to put your shit away when you're done playing with it?" He threw one of the toys across the tiny interior. It hit the wall with a loud clatter.

"Jared. Stop," I said, stepping in between him and the girls.

Kim was sitting on the couch with the girls curled to her

sides. Cartoons played on the TV mounted across from them.

"Here, take them to go get ice cream, please." I dug my credit card out of my purse, hanging on a hook by the door, and shoved it in her hand.

She nodded and ushered the girls out of the bus. He slammed cabinets open and closed, one after the other. I knew what he was looking for, and a part of me died a little, watching him like this. He finally found a bottle and opened it, tipping his head back to take a swig.

"Jared, can we please talk about this?" I made a grab for the bottle.

"Why the fuck are you here? Shouldn't you be out there with your little fans? Those people really love you, you know?"

"I'm here because I love you. You're the only one that matters to me. Please, just talk to me. I don't understand why you're acting like this. You've been overseas three times, and you didn't come back like this before."

"Yeah, well. The first two times, I was with my brothers. Smart guys who were fucking well-trained. Then I fucked them over for you and got what I deserved. Getting sent over there with a pack of fucking idiot soldier wannabes." He threw the bottle up against the wall, and it shattered. "Are you fucking happy now?"

I took a shaky breath to calm my racing heart. "Jared, I think you need to talk to someone."

"Why? So we can figure out that you're the source of my problems? It always comes back to you!" He got up in my face, screaming at me.

A sob tore from my chest. "You don't mean that."

"Yeah, I do. Because no matter what happens, every fucked up thing in my life can be traced back to you. I don't even know why I bother," he said venomously, then turned and left, the door cracking against the side of the bus and swinging back halfway.

I dropped to the floor and continued to sob. I couldn't understand it. He was always so angry now. I knew something major was wrong. Something had happened on this last deployment. He got angry at the slightest thing. I'd put myself between him and everyone, trying to keep them from this pain, but I wasn't sure how much more I could take.

My phone rang, and I picked it up to answer without looking at who it was. I couldn't think straight at that moment.

"Did he hurt you?" a modulated voice asked.

I checked the phone, and the call was from an unknown number. *The motherfucking stalker.*

"Why do you care? Isn't your job to, what... scare me? Aren't *you* planning to hurt me? Why don't you fucking leave me alone, because I can't deal with this shit anymore."

"I'd never hurt you. I've only been looking out for you. I'm trying to make sure you're happy," the voice intoned.

"Says the chickenshit who won't even use his real voice when he calls. Did you forget that I already know what your real voice sounds like after you picked me up in New Orleans? Yeah, I know that was you. You know what? Fuck you. Go get your own life and leave mine alone."

I hung up and sagged backward, leaning against the couch. The whole bus smelled like whiskey. I wasn't going to sit around feeling sorry for myself. I picked myself off the floor and started pulling out the cleaning supplies. The door creaked. Asher was standing there, taking in the debris littered around the space.

"Are you okay?" he asked.

"I'm fine. I just need to clean this up." I bent over, sweeping the broken glass into a dustpan.

"Let me help," he offered, taking a step toward me.

"No." I held up my hand to stop him. "This is my problem. You don't have to be a part of it."

"I should just sit here and watch him tear you down? Because I live on this bus, too."

"That's not—I don't want to talk about it," I said over my shoulder as I continued to clean.

He snorted but didn't say anything else as he leaned against the wall.

"What do you want me to do about it? Break up with him? Cancel the tour? The best I can hope for right now is just to contain the fallout, Ash. Hope that eventually he hears me and decides to get help. Because there really is no other option."

Chapter Eighteen

Now

"Good girl," he says, and his mouth twitches into a smirk before falling away to the neutral mask he wears often. His head tilts to the side as he studies me from his position. He's no more than ten feet away, but the silence seems to stretch out the space between us, making it feel like miles.

"Say something." The words leak out of me.

He doesn't reply but instead walks toward the door, and my stomach plummets. Bile rises to the base of my throat. I was wrong, so wrong about him. The room spins as his hand reaches out for the doorknob. I don't blame him; I'm ruined. I'm the spoiled milk that has been sitting on the counter for years. Curdled, sour trash. Tears fill my eyes as I sway, unsure of how I'm still standing because I can't feel my feet. The numbness has settled over me, somehow comforting in its familiarity, like an old unwelcome friend.

The lock on the door clicks, and Dex turns to face me. His brows climb as he takes in my face, his eyes filled with fire. His neutral expression turns to something much darker. I can see it—the anger. I think that's the only emotion he wears with ease. He stalks toward me like a predator, all lethal grace. He stops when his toes are mere inches from mine. I know because I'm staring at them.

I can't move. My eyes slowly track up his tightly coiled body to his chest, but I can't bring myself to meet his eyes.

"I think we've danced around the truth long enough," he says as his hand slides up my arm and over my shoulder.

I'm expecting him to tip my chin and force me to meet his eyes, so I'm caught off guard when instead, it wraps around my throat, and I find myself stumbling backward. I hit the wall, knocking the breath out of me just before the pressure increases. Not squeezing to choke, but pressure over the vein in my neck, making me dizzy. He captures that last breath as his mouth descends on mine. Pleasure skitters down my spine, lighting me up. His body presses into mine. I can feel the coiled tension beneath his skin. Our tongues tangle and fight for dominance, but now we both know who will win.

He grips my thigh with bruising force and pulls it up to his hip. Then his fingers skate over the back of my leg in a whisper-soft touch. The contrast does strange things to me. A strangled moan escapes me as his fingers deftly slide under my shorts and dip into my core.

Dex releases a growl that vibrates through me at every point of contact. His lips break away. "You can't fake perfection like that." His voice is rough and carries a razor's edge. "How far can you go?"

"Give me everything," I rasp out. My fingers dig into his shoulders. I curl them, pressing my nails in hard enough to draw blood, and I pull. "Fuck me."

His reaction is instant. I hear the tear of fabric, and his hand is gone from between my legs. The other hand around my throat pushes higher until my toes barely graze the ground. My heart is a band of wild horses, racing through open plains. He grunts as my hands press harder into his shoulders to relieve the pressure on my neck and breathe. Then his knee is shoving my other leg out of the way, and I can feel the heat of him as he lines his cock up to my entrance.

"Admit that you love me," he demands.

My eyes lock on to his. They're so dilated that they look

like black holes eclipsing turquoise stars. But I see it, lying beneath the hunger—pure unadulterated adoration. This man has met me every step of the way. His quiet calm and understanding has opened my soul. He never flinched, never drew back, just accepted me for what I am. I'm a misshapen puzzle piece that never found a good fit. He has wrapped himself around my life and clicked into place. I feel giddy as I realize that he's everything that I need and all that I want. I couldn't deny how I feel if I wanted.

"I do."

"Say it, Firebird."

"I love you."

He slams into me so hard, I cry out, the heat of him burning through me like wildfire. He stills inside me. The sound of his labored breath fills the void between my sharp gasps. His eyes still pin me in place, watching. I'm staring death in the eyes because this man has the power to kill me.

"I'll kill for you. Anyone who threatens you. Anyone who tries to come between us... I'd warn you that I'm a dangerous man, but I think you know what I am. So perfect. You fit who I am and what I want to be like a glove. You. Are. Mine." He punctuates the last word with another thrust that has me crying out again.

I'm going to combust. Each stroke of his cock is like a licking flame. I feel like a real firebird as his fire consumes me, razing through the fractured pieces of my soul—the dark and the light, creating a new unified landscape that is entirely his.

"Yes," I scream. "Harder. Don't be gentle. Make me feel you. Make me yours."

His mouth is back on mine in a flash, and his hand releases my throat, only to punch through the drywall next to my head. He pulls on the edge of the hole as he grants my wish, pounding into me. *Yes.* It's breathless and tender and hard. Like he's making love to me in his own way. Our way. And it's perfect.

"Fuck me. Fuck me. Fuck me," I chant along with his

brutal thrusts. "Dex, you feel so good."

I'm not even sure why I'm talking. I've never done this, but something about him makes the words spill from my lips. A need to voice all the dirty thoughts he inspires.

His hand not currently tearing out the drywall sneaks in between us, his thumb finding my bundle of nerves. It circles lazily, so at odds with his punishing pace. It pulls me to the brink of release, but it's not enough to tip me over. My mind follows that lazy circle pattern, scrambling my brain. A smirk takes over his face like he knows. The pressure's building and building. He leans forward, running his tongue up my neck, and nips my ear.

"When you come, I want to hear you scream my name. So I know it's branded on your soul," he whispers in my ear. His voice rough with lust and strain only pushes me higher.

I'm Icarus soaring way too close to the sun.

"Come," he commands, watching me with those eclipse eyes. His fingers come together, pinching the swollen bundle of nerves.

I scream his name in a broken staccato to the rhythm of his hips and the waves of bliss that roll over me. He grunts and speeds up as he meets me in our temporary heaven.

He pulls me to him, and I'm wrapped around his body like overcooked spaghetti, sticky and limp. Leaning over the bed, he deposits me there. We groan together as he pulls out. My legs twitch with the friction. He pulls off my shorts as he stands and discards my sports bra, too. I watch him through hooded eyes as he drops his shorts… and my brain falters.

He's motionless as my eyes travel from where the tail of the dragon rests on top of his left foot. It wraps around his calf and thigh, disappearing behind his hip. I'm distracted by his hardening cock for a moment before I move up. One wing stretches up to the side of his neck, and the other curves around his body, ending on his right hip. He has Audra's name over his heart, and I melt a little at that. He has various other tattoos over his arms and body, but my eyes reach his face and catch sight of his look. It's smoldering. He likes my attention on him.

My mouth goes dry. I lick my lips, and he falls to his knees, yanking my ankles and dragging me down until my legs are off the bed. He pushes my thighs apart, his tongue darting out to moisten his lower lip. I'm hypnotized by the tiny movement until he leans forward, and I realize what he's doing. I bring my legs together, trapping his head to stop him. He growls and looks up at me.

"You came in me," I say, slightly scandalized by his intentions.

He grins, exposing those dimples. "I know. I was there, but now I'm about to find out what that heaven tastes like."

He forces my legs apart, and his mouth is on my sensitive folds in a blink. The heat of his tongue parting me adds to the sensation. I'm so sensitive I can feel the texture of his tongue. A moan spills out of me in response. His chest rumbles, the vibrations ricocheting through my body, breaking apart every thought in my mind. Knowing that he's lapping up the evidence of both of our pleasure and that he likes it, is blowing my mind. It's animalistic and carnal.

He pushes two fingers into me and curves them in just the right way. I can feel the pressure rising. His other hand moves to my breast at the same time his pinky penetrates my puckered hole as he pinches my nipple roughly and sucks hard on my clit. The stimulation is overwhelming. My back bows off the bed as a scream of pleasure erupts from me.

"Yours. I'm yours," I pant.

Halfway up the crest of pleasure, he's gone. I'm roughly pushed over to my belly, and he grabs my hips, lifts, and is back inside me before I come down. My orgasm stretches out in waves punctuated by the crude slap of skin on skin as he drives into me. *Holy fuck.* My whole body convulses and spasms with the overload of stimulation. It feels like I'm falling as my vision dims. Black spots and flashes of light are all I see as I claw at the sheets to get away. He only tightens his grip and picks up the pace. When his fingers brush over my belly, heading for that special spot, I know I'm going to die. *What is he doing to me?*

He presses my clit lightly with a circular motion and down in tandem to his thumb invading my ass. I choke on a scream as my limbs give up the struggle and the last of my vision blinks out. Stars. That's what the tiny sparks of light look like, and my body feels weightless. Euphoric. I know where I am. I read about this when I was trying to give a voice to my peculiarities. I didn't expect this. I feel everything as Dex comes with a groan, his weight pressing me into the mattress briefly before he rolls off me. Floating. Boneless.

I can't think.

A phone rings. My spent body couldn't move to answer it if I wanted to. When it stops, another round of rings takes its place. Dex sits up and walks to the bathroom. I take a moment to appreciate that the god of chaos that rules my life decided to wait until after that blessed moment to stir shit up.

"Hello?" Dex answers.

I roll my head so my ear faces the bathroom. It's about as much effort as I can muster.

"It's done?" Dex asks. "Good. Yeah… yeah. No. Okay. I'll see you in the morning."

I blink several times, vaguely registering that my hands are beginning to tremble. I curl in on myself until I'm no more than a ball. Tears fill my eyes.

At some point, Dex ends the call. But all I hear around me is silence.

"Hey," Dex says as his hand lands on my thigh. I jump at the touch, and he fills my field of vision with a frown. "You okay?"

"Yeah," I whimper. "I will be." I wipe the tears from my face.

His fingers trail my cheek.

"I'll be okay." I push his hand away and curl up further.

"Hey," he says, forcing me to meet his eyes. "Tell me what's wrong."

"It's the loss of endorphins."

"That's why you're crying?"

I nod. "That. And because Nic and I dumped a load of shit at your feet and you didn't say anything. Then next thing I know, you're demanding that I tell you I love you and fucking my brains out. I still don't know how you feel about any of it. Any of this. Does that add clarity for you?"

"Fucking your brains out seems like a pretty good review." He smirks, and I roll my eyes at him. "I love you, Maddie. The good, the bad, and everything else. There's nothing you or he could've said that would change that. When is that going to get through to you?"

I can see it. Shining in his eyes is a look of utter reverence. And I know it's meant for me.

"Now," I answer.

"Now?" he echoes in question.

I nod.

"Come here." He pulls me into his arms. His lips brush across mine softly. "I love you."

"I love you, too, Dex," I respond, and he squeezes me tighter.

"Good, because I gotta surprise for you, Firebird."

"You do?"

"Yes, I do. It'll make you fall for me even more."

"I'm not sure that's possible." I manage to muster a grin through my exhaustion. "But I love surprises. When do I get it?"

"In the morning."

I realize now he has his jeans on, but the top button hangs open. *Fuck that's sexy.* I know for sure in this moment that I've a new fetish—him. I grow incredibly aware of the fact that I'm stark naked still and he's staring at me with those ocean-colored eyes overshadowed by desire. *Goddamn. This man is intent on killing me.* But what a way to die.

Then

I tossed restlessly alone in the bed at the back of the tour bus.

Jared hadn't come back, and I was worried about him. Everyone else was asleep. The generator hummed in the background. At a bump and a curse, I sat up. The door to the bedroom opened, and Jared stood there. He looked like hell warmed over.

He shut the door quietly behind him and started removing his clothes without a word. I lay back down and turned away from him. I didn't have anything to say to him. I felt the bed dip as he crawled in behind me. His arm came over my stomach and tugged me to press against his chest. I stiffened in response.

"I want to say I'm sorry, but I know that's not enough," Jared said quietly.

"Where've you been?"

"Sitting behind the set trucks, feeling sorry for myself," he sighed. "You know there are videos of your encore performance all over YouTube already?"

I didn't answer.

"I've watched them over and over, feeling like an asshole for the shit I've said to you. You don't deserve this." He brushed my hair away from my neck and trailed little kisses there. "I think you're right. I need to talk to someone."

"Really?" I asked, rolling over to face him.

"Yeah." He gave me a sad smile. "Will you forgive me? I can't lose you, Maddie."

His eyes were glassy with unshed tears, and my heart softened toward him.

"I know this isn't you, Jared. Something's wrong. If you promise to see someone, then yes, I'll forgive you. I want to get through this, with you. Get our life back. I love you."

I ran my fingers through his hair, enjoying the quiet moment. He kissed me softly. The kiss deepened, and he rolled up over me.

"God, I love you so much, Maddie. I couldn't live without you."

"You don't have to," I whispered wholeheartedly.

He kissed me again as he pulled me to sit up, breaking

only to tug my nightgown over my head. Our lips and hands became frantic, seeking each other, the warmth of our bodies soothing over the rough edges of emotional wounds. He pushed me back on the bed, his palm gliding down between my breasts to my stomach. A trail of tingling sparks lit up my skin in its wake. *Would his touch ever stop having this effect?*

I was so afraid of what we were becoming, but it was moments like those that reminded me why we were so worth it. I loved him with every inch of my soul. I pushed all those emotions into our physical connection. Lips pressed and caressed, tongues twisted and tangled, hands felt and grasped, holding on to the shreds of our love beneath the landslide of shit we'd faced. The boat was sinking, but we could still make it to shore if we pointed ourselves in the right direction. I had hope, and I clung to it as much as I clung to him in the stillness of the night.

Our breaths competed in the silence between us as he lined up at my entrance.

"I love you," he whispered as he filled me up.

I squeezed my eyes tight, fighting back the tears that threatened to fall. Something about him—us—ripped my heart to tatters. I knew I couldn't live without him, but we were slowly drifting apart and clinging desperately to each other to stop it. His pace was slow, languishing in the depth of feeling that resided in each touch. It was love, pure and simple, and I could feel it down to my bones.

Jared was broken—we were broken. But mending wasn't impossible. I needed him to save me. To pull me up from the depths I fell into with every fight, every cruel word. It was just hard to know who was compromising themselves in the moment of forgiveness when you were a part of the problem.

I could feel his pace quickening as he neared release. My hand slid between us, as I raced to meet him there. Running my fingertips over my sensitive nub, I met him on the edge of bliss. We groaned together, and his weight pressed down on me as the edge wore off. His labored breath was heavy in my ear.

"I'm sorry," he said.

"You're forgiven," I replied. Looking for a change of subject, I grasped at the first thought to cross my mind. "The stalker called me when you left the trailer."

"What did Officer Martinez say?"

"Shit! I completely forgot to call him about it. I started cleaning up after I got off the phone, and it just slipped my mind."

"Call him now."

"It's the middle of the night."

"If they can run a trace on the call, it's probably better to do it sooner than later. You know that well enough after what happened in New Orleans. Call him, Maddie."

I knew he was right. I'd waited until the next day to report the stalker's appearance as my cab driver. And they weren't able to trace the call for whatever reason. I picked up my phone and dialed the number.

"Hello," Officer Martinez answered, sounding still asleep.

"It's Maddie Dobransky."

"I'm up," he replied. "I assume he made contact again."

"Yeah, a phone call. He used one of those voice modulator things so I couldn't identify his voice."

"Can you bring your phone down to the station? I can meet you there in twenty minutes."

"I'm actually in Chicago right now."

"Oh, yeah. That's right, you're on tour." He chuckled. "I sometimes forget that I'm on a rock star's speed dial. I can run a trace on your phone records in the morning. Just have your lawyer contact me, I'll wait up. He's definitely escalating. If we're quick enough, we might find something to work with in your phone records this time. We can finally get a detective assigned."

"Can I be honest with you?"

"Absolutely."

"I don't want anyone working on this, but you. You've been the only one to believe me from the start, and I don't want some kiss-ass trying to work my case because I'm famous now."

"Uhhh... well, that's something you'll need to share with the captain. I don't really have that kind of sway."

"I'll talk to my lawyer and see what we can do."

"Sounds good. Try to get some rest."

"I will. Thank you. Bye."

No sooner did I hang up the phone than it started ringing again, vibrating in my hand. This call was from Sloane.

"Hello," I answered.

"You have to come home," she said without preamble.

I would've thought she was joking, but I could hear the edge of panic in her voice. "What's wrong?"

"Holly's in the hospital," she choked out through obvious tears.

"I'm booking a flight right now."

Chapter Nineteen

Then

I ran through the halls of the hospital, bypassing the nurses' station. I didn't need to ask where she was; Sloane had told me where to go. I turned the last corner to the ICU waiting room and saw Sloane and Bridget, heads bent together, talking in hushed tones.

My footing faltered, and I stumbled, barely catching myself. Up until that moment, it hadn't seemed real. There was urgency created by a need to find out the truth, but seeing them here made it more tangible. Knowing that I'd see her soon, made me hesitate. *Can I handle this?*

Sucking up every last ounce of courage in my arsenal, I put one foot in front of the other. Sloane glanced up and locked watery eyes on me then. She stood up, and my feet found new urgency as I rushed to her open arms. She squeezed me and sobbed. Bridget reached out and wiped tears from my cheek. I stared at her hand in fascination. *I'm crying? Who knew I could still do that over something not related to Jared?* I felt like I had become numb to everything else but him.

Who knew that my best friend ending up in a hospital would lead to the moment that I realized I was still capable of having real emotions; I'd been in that numb limbo state since Jared returned, with a growing certainty that I was dying slowly from the inside out.

"She's going to be okay, but it doesn't look pretty," Bridget said, offering me a sad smile. "Ruby's in there now, but she should be out soon. Only one person can go in at a time."

I nodded.

Ruby appeared through the sliding doors moments later. Her face was splotchy, her movements slow and strained. I moved like I was on autopilot, without thought. I hugged Ruby and strolled past her, following the directions she gave me.

I don't know what I was expecting to see, but the moment I laid eyes on her, the breath was knocked out of me. Her arms and neck and face were mostly purple, but what was left untouched was sheet white and sallow. Her face was unrecognizable as half of it was swollen, with bandages that peeked out from the neck of her hospital gown.

She opened her one eye and pinned me in place. Tears filled that eye as her swollen lip trembled. I gasped for air and wiped the tears streaking my face. My body went into motion again as I went to her, but I halted. I was afraid to touch her. Afraid that there was no way to comfort her without hurting her. And the only thing I knew about physical pain was that most people avoided it.

I gently tucked my hand underneath hers. If anyone tried to tell me that true love existed solely in romantic relationships, I would've told them that they were full of shit at that moment. Because I knew beyond a shadow of a doubt that what was in my heart for this girl was pure unconditional love. And I knew she felt the same by the way her shoulders relaxed, and a sigh leaked out with the contact.

"Wha—what happened?" My voice came out coarse and unsure as I struggled to ask the question I'd been avoiding. I was afraid this cause would lead back to me, and I knew I'd hate myself for it.

"Roz—he found out about Asher." She took a shaky breath. The way her eyes seemed to lose focus, I could tell that it hurt her to talk, whether from the memory or something more physical.

"I thought you broke up?"

"We—we did." Her eye tracked to the wall before returning back to me. "I didn't know…" A pained sound escaped her.

"Did he…?" I couldn't bring myself to say the words.

Her eye closed as if to hide from the question, and when she opened it again, there was a lifeless quality that had never been present in my fearless friend. I knew then, without words, but her slight nod and grimace confirmed the worst. Red colored my vision. I fought the urge to jump up and hunt him down. I'd kill him with my bare hands if given the chance.

I was beginning to think the opposite sex might not be worth all the hype. It's like they were put on this earth to tear us down or just plain rip out our soul until we were nothing but an empty shell. They all had different methods, but the results were the same.

I didn't ask her any more questions. The pain of talking was written all over the unmarked parts of her face and apparent in the raspy tremble of her voice. We sat in silence for minutes, hours, I lost track. I was just there for her. Pain sliced through my heart. I couldn't take this. I needed her. I was falling apart, and she was my lifeline, but now we were both broken. I couldn't help her. I couldn't make this right.

Her eye had closed, and her breathing settled, the rhythmic bleating of her heart monitor lulling both of us. I was sure she had fallen asleep, and I carefully removed my hand from hers. Her eye flew open as she pinned me with a panicked stare.

"Don't tell—him." Her rough voice cracked, and her mouth moved soundlessly for a moment before trying again. "Don't—tell Asher."

Now

We don't stop anywhere on the way to Dex's home the next morning. As we pull into the parking lot, I wonder what that phone conversation last night was about. He said he had a surprise for me, and I'm not going to lie, I like surprises. I love them, in fact. My stomach feels tight with giddy anticipation.

He tugs on my hand, smushing it between his palm and the gear shift as he sets the car to park. He hasn't stopped touching me but for a few brief seconds. I love it. I love him.

There are two very familiar cars in the parking lot of his home, and one I've never seen before.

"Nate and Asher are here?"

"Yep," he replies, not adding any more detail. He releases my hand and gets out of the car, coming around to my side for the door.

"Care to elaborate why?"

"Nope," he says with a dimpled smirk, taking my hand to help me out of the car in this tight dress.

I don't keep any clothes other than my fight gear at Nic's, so I was forced to wear yesterday's dress. Not that it was dirty or wrinkled. I only had it on for an hour before it got hung in the closet for the remainder of the night.

Dex is wearing the sexy suit again. No tie. And when I straighten, I'm eye level with the exposed skin that peeks out where the top two buttons are undone. I lick my lips. I want to lick that dip at the base of his throat. I feel like an addict. I'd one taste, and I already need more.

He runs his thumb over my bottom lip, tilting my chin up until I meet his eyes. The hunger there matches my own. He leans forward like he's going to kiss me, but pauses. His breath rolls over my lips, leaving a wake of tingles with each soft tease. I try to close the distance, but the grip on my chin stops me. I can feel his resulting grin, and a little whimper escapes me, a one-syllable plea for him to end my torture.

Flutters expand in my stomach, and it feels as though my heart is trying to pull itself out of my chest to go to his. It's like nothing I've ever felt before. When his lips capture mine and his teeth grip my bottom lip, my legs give out, and I sag against the doorframe. His arm wraps my waist and pulls me up with a deep rumble in his chest. My toes are barely brushing the ground. Nothing exists in this moment but us. It feels like flying, a weightless tumble where you can't tell which way is up or down, but you also don't care.

Our tongues dance in perfect rhythm. I want him to carry me inside right now. I want him to fuck me in the foyer, on his couch, in his art studio and bedroom; then I want to do it on the edge of the river just beyond his porch, where my screams will echo back to me from the opposite cliff. I feel out of control. I'd be climbing up him if it weren't for this stupid dress.

He breaks the kiss and pulls back to look at me. I feel drugged.

"Worth it," he mutters.

I reach up and run my fingertips over his scar. "I agree."

He squeezes me tighter for a second before he sets me back to earth and takes a large step back. His breathing is labored like he's trying to rein in his control. I love that I make him fight so hard for it, but I don't like the distance. I move to step forward, and he holds up a hand.

"Don't. If you do, I'll be taking you inside, and we won't be back out for at least a few hours, and I want to show you your surprise."

Reality crashes back into me. There are people inside waiting for us.

"Maybe it won't take long." I shrug and fall back on my heels.

His dimples appear as he looks down, trying to fight the smile. The morning sun is rising directly behind him, giving him an ethereal look. He peeks up at me through his thick lashes, and I groan. That look isn't helping anything. It's so sexy my chest aches in response.

He straightens and looks away, holding his hand out to me. "Come on."

217

I expect him to lead me inside the house, but instead, we start in the opposite direction. We walk toward a much smaller building on the opposite side of the parking lot that I hadn't noticed until now. It matches the exterior of his garage home, so it must belong to him.

"What is this?" I gesture toward the building.

His face scrunches up. "I think it used to be an office of some sort. I'm not really sure, though, because there was an office in the main building as well."

There are no windows on the building, so the fact that it was an office and not a storage shed is curious. He pulls open the door and gestures me to go in ahead of him.

The inside is much larger than it appears to be from the outside. It has two rooms; the one I'm in has a row of off-white cabinets along one wall. A walled-off portion with a door to what looks to be a bathroom sits in the back corner, but that's not what has me shocked silent.

The other room's walls are covered in soundproof tiles, and the row of cabinets in this room is littered with recording equipment. Musical instruments are scattered everywhere. Asher, Nate, and a man with a dyed-black mop of wild hair look up from their tasks as we enter. I take in the newcomer's worn-out denim jacket covered in patches and paint, to the ripped and faded black work pants, the chain dangling from his hip, and black work boots. I freeze on the spot. That isn't just any man with black hair. Familiar, warm brown eyes, shadowed by dark circles, are laughing as he looks me over from head to toe.

"Wild night?" Spencer asks with a questioning look directed at my evening attire at this early hour.

My brows climb. "You haven't talked to me in almost six years, and that's the first thing you can think to say?"

"I haven't talked to you?" He snorts, shaking his head. "You fucking left me in your dust, Miss America's Military Sweetheart."

I cringe at the name. That's not how I remember it at all. He took off to California right after Law left for the fight circuit, leaving me behind. "Then why did you agree to come here?"

"Color me curious as to how the other half lives." He shrugs. "And you played it smart, sending this one to feel me out." He nods toward Asher.

I look at Asher curiously, trying to figure out what he could've possibly said to get him here. "You got here awfully fast," I comment.

"It doesn't take that long to drive five blocks." He smirks at my confusion. "Did your self-righteousness get in the way of finding out that I moved back three years ago?"

Anger stirs in my gut. This was a bad idea. "Communication goes both ways, asshole," I grumble.

"Bitch," he replies without hesitation.

We stand there, staring each other down. The room is silent since everyone has stopped to gawk at our conversation. Then Spencer shifts suddenly and leaps over the equipment and wires that separate us. I find myself crushed in a hug.

"I missed you, nerd girl."

"You look like shit," I reply.

We both laugh and break apart. I feel warmth at my back and know it's Dex without even looking. Spencer's focus moves over my shoulder, and his eyes squint as he tilts his head. His brow crease and his lips pinch in concentration.

"Oh, Spence. This is Dex, my boyfriend. Dex, this is Spencer."

"We met?" Spence asks, offering his hand.

I turn to catch Dex's thoughtful frown. "I don't think so."

One of those awkward silences settles, and I allow my eyes to scan the room.

"Huh. My bad. Guess you just have one of those faces," Spence says with a grin.

Dex smirks and shrugs. "Guess so."

And just like that, the awkwardness dissipates.

"What is all this stuff doing here?" I ask.

"That was my idea," Dex answers. "I thought you might

feel more comfortable recording in a change of location."

I turn back to look at him. I'm sure the shock is written across my face. I blink several times and have to remind myself to breathe. It's been a long time since anyone has been close enough to anticipate my needs or know how to take care of me. I'm shocked speechless, which seems to be a habit I've developed around him.

I feel a pressure in my chest, and I know that my heart is full, mended in a way I thought was impossible. I'm so far gone for this man. I startle when I realize I've moved toward him. I remember that we have an audience and they probably don't want to see that.

I go up on my tiptoes and position my mouth next to his ear. "Later, killer." I pull back and bite my lip, hoping that he catches my meaning.

Someone does because I hear a throat clear behind me.

"You gonna stand around and flirt with your man all day, or do you want to show me these tunes you wrote." He looks back at Dex. "It makes you so proud when they grow up and write songs of their own," he says in a silly voice, like a proud papa about to show off his kid walking for the first time.

I shake my head at him.

"I'm gonna go back in the house and get some stuff done," Dex says, motioning over his shoulder.

I nod and watch him turn and leave. *That's a great view.*

Then

As I parked my car outside the police station, I saw Bridget walking toward me. I'd never really seen her dressed for business, as we were pretty casual around the office and on the road. I sat there in shock with my jaw slack for a few moments before I remembered I needed to get out of the car. She stood at the front of my car, wearing a skirt suit and heels, her blonde hair smoothed back into a low chignon. I pulled on my baseball cap and zipped up my hoodie; it was my incognito costume du jour.

"You act like you didn't think it was possible for me to look professional."

"You're hitting all the key points of my hot lawyer fantasy." I wagged my eyebrows at her.

"Well, thank you." She gave me a smirk, and a dimple appeared. I was instantly jealous. "You pull off the Unabomber look quite well, yourself." She snickered.

"You're very welcome," I said, looking her over from head to toe. I thought she was a bombshell before; now I was thrown. "How do you get any work done around here?"

"It actually works in my favor. Dumb guys are too busy drooling to argue." She winked and then turned to walk inside.

I followed her, since I'd no clue where anything was inside a police station. She walked straight past the front desk like she owned the place, and no one bothered to stop her. We rode the elevator up with two uniformed police officers and a dirty guy in overalls they had in handcuffs. He looked up from Bridget's ass long enough to give me a toothless grin, and I pressed myself against the wall.

We stepped off into a hallway lined with doors and turned right until the hallway opened up to an open area with lots of desks. In the corner of the room was a glass-walled office. Bridget didn't stop until we arrived at the door of that office. The placard next to the door read Police Chief Montenegro. I looked to Bridget with a crease in my brow.

"I went above your friend's captain's head and straight to the decision-maker."

She rapped on the door, and the man at the desk looked up and waved us in.

"Miss Colfax, how nice to see you," he said, looking like he was anything but pleased. "Have a seat."

"Art, we don't need to be formal. I thought you heard that I was out of criminal law?" she joked as we both sat in chairs across the desk from him.

"Really?" he asked, perking up but still sounding skeptical.

"Then what brings you here?"

"My client"—Bridget nodded toward me—"would like a specific police officer assigned to her case."

"Didn't you just say you were out of criminal law?" he grumped.

"She's not a defendant, she's a victim. I'm in entertainment law now. This is Laine Dobransky. Perhaps you've heard of her—America's Military Sweetheart?"

His bushy eyebrows climbed up his forehead.

"This is her case number and Officer Martinez's badge number. Laine is asking that Officer Martinez be assigned lead detective in her case." Bridget held out a piece of paper.

I didn't think it was possible for his eyebrows to climb any higher, but they did. He took the paper from Bridget.

I cleared my throat. "This stalker has been following me for years now. Little things here and there. Your department wouldn't open a case because I couldn't prove a pattern or supply identifying evidence, but Officer Martinez has been keeping track of everything. If you pull the file, I think you'll find enough to open a case. But I want him to work it because he's the only one who believed me from the start."

"I see," he said, and then turned to his computer and started tapping away at his keys. He picked up the phone.

"Captain Norris. Is Officer Martinez around? Yeah. Bring him to my office." He hung up the phone and looked up at us. "Just sit tight for a minute."

I looked down at my hands, studying my fingernails while we waited in silence. It was only a couple of minutes, and Officer Martinez entered the office with a woman, both of them uniformed police officers.

"Grab a chair from outside, will ya?" Chief Montenegro asked as they came in.

Martinez turned around and rolled in a chair from an empty desk outside while the woman I assumed was Captain Norris sat in the remaining chair in the office that lined the wall. When everyone was seated, the chief spoke.

"This young woman here says you've been investigating

her case for years?" Martinez nodded. "Did you know about this?" he asked, looking at the captain.

"Yes, sir. When the first call was made, there wasn't enough evidence to open a case. The incident involved a man at Zilker Park giving her daughters flowers. She said she had received similar items previously but didn't think it strange until that incident."

"You took it upon yourself to investigate on your personal time and built this case file?" The chief looked to Martinez.

"Yes, sir," Martinez said.

"Hmmm." He leaned back in his seat, making it squeak. "What does the rest of his record look like, Captain? Would you recommend him for promotion?"

I squirmed in my chair, uncomfortable being included in what should be a private conversation. No one else seemed to feel this way as I looked over everyone.

"He's a good officer; no complaints filed, and no disciplinary actions have been taken. He's been on the force for six years. He shows up on time, does his job well. I see no reason to withhold promotion, sir."

The chief nodded. "Very well." He looked to Martinez. "I want you to turn in your badge to Captain Norris and report to Lieutenant Collins this afternoon. I'll forward this case to Collins and your assignment to the case. We'll talk more on this later. You can go."

"Oh, before you go," I said, looking to Martinez. I dug my phone out of my purse and handed it to him with a smile. "You asked for this."

"Thank you, Miss Dobransky," he said with a serious look to convey the multiple meanings of his gratitude as he took the phone.

"Thank you." I nodded with a gracious smile.

Martinez nodded back and left with my phone in hand.

"I assume you're done telling me how to do my job, Miss Colfax?" the chief grumped.

"For now." Bridget grinned. "I assume you've heard I'm volunteering for the prosecution." Her tone was still light and teasing, but her smile had vanished. Thinking about what Roz did to Holly did that to all of us.

"I have," he mumbled, his mouth flattening to a thin line as he breathed in through his nose. "I take it you'll be around."

"More than you'd like, I'm sure," Bridget answered and stood. "But thank you, Art, for your time. We'll leave you to it."

"Thank you," I repeated and followed Bridget out the door.

"Doesn't seem like your biggest fan," I said to Bridget as we walked back to the elevator.

"They never are. Every cop hates a good defense lawyer." She smirked.

Chapter Twenty

Now

I play the bar of music again, and Spencer frowns. He's possibly the only person who can make me feel like I suck at music without ever saying a word. Then again, he's the only person I've ever met who doesn't tell me that everything I do is golden. That's why I've always loved him. He pushes me to do better, try harder. We've always made a hell of a team.

I can't help the slow grin that has my cheeks stretching as it grows. It feels great to have that dour face staring me down, not quite happy with my music.

"No, it's still not working," he says, his brows pulled down as intense concentration takes over his face.

He plays the same notes but changes the timing of each slightly, altering the flow of the music. It's better. He nods, and I repeat his pattern on my guitar. His eyes betray his smile, even though he's chewing on his bottom lip, so I know we've found it.

I lean over and mark the changes down in my notebook and turn to Asher.

"You wanna take it from the top?" I ask.

He bobs his head once in confirmation and picks up his drumsticks. The short, quick taps on the cymbal set the pace. One... two... three... four...

We play the song from start to finish. It's good but still off. I study their faces; neither are entirely happy, nor are they unhappy. Apathetic is a good word for it. But apathy is death to music because music thrives on the emotions it evokes.

"It's still missing something." I tap my finger on my lower lip, frowning at my notebook.

"Yeah, depth," Spencer says.

"Guys, I'm gonna take five." Nate's voice breaking in through a speaker causes me to jump.

He's been in the other room with the recording equipment all day. With no glass wall to see him, I keep forgetting he's there until his voice sounds out loudly, joining our conversations. Out of sight; out of mind.

I nod before I remember he can't see me, and then speak into the microphone.

"Sounds good." I purse my lips, mulling over the music. "We need bass and rhythm guitar. These songs can't be pulled off with three instruments."

"You know we can call him?" Spencer asks.

My head whips in his direction so fast my muscles clench. "He still plays?"

"Did you think we were the only serious musicians in the band?" He gestures between us.

I shrug. "Monk doesn't play drums anymore, aside from the lessons with the kids he works with. I just assumed..."

"You know what they say about assuming?" Spence poses, spreading his hand out in front of him.

I pick up my pencil and lob it at his head. "Shut up, dick."

He angles his body slightly, and it sails past him, bouncing off the wall. Spencer chuckles.

Asher laughs, too, and I turn narrowed eyes in his direction. He fights to keep the smirk off his face. He obviously enjoys how much shit Spence has been giving me since I walked in the door. I think my face is going to be stuck in a permanent glare after today.

I rest my arms on top of my guitar. "Call him."

Spence pulls his phone from his pocket and holds up a

finger. "On it."

Spencer is listening to the phone ring when the door squeaks open. Asher and I turn to face the noise, only to find a grim-faced Dex.

I'm immediately on alert. Dex doesn't wear his emotions unless he means for you to see it. I set my guitar down as he looks over his shoulder into the other room. I hop over the equipment as best I can in the ridiculously oversized borrowed T-shirt and flannel sleep pants to get to him.

"What's wrong?" I ask.

His body relaxes slightly when I touch him, but he's still tense. I look past him into the other room and notice that Nate's not there. But in his chair is another flower and another note. I look around and don't see any sign of Nate. I push past Dex, immediately going to see if Nate has left. When I open the door, the daylight blinds me for a moment, but when my eyes adjust, I can see Nate's Beemer sitting in front of me. I go back in, thoroughly confused, until I remember the bathroom. The bathroom door is closed, so I knock.

No answer.

I knock again.

Nothing.

I try the handle. It turns, but something is blocking the door. My stomach plummets. I back away, shaking my head. I suddenly don't want to be here anymore. I want to get away. I turn with the intention of bolting out of the building but halt when I notice Dex is standing there, reading the note.

Dex's fingers curl into the paper, warping it like he's barely able to keep from destroying it. It's his only tell. His face is back to the cool, calm mask that he usually wears.

"What're you doing?" I ask, my voice belying my fear.

Dex looks up from the note. Whatever he sees on my face causes his brows to drop. "It's not like you're gonna hand it over to the police." He shrugs. "Not likely that they would find anything anyway, and I wanted to know what it said."

He holds the paper out to me, and I shake my head.

"I don't want to touch it."

Why I think a plastic barrier makes holding one of the notes, any easier, is beyond me. Or maybe it's just the increased fear of what's in the bathroom. I catch sight of Asher moving toward the bathroom door, and the curiosity over what the note says battles with my need to be far away from that door when it opens. Call me a fucking coward, but I'm sure I can't live with any more death, especially in a place where I'm recording music.

Dex is cupping the back of my neck, pulling me to his chest before I register his movement. I breathe in his woodsy scent. I'm not real good at differentiating scents, but I can smell a hint of cedar and lavender to whatever it is he wears. It's not a cologne; it's more subtle. My mind mulls over this little debate, and I find myself melting into him. His touch, his presence, is soothing.

"I can tell you don't want to, but you need to read this. Maybe you'll understand it better."

I plead with my eyes for him to take me away from here. I can hear Spencer has joined Asher, trying to open the bathroom door.

"I've got you," he whispers, running his thumb over my lower lip.

A fine shiver courses through me, and I burrow further into his arms. It gives me a modicum of strength and I turn to read the note in his hand.

He said a debt must be settled between you. That I was to contact you or he would send evidence to the police. You need to leave town, go somewhere he can't find you.

My brows draw together as I tip my head back to meet Dex's troubled eyes. "Is this some weird talking in third person or multiple personality thing? Who is *he*?"

Then

I pulled into the newly repaved parking lot at the recording studio. The expansion of the building fit seamlessly to the old structure, making it impossible to tell that it wasn't always that big. We kept the steeple and added more stained glass windows. I was fond of the quirkiness that the old church look gave to the business.

I waited for Bridget to get out of her car at the end of the walkway leading to the front door. I looked over the squares of freshly laid sod covering the evidence of the recent construction.

"You ready to see what you've been paying my salary for?" Bridget said with a smile as she joined me.

"I think I got that by the many documents I get by mail and email to sign every day. This is impressive, too, though."

Her eyes lit up. "Wait until you see the inside."

We walked the path to the doors. So many changes to the interior had me blinking in shock as I opened the doors. We walked into a real reception area. The style was a bit more modern, quirky, and fun. I immediately loved it. As much crap as I gave her, Sloane really did have good taste.

There was a desk in the center of the area with a sign behind it that read Mad Lane Records. I smiled at that. The record label name was Nate's idea, his homage to me, his new business partner. I bought half of the recording studio, and we both invested the money for the expansion. Bridget did the legwork on setting up the record label, and we were in business.

"You ready for the grand tour?" Bridget beamed.

"Lead the way."

I followed her down the hallway lined with the glass-walled offices of the new addition to the building. Each office had the name and position of the occupant. The first two were Bridget and Priscilla's offices, Legal and Publicity Director respectively, followed by two that were sitting empty aside from the basic office furniture. We passed a larger area that had a break room on one side of the hall and a conference room on the other side. So far, we had yet to run into anyone, and I began to wonder where everyone was at.

Their cars were in the parking lot after all.

We continued on to the end of the hall, which opened up to a second reception area and two large offices that lined the back wall. Both had glass walls to the inside, but there were blinds pulled closed, so I couldn't see through.

I knew from the plans that those two offices were the only ones that broke the exterior church-like facade and had full glass walls facing the outside, since they were hidden from the street and the parking lot by the rest of the building and overlooked the creek outside. One had Nate Thompson—Owner and Executive Operations—and the other, Madelaine Dobransky—Owner and Executive A&R.

I felt like I could fly at that moment because it finally felt real. I loved playing and performing, but this was my dream. Nate and I divided the ownership of the company; he would handle the business and management of the company, and I'd own the direction and talent of the record label.

I pushed the door open, and the lights came on. Everyone jumped on the spot, yelling. "Surprise!"

I shrieked and let the door swing closed in front of me. The door opened, and Jared stood there with a huge grin on his face.

"We got you, didn't we?"

"Holy fuck, I think I'm having a heart attack." I placed my hand on my chest and willed my racing heart to slow.

Jared wrapped his arms around me and kissed my forehead. People filed out of the office, which had exceeded its max capacity. Just about everyone I knew was in there, with a few notable exceptions—Holly, Sloane, and Ruby. I felt a dark cloud pass with the thought, but I put on a brave face.

"We decided to celebrate since construction finished last week, and we're set to open next week. This is last-minute." Nate shrugged with a grin and held up a bottle of champagne.

"There's actually food in the break room fridge. I slaved away at the stove all day," Bridget said as she pulled me from Jared into her own hug.

I pulled back sharply. "You don't cook."

"Fine." She grinned and let me go. "I ordered catering. You could've let me live in my fantasyland of domesticity, but no." She made a show of her pretend outrage, and I laughed loudly, shaking my head. She leaned forward and whispered loudly, "Congratulations, bitch. You did it."

I was unable to stop the production of tears as they filled my eyes, blurring my vision. I nodded, unable to speak past the growing lump in my throat.

I was passed around from one person to the next while they all congratulated me on the business opening. I finally made it back to Nate.

"We're supposed to be recording tonight," I said, wiping underneath my eyes.

"We are. You're the entertainment. Everyone gets to watch as we christen the new recording booth. Have you seen it?"

"No, we didn't go into the old part of the building, so I haven't seen the remodel."

He grinned. "Just wait." He turned to face everyone and whistled loudly. "Everybody, we're moving to the studio to watch the magic happen. Let's go."

We all moved to the studio, which looked amazing. We had torn out the old kitchen and two of the storage closets and put in a new recording booth with its own waiting area. I stopped and looked into the old "crash pad" room that had been outfitted with bunks based on Japanese hostel designs, so people now had their own private cubbyhole to crash in. This was perfect.

We got to work then. It didn't take long to record the song since it was just me and an acoustic guitar. Afterward, I was sitting on the couch with Jared when someone opened the bottle of champagne finally. When the pop sounded, Jared jumped, then stiffened, and his pupils dilated. Fear crawled into my chest like a rabid animal. I moved onto his lap.

"Hey, Jared. Look at me. I read about this. If you count

backward with me, it'll help." When I got his attention, I began to count backward from ten.

Eventually, his color returned, and his body relaxed. I brushed my lips against his.

"See, we can get through this together." I beamed at him with a watery smile.

"Thank you," he said, burying his face in my neck and taking a deep breath.

Now

I'm pacing the floor, trying to get my breathing under control. The guys got the bathroom door opened, and there was nothing in there. Empty. It was just stuck closed by something to do with a shifting foundation or hinges... I tune the guys out when they start mansplaining it.

But, Nate is still missing and in his place is a new flower. My mind races with infinite possibilities as to what it all means. He could be in danger—taken by the man that watches me and leaves cryptic messages.

It felt preposterous to me that he would be the stalker. But Dex did submit that as a possibility, that this note was a goodbye. With each change of direction, I vacillate between anger and worry. I can't make my mind up.

Asher is explaining to Spencer what it all means, and Dex is just sitting still. I can see the thoughts moving behind his eyes, but so far, he hasn't made a move to share them with anyone.

Moments later, the doorknob turns, and we all turn to watch it. Dex moves from the chair with a quiet stealth to stand in front of me, blocking my view. His hand goes to his ever-present weapon in preparation for the worst.

"Hey." I hear the familiar husky male voice. "Any of you know this dude passed out on the ground out here?"

I catch the whiff of marijuana on the air, and I know who it is, instantly. I place a hand on Dex's to keep him from drawing his gun.

"Spaz?" I ask, trying to sidestep Dex. "My God, that's probably Nate."

Dex places a hand on my arm to stop me, and I meet his hardened stare. "You stay here." He nods to the chair. "I'll go see if it's him."

Fuck. I know he's right. We know the stalker's been here. Nate is missing, and the last thing I need to do is go running off half-cocked by myself. I nod and drop into the seat, defeated.

Dex leans down and gives me a brief kiss. "Good girl."

I catch movement out of the corner of my eye. Spence is watching us and fighting a smirk on his face. His shoulders rock in silent laughter. *Fuck off,* my eyes tell him. I know he's thinking about the song he wrote and how he used to relentlessly tease me about my proclivities. *At least I got laid.*

Asher goes with Dex. They return a few seconds later with a ruffled and dirty Nate clutching his head.

I gasp. "What happened?" I rush over to fuss over him and pull him to the chair.

"I don't know. The bathroom door was stuck, so I walked around back to, you know... then someone hit me over the back of the head. I didn't see anyone because they got me from behind."

His hair is matted with coagulated blood. It makes me nervous to look at it closer. I'm always afraid of hurting people. I delicately part his salt-and-pepper gray hair. He sucks in a break and jerks. I almost jerk away, too. But I'm distracted by the nasty gash—his skin is split open, exposing the yellowish fatty tissue below.

I look up at Ash. "He needs to go get stitched up and checked out for a concussion."

"I can take him." Ash already has his keys out.

Dex and Asher help Nate to Asher's truck. I watch them go and then turn to face the others. Both are watching me, and I sigh in resignation.

"I'm sorry," I say, sitting in the vacated chair. "I'll

understand if you want to get as far as you can away from me."

One of them snorts, but I don't look up. I twist my hands in my lap and crack my knuckles.

"Are you kidding?" Spaz starts. "This is awesome. The most excitement I've had in ages. Besides, it's not like we got anything better to do."

"Yeah, but it's dangerous to be around me. I don't know what's going to happen, but I'd feel horrible if something happened to you because of me."

I already do feel horrible. Jesus, Nate probably hates me. Or he will when he gets his wits about him.

"I'm sorry this is happening to you," Spence says, punching Spaz in the shoulder. "But what we're working on here is good stuff. I'm not gonna pass because your producer got knocked around."

"I think what my friend's tryin' to say is that the risk is better than working Jet's Pizza for the rest of our lives."

"You work at Jet's Pizza?" I blink.

"Lainey, babe," Spaz says, pulling a joint from his pocket. "We don't have a band anymore. We fuck around mostly. Play with other people here and there, but things didn't work for us the way they did you."

He lights up, and smoke billows through the room. I hear the door snick behind me, and I'm tempted to give him shit by informing him that Dex is a cop, just to see the look on his face. But Dex's undercover, and he likely doesn't give a shit about my pot-smoking friend.

"I'm glad you're in," Dex says from right behind me, and I startle a bit. "Because I gotta plan."

The door opens again, blinding me with sunlight. Two people enter.

"Oh, whoa… fuck, man. Some bitch's gettin' toasted in here," Holly says. "Oh shit, it's my lil troll doll."

Holly squeals and practically tackles Spaz out of his chair.

Marcus walks over to Dex. "What's up, man?"

"Right on time," Dex says.

Marcus and Dex do some elaborate secret-handshake thing before man hugging, complete with back slaps. I look back, and Holly seems giddy as she stands behind Spaz, running her hands through his hair and pulling it up until he does sort of resemble a troll doll. Spaz has his eyes closed, looking perfectly content.

"This part doesn't hurt either. You always come with a gaggle of hot chicks that want to play with my hair." He grins, eyes still closed.

"What's the plan?" Spencer asks.

That grabs Dex's attention. "Right. I think you guys need to have a concert."

Chapter Twenty-One

Now

It takes a couple of weeks to get everything set up. In that time, I learn one very important thing—Dex and I make a great team.

Everything is running like a well-oiled machine, and I get to sit back and do what I do best. The best part is that I feel confident in Dex's plan. We're no longer sitting on our asses—we're fighting back. This shit ends tonight, and I can have my girls back. I miss them terribly.

We're holding a special comeback performance at Slo, Nic's club inside the Black Building. Press-zilla has worked her ass off to get the word out. We're expecting a huge crowd, but the hope is to lure the stalker here tonight. He can't sneak past the security here; this place is more secure than Fort Knox.

My whole company has been scrambling to make this all happen on such short notice, while the guys and I put the music together. It feels like coming full circle in more ways than one. The music is me, heart and soul, but having Asher, Spence, and Spaz with me has been amazing, blending old and new to make something different that is uniquely ours.

I feel an arm snake around my waist, and I feel slightly dizzy. I melt back into him when he kisses my shoulder.

"Are you nervous?" Dex asks, his lips teasing the shell of my ear.

I sigh. "No. It's my superpower. I've never gotten stage fright."

Turning in his arms, I meet those hypnotic eyes. They're smiling.

"I'd say your superpower was that thing you did last night." He laughs. "You people need to learn some healthy boundaries... no, I'm not telling you."

That's when I notice the earpiece he's wearing. *Better him than me.* I smirk at him because I know those guys. And I guess when you work in a place like this and see what they do, day in and day out, taboo topics fade to normalities. It could also be Nic, since Nic is coordinating the security team from the command center upstairs. That would *not* surprise me.

"I got something for you," Dex says, pulling a small black velvet pouch from his back pocket.

I watch him curiously as I take it and upend the bag. A silver necklace spills out into my hand. It's a dragon pendant, but not just any dragon—his dragon. It's pure silver with rubies for eyes. It's beautiful.

"Thank you," I say with a watery smile. "You want to put it on me?"

"I do."

He pushes my hair over my shoulder, running his fingertips over my skin so lightly it makes me shiver. He clasps the necklace, and I look down at it. It sits right in that perfect space between my throat and the neckline of my shirt. I love it.

"You're on in two," Nate says, walking into the greenroom.

Everyone springs into action. The opening act trails in behind Nate. Spence and Spaz greet them since they're friends of theirs. I start to head toward the stage, but a finger in the belt loop of my ripped jeans stops me. I'm pulled back into Dex's arms.

"I think I might be developing a rock star fetish," Dex whispers, while toying with the black bra strap peeking out from my white wifebeater tank.

"I'm okay with that. It works well with my artist fetish. Especially, when you paint my body with your tongue," I whisper back, nipping his lower lip.

I'm swept up in his kiss, losing track of what I'm meant to be doing until a voice announces, "One minute."

We break apart, and I hurry down the long hall toward the stage. The click of my boots echoes off the walls of the mostly empty hall until it's drowned out by the rising volume of the raucous crowd.

I climb the steps of the raised dais, but Dex jerks me back, and his mouth claims mine again. It's hard and fast, possessive.

"I'll be right here," he assures. "He won't get to you."

Smiling at him, I'm reminded that I'm in love with this man. It's that simple. He sets the darkest parts of my soul ablaze and makes my heart feel like it's not just an empty husk. I reluctantly let go and walk onstage to the chorus of cheers.

"What's up, Austin?" I say into the microphone, pulling my guitar strap over my head. "I hope you're ready for some new stuff because this is a new band and a new beginning. You ready to hear what *Splash!* is all about?"

Cheers and whistles are my answer. Spaz named the band. He thought it was cool because it was a mash-up of all our names—Spence, Spaz, Laine, and Ash. We couldn't think of anything better, so we ran with it. I look back at Asher with a nod, and he launches into the first song.

By the third song, the crowd is pumped—they love the new stuff. I'm sweaty and hot, but I feel like someone plugged me directly into an electrical socket. The energy in the room has me buzzing. I look out over the multitude of faces, but there's only one I want to see.

I turn to look at the side stage, and he's there, still watching me. The blend of shadows and light that fall across him highlight the sexiest parts of him. *Jesus Christ. He's mine.* His eyes darken as if he's reading my thoughts.

The girls are out there somewhere. Holly and Marcus are supposed to be moving through the crowds, searching for anyone familiar who was not officially invited. Bridget, Ruby, and Dawn are just here for moral support and because they wanted to see the concert. They have security assigned to them, so they're free to enjoy their night. I look for the green head of hair; Dawn's always easy to spot in a crowd. They are bouncing up and down, dancing about ten feet away from the front center of the stage. It's amazing I hadn't seen them because they're right in front of me.

Bridget makes eye contact, and I grin at her, blowing a kiss in their direction when I get a break from singing. When we get to the eighth song, the crowd is getting tired, so we switch gears and play a slower-tempo song. God, I've missed this. I can read it all over Asher, Spence, and Spaz. They're flying high on it, too. We pick up the pace again with the ninth song, gearing up for the tenth and last song, which is going to be the first single from the album.

That's when it happens.

Pop!Pop!Pop!

Gunshots ring out over the loud music. People scream and scatter, running from the sound. I crash to the ground under the force of a large, hard body. The neck of my guitar snaps off, and the discordant sound reverberates from the speakers throughout the room.

"What the fuck are you doing?" I scream at Dex.

"Keeping you from getting shot."

"What about you? You're going to take a bullet for me?"

His face scrunches in confusion. "That was the plan."

"Fucking stupid, jackass plan. Fuck your plan. If you're not shot, I might just do it myself. Get the fuck off me."

"Can't move yet. I'm waiting for the all clear," he explains.

Anger takes over me, and I can't stop the flow of expletives from my mouth. Spitting mad. I'm seething. He can't sacrifice himself for me, because I'll never survive the fall. I'd rather die than watch him take a bullet for me. He laughs.

"What the fuck were you thinking? I can't watch you die. You can't take a bullet for me, you giant tattooed asshole."

"I love you."

"I love you, too! That's the point. Now get off me before I knee you in the balls. And I really don't want to ruin my chance at another child—"

I'm silenced by his kiss. It's a good kiss. And in any other situation, I'd be lost in this kiss, but there's a person in this room with a gun. They could've been shooting at me or in the opposite direction, but they could still be getting ready to shoot again and now is not the time. I slap at his shoulders to make him stop.

When he does, my guitar strap is over my head before I can blink. I probably have whiplash from him pulling me up so quickly. He's still shielding my body with his own. I want to kick him in the shins for it, but my feet are busy trying to keep up. He's dragging me as he navigates the halls like he knows exactly where he's going. Spencer, Spaz, and Ash are following us. When we get to a door and it clicks open ahead of us without anyone touching it, I catch on to the fact that he's being guided where to go.

The door clicks shut behind us, and we stop. Well, me and the guys do—Dex, however, is checking out the room.

"Yeah, it's clear," he says, obviously to whoever is talking to him through the earpiece since he's not looking at any of us. "The stairwell on the southeast corner? I'm on it."

He pulls his gun from his holster. His back is to me as he does it, and I get caught up in the thought that he's only able to hide that because he has a nice, pert ass. Like a really nice ass. Now I'm remembering it naked. Yep. It's a good one. I shake myself out of it.

"Your friends are coming up the hall." Dex pulls me out of the way, and only then do I realize I'm still standing in front of the door.

He opens the door. Bridget, Dawn, and Ruby rush in,

followed by Noah. I hug the girls tight, thanking God that they're all right. Dex starts to move past them and out the door, and I reach over and grab his arm.

"Where do you think you're going?"

"There's a security breach in the stairwell. It might be our guy. I'm going after him."

"Did I not make myself—"

Son of a bitch cuts me off with another kiss, and the door snaps shut behind him and Noah. He's gone. When I try, the handle doesn't work. I flip the middle finger to the camera in the corner of the ceiling because I know I just got tag teamed by Nic and Dex. *Fuckers.*

"Psst, Laine," Spaz whispers. "When did you start dating John McClain? Didn't you say he was an artist?"

I roll my eyes at Spaz, but really, it's just to buy time to think of an explanation. I can't think of anything, though, so I go with distraction.

"Why are you whispering?" I say in a normal voice.

Then

I sipped from my glass of wine as I sat across the golden cloth-topped table from Jared at the Driskill in Downtown Austin. I leaned back in the wide leather chair, enjoying the rare date night with him. Though, it wasn't just an ordinary date night. It was my birthday. The dimly lit wood-paneled room with its heavy red curtains was romantic and cozy.

The location wasn't really my scene; the reservations had come from Priscilla. I accepted them with a smile, knowing that I was conveniently not telling her about our plans to go to Ruby's to shoot some pool and drink beer afterward, as was tradition. You had to pick your battles.

Jared laid his hand on the table, and I placed mine in his. He smiled at me.

"Have you given any thought to setting a date? I know we had decided to wait until after the tour, but it's only six months and we'll be done."

"I don't know." I shrugged. "I'm conflicted. I really don't want a big wedding, but we have so many friends that would feel slighted if they didn't get to be there. If I had my way, we'd run off and get married on a beach alone somewhere, with turquoise waters and white sand," I said and started dreaming of standing on that beach with a white sundress and no shoes.

"Sounds perfect. I think we should do it," he said, taking a bite of his steak.

"Really?" I asked skeptically.

"Yeah, we can have a party for everyone else when we get back, but do what we want to do for everything else."

I thought about it for a moment. It could work for most people. We might not be able to pull off *alone* on a beach, but close. Just as I was about to open my mouth to reply, a shadow fell over our table. I looked up into familiar green eyes.

"I didn't know you were in town," he said.

"Holden," I exclaimed and stood from my chair to give him a hug. "What're you doing here?"

"Just have some business to talk about with my boy and some potential sponsors. It's been a long time, hasn't it? Sloane keeps me informed about you, but you should come by the gym sometime." I looked over his shoulder to see Law standing about twenty feet away, watching us warily. I sent Law a half smile and turned my attention back to his father.

"We're only in town for two more days, and then we'll be back on the road. We just flew in to handle some issues."

"Ah, well, I'll let you get back to your dinner. I just wanted to say hi."

"No problem. It was good seeing you."

"You too, baby girl. Sir." He nodded to Jared and left.

The table the host sat them at was two rows away and directly in my line of sight. Great. I kept my eyes on Jared and tried not to pay attention to the fact that I could feel *his* eyes on me throughout the rest of dinner.

We chatted endlessly about trivial things, but everything I did felt awkward and staged. The fact that I knew Law was watching us made me self-conscious of every facial expression, laugh, and gesture. While we were waiting for dessert, I excused myself to go to the bathroom. I needed a break from the pressure.

I sat in a stall and forced myself to pee. I stood up and heard the door open to the outside, and someone entered another stall. I flushed and walked out to the sink to wash my hands. I looked at myself in the mirror and really caught sight of the difference between the girl I once was back before senior year, the night I met Jared. I looked less like a girl and more like a woman. I'd no idea when that had happened.

I heard a shuffle and a click and turned to face the stalls. There were no feet visible at the bottom of any door, and I could've sworn I heard someone come in.

"Hello?" I said, hoping for an answer.

I finished rinsing off my hands and reached for the towels. I heard another thump and turned to see a pair of decidedly male boots topped with jeans through the bottom of a stall door. This place had a dress code; jeans were not allowed. I shouldered my purse and walked out quickly. I was going to notify management that some creep was in the ladies' restroom. When I turned the corner, I ran smack into a really solid, broad chest. The hand I put up to protect my face from the impact rested near a steadily thumping heart covered in a gray wool suit.

"In a hurry?" he asked.

"There's someone in there. A dude. I think he was watching me," I said to Law as he looked down at me with concerned hazel eyes.

His eyebrows rose. "Was there anyone else in there?"

"No."

"Then I'll check," he said, pushing past me and walking into the bathroom.

I followed him in as he pushed all the stall doors open.

"There's no one here." He opened the last stall.

"Did someone come out behind me? We were standing no more than five feet from the door. There doesn't look like any other way out."

"You sure you saw someone?"

"Yes, Law. They wore work boots and jeans. Their feet were under that stall door right there."

He held the door open to the stall I pointed to. "There's no one there."

"Holy fuck, I think I'm losing it." I massaged my temples. "I swear to God someone was in here."

I leaned over the sink, feeling dizzy. When I opened my eyes, Law was standing there looking at me. My mind flashed to another time when we were in a similar position. Another bathroom, so many years ago. His eyes grew darker.

"You sure you weren't just trying to get me alone in a bathroom again? Remember what happened last time?" he asked with that one-dimpled smirk.

I cringed. "Give me a fucking break, Law. That's not what this is." I felt dirty thinking about the things we used to do together.

"What's that look?" He tipped my chin up, turning me to meet his eyes. "Because to me, that look says you're ashamed of something, and that's not the Laine I know. You never held back."

"I guess you don't know me that well anymore. I'm not that person. What we did was dirty and twisted—that's not how normal people act." I jerked my head out of his reach and backed away.

"Says who? Him?" He took a step toward me, his eyes narrowing to thin slits and the muscle in his jaw ticking.

"I'm not doing this with you." I turned for the door.

I made it to the door and had it open several inches before his hand came over my head and slammed it shut.

"You know, I backed off because you seemed happy. I love you enough that that's all I want for you. He seemed like a nice guy and was good to your girls. But I've seen the news—the videos TMZ shows of him freaking out and attacking fans and berating you. I'm only going to ask you this once. Has he hurt you?"

"It's none of your business, but no," I said, turning to him. I had to look up to see him, he was standing so close, leaning over me to keep his hand on the door.

"You say that, but obviously he's made you feel ashamed of who you are. That's not right, Laine, and you know it. There's absolutely nothing wrong with the way we like to fuck."

"I give up, Law. Why can't you just move on?" I whined, letting my head fall back to the door with a thump.

"Do you know how hard it is to find someone who is not just willing to try the things we did, but actually enjoys them? Fuck, Laine. You're one of a kind, and that's really hard to ignore and just let go. We were fucking perfect together." He took a ragged breath. "Jesus, I want to touch you right now, kiss you. The fact that you don't even know what you do to me drives me insane."

My eyes flew open, and I glared at him. "That's not going to happen." I put my palm in the center of his chest and shoved, but he didn't budge. "Let me go, Law. Now."

"Fine." He held his hands up in surrender and took two steps back.

I walked out the door, and as soon as I turned the corner, I halted. Jared was coming around the corner into the hall. Law bumped into my back, causing me to stumble forward. Jared's eyes went from normal to deadly in a fraction of a second.

"You sit there and talk to me about wedding plans, then get up and go fuck this asshole in the bathroom?" he asked loudly. Too loud. Jealousy is an ugly stain on a relationship, and like most stains, once there it's next to impossible to remove.

"That's not what this is, Jared. It's not what it looks like."

"Sure. I bet it's exactly what it looks like. He turned you into a sick twisted slut—makes sense you would go running back to him eventually."

Law tried to push past me. "Don't fucking talk about her or to her like that."

I flung out my arms and used my body to keep him away from Jared.

"Why not? I bet you jerk off to that picture of her on the *Rolling Stone* cover, too."

"She's got a nice ass. What can I say?"

I looked back to Law. "That's not helping," I growled.

"Come on, Maddie." Jared held out his hand in invitation to come to him. "It's time to go home. I already paid the check."

I walked toward Jared, and when I was within reach, he grabbed my arm, wrenching it and pushing me toward the door. Law crashed into him, knocking over a table. Dishes clattered to the floor, and people screamed before my brain could even process what was happening. I ran back over to where they had fallen.

"Stop it!" I yelled over the commotion.

"Or what?" Jared seethed, grappling with Law. "You going to use the handcuffs he used on you in the bathroom?"

"There's nothing wrong with the way she likes to fuck, asshole," Law said through clenched teeth.

People nearby gasped. My hands flew to cover my face. *Oh, God. This was not happening.* They were a tangle of limbs as both fought to gain the upper hand over the other.

"Just fucking stop it," I sobbed, gasping for breath as tears spilled from my eyes. "You're both acting like children."

Law threw another punch and it landed with a thump. "He put his fucking hands on you, Laine."

I looked for an opening to intervene, but they were too fast. The tears streaming down my face dripped onto my helpless hands.

"Jared—Law—please just stop," I begged.

Holden fought his way through the gathered crowd and pulled Law off Jared.

"You three need to leave, now," Holden said in a stern voice that brooked no argument.

I nodded and grabbed Jared's arm, pulling him toward the door with every ounce of strength I had.

"If I find out you put your hands on her again, you're a dead man," Law called after us.

"Ditto," Jared replied snidely.

People had their phones out, recording the whole scene. This was going to be bad in so many different ways. I wanted to go home and curl up in a ball, and forget the rest of the world existed, especially Jared and Law.

Chapter Twenty-Two

Now

I pace the small office like a caged tiger. Thirty fucking minutes. Dex has been gone for thirty motherfucking minutes. And if he doesn't walk through that door soon, I'll kill him myself.

There has been no word sent our way, no communication as to what's going on outside those doors. And Holly hasn't come back here. I've no idea where either of them is. I'm one heartbeat away from losing it when the door opens.

Dex strolls in. I pounce, crossing the room. My hand cracks across his face before I realize what I'm doing. He wraps one arm around my waist, while his other hand dives into my hair, squeezing until my scalp feels tight. He kisses me.

It's not a gentle or loving kiss. It's demanding, domineering. It's an attempt to put me in my place, to show me who's in charge. It's very effective. I whimper.

A throat clears.

"Whoa," Dawn mutters.

"As hot as it is to watch you two tongue fuck each other..." Bridget says. "It's a little cramped in here. Can we get out of this room?"

"I don't know. I can stay behind if you need an audience?"

Spaz offers.

Spencer smacks him in the back of the head.

"We need to go. Marcus was shot. Holly's with him in the ambulance. She's fine, but we need to get to the hospital. Now."

At that, Dex grabs my arm and steers me out of the room. We weave through the maze of halls, heading toward the parking garage where my car is.

"Did you catch him?"

"No."

"What're we going to do now? Go back to waiting for him to show up?"

"No."

"Can you say something other than no?"

"No."

Okay, then. I'll shut up. He obviously doesn't want to talk. Can I blame him? We're rushing to the car to go to the hospital where the life of his brother, his Evan, hangs in the balance. Or at least I assume it's that bad by the grim expression he wears. I know he's upset because he isn't hiding it. Or perhaps, he isn't hiding it from me.

The drive to the hospital doesn't take long. The time in the waiting room lasts much longer as we await the outcome of Marcus's surgery. Dawn, Ruby, and Bridget comfort a distraught Holly while I sit by Dex's side. He hasn't spoken to me since we left the Black Building, but he grips my hand tight, like I'm his lifeline.

I'm barely holding on myself. Being in hospitals brings back so many dark memories. I know why they don't sell hospital cleaning supplies to the general public—no one would buy them. That smell has to be host to so many horrific memories.

Dex's hair is wild. He's been running his hands through it nonstop since we got here.

"Dexter McClellan?" a doctor calls. He's wearing green scrubs, while a surgeon's mask hangs loosely around his neck.

"I'm him," Dex answers, walking to meet him.

"He made it through surgery, but he's still not out of the woods," the doctor says, placing a comforting hand on Dex's shoulder. "You can go back and see him, but only one at a time."

Dex asks a few questions, and the doctor answers them, leaving Dex with directions to Marcus's room. When he turns his eyes to me, they look haunted, pleading.

"Go to him," I say. "He needs your strength right now. I'll be fine."

He nods absently. I watch him walk down the hall to the all-too-familiar doors leading into the ICU. They slide open silently in front of him, and he disappears inside.

I go to Holly in his absence. Stroking her hair as she curls into my shoulder, I ask the question that has been stuck in my mind since we left the Black Building.

"What happened?"

She's silent for a moment. "Some sick son of a bitch. It all happened fuckin' fast. I didn't see his face. The fucker grabbed me. Started dragging me toward the emergency exit. Marcus tackled him. Then the shots." She blinks, shaking her head. "Marcus didn't bleed like I expected him to. We were stepped on. People were panicking to get out. There were just dark holes in his shirt. His eyes rolled back in his head. So pale."

A sob wrenches from her mouth. Her body is trembling again.

"He was after *you*?" I ask, tears welling in my eyes.

My heart was breaking for her, with her, because of her.

"Yeah," she chokes out.

Fuck. He's trying to hurt me through my friends. We hear a commotion down the hall, doctors and nurses rushing into the ICU.

"Dawn," I say turning my attention back to my friends. "When you leave here, take her back to your place. I think it's safer for all of you to be in the Black Building right now. I can't—"

Dawn takes my hand with a nod. "Of course, we'll stay

safe. But you need to, too."

Dex stumbles out of the ICU, interrupting my reply. He leans against the wall, pressing the heel of his hands into his eyes before his legs give out and he slides down.

It all happens in slow motion. Or at least it feels like it.

Jumping from my seat, I feel like my feet are stuck in tar. I can't get to him fast enough. Holly moves with me, but Bridget and Ruby catch her as she falls to her knees. A keening wail that'll haunt my dreams escapes Holly's lips. Dex doesn't look up. His shoulders jerk and I know he's crying.

My feet falter, and I slide the last few feet to his side. I wrap my arms around him. He pulls me to him and releases a sob. It hurts. His pain is blinding as it ricochets through me. I've heard that loving someone means that you feel their pain more fully than your own. At this moment, I know that nothing can be more true.

He doesn't have to speak. I know. I know that Marcus didn't make it. Holly knows it, too. And my heart breaks for both of them.

Then

"Did you ever think that maybe you should think twice before accusing your fiancée of cheating on you in a public place? That maybe I've never given you a reason to doubt me? And maybe it wasn't fucking smart to air our dirty laundry for everyone with a fucking cell phone to record?" I said, breaking the long-held silence as I flung the car door open.

I'd kept quiet the entire ride back home, but I was just stewing in my anger. I had to say something, and he was going to hear it. Jared got out of the car, slamming the door. I turned and left the garage. He followed me after hitting the button to close the garage door.

"No reason?" He spat the words at me. "Every time you're near him I have reason to doubt you. You've never seen that type of longing on my face for anyone."

"Oh, please." I stopped and turned to face him. "I've seen him a total of three times over the last three years. Two of which you were there for, and the other time, four other people were there who each told you that nothing fucking happened." I turned back to the house and kept walking.

"Those were the only times I found out about. There could be more. There probably is; otherwise, why the fuck is he still hanging onto hope after three fucking years!" His voice held a slightly hysterical tone.

"I don't know what his problem is, but that's just it. It's *his* problem."

I unlocked the door and went into the house. He followed me, shutting off the alarm.

"You still haven't explained why you two were in the bathroom together."

"That's because, one, you never fucking asked. And two, you haven't even given me a chance. You just flew off the fucking handle. And I can deal with your PTSD bullshit, but when you start accusing me of shit without so much as a second to explain, that's too fucking much to handle."

"Then explain it to me now, Maddie."

"Why bother? It crystal fucking clear that you have such a low opinion of me that no matter what I say, you won't believe me. Why are you even with me if this is how you feel?"

"Or maybe you have something to hide?"

"Or maybe you're just a jealous asshole," I said, turning around and leaning toward him, "because you know deep down that he was a way better fuck than you. He wasn't satisfied focusing on what made him happy. He took the time to get to know me, and he knows parts of me that you'll never know because he wasn't a selfish dick—"

The room exploded into stars as his hand cracked across my face. Tears sprang from my eyes unbidden, and my body reacted out of instinct as I moved to take him down to the ground where I'd a better chance of fighting back. I'm not sure why I wasn't prepared for his countermove, but it still caught me off guard. I lost my footing and fell backward. I twisted to catch myself but wasn't quick enough, and my cheekbone slammed hard into the edge of the coffee table.

I sat there, stunned for a second, before he came at me again. I met his momentum with the heel of my palm to his nose. He fell back, and I took the opening to wrap my legs around his waist, but before I could get a lock on his arms, his head flew back as he bucked and nailed me in the forehead. I dropped back as black spots floated in my vision. He twisted around, and his hands wrapped around my neck, cutting off my air.

His eyes were vacant as if he wasn't seeing me as I clawed at him.

"Jared," I managed to croak out with a gasp.

His eyes refocused and his hands were gone from my neck as his jaw dropped. He crab-crawled backward away from me.

"Maddie—fuck—I'm sorry—" He clawed at his head, pulling on his hair. A sob tore through him. "What the fuck am I doing, Maddie? What's wrong with me?"

I fought to catch my breath, my throat tight. "Get out," I wheezed.

"Maddie, please. I'm sorry. I didn't know—I thought I was *there*."

"You need help, but I can't give it to you. We—I can't." I pulled his ring off my finger and tossed it toward him. "I won't marry you until you get better. *If* that ever happens."

"Fuck, please don't do this." He crawled back toward me, and I cringed away from him. He hesitated. "I didn't mean to do it. I swear, I'll get help. I'll go to a live-in clinic for however long. Just, please don't give up on me—on us."

"I don't want you near the girls either." I closed my eyes to shut out the vision of his pleading eyes.

"Maddie—"

"I don't want to hear anything else from you. You're dangerous, Jared. You could've killed me. You need to leave. Right. Fucking. Now!" I yelled as loud as my voice would go.

It was coarse and choked sounding, even to my own ears.

He sobbed again, "I can't live without you. I need you, please."

"Get out!" I used every last bit of energy and vocal capacity that was left in me to scream those words at him.

He didn't say another word as he got up and left the house.

I didn't move, just leaned back against the couch and let the tears roll down my face. *What the hell did I do to deserve this? Where did we go fucking wrong?* We were happy once. And I know I said shit that I shouldn't have said. But we couldn't continue like this. I was becoming someone I didn't recognize anymore. And I was beginning to fear that next time—if I let there be a next time—he would kill me.

Chapter Twenty-Three

Now

Dex wants to hide me. He says it's because he needs me even more, now that he lost his best friend. My heart is broken for him. For Holly. Holly is devastated. They took her to Dawn's place in the Black Building. It's secure enough to keep them safe. Everyone is on lockdown.

Dex, however, decides he's taking me to his dad's place. He's back to not talking, but I think he's insistent because he needs Audra, too. Which is sweet, even if I'm not entirely sure it's a great idea. I'm a walking target. People in my orbit are getting hurt and even dying.

Part of me wants to jump out of the car and just run away. Let the bad man have me, keep everyone else safe. Then the more rational part connects this to fear of meeting his father. The asshole who abandoned him and his mother. I already don't like the dick, so I doubt this will go over well.

The drive there is long. Not because it's far away, but because he's been driving in circles and twists, making sure no one is following us. It's given me too much time to waffle between the jumping and the staying.

It helps that Dex has tethered me. Our fingers intertwine on my lap. "On the Vista" by Blakroc plays over the radio from Dex's phone. The melancholy beats fit the mood, perhaps even set it.

We pull up outside the sprawling ranch house in the heart of a gated community. This place is money. Dex parks behind a blue rental car on the circle drive. The driveway is long, winding its way to a three-car garage. Two motorcycles sit under fitted covers in front of one of the garage doors, but no other cars are visible.

Dex stares at the house before killing the engine. He's holding on to me, but he feels so far away. I can't help myself; I need to close the distance. I slide in between him and the steering wheel, straddling his lap.

"Talk to me," I whisper in his ear.

He ignores my request and captures my lips with his.

"Dex," I sigh. "I love you."

I break the contact and run my fingers over his face, tracing his scar, the beauty marks, his full lips that are darkened from kisses. I want to stare at this face for the rest of my life.

My hair curtains us in. It feels like the world no longer exists. I place his hand over my heart.

"You're in here. You have a home here. Feel free to hide here from your pain. I'll always protect you with everything I have, but please don't hide from me. Don't pull away."

"Never," he says, pulling my face back to his and recapturing my lips. When he breaks away, he continues. "You're my soul, Maddie. You're everything that's good in me. The only light I got left."

Despite the heavy cloud of death that hangs over us, I find a smile pulling at the corners of my mouth.

"We should probably go in, though, and stop making out in front of my dad's house. It's a little awkward," he says, an answering grin fighting for purchase on his face.

I nod, but make no move to get up. "Yeah, that's probably a good idea."

He pops the handle to his door and helps me climb out. I stare at the house and decide I'm ready. I want to meet his family. I want him to be a part of my family. He's opening the trunk to get our bags when I walk past him to the door.

There's a porch that spans almost the full length of the house. I step onto it, looking back to make sure Dex is coming. I poise my hand above the doorbell, but before I can push it, the door swings open.

Broad shoulders and a defined chest fill the frame. My gaze tracks up the muscular build to meet eyes filled with flecks of gold, green, and blue. The world shifts beneath me, and I'm rocked to the core.

"Laine?" *that voice* asks.

What we did was wrong.

You're a dead man.

He hurt you.

It was our fault.

Flashes of the past take over all rational thought. My legs give out as darkness flecked with bright spots begin to crowd my vision. I expect to hit the ground, but instead, I'm back in familiar arms again. He catches me, pulling me into his body.

"Law?" The question leaks out of me in a breathless rasp.

Then

I don't know how long I'd sat there, when the doorbell rang, and my body carried me on autopilot to the door. My mind was wrecked; I couldn't think straight. I opened the door without even thinking to look at who could be there.

Law stood there, his hand rubbing the back of his neck, his eyes trained on the ground. His hair was a mess, and he'd lost the suit coat and tie. His sleeves were rolled up his forearms, exposing his colorful tattoos.

"I wanted to apologize for the way I acted, with both you and him. I'd like to talk to—" He cut off as he looked at me. His eyes went from apologetic to furious in a blink. His hand slammed into the door, and he pushed past me. "Where is he? I'm going to fucking kill him."

"He's not here."

He turned back to me, and his eyes softened. "Are you okay?"

"Yeah, I'm fine," I answered as he walked back to where I stood near the doorway.

"You're not fine. He hurt you."

He reached up toward my face, and I flinched. He grimaced and gently grasped my chin, brushing his fingertips over my uninjured cheek.

"Where is your first aid kit?"

"In the kitchen. Why?"

"I'm going to clean the blood off your face."

"I've blood on my face?" I asked in disbelief as I reached up to touch my cheek. I winced at the wetness and pulled my hand back, red coating my fingertips.

"Come on," Law said, shutting the front door. "Take me to the kitchen. Let's get you cleaned up."

I turned and walked into the kitchen, grabbing the first aid kit and setting it on the counter. Law's hand covered mine before I could let go. I could feel the heat of his body behind me. He brushed my hair off my shoulder.

"I'm sorry for this. I'm feeling kind of responsible because it wouldn't have happened if I wasn't an ass. Seems that's all I ever do with you is fuck up."

"It's not your fault," I said, turning back to look up at him. "You were just trying to help. It just turned into a bad situation. This—" I pointed to my face. "This isn't your fault at all."

He gripped my hips and hoisted me up onto the counter, so we were closer to eye level with each other.

He looked away to open the first aid kit. "I shouldn't have let you leave with him when he was obviously—"

"You didn't let me do anything. This isn't your problem. We've been out of each other's lives longer than we were ever in them."

He tore some paper towels off the roll on the counter and wet them. He tilted my chin back with his thumb, his fingers gently curving around the back of my neck. He started wiping my face down, working around the injured parts.

"That's not true. We may not be physically near, but you're always with me, Laine. I started fighting for you." I made a face at him. He gave me a sad smile. "I was always talented in the ring, I just didn't have the drive. But I wanted to prove myself worthy of you. Make you see me as your equal. A man, not just some punk kid that screwed around with his friends in a garage band. I thought—" He shook his head. "It doesn't matter what I thought. It was bad enough for me to lose you, but then you went and got famous. Now there's pictures of you in magazines and on the internet. I turn on the TV—I see a story on you. I listen to the radio— hear your songs." His eyes darted back and forth as he searched my eyes; looking for what, I didn't know.

"Sorry," I said, at a loss for what else to say. I looked down at my hand to avoid his inquisitive stare.

He snorted. "Stop being sorry for things you can't control, Laine."

I raised one eyebrow at him. "Isn't this how this conversation started?"

"Touché." He smirked and that dimple I loved so much appeared. "Still, it's not going to stop me from feeling like shit for not protecting you."

He pulled out the hydrogen peroxide. "This might sting a bit," he said, putting the liquid on a piece of gauze.

It won't, I thought. But he didn't know that. He tilted my head back again and with a featherlight touch started cleaning the cut on my cheek. It didn't take long for the hunger to settle in his eyes.

"Fuck, stop." I shoved his hand away, annoyed by the tenderness he was showing when I knew I didn't deserve it.

He chuckled and blew gently on the cut, thinking that it was the pain that bothered me. He gripped my chin a little firmer. "Hold still, I just have a little bit more to clean up. Then we can move on from this."

He touched the cut again, and I started to bitch about it, but then his mouth was on mine. My open mouth gave him instant access, and his tongue stroked against mine. I was shocked at first, but then the familiarity of his kiss washed over me. I didn't think; I just reacted and kissed him back.

His hands dove into my hair, and as I responded, his grip on my hair tightened. It had been so long since someone had kissed me like they were suffocating, and I was the air they needed to breathe. So long since someone handled me like they were sure I wouldn't break under a firm grip. I moaned, the shock of the sound snapping me back to reality, and I pulled away. We stared at each other, our breathing labored.

"Sorry," he said, looking anything but. "I couldn't think of a better way to distract you. It's the only thing on my mind when I'm around you."

"I—" I stopped because I couldn't think of what to say.

He turned back to the first aid kit and grabbed a butterfly bandage, applying it to my cheek. It gave me a break from all the intensity. I knew that if I was truly honest with myself, I never stopped loving him. But this just wasn't the time or the place for that kind of conversation. "All done." He closed the first aid kit and returned it to the cabinet.

"Law," I said, placing my hand on his forearm. "Thank you. For taking care of me. For coming to apologize—"

His stare was intense, looking at my left hand as it rested on his arm. "You're not wearing his ring."

"Um, did you fail to catch on to what happened?" I pointed at my face.

He leaned forward, resting his hands on the counter on either side of me. "What did happen, Laine?" His brows pinched and his jaw clenched, as his lips pressed into a flat line.

"I said something I shouldn't've," I said, focusing on my hands. I couldn't tell him what started it. I really didn't want to talk about it. Especially not with him, the source of the anger that fed into that fight. I looked up at him as he stared at me in silence, waiting for an answer. I sighed in frustration. "What do you want from me, Law?"

"Why would he get so pissed about me? Why would it

escalate to this when you got home? I've only seen you a handful of times, and you're not the kind that strays, but he doesn't seem like the kind of guy to act like that without reason."

"He was here when you left. He got to watch me every day, going through the motions but not really living. He sat by for months while I…" I shook my head, not wanting to go there. "But really the biggest problem was that he heard you that day at the derby. You basically told him that I've a preference for rough sex and ass play." I could feel the anger swelling up in me again. *Fucking Law.* "And he's not like that. He's not into kinky shit at all. Is that what you want to hear? He doesn't know about the rest of it. Fucking Lord knows that would send him further into crazy town than he's already gone."

"That was years ago," he said, confusion stamped on his face. "He's been giving you shit for that this whole time? Why would you even agree to marry him?"

"No. He wasn't like that at all. It wasn't until he got back from this last deployment. I didn't even know that he had heard you. But he's changed. I know he has PTSD, and we've been trying to get him to get help… but the tour… none of it makes it any easier for him."

"He's been doing this since he got back?" His voice was low, with a deadly undertone that caused me to look up. His arm muscles were bulging with the strain of his grip on the edge of the counter. From his look, it was clear that he thought Jared had been beating me on a regular basis.

"No," I defended. "This is the first time he's ever laid a hand on me."

"Then what would set him off like this, Laine?" He raised his voice, his disbelief apparent in his tone.

"I told him you were a better fuck, okay?" I yelled. "Is that what you want to hear? Does that make you happy? I rubbed it in his face that you'll always be something more than he'll ever be. And it doesn't help that he had to sit by and watch me fall apart when you left. You fucking destroyed me, Law.

He tried to put me back together, but he never had all the pieces."

"I destroyed you? You broke up with me."

"Because you wouldn't accept that moving here was the right thing to do. It could've been temporary—you could've been here every night to fuck me in this house while he had to watch you come and go—but you chose to walk away. You didn't even put up a fight. You just left town. You cut me off. So don't fucking sit there and act like you were the victim."

"Fuck, Laine. I see that clearly now, but back then I thought that you were choosing him." He pushed back from the counter and paced the kitchen floor. "He had the means to support you, and I didn't. I started boxing to prove to you that I could be that man. That I could take care of you and your girls. But when I came back, it was too fucking late." His hand went to the back of his neck. "I thought I knew what love was until I met you. But you—you're the kind that no amount of space or time will let me forget just how stupid I was." He tipped his head back and laughed. Silence followed. Then he pinned me with his gaze. "You're not with him anymore. You want me to fight?" He took two steps and was back in front of me.

I opened my mouth to reply, and he crashed into me, his tongue taking advantage of my open mouth. And this kiss was different. It was claiming, consuming. His hands fisted my hair, pulling my head back to the exact angle he wanted it at. My body responded to him like the puppet he trained it to be. His arm fell down to my waist, and he pulled me toward him so we were pressed together. I ground against him, and he groaned.

Common sense warred with desire in my brain. It felt so good, my willpower was slipping further away by the second.

"Stop," I gasped in a brief second his mouth parted from mine.

He pressed himself tighter against me until I could feel his hard length against the apex of my thighs, the heat rolling off of him, the way he thrust against me—so eager he couldn't stop the instinct to drive into me, even with clothes on.

"I'm not stopping until my cock is deep inside your pussy where it belongs," he pulled away and said between the kisses and nips he trailed down my neck. "I'm making you mine again, Laine. So you need to use our safe word if this is too much."

He bit down on my nipple through my dress, and my head fell back as a keening moan escaped my lips. I couldn't bring myself to say the word. I couldn't stop. I'd been needing this for so long. Deprived of someone who knew my body and how to give me what I needed without asking. Without choice. His hand slid up my skirt and pressed into the throbbing bundle of nerves. He pushed my panties aside, and his finger slipped into me.

"Jesus, you're wet, Bumpkin."

My body shivered at the name and the sensations his hand was drawing out as his fingers entered me. His mouth was back on mine while his fingers worked me toward release. It didn't take long after being denied for so long, the pressure built up within me like a freight train barreling toward a cliff's edge. I was powerless to stop it, and I didn't want to.

It started in little pulses to the rhythm of his fingers pumping in and out. Tiny waves of pleasure that had me gasping out disconnected moans. Then it exploded as he pinched my clit and bit down on my nipple at the same time. A scream throttled out of me as I hit the crest of pleasure.

His fingers disappeared, and his cock slammed into me before I came down from my orgasm, each thrust drawing out the pleasure in waves. His fingertips dug into the cheeks of my ass as he pounded into me.

"You're mine, Laine. You were made for me. We were made for each other," he growled in my ear before he bit down on my shoulder.

I cried out in veneration. He was undoing me, dismantling every condemnation that I'd felt toward myself and what I craved by giving it to me while slaking his own thirst. He lifted me up, walking across the room until my back slammed into the door of the pantry. His rhythm was relentless. It was raw and primal. Each thrust felt like an exaltation. I felt it, too—the relief of letting go, giving in to the intrinsic urges that were inherent in who we were at our core.

I ripped open his shirt, buttons clattering to the floor. My fingernails were desperate to rake into his skin. My mind barely registered the new ink across his chest as I clawed his back. One of his hands gripped the neckline of my dress, and the sound of ripping fabric echoed in my mind as the cloth gave way and his mouth found my breasts. I bit down on his shoulder and he groaned, quickening his pace.

His thumb returned to the bundle of nerves at my center, and the fingers of his other hand teased my puckered hole.

"Come," he breathed in my ear.

I detonated at his whispered command, submitting my pleasure to him. The orgasm barreled through my body, my brain losing control of everything. Synapses failed to communicate anything else but the overwhelming sensation of release. I screamed as my limbs convulsed, and his pace increased until he found his release. He collapsed against me, pressing me into the door.

We stayed there, still joined together, breathing heavily into the silence. He searched my eyes, his own filled with such reverence. A crooked smile tugged up the corner of his mouth and his dimple appeared.

"You okay?" he asked.

"Yeah," I answered between ragged breaths.

Crash!

Something fragile shattered from the front of the house, followed by the front door slamming. The reality of everything came crashing back to me with that sound. Guilt flooded me. *Fuck.* I pushed at Law and scrambled to put myself back together as I raced for the door, Law right behind me.

I flung the front door open and ran to the end of the driveway, to the open security gate that surrounded the house. *He was here. I know he was. He saw everything.* I looked both ways down the road—nothing. I collapsed to the ground as sobs released from my body.

"Laine?"

"It had to be Jared. He saw us, Law. Fuck. What have we done? What was I thinking?" I said, looking down at the raw scrapes in my palms from the concrete below me. The scuff of Law's shoes on the pavement gave away his movement toward me. "You need to leave."

He stopped. "Laine—"

"Go!" I screamed. "Leave, now. I've gotta find him."

I pulled myself up from the ground and ran back into the house.

Chapter Twenty-Four

Now

His hands frame my face as he searches my eyes. *Law.* I'm
standing in front of Law. My mind has slowed to—before I
even have a chance to think, his hopeful mouth ensnares
mine. Chills sweep my spine with the familiarity of it all. My
mind blanks. He pulls me to him until our bodies are sealed
together. He's so much larger and more defined, a champion
fighter in his own right, but still as familiar as a well-worn
glove.

"Bumpkin," he whispers, breaking away and resting his
forehead on mine. "God, I've missed you so much. Sloane
told you I was in town?"

I shake my head. I've no words. Tears fill my eyes. The
anger I usually feel toward him isn't there, and it shocks me
enough that I forget why I'm here and who I'm with.

Years ago, Law told me he had a brother. One that he
hated—for reasons he never told me about.

Dex mentioned it, too, when we first met. His brother
that'd been in a local punk band. And what he did to destroy
that relationship—Audra's mom.

They look nothing alike, Dex and Law. Though, now that
I know, I can see a little of Holden Russo in Dex. He's got
his father's build. The dimples. *What in the actual fuck. What're*

the odds? I was more worried that Dex knew who I was when we first met, I didn't give much thought to whether I knew anyone in his family.

Fuck.

Law's eyes finally flit over my shoulder.

"Hey, Dex. Audra's inside with Sloane," Law explained. "Where's the girlfriend she said you were bringing? Have you met—"

His arms loosen from around me and then fall away. I'm going to throw up. This can't be happening. I see it click into place in Law's eyes with a slight widening, followed by a cold, hard veil descending.

I close my eyes. Maybe this will all vanish. I'm roughly shoved to the side. I turn just in time to see them crash into each other.

"Is this supposed to be payback? Kissing the first girlfriend I bring home?" Dex grits out between clenched teeth.

"No. *This* is payback." Law's fist swings low, catching Dex in the ribs.

My gasp is drowned out by the yelling and grunting. Dex picks Law by his thighs, and they both go crashing to the ground. I take a second to thank God that they moved to the grass before starting this Neanderthal horseshit.

"What the fuck?" comes from over my shoulder. I look back to Sloane's horrified eyes as they turn on me. Without taking her eyes off me, she screeches, "Daaaaaaaaad!"

I shrink back in on myself. *What the fuck have I done?* Tears well in my eyes. I can't love without destruction. I'm so naive I poison lives. I always make the worst choices, fall for the wrong people. Nothing in my life can ever be simple.

She takes large strides and is in front of me in an instant. "No, no, no. You don't get to shut down on me again. What are you doing here? I told you I'd be by after Thanksgiving. I didn't call because I knew he'd be here." She tips her head in Law's direction. "And you wouldn't want to see him." She looks over to where the two brothers grapple, and then back to me with confusion. "Why are they fighting?"

"Cut it out!" Holden roars, appearing in the doorway.

Audra's face peeks out, too, and Sloane moves quickly to shuffle her back inside and close the door.

Law and Dex are grappling on the ground. Occasionally trading punches, they flail and struggle until Law is straddling Dex's back and Dex has Law's arms trapped in his armpits. Both of their faces are red with strain. Though they look calm, they're still struggling for the upper hand. Holden walks straight up to them and smacks Law in the back of the head, dragging him off Dex. Law lunges and twists in Holden's grip before he stumbles away.

"What the fuck is going on with you two dipshits?" Holden asks. "You're acting like goddamn teenagers."

"He kissed my girlfriend," Dex groans.

Sloane gasps behind me. Law lunges, going after Dex before he's fully upright. Holden plants his palm on Law's chest and shoves him back, stepping between them.

"He's fucking my girl," Law says, then leans around to pin Dex with a glare. "Again."

I cringe. "I haven't been your girl for a long time, Law."

Law turns his glare on me. "I said I'd give you time and space to get over what happened to *him*. But you never stopped being mine."

"I'm better. I've been for a while. But I didn't come back to you, because we can't go back. What we did was beyond fucked up." I know, once I say the words, that I'm wrong. I don't know when it happened that I moved past the blinding guilt. Sometime over the last few weeks. I think Dex is part of the reason I started to see things differently. Some of it was Marcus's death, but I've given more credence to the murder theory with all that's happened lately.

"We didn't kill him." Law is seething.

Everyone else is silent. I can feel the weight of their questions in the air.

"Maybe you're right. But we crossed a line. Whether he killed himself or was murdered, we fucked up. And you weren't the one that finally made me see that."

"This is why you blame yourself?" Dex asks. "Why didn't you tell me?"

"Because knowing that I fucked Law the night Jared died wouldn't help you solve the murder if there was one. I never told anyone about what we did. It helps nothing to rehash it."

"I told you everything," Dex says, defeat laced in his voice. "You know the history here. I can't—I need to clear my head. I don't—"

"What—" I try to ask.

"I'm going for a ride. Stay here. I'm sure my brother can keep you safe." He cuts a glare at Law and pivots on his heel.

"Don't leave," I plea. "We need to talk about this. I'm sorry. I should've told you."

I chase after him as he walks up the drive to uncover his Harley and hop on the bike. Not looking up, he starts the engine. I stop his hand before he puts on the helmet.

I shout over the grumbling motorcycle, "Please, just talk to me."

"I'm not the one who has a problem talking. And this isn't just about you. I'm trying to be a better man, and taking something else from my brother doesn't fit with that."

"I'm yours, Dex."

"I'd like to think that, Maddie. But I'm not so sure anymore."

He slides on his helmet and drives away. And I feel it this moment, a pain so intense it leaves me breathless. A pain so deep it tears into my soul. What I feel for Dex isn't normal. It isn't what I had with Jared, and it isn't what I had with Law. It's more. And when he turns the corner out of sight, it feels like someone's piercing my heart with a poisoned blade.

He's a better man. He isn't perfect, but he's perfect for me. The match to my crazy. The only one who will ever understand every facet of my being. He's the one. The one I'm willing to put in the work for. Do anything.

I know—I know without a shadow of a doubt that I can't let him walk away. I have to go after him.

Then

I threw on the first coat I could find and grabbed my purse and my keys, and was driving down the road before I knew what I was doing. I'd no idea where to go. I looked down at the gauges and realized that my gas tank was on the wrong side of the red line. Shit.

I pulled into the nearest gas station and started filling up the gas tank while I thought about what I needed to do. I tried calling Jared's phone, but it went straight to voicemail. Nic had moved to LA last month, so that wasn't an option. Maybe Asher would know? I pulled out my phone and hit Asher's number.

"Mads?" Asher answered. His voice was rough and I heard a sniffle, like he'd been crying. I felt bad for him; he must've been really taking the split with Holly hard.

"Do you know where Jared is? Have you seen him tonight?"

"No—no. I thought y'all were having a date night. How would I know where he is? Did something happen?"

"What didn't happen? I need to find him. Now. I don't know, Ash. I don't know what I'm doin'." I pulled my hair in frustration. The lady pumping gas on the other side of the pump had leaned over and was looking at me. "What the fuck're you lookin' at?" I yelled at her.

He took an audible shaky breath. "Where are you?"

"I'm at a gas station." My mind was racing a million miles a second. It was hard to keep my thoughts together. "My tank was on empty, but I'm going to find him. I gotta…"

"Which one?"

"What?" I asked, already forgetting what he was talking about.

"Which gas station, Maddie?" he asked louder and slowly. "I'm coming to get you. You're upset. You don't need to be out driving around by yourself."

I paced back and forth in front of the gas pump. "I don't have time for that. I need to find him."

"I'm in my truck already. When you're done getting gas, I'll be there. We'll go find him together. Okay?" His voice was soft, higher-pitched, like he was talking to a child.

"Asher, you're not hearing me." I was getting more and more frustrated. "I don't have time for that. I fucked up. I need to find him, now."

"I get that. We can find him faster together. Just tell me where you're at. Please."

I sighed, relenting. "I'm at the corner of South Lamar and Barton Springs."

"I'm on my way. Stay on the phone with me okay?" The sound of his engine starting came through the line, his voice sounding farther away as the phone switched to hands-free. "Tell me what happened."

"Him and Law got into a fight at the Driskill." I cringed. Just saying Law's name brought forth a flood of guilt and shame. "I broke off the engagement."

"What do you mean, they got in a fight?"

"I mean they were beating the shit out of each other until Holden broke them up. I'm willing to bet it's already on YouTube somewhere. There were plenty of people there, and they caused a huge scene."

"Do you have any idea where he might go?"

"No, my only idea was that he was with you. Evan is currently stationed in Seattle, and Nic is in LA now. He doesn't have any other friends here, besides you. That's why I called you."

"I'm pulling into the gas station. Do you see me?"

His truck was just pulling in. I waved and hung up the phone. He parked in front of the store and got out. I could see the worry etched on his face behind the red puffy eyes as he approached me, but as he got closer, his look grew darker.

"What the fuck?" He grabbed my shoulder, forcing me to face him. "Maddie, are you okay?"

"Yeah, I'm fine." I waved him off.

"Your cheek is split open, you have a lump on your forehead the size of a Ping-Pong ball, you have bruises on your neck, your dress is ripped. Please tell me that he didn't—" He turned away, his lips drawn tight into a straight line. "And you call me telling me that *you* fucked up!"

He turned and walked back to his truck, punching the tailgate. He leaned against the truck for a second. His shoulders dropped. He sat there in that pose for a few moments before he walked back to me.

"You broke up with him for this?" he asked, and I nodded. He looked conflicted about that news as he stood there motionless for a moment. "I know he was a good guy, but whatever happened to him over there fucked him up. I'm so sorry, Maddie." He squeezed his eyes shut tight and pinched the bridge of his nose, like he was fighting back tears. "This shit isn't cool." He waved his hand to encompass my current state. "Give me your keys."

The state of my brain at the moment made it hard to keep up with the sudden change in subject. "Huh?"

"Give me your keys. I'm gonna park your car over there." He pointed to a parking spot at the side of the gas station. "Or haven't you noticed that the gas quit pumping already? Probably a while ago."

I startled at the thought. I'd forgotten what I was even doing standing here. I held out the keys without a word and walked over to his truck. It was unlocked, so I slid into the passenger seat to wait for him. I leaned my head against the cool glass window. There was a bitter metallic smell in his truck that I couldn't quite place.

Asher got in the truck. He placed my keys in my purse and set it on the center console between us. He started the engine and leaned back in his seat, letting out an audible breath.

"Where—" he started, but was interrupted by my phone ringing.

I looked down at the unfamiliar phone number. At least it wasn't unknown. I answered.

"Hello?"

"Good evening, is this Laine Dobransky?"

"Yes," I replied.

"This is Carol from Counterforce Security. We got an alarm in progress at your place of business, Barton Creek Recording. I'm calling to ensure this isn't a false alarm?"

"I'm not on the premises, so I can't answer that."

"Thank you, ma'am, the local authorities have been notified."

"Okay, thank you." I hung up.

"Who was that?" Asher asked.

My voice came out distant and flat as my mind raced. "Someone broke into the studio."

"You think it's him?"

"Yeah, let's go." On the outside, I sounded confident, but inside, I wasn't so sure.

Jared knew the security codes. He would've turned them off before an alarm was reported. A sense of dread filled me, along with wavering, uncertain thoughts. Either something was horribly wrong, or yet another problem was looming on the horizon.

Chapter Twenty-Five

Now

I know I shouldn't be doing this, but I can't help it. I need him. I need him to see that there's no comparison. He's it for me. We've lost too much in the past twenty-four hours. He lost Marcus, and I'm not going to lose him. And Dex's importance to me painted a target on his back.

I pop the hood of the car and pull the screwdriver from the glove compartment. I prop up the hood and hone in on what I need. Bingo. Dex took the keys, so I'm forced to jack my own damn car to go look for him.

I don't have specific memories of my father, but for some reason, I know that he's the one who taught me how to do this. Just like I know that he's the one who taught me to work on cars. But that's more because Evan's dad, Gary, helped me carry on the tradition. He gave me a thread, a lifeline, to hold onto my father's memory. Not that it worked, but I still have his car and the skills to fix them.

Mounted on the firewall behind the driver's-side valve cover is the starter relay. All I gotta do is bypass the relay connection. I use the metal screwdriver, and it sparks, the engine roaring to life. The advantage of classic cars is that it's an easy fix if keys are forgotten or lost. The disadvantage is that they're much easier to steal if the thief knows what they're doing.

"I'm not letting you go," Law says from across the hood. "You need to stay here. Wasn't he bringing you here because someone is after you?"

Ignoring his question, I finish with the car. "When are you going to learn that you never *let* me do anything?" I slam the hood down to punctuate my words. "His best friend just died! Because of me. And then he learns that his girlfriend is also his brother's ex! How do you not see that as a problem? I need to find him. I need to explain everything to him before I lose him."

"You're not just my ex, Laine." He grips my arm to stop me.

I shake him off. "Well, I'm certainly not your girlfriend."

"You're mine. We fit, Bumpkin."

I laugh manically. "That's rich. We don't get to go back. I know better than most that it doesn't work. People change, and given time—space, they grow apart. Besides, you never wanted a family. You only wanted me, and that doesn't work for me. We only worked when I pretended that the rest of my life didn't matter. When I deluded myself into thinking that I could lead two lives."

"You're right, people change." He backs me into the car, caging me in with his arms. "And you're wrong about me. I want the family. I want more than just you and your girls. I want kids of our own too. I want—I need you. All of it. And I've waited long enough already. Too long."

Shock sets in. My mouth bobs open as I grapple for a response.

"I can't do this with you again. It's been four years, and if you were as dead set on me as you say, you would've shown up before now. But yeah, it probably was a pretty sweet gig. Fuck anything you want, whenever you want, knowing that you can come back and claim me anytime. Life must have seemed peachy-fuckin'-keen from your point of view," I scoff.

"I didn't—"

"I love him," I say, cutting him off. "I'm in love with him."

He shakes his head. "Why do you always do this—undercut my emotions with your assumptions? Never give me a chance to get a word in edgewise. Not just listen, but actually hear me, Bumpkin."

This conversation is just wasting time, and I'm losing ground to catch up with Dex. I need to end it.

"I need to find him. Get outta my way." I shove him hard, and he doesn't budge but reluctantly steps back.

I can see the hurt in his eyes as I step sideways and slide into the driver's seat. He rubs the back of his neck and watches me, his jaw clenched tight. I put the car in reverse and back up, faster than necessary. But I've time to make up for. The tires squeal as I hit the road and spin the wheel hard to straighten. I've a moment when I pause to shift into drive where I think that Dex would be proud of that move. I hit the gas, and the tires spin for a second before they catch traction. I need to find Dex. If the stalker is going after people I love, Dex's going to be a prime target.

I drive the neighborhood but don't spot him. *Maybe he went home?* Maybe he needed to paint out the frustration, or something. *This is pointless.* But it's better than sitting still, waiting for a phone call that he's dead. I'm sick with the idea that I'll relive the agony of losing another loved one.

It's pretty clear to me at this point that my suicide theory isn't holding water against the weight of Marcus's death. I shiver at the thought that he meant to get Holly, but it's clear to me that he's got no problem killing. How could the weight of my guilt have kept me blinded for so long?

I merge from Mopac onto 290, then take the South Lamar exit to get back to our side of town. My eyes are tracking every motorcycle on the road, but I don't see him.

I'm approaching Oltorf, trying to decide if I want to take a right and see if he went to his father's gym, which is a block away, or head straight to his home. The light is red, so it gives me time to contemplate—

Wham!

My head bounces off the steering wheel as I'm shoved into the intersection by a car that just hit me from behind. *Fuck, that's just what I needed—to waste time with a car wreck.*

Crash.

The rain of glass makes a tinkling sound. Or maybe that's just my imagination. My ears could be ringing, but it seems to syncopate with the glitter of the glass as it catches the fading sunlight. Everything moves in slow motion as my body is suspended by the sudden change in movement.

A truck's grill now takes up what used to be half of my car, the heat radiating off it catches my attention first. If I reach out, I could touch it. My head is half hanging out the window. I'm hanging onto consciousness by a thread when I see the man from the truck get out. He leans into the missing window to ask if I'm okay. I can feel the trickle of blood down my face.

This is bad. Really bad. Because I've no way of knowing how extensive my injuries are. I feel uncomfortable pressure. I don't know what to say but I'm not sure I could answer him if I had the words. The guy accepts my silence, but when he stands, I see the man from the car that rear-ended me.

My mouth tries to form the words, to emit a sound, but nothing comes out. It's in that infinite moment that I realize I know the guy from the car.

Blake is dialing his phone when the other man approaches him. My mouth is open to say something, and I gasp for air to produce a sound when I realize my mouth is covered. Smell—sickly sweet—invades my nose. I'm being pulled back through the open space that used to be the driver's-side window of my car. My body refuses to cooperate, to fight back.

I choke on the noxious fumes, knowing that this is it. My stalker has finally come for me. I can't fight it—him. And the last fleeting thought through my mind before everything fades to black—I'm glad he got me because at least now I know everyone else is safe. Dex is safe.

Then

Jared's truck was in the parking lot of the recording studio when we pulled up. Asher pulled in alongside it. I could feel it immediately—something was off. Even as I opened the door, the fog swirling with the movement, and heard the piercing wail of the building's alarm, I felt it—this gut-wrenching sense of apprehension.

Shutting the truck door, I took a deep breath, steeling myself for the reckoning that was about to happen. The moist air filled my lungs. It felt as heavy as my heart, the leaden weight of the lump in my belly. *How did we get to this point? How did we get so fucked up?*

I couldn't see more than a couple of feet in front of my face, but the flashing red lights of the alarm colored the fog between me and the building, showing the way.

Asher joined me once we reached the sidewalk leading to the building, but stayed silent.

Step by step on shaky legs, I moved closer. Closer to the love of my life. Closer to facing the consequence of my decisions. Shattered glass crunched under my borrowed shoes as I reached the front door that was no more than a metal frame. Someone had broken through it.

"You sure you want to do this?" Asher asked.

I took in a shaky breath to steel my nerves. "Yeah. If it was a burglar, they're likely gone. And Jared is in there. I need to see him. Make sure he's okay."

Asher nodded, frowning, and stepped through the empty doorframe.

I followed, the deafening sound of the alarm increased tenfold once we were inside. I rushed to the panel behind the reception desk to shut it off. Though, my ears still rang with echoes of the alarm in the ensuing silence. The lights weren't turned on, just the standby lighting that was left on during the night, a dim bulb placed every thirty feet or so. Shadows danced in between. My nerves ratcheted up at the thought that anyone could be here, and maybe it was stupid of us not to wait for the police.

"Jared?" I called. No answer. I looked over at Asher, who mostly seemed to be studying the ground. "You take the offices, I'll go look back in the studios."

He nodded and turned down the hallway, his movement quicker than I expected.

I took a right, to the doorway that led to the old building where the recording studios were. Everything looked normal, perfectly in place, not like someone had broken in to vandalize or steal anything. And this would be the area a robber or vandal would go to, with thousands of dollars of equipment lying around.

I walked back farther to the second studio, and still nothing. The lights weren't even on back there. I fumbled in the dark for the light switch. Again, nothing seemed out of place. My stomach twisted in knots.

"Jared? It's me. Can we talk? I don't want to fight anymore. I'm so sorry," I asked the empty room as if he was just hiding.

I blinked furiously against the tears building in my eyes, fighting back the jagged unease that felt like it was expanding inside of me, ready to rip me to shreds from the inside out. I knew. I just knew something bad had happened, and I warred with the panic of finding out just as strongly as the compulsion to know the truth.

I shut the lights off, intent on heading back toward the offices to see if Asher had found him when I walked past the crash pad. *Why didn't I think to look in there?* Of course he would come here for a place to stay—we had beds.

The door creaked as I pushed it open. It was dark, the new moon outside not offering any light through the window.

"Jared? You in here?"

The door jammed against something, but I couldn't see what it was. I felt along the wall for the light switch. When the fluorescent lights flickered on, I realized it was Jared's boot that was behind the door. He was lying across the floor on his stomach, his head turned away.

I dropped to my knees and crawled across the floor to his side, shaking his shoulder.

"Wake up, Jared."

He didn't move. I pulled his opposite shoulder until he rolled over, and his head lolled into my lap. I leaned down and kissed his blue-tinged lips. Tears poured down my face, and there was a distant keening wail.

"Wake up, Jare. I didn't mean it."

I brushed his hair off his forehead. His normally crystalline blue wolflike eyes were cloudy, dull and lifeless.

"You can't leave me," I cooed. "We're running away to the beach together, remember? I was thinking Bali. Does Bali sound good? Please wake up. I love you. I love you so much, Jared."

I rocked him, stroking his hair.

"I didn't mean any of it. We'll get you some help. We'll fix this. It's you, Jared. It's always been you. You're it for me. You can't leave me."

Asher skidded around the doorframe and froze. A loud sob released from him as he took in the sight of us. "Maddie, stop touching him," he begged.

"I can't." I squeezed Jared tighter to me. "I gotta wake him up. We're going to run away and get married in Bali, Asher. Did you know that? We're planning to go after we finished the tour. Just something small and private. I—I'm not going to wear shoes, so I can feel the sand between my toes as we say 'I do.'"

Tears streamed from his eyes as he looked at me with such deep sorrow. "Oh God, Maddie. Come here."

Asher held open his arms, and I shook my head, clinging to Jared even tighter.

"I can't. He's going to wake up. I gotta wake him up, Ash. I can't live—I don't want to—he needs to be okay. The police will be here soon; they'll get an ambulance and take him to the hospital."

The light from flashlights bounced around the darkened hallway behind Asher. Murmured voices echoed as someone approached. Two police officers rounded the corner with guns raised. They started shouting, and Asher talked to them.

I sang my song I wrote for him into his ear, tuning out the commotion.

Is this the end,
of what I knew?
Is this the end,
of what we used to be?

One of the policemen hooked his hand under my arms and tugged on me. I hugged Jared tighter and kissed his forehead.

"No, I can't leave him. He's going to wake up. We're going to Bali to get married soon. I can't just leave him here." I looked up at the officer, pleading with him.

"Ma'am, you're contaminating a crime scene. I need you to leave the room, now."

"Crime scene?" I asked.

"Maddie, come on," Asher coaxed. "Come with me outside. We've got to let them do their jobs. It's going to be okay."

"Where's the EMTs? We need to get him to a hospital. They can help him. He has to get better. He said he'd never leave me again."

Asher pulled me out from under Jared's body and picked me up, carrying me from the room.

Something about leaving the room, the change of the texture of the air without the laden coppery smell of blood, or that I knew I had left him back there, alone with strangers—the tears finally broke free. I wailed into Asher's shoulder as reality came crashing into me. I couldn't stop. I couldn't breathe. What would I tell the girls? This couldn't be happening. I wanted to go back to denying it. I pulled away from Asher's shoulder and realized I was covered in blood—

Jared's blood. Why didn't I see that before?

Asher set me on the couch in the old part of the studio. He sat down next to me and pulled me to him and cried with me. I don't know how long we did that, when a police officer approached.

The officer bent down into my line of vision. "Ma'am, I'm going to need you to stand and turn away from me. And place your hands behind your back."

"What? Why?"

"I need to take you downtown for questioning." His tone was wooden and matter-of-fact.

I looked to Asher, hoping he would rescue me somehow.

Asher nodded to me. "Just do it, Maddie. I'm calling Bridget. They can't hold you for long. You didn't do this."

I felt numb as the cold handcuffs slid over my wrists. The officer led me outside to a waiting police car. Along the street, news crews and photographers gathered. They went into a frenzy of shouting questions and camera flashes. I blinked, unable to comprehend what was happening as the officer placed his hand on top of my head and pushed me into the backseat of the squad car.

Chapter Twenty-Six

Now

The first thing I notice when I start to regain consciousness—my mouth is dry. Like someone had packed my mouth with cotton while I was out. The second thing I notice is the taste. The taste is so vile it has me rolling over to expend the contents of my stomach before I even open my eyes.

Luckily there isn't anything for me to expel because the third thing I notice is that I'm laying on something really soft. It's cloud-like and comfortable, but also has the smooth silkiness of—sheets. I'm in a bed. I blink several times, trying to get my bearings.

It's dark. A thin sliver of faint light is the only thing I can make out of my surroundings, but it smells wrong. The air smells metallic, like rust and steel. This is not my bed. I search my memory, trying to reconcile where I am and how I got here. There are only bits and pieces. Nothing whole to grab onto.

I see a face. *Blake.* I try to remember the last time I saw him; I think it was at the gym years ago. No that's not right— it was when he installed my alarm system. My heart rate picks up. He had access to me—to my home because he knew how my alarm system worked. I feel like I'm going to throw up again, but not from the taste. Dex was right, I did know my stalker, he just played such a minor role in my life that I never gave him a second thought.

Memories start flashing behind my closed eyes. The car wreck—being rear-ended by Blake and pushed into the intersection for another hit. The twinkling lights that played off the shattered glass as time suspended. Then the smell. *Taken.*

I'm not supposed to be here. I reach out and feel for the edge of the bed and then move my feet to hang off the end and reach the floor. Cold. Hard. It's made of some sort of stone, and I'm definitely barefoot. I run my hands over my body to check for clothes now that I'm thinking about it. I'm wearing something, but it's not my clothes. The T-shirt is too large to be mine, and the bottoms feel soft like sweats, not my jeans.

Somebody *dressed me, undressed me.* I can't settle on which's more disturbing. I need to move. *How come sickos can't just kill you in your sleep? Why do they wait until you're awake and make a big to-do about killing you?*

Shoving off the bed with my hands, I settle my weight on my legs, and the world spins. It's like this one time we went to the Watermelon Thump out in Luling. They had a carnival ride there called the Gravitron. It resembled a silver spaceship, wider on top than the bottom. It spun around so fast that you could turn upside down on the wall and never fall. My head is the Gravitron, pulling me back to the bed.

If it weren't so dark, I could find a focus point to help. I try again to stand up and barely manage to find my footing. My legs are weak, shaky. I don't know what's wrong with me. I know I was drugged, for sure, but I don't know where I'm at, or how long I've been here. And I don't know what my injuries from the wreck look like. I could be dying and not know it.

Putting one foot in front of the other, I move toward the light, swinging my arms around to avoid running into anything else that could be in this space. With each step, my footing feels more firm. When I reach the door, I run my hands over it. It's smooth, not like a door in a house, but like one you would find in an office building. It's big, too, as it takes me a moment to locate each edge and I'm forced to sidestep. My arms aren't long enough to span it.

I feel around for a handle and find nothing. I push, and it doesn't give. Just as I begin to rethink my assessment that this is a door, I remember the pocket doors that Portia was so proud of when they built their lake house years ago. I press my palms to the door. They're sweaty now, so I gotta wipe them on the pants and try again. I push left first, with no success, but it glides with ease to the right.

Silence.

I'm in luck that I've managed to get this far without calling attention from my captor. The open door reveals a hallway that is lit only by the moonlight coming from a large picture window at the end of a hall. The opposite end opens up into a room with faint light coming from it. There are two other doors in this hall as well.

What is this place?

I choose the window first. It's better to figure out where I am and plan an escape route.

Stepping carefully, I try not to make a sound. As I grow closer, I realize that the window is set in a brick wall, and when I look out, I see that I'm on a third—maybe fourth floor of a cinder block building. Outside, there's a dirt lot with mounds of gravel sporadically placed. Beyond that is nothing. Just flat land and a few copses of trees. The light pollution is faint. We're out in the country.

With sinking certainty, I know I'm not in Austin anymore.

I turn back to the hall, and something catches the moonlight, reflecting it off the bare hall in shades of white and red. I jerk, my heart thundering in my ears. The light flashes again, and I realize it's moving with me. I look down. The dragon pendant. Its ruby eyes seem to glow in the moonlight.

Dex.

I've no idea how long I've been out. My hands aren't covered in blood, so long enough to be cleaned up, but I'm still covered in scratches, so not long enough to heal. I tuck the pendant beneath the shirt before I go back down the hall.

Stealth is my motherfuckin' middle name. I'll be out of here before anyone realizes I'm awake.

I try to pump myself up to control the fear, but it's not working as well as I hoped. Reaching the end of the hall, I press my back against the wall and sidle up to the opening. I take a long, deep breath and try to slow my rapid pulse and build up the courage to look around the corner.

It's nothing but a large empty space—concrete floors, more cinder block walls, and identical windows that fill the exterior wall. There's a large, well-worn sofa in the center and a plastic folding table with several computers on it. I consider making a dash for the computers, but the screen saver is on. I'm sure that my kidnapper isn't dumb enough to leave it alone without password protection.

The thought suddenly occurs to me that the door near the window is probably a stairwell. Most industrial buildings, the stairs are near exterior walls with emergency exits toward the bottom. I hear a toilet flush and running water coming from one of the other two doors.

Shit. Shit. Shit.

I run as fast as my inept feet can take me to that last door. I gotta take the chance—if it's a closet, at least I can hide there. I'm a foot away when the door to the bathroom opens, and light floods the hallway.

"Good. You're up," the familiar voice says.

My feet, still semi-numb and tingly, lose their coordination, and I stumble. The urge to look back and make sure my ears aren't deceiving me is too great.

I turn. I blink several times to ensure that I'm really seeing what I'm seeing. But never in a hundred years would I imagine this. My mouth drops open, and I struggle to find my voice.

"Detective Martinez?"

Then

"Do you know why we're here today?" asked the lady sitting across from me wearing an ill-fitted, boxy-looking pantsuit.

Beyond her was a window. I noticed the sunlight reflecting off a car in the parking lot the window overlooked. It was a beautiful day, the kind that inspires people to go outside. The perfect complement to good news.

The news that day was the furthest from *good* news you could actually get. At least, if you were me.

"I'm not really sure how to answer that. I'm not dumb, I get it. But since we're both reasonably intelligent adults, and the answer quite obvious," I sighed, "I'm not really sure why you're wasting the effort to ask it."

"Okay, Miss Dobransky. Madeline, right? Can I call you Madeline?" She looked down at the manila folder in front of her.

I forced myself not to roll my eyes, that's how much that question annoyed me.

"No, it's Madelaine—notice the *A* in it. Nobody calls me that, though, so I'd rather you not."

"Well, the media calls you Laine, but I assume, like most famous people, that you probably don't go by that name. What do your friends call you?"

"Look, we're not friends, so you can just call me Laine, like everyone else." My tone was bored, flat. I wasn't in the mood to talk to anyone at that moment. I wasn't trying to be defensive, but everything my brain spat out sounded rude. My attention was drawn back to the window as fluffy white clouds floated by in the bright blue sky. It felt perverted for the weather to look so beautiful; inside me was a raging storm of emotions that I couldn't even begin to process or comprehend.

"Okay, Laine. Can you tell me about your relationship with Jared Wilson?"

My focus snapped to her dull brown eyes. Strands of blonde hair had fallen from her ponytail to frame them. Her face was pretty but weathered with age, cheeks reddened like the faintest hint of sunburn. She wore no makeup. Her face was plastered with an earnest expression like she cared. That's what they wanted you to believe. That they cared about you. Your safety and health were their utmost concern.

I didn't buy it, though, because like everyone else, she already had an opinion of me. Anything I said would confirm that opinion. If I contradicted her opinion, her brain would just tell her that I was lying, so why even bother.

She didn't stop staring at me, so I decided to just answer her. I felt like we would be here all day if I just stared out the window the entire time.

"I loved him. Still do, actually. He's the love of my life and my biggest regret. Does that clear it up for you?" I moved my focus back to the clouds.

"What do you regret about your relationship?"

"Seriously? Anything. Everything. Have you ever met your soulmate?" I looked at her, but her expression never changed from the impassive, pleasant expression she'd had since she walked into this room. She wasn't going to answer my question, so I just continued. "Well, it's not something you want to happen to you at a young age. A soulmate is a responsibility, and when you're young, you're just too stupid and immature to handle something that big. You're bound to fuck it up. Not with anything earth-shattering, but little mistakes here and there add up. And before you know it, it's broken. And you're still too young and stupid to know how to fix it."

I looked back to the clouds, ready to sign out of that conversation. I just wanted to go home.

"Does that answer your question?" I asked, refusing to look at her again. To be honest, her unchanging facial expression was starting to creep me out.

"Can you tell me about your relationship to..." She flipped a small notebook open. "Lawrence Russo?"

That caught my attention as overwhelming guilt and shame rocked through me. I looked back at her and considered my words carefully.

"What is it that you would like to know?" I said in a fake pleasant tone.

"We just want to know what happened. Were you raped?"

"No!" I snapped, my voice grating harshly, even to my own ears.

I was done with this circus. They'd had me trapped in this room for almost eight hours. The sun was shining, and I'd yet to go to sleep since I woke up the morning before. I was fucking exhausted, but they didn't seem care. They weren't looking like they were going to start giving a shit anytime soon.

She just stared at me without changing her stupid face to any other expression. Not frustration, not anger, which I felt was oozing out of every pore of my face at that point. I slammed my hand down on the table in front of me. She startled. Finally, a human emotion. I fought the urge to gloat over her reaction.

"You know what? I'm done talking to you. Where's Detective Martinez? I'm only going to talk to him. So you can leave now and go find him because I'm not playing this game with you." I made shooing motions with my hand and then looked away.

"I'm the lead detective on this case, not Detective—"

"Did you not hear me? I'm not talking to you. I want to talk to my lawyer, now. Is she here yet?"

"Okay, Miss Dobransky, I'll leave. You understand you're not permitted to leave this room. There are armed officers outside the door. I'll notify your lawyer of your request."

I didn't respond, and the door softly clicked as it shut behind her. I leaned my head back against the pillow behind me and shut my eyes. The door opened again, the sound of voices in the hallway giving away the entrance of a new person. My eyes flew open, expecting to see Bridget, but it wasn't her.

The woman who entered wore medical scrubs.

"I just need to check your blood pressure and temperature," she said softly, like she was approaching a wild rabid animal.

I tried to readjust the grimace on my face to make her not look so scared of me.

"Do you think I can get the remote for the TV?" I asked, trying to ease the tension a bit.

"It's right here, built into the bed." She pointed to the array of buttons on the railing of the bed I was lying on.

She pushed one and the television blinked on. The volume was too low to hear, but I was thankful for that as a local news station was playing a video taken of the incident in the restaurant from the night before. I shut my eyes as she adjusted the cuff around my arm and it started to inflate.

The door opened and shut again, followed by the clack of heels approaching. I opened my eyes and looked into the concerned blue eyes of Bridget.

"It's about fucking time," I said to her.

She didn't react, just pulled up the chair next to my bed and sat.

"It took us a while to find out where you were. Asher said they put you in a police car, and I went to the station, but you never showed up. And they weren't real eager to talk to me about you or your case."

"I don't know what happened. I just remember being put in the back of that car and waking up here in this room, without my clothes or a phone." I shook my head like that would knock the memories loose.

"Yeah, the police officer that was bringing you in said you lost consciousness en route to the station, so he brought you directly here. How are you feeling?"

"How the fuck do you think I'm feeling, Bridget?" I snapped at her but instantly regretted it. "I'm sorry. *Fuck*."

The nurse—or at least I assumed she was a nurse—held a thermometer in front of my face. I scowled at her as I opened my mouth.

"Well, since you can't talk, let me tell you what I've got so far." Bridget settled back in her chair. "The coroner declared a time of death that put you sitting at a gas station on camera with Asher at the time. So, you're no longer a suspect. Before that, though, Sloane's brother showed up to make a statement and give you an alibi."

"What?" I tried to shout around the thermometer.

"Miss, you can't talk until this beeps." The nurse tapped the little unit in her hand that was attached to the metal stick in my mouth.

The beep sounded, and I flung the thing at her. "Are you done yet?" I glared at her.

She wrote the reading down on her clipboard, unhurried and no longer fazed by my attitude. I stared her down until she left the room, then turned back to Bridget, who was looking at me like I'd grown a second head.

"I know asking if you're okay is a dumb question, but I've never seen you like this. You're being a bitch. And that's usually my job."

I shrugged, not at all phased by her assessment. "Isn't it one of the stages of grief? I've already been through denial, now it seems I'm on to anger. I can't help it if everyone—everything, is pissing me off. I've been here too long. I want to go home."

"I'll get you out of here soon."

"We need to rewind a bit. You said that Law made a statement to the police."

She nodded.

"What do you mean, Law gave a statement?" I asked through clenched teeth.

"I mean that he came down to the station and told the police that he was with you most of the evening."

"No, we have to take it back. Get it stricken from the record or redacted or whatever the fuck you call it. If he gives a statement, then it becomes public record that he was with me. Do you not already see the news? It doesn't matter if I was on camera at a gas station. This whole thing will be a shitstorm. I mean, look." I flung my hand to the TV, where there was a picture of Jared and me. "It's already all they've been reporting on since I woke up. Earlier, they were showing a video of the fight at the Driskill." My vision grew misty with unshed tears. "I'm not even worried about what happens to me, Bridge. But the girls, Diana and John, Nate and the studio, Law's career—fuck—everyone is going to be torn down because I made a stupid fucking decision."

Tears fell down my cheeks.

"This isn't your fault."

"The hell it's not. He killed himself because I broke up with him. The last thing he told me was he couldn't live without me. I just screamed at him to get out. Don't tell me that you know, because you don't. You weren't there. The gun was in his hand when I found him, Bridg—" A sob choked me, and I couldn't continue to speak.

"Maddie—"

"The media, the police, everybody will try to turn this into something that it's not. Because it will give them something to talk about. He was broken. He came back from Afghanistan broken, and I couldn't save him. I turned my back on him. Now, *I* get to live with that. You just need to help me fix this. Keep it from hurting anyone else. Because it will. If I've learned anything, it's that those people"—I pointed to the TV—"will say and do anything to earn a dollar, regardless of who gets hurt. Help me, Bridget, please. Get Law out of there. Remove his statement from the record."

"Okay, Maddie." She nodded, tears filling her eyes. "I'll get to it." She picked up her briefcase and turned to leave the room. "I'll be back soon," she said, without looking back at me as she shut the door behind her.

Chapter Twenty-Seven

Now

We had a guest teacher once in my jujitsu class long ago. He told us that he could teach us every move in jujitsu and possibly every other fighting style as self-defense, but the best skill we had at our disposal, we already possessed:

Run.

"I'd love to stay and chat about the case, but I've somewhere I gotta be," I say, turning on my heel and taking the last few steps to the door.

I can hear the heavy thud of his shoes behind me, and I brace myself. Swinging open the heavy door, I bolt into the darkness. The light from the hallway doesn't reach more than three feet in here, and this room is black. No light. Complete darkness.

If my guess is right and this is a stairwell, the next step will drop, or I'll hit a wall or railing, but I take my chances. I'm sure *Joe* didn't bring me here for teatime. So, my goal is to get out at all costs. I'm right. When the floor fails to meet my foot, I pitch forward and flail before losing the battle. I've no idea how long I'll fall, so I curl up like I do in derby and fall small. Wrapping my hands around my neck and tucking my head, I more or less slide down after the first bounce.

For once, I'm thankful I don't feel pain. Because that

likely would've hurt. This is a typical commercial staircase, though, and it only goes down for a half flight before turning. I can see that now because Joe hit the lights. I look back for a second and see him bounding down the steps two at a time, his brow pinched. I scramble to my feet and do the same, holding onto the railing to help me skip steps.

I make to turn the second corner when I feel the tug on my shirt. I bend my knees, ready my hand, and turn in to him. Pushing up with the strength of my whole body behind my arm, I deliver the heel of my palm to his face and then follow it smoothly with a knee to the balls.

Take that, fucker. Nobody kidnaps Maddie Dobransky.

I don't pause to gloat. As soon as his grip on my shirt is gone, I'm off again. Three more turns and I see the red exit sign. Red has always been my favorite color, but if I could kiss the color red right now, I would. That's the level of relief that shuttles through me.

The door opens easily when I hit it at full speed. It slams into the outer wall with the force of the swing. *Really?* Detective Martinez is the world's worst kidnapper. This was the easiest escape ever. I feel let down by all the movies with complicated escape routes, locked doors—so not realistic. Maybe there's a robot ahead? An electric fence? Anything? I see nothing, other than a few smaller buildings, mounds of gravel, and a backhoe.

I keep running. Nothing's stopping me from getting out of here... until a body crashes into mine full force.

We both go down with a grunt. The air is knocked from my lungs, and I struggle for breath like a kid with severe asthma. I roll over, surging to my feet. The world looks like the view from a Tilt-A-Whirl. I can't see straight as I try to take a step, and hands drag me back to the ground. My chin bounces off the dirt with the impact. I roll to my backside, ready to fight back, but he doesn't advance.

"Stop running... please," Joe says with a gasp.

We are both spent.

I want to laugh darkly, but it comes out like chunky

wheezes. "I'm just supposed… to stay here… so you can do whatever your… twisted mind… has planned for me?

"I'm trying… to protect you."

I've the sudden urge to cough, but instead, I start dry heaving again. Blood comes up this time. *Fuck.* My body is fucked up.

"You can't… protect me… from yourself," I say, gasping.

I go up on my hands and knees, escape still at the forefront of my thoughts. I gotta get back for my girls. I *have* to survive for Cat and Cora. They need me, and I won't let them end up orphans like I was. They'll have a mother that grows old with them, who watches every important life event and hugs them through the bad times.

"I'm protecting you from the Hummingbird," he says, clearly catching his breath.

I freeze. What to do? He knows something I need to know, and I'm fighting the urge to turn around and ask as I struggle to keep moving.

"Who's… that?" Curiosity finally breaks me into asking.

"I don't know. He's never contacted me in person."

I nod like that's a totally normal explanation. It seems to encourage him, though, because he continues.

"All I know is that he had stuff on me. He made me start sending you the flowers again."

Again. Holy shit. Martinez is my stalker. Was always my stalker. I called my stalker to complain about my stalker. This seems almost poetically absurd. It wasn't Blake after all. But curiosity gets the better of me, and instead of hightailing it out of there, I want to know more. Curiosity will be my downfall.

"What kind… of stuff?"

"He had evidence of me, stalking you."

"This Hummingbird… is stalking me, too?"

"No, I think he's just very good at finding out secrets and using them against people. To make them do what he wants, or to hurt them. And, for whatever reason, he has it out for you." I think about that for a moment. Joe's description does seem to fit. This *Hummingbird* knew who my stalker was and how to fuck with my life. He knew who Chloe really was and fucked with her life. And he's still a problem. A big unknown. One that I don't want to think about anymore. I just want to get away from here. I want life to be normal again. But there's still Martinez to deal with—to get away from—but he's not making a move to hurt me, and I've so many questions for him.

"You were... at the concert?"

"I was." He looks away. *Regret.* I can see it written all over him, from the slope of his shoulders to his down-turned eyes. "I was—I needed your friend to get backstage. I needed to get you out of there. This guy—the Hummingbird—is dangerous, and I know he wants you. And he can use anyone with something to lose against you."

"You killed Marcus!" I shout, but it causes a twinge that leads to coughing, and more blood bubbles up from my lips, staining the dirt below me.

"It was an accident. He tackled me, and he knew—he knew that I was the one watching you. He saw my gun. We fought for it. I didn't—"

Cry me a river, buddy. I'm angry—no, angry isn't a good enough word... I'm murderous, enraged. And if I'd enough left in me, I'd gouge out his eyes and feed them to him. But one question keeps niggling at the base of my skull, forcing me to ask it.

"Why were you... stalking me... in the first place?"

"My sister," he answers.

I'm so confused, I give up and fall onto my ass.

"She wasn't kidnapped," he says, rolling over and rising to his knees. "She was driving the car that killed your mother. I was with her. She died that night, too. I survived, and I heard you in that waiting room that night, that you were orphaned, and I knew that I had to look out for you."

My face feels numb. I never found out who was driving the other car. All I knew was that it was a minor. I didn't want to know either; it seemed like not knowing made it easier, more abstract and less real.

"I don't think you got it at first, but I was trying to let you know I was watching over you. Like a guardian angel. I just wanted to keep you safe, make up for the lives lost."

That's an incredibly fucked-up sentiment. He should not write greeting cards, that's for sure.

"After the park, though, your kids didn't recognize me. And when I showed you the picture of my sister, I knew you didn't know who I was. But I had this opportunity—I just had to leave you a flower, and you would contact me and give me an update. But when your fiancé died, I figured I was doing more harm than good. I wanted to give you some measure of peace."

"When he... died? *You* said... it was murder!" I gasp and struggle to continue. Anger forces the words from my mouth. "You're also... the one... who said that... the stalker... and the murderer... were the same. And you tried... to blame the murder... on me."

"I know—I know you didn't do it. The Hummingbird's message was clear—I was to blame you and try to find enough evidence to convict you. But I was there. I followed Jared after your fight at the Driskill and at your house. The door to the studio was unlocked. I thought about confronting him for hurting you, but the other guy—your drummer, was there. He was the one who killed him. I thought if I smashed the front door and set off the alarm, someone would get to him in time. That's when your friend fled the scene."

Asher? Asher killed Jared. I'm stunned speechless. My mind has ground to a halt like rusty gears. *Asher? No way.*

"Obviously, I couldn't come forward with the truth, since I had no reason to be there."

Obviously. I roll my eyes. I don't believe this story at all.

"I went back to check on you, since your fiancé was the one with the gun and was waving it around, talking about how it was all over. I found you with that other guy—the boxer. I smashed that vase to get your attention, so you would leave and go look for your fiancé. I thought maybe you could save him. Then I left. I was done interfering. Your life is your own."

"Too shitty... to stalk... I guess," I snort, but my muscles over my ribs seize. "You were... the one that saw me... with Law... that night... not Jared."

He nods.

And then I laugh. I'm probably dying. I don't know if it was the car wreck or the stairs, or when he tackled me. Life has a cruel sense of irony. My stalker stopped stalking me after catching me sleeping with another man on the night my fiancé died. Even if, technically, Jared wasn't my fiancé anymore because I broke up with him... I laugh. Or at least, I think I'm laughing. It might sound different outside of my head, but I can't be bothered to care.

Jared didn't kill himself because he saw me with Law. All that guilt I felt because I had thought he did, I can't say it was for nothing—what Law and I did will always haunt me. But at least he didn't die knowing that I lived up to his worst thoughts of me. It made me feel like he had a small measure of peace from that pain. But that guilt will never leave me because the fallout was just too great. The what-ifs still lingered. And they probably always would.

I gave up on him, and that was enough to push him over the edge. And knowing that didn't make the guilt any easier to bear. And Asher. Asher killed him. *God, life fucking sucks.*

Martinez moves forward, approaching me. I think I might be hysterical, hence the laughing. But his eyebrows are drawn together and his lips pinched. I'm holding on to my side and laughing. He reaches out to touch me, and I scream.

I shriek—not because he's touching me, but because warm blood coats my face. Blood that is not mine. Martinez slumps over, a hole in both temples. His mouth opens in a silent scream as he hits the dirt at my feet.

I scramble to get away from him. I need to hide. Silent bullets are coming from nowhere. That can't be good. I find my feet and run—well, hobble, but I intend to run. I squat next to one of the massive piles of gravel, my eyes scanning the darkness. I'm not even sure if this spot is effective. I could be giving the shooter a nice backdrop, something to cushion his bullet after it pierces my brain.

And then I see him.

He's a shadow. Framed by the dark—black pants, black shirt, black boots, a black sniper rifle with a silencer strapped to his back, and killer eyes. Turquoise pools of death. My deadly love. *Dex.*

He runs across the open space, skidding to a stop in front of me. His eyes search mine as he cups my face with one hand and strokes my hair with the other.

"Shhh... shhh... I got you, Firebird. I got you."

Then

They insisted on wheeling me out to the parking lot in a stupid wheelchair. The orderly pushed me through the automatic doors to the sidewalk. I'd no idea who was picking me up. Bridget had come back with clothes and mumbled something about a ride home. I didn't blame her for not wanting to be around me. I didn't want to be around me, and I was taking it out on anyone with an ear.

I looked around and didn't see any familiar cars, but then I saw him. Law leaned against his bike, holding two helmets in his hands. It wasn't the same bike he had back in the day, but it was the same make. I narrowed my eyes at him. The last thing he needed was to be seen with me. I looked around and didn't see any media or paps, but that didn't mean they weren't lurking somewhere.

I walked over to him, and he held out a helmet. I took it automatically without thinking.

"What're you doing here?"

He rubbed the back of his neck with his now free hand. "I thought maybe you might like to go for a ride after being cooped up in there."

"You thought wrong." I shoved the helmet back at him.

He didn't take it, just studied my face for a moment, then turned and straddled his bike.

"Hop on," he said without inflection.

I folded my arms across my chest and stood my ground. "No."

He looked around us. "Dammit, Laine. Do you really want to do this here?"

My eyes followed his gaze, and I realized that people were starting to notice us. I pulled the helmet on and got on the bike behind him, wrapping my arms around his waist. He started the bike up and took off out of the parking lot with a squeal.

He got on the highway and took us straight out of town to the long winding country roads. When we had gone far enough that we hadn't seen a place of business or home for miles, he pulled off onto the shoulder. I hopped off immediately and pulled off the helmet.

He sat there for a moment before killing the engine. I waited for him to remove his helmet. He did, rolling his shoulders before swinging his leg over the bike to stand. He placed the helmet down on the handlebars and turned to face me, his hand going to the back of his neck.

"I'm sorry about what happened."

I rose a skeptical brow. "Are you?"

He took a deep breath. "I'm not sorry about us. It sucks that it happened the same night we reconnected, but I'm not going anywhere. I know how you felt about him, and I know it—"

"Fuck what you know. You're not sorry? Really? We *fucking* did this. We didn't pull the trigger, but we may as well've, Law."

"They ruled it a murder—"

"Did you know the last thing he said to me was that he couldn't live without me? Then he comes home to find your dick inside me. How is it that you're failing to see the connection here?"

"They said—"

"They?" I threw my hands up. "They are going to say what makes them the most money. The media gets a rapt audience, the police get good PR for working to protect the public and bring a hero's killer to justice... Listen to *me*, because I'm the one who found him. I was there. I saw—I saw—" I couldn't breathe.

I struggled for breath as I collapsed to my knees. Tears fell to the dirt below. Law's arms came around me to gather me close. I couldn't look at him without the reminder of what a fucking horrible human being I was. I couldn't let him touch me because I didn't trust my weakness for him. And I didn't deserve—I didn't deserve his comfort or some happily ever after where he wades through the grief with me and our love grows.

"Don't touch me!" I skidded away from him on my butt. "I can't—"

"Don't. Don't you fucking say it, Laine."

"I'm not fucking Laine!" I pulled my hair by the roots. "It's a fucking stage name, a facade, a fake persona."

He stayed crouched near me but didn't move to touch me. He was silent as he rubbed the back of his neck. I used to think it was adorable that he had that tic, exposing when he was nervous or anxious. But at that moment, it annoyed me to the point that I wanted to break his arm or his neck to stop him.

"Bumpkin." He snorted a self-deprecating laugh. "Don't push me away. I want to be there for you."

"No." I looked up into his concerned eyes. "No, I'm not dragging you down with me." I stood up, pacing. "This is *my* hell. *My* punishment. You being with me—just being near me—you'll lose it all. They'll start calling you a murderer, too. And you didn't owe him anything; that was all me. So no, Law. Get on your bike and go home. Just leave me alone."

"I'm not—"

"What part of 'no' do you not get!" I walked back to him, getting up in his face. "This isn't the start of something. It's the en—"

"Will you fucking let me talk, for fuck's sake!" he yelled over me, standing up and looking down at me. "I'm not leaving you. Not here, not now, not ever! I just got you back. You're mine, and you always will be."

"Why? Do you think we have something here? Well, let me clue you in. We don't. There's nothing between us except matching levels of twisted perversion."

"That's not true. I love you, and I know you still love me. You wouldn't have let me in last night if you—"

"You don't even fucking know me. You never knew me. You knew who I pretended to be, and maybe for a while, I convinced myself I was her and that she loved you, but it wasn't real. It was all a lie. I'm a bitch, a liar, and now a cheater. You don't want to know the real Maddie Dobransky. So get on your stupid fucking bike and leave! Goddammit!"

"No!" His face was mere inches from mine.

I started to respond, but then his lips were on mine, his hands cupping my cheeks. I let myself succumb to it for a moment, relishing the feel of him one last time. Then I bit him hard, rearing back and slapping him with everything I had. He didn't move, didn't blink. He just breathed audibly, searching my eyes.

"I told you. This is over. Are you fucking dense? I. Don't. Love. You," I lied. "Fucking leave already."

He had to go. To save himself, and because I didn't deserve happiness. Not after destroying one life. And I didn't care what anyone said—I was the one who caused all of this. Me and my stupid heart, in love with two men and destined to have neither. I deserved to grow old and die alone.

"I'm not leaving you out here—"

"Fine. You don't want to leave? I will." I turned and walked out into the field we were next to.

"You can walk away. I'll give you all the time and space that you need. But you're mine. Don't ever forget it, because one day, you won't feel this guilt. One day, you'll heal, and I'll be waiting for you."

I kept walking until I couldn't see him, or the bike, or the road. Then I lay down on the ground and stared at the taunting white clouds that seemed to be laughing at me. Mocking my existence. Letting me know that even hell could be beautiful; it just wouldn't ever be satisfying.

I closed my eyes and tortured myself with memories of a lifeless body and kisses on cold, stiff lips. I lay there alone until the sun had set and the stars had come out. I was numb to the core. There it was. The traditional Maddie grieving process. Only this time there was no Jared to take my thoughts away or distract me from everything. I was well and truly alone.

A face appeared above my head next to a blinding light. I cringed and covered my eyes.

"Turn that shit off," I demanded.

He didn't turn it off but turned it to the side as he leaned down next to me.

"Come on, Neddie. Let's get you home," Nic said as he picked me up.

"You came home." I buried my face in his neck, tears welling in my eyes. "He's gone, Lucky."

He squeezed me tighter. "I know, Ned. I know."

Chapter Twenty-Eight

Now

I blink open my eyes. Thankfully, someone has killed the harsh fluorescent lighting in the hospital room.

Beep. Beep. Beep. Beep.

The steady sound of my heart monitor assures me that I'm alive. I almost can't believe I made it. My vision had almost completely faded by the time I pulled into the emergency bay. I don't remember getting out of the car.

When Dex came to get me, Law had driven him out there. Dex drove Martinez's car to the hospital but made me drive the last quarter mile alone. The story was that I escaped and don't know who killed Martinez.

I try to take a deep breath, but there's something wrapped tightly around my body that keeps me from doing it. My eyes search the room. That's when I see him, feet kicked out, reclining in a chair in the most uncomfortable position, sleeping.

But like he can feel my eyes on him, his open. I'm trapped in his intense gaze. I'm not sure where we stand. He left me, but then he killed for me. I don't know what it all means. His look gives nothing away. It never has.

"How are you feeling?" he asks.

My shoulder pitches up slightly. It's the most movement I

can manage. "The same as always."

"There are detectives outside that would like to talk to you. Bridget is with them. Everyone else is out there, too."

"How long have I been out?"

"Three days," he says. "Two surgeries. You had a concussion, three broken ribs—one of which pierced your lung—ruptured spleen, and a lacerated liver."

"That's it?" I grin, hoping to wash away some of the worry. "I got no spleen now? Is that devastating?"

He huffs a laugh and leans forward, his expression grim. "It's still there, but they had to repair a small tear. I thought I was going to lose you."

I don't know what to say to that, so I just nod.

"What were you thinking?"

My eyes dart to his in question.

"You were supposed to stay put."

"You left me," I whined. "I needed you to know that I choose you. I'll always choose you. And leaving was stupid. He could've gone after you. I was relieved when he came for me. I knew you were safe."

His brows draw together as his head tilts like I just spoke another language. "I didn't leave you. I just needed to clear my head."

"So you could think about leaving me?"

"I said I was trying to be a better man, but I don't think I'll ever be good enough to give you up for him."

He crosses the room in a few short strides. His fingers trace the lines of my face, stopping as his thumb runs over my lower lip. If I weren't lying down, my legs would give out. I've become a sucker for that move.

"Kiss me," I whisper.

He does as commanded, his lips an echoing whisper as they brush over mine. He pulls away too soon, and I groan from frustration. I can't follow; there are too many tubes and wires sticking out of me right now. His dimple appears with the answering smirk. I close my eyes to block out the vision. He's almost too much.

That's when I see it. The hollow eyes and twisted mouth. Martinez.

I lock on to those turquoise eyes. "How did you find me?"

"With this." He pulls the dragon necklace from his pocket. "I had it special made for you with a GPS chip implanted."

I reach out and run my fingertips over it. I think I love it more now that I know it saved my life. But speaking of saving lives—my focus jumps to Dex's face. "You killed for me?"

He gives a slow nod, his lips flattening into a straight line. "I didn't want to go in and risk you getting hurt or possibly killed. It could easily have turned into a hostage situation." His jaw ticks like he's grinding his teeth. "And he took you from me. I was two hundred and fifty yards away. I didn't know what he was saying, I just didn't want him to hurt you." His eyes search mine.

I decide to answer the question he never asked. "It doesn't make me love you less." I pause before continuing. "I don't know what it says about me, but I think it makes me love you more. Which doesn't necessarily surprise me." I snort. "There's a darkness inside me that I think you understand. It draws me to you."

He starts to speak, but the door opens. A nurse walks in, carrying a clipboard. She looks up.

"Oh, you're awake." She smiles, walking over to fiddle with the machines out of my range of view. "You've caused quite the stir around here. Kidnapped rock star rescues herself, barely survives. It's big news. How are you feeling?"

I answer her the same as I told Dex. Her brows pinch for a second before a look crosses her face like she made a connection. I'm glad because I really don't want to explain myself. She runs the usual checks and informs us that the doctor will be by soon.

As soon as she's gone, Bridget strides in, looking less than her usual perfection. She pulls a chair from the corner. It grates loudly across the floor before she stops next to the bed.

"We've got"—she looks at her cell phone—"maybe five minutes before the cops get here to start asking questions. Nurse Sunshine announced that you were awake to the entire waiting room. Start from the beginning and tell me what happened. I want to make sure your statement doesn't incriminate you."

I tell her everything, from the scene with Law at Holden's house to my arrival at the hospital, with some alterations to the story.

"He said he was stalking me because his sister was driving the car that killed my mom. He was in the car, too, the only survivor. He felt he needed to watch over me. But he killed Jared and decided to leave me alone—"

"He killed Jared?" she asked.

"Yep." I nod to emphasize my position. *Shit.* If they don't buy it, the police won't. And right now, they both look skeptical.

"Why?"

"He was watching us when we got in that fight. He went to confront Jared. He said it was self-defense. That he didn't mean to do it. And honestly, I don't really care why. The man destroyed my life."

The doubt erases from her features, and I know that did it. I convinced them.

I'm a liar. A pretty good one, by the looks of it. I'd mulled over this on the ten-minute drive to the nearest hospital after Dex rescued me. Asher would never make it through a trial without it destroying every part of his life. Even if he was found innocent. And for what?

Pursuits of the truth are only noble in fiction, in ideal worlds where consequences can be ignored. But sometimes the truth is better left unspoken. Sometimes it's better to let go of the past.

Martinez said that Jared's death was an accident. That it was self-defense. And I believe him. He had no reason to lie, so I'm letting it go. That mystery will die with the only man who knew the truth. I still love my friend and have no doubt that whatever happened that night, Asher was trying to do the right thing.

The police detectives come as Bridget predicted. They listen to my story, make notes, then leave. They are followed by a string of other family members and friends, each wanting to hear my story. I tell it so much I start to forget the lies. I believe it as truth, and it becomes one.

We can all move on now. It's the start of a new day, and now I know what hope really looks like. It has broad shoulders that taper down to a trim waist accented by a dragon tattoo. It carries a gun with deadly aim. It loves me. And I love him back.

Then

I was sitting on my bed as the door to my room opened. Evan stood in the doorway, his eyes trained on me. He got special leave to come home for the funeral and to stay for a couple of weeks after. I didn't know what to expect from him, so I stayed seated and turned back to staring at the wall. He loved Jared almost as much as me, they were brothers-in-arms. I wouldn't blame him for hating me. I hated me.

Once the first tear slipped past my lashes, the rest followed in an endless rush. I wished I could stop crying. I moved my focus down to my feet. The black stiletto heels, the black dress. It was supposed to symbolize mourning, right? But to me it felt like a scarlet letter, announcing the dark soul that lay beneath. Before I knew what was happening, I was swept into muscular arms. Evan held me in a tight embrace.

"Don't shut down on me, Mads. I feel it, too. It fucking sucks, but I need you to stay here. The girls need you."

I glanced away. "I don't know how I'm going to do it. I can't go out there."

"You put one foot in front of the other. Ignore the idiots outside and take comfort in the fact that there are people here that love you and want to help."

"I don't deserve their help or their love, Ev. This wouldn't've happened if I gave him a chance to get help. If—"

"You can't keep doing this to yourself. What-ifs don't matter—it happened. Now you've gotta pick yourself up and carry on. You have those girls that need you now more than ever." He sighed. "You don't owe anyone out there anything, but you gotta do this for yourself. Show them that you're not scared, you're not guilty."

"You're not hearing me, Evan. I killed him. I'm guilty. The guilt is crushing me. I feel like I can't breathe. How can you even stand to look at me?"

"You've gotta cut that shit out. You didn't kill him. You had a fight. You had every damn right to kick him out after what he did. After that was out of your control."

I was so tired of fighting everyone on this. They were all convinced that he had been murdered by some mysterious other person. I knew damn well that when he left, he wasn't in his right mind, and I also knew what he had seen. I felt sick just thinking about it. And that was a secret I'd take to my grave.

I stood and walked out the door to the room. I was on autopilot, not really seeing or hearing things around me. The funeral was nice, but I just stared straight ahead, only blinking before my eyes dried out. When it was over, and people gave up trying to talk to me, I went back to bed. I didn't leave it either.

Without food or water, I didn't need to go to the bathroom that often. I just stared at the wall, my mind a beautiful blank. Everyone visited, everyone tried to help, tried to make me move. Then they gave up. I closed my eyes and went to sleep. In dreams, I had crystal-clear beaches and bright sun. Clear blue eyes filled with love, and vows that bound us forever, until the ocean turned to blood and the sky grew black.

Days passed like endless empty rotations of the sun and

moon's dance. Months went by. I remained a living ghost, only doing the bare minimum to survive.

One night, I woke up. It was dark outside. Something was wrong. I couldn't put my finger on it, but there was something not right. I pulled back the covers, and then I felt it. The cool air hit the wetness on the sheets, between my legs. I turned on the bedside lamp and stared at it.

Nic came in the room. His hands were on my shoulder, shaking me. When his hand cracked across my face, I blinked up at him.

"Did you just slap me?" I asked.

His finger dug into my shoulders. "You wouldn't stop screaming."

My eyes darted to his. *I was screaming?* His olive-green eyes looked sad, defeated. He left the room and then came back and picked me up. He carried me to his car. Holly stood by it with tears in her eyes, holding her hand over her slightly protruding belly. I watched her as we drove away, and she walked back inside my house.

Hours later, I found myself sitting in a bright room. An older Asian lady with a stethoscope and a name tag that read Dr. Chen said the words that would haunt me forever.

"You were pregnant."

Were. Were. Were. Were. Were.

My mind was stuck like a record skipping. A seemingly innocuous word just became a death sentence, and what was left of my rotting soul shriveled even more. Nic cried while I stared at the wall. The doctor patted his arm and told him about fertility treatments. I laughed. It sounded hollow and sadistic. They stopped talking, and the doctor left the room.

Without another word, or at least one that I actually heard, Nic helped me into a wheelchair and got me to the car. Then I was back in bed, where I listened to the deafening roar of silence. It was taunting me for being so fucked up that I could lose a child and not even feel it. Where was the pain? I felt so cold and numb. I needed to feel it. I needed to feel the consequences of my actions. I needed to be punished for being so selfish.

I got up. I went into my closet, pulling down boxes from the top shelf until I found what I was looking for. I sat on the edge of the tub and flicked open the pocketknife. I stared at the shiny blade in morbid fascination. Then I put the blade to my inner thigh and slid it across the surface. I watched the red liquid bubble up from the line without so much as a blink. I did it again and again, screaming in frustration when the only reward was the barrage of memories from the metallic smell of blood.

Slipping off the tub, I bounced off the floor when I heard my name. I looked up into horrified hazel eyes.

"Maddie, put the knife down," Evan coaxed in a gentle voice. "What're you doing?"

"I didn't feel it, Ev. How can you lose a child and not even feel it? I need to feel it. I need to feel something. I can't deal with this numb shit anymore. I want the pain. I deserve it."

He took two strides and pulled the knife from my hand. He threw it behind him. It clattered as it skidded across the floor. His hand pulled at the flesh on my inner thighs.

"They're not deep," he said over his shoulder. "Can you clean her up?"

My eyes tracked behind him to the door to see Nic and Holly, both with equal looks of horror. Holly nodded. I laughed.

"Wow… you guys looked so stunned. It's almost like you didn't know I was a fucked-up freak. I mean, come on. I lost a baby, and I didn't even know who the father was. I'd never know. How's that for karma?"

They didn't seem shocked by that little revelation, which made me laugh harder. But I had a feeling they weren't really listening to what I was saying. They looked scared, either of me or for me, I didn't know.

"Neddie, you need to shut up now," Nic said firmly. "I don't know what's more disturbing—the blood or her laughing."

I laughed harder. I laughed until I couldn't breathe. I laughed until tears filled my eyes and those deep belly rumbles turned to soul-wrenching sobs. I'd say that I was losing it, but I'm not sure I ever had it. I just put on a good mask. I walked the earth seemingly normal, but so shattered inside it was like a kaleidoscope in there.

Chapter Twenty-Nine

Now

I was finally released from the hospital after three torturous weeks. They kept me in longer than normal due to my condition and inability to recognize reinjury.

On the day I was released, Press-zilla set up a press conference where I gave a public statement about putting the events behind me, though she made sure to tie it to the release of the new album. The first single is already at number eight on the Billboard charts.

I don't think I'll ever consider my music career a success until I can manage to make it without being tied to a newsworthy current event. I hate to sound ungrateful, but it does seem to cheapen the win a bit.

Then

"You're ready for this. It's time," Dr. Farley said, urging me toward the door. "Go on. Your brother is waiting for you." She smiled, lifting the deep-set wrinkles at the corner of her eyes.

She liked the way Nic and Evan adopted me as their sister. She said that those bonds were what would keep me grounded. *Never let them go, and honor their strength.*

"Remember your mantra?" she asked.

Her silver hair reflected the harsh sun coming through the sliding glass doors. Six months. It had been six months, and I was going home. Holly would be having her baby soon. I needed to be well enough to be there for her.

I smiled at the good doctor. "Inhale, summoning strength and courage to move forward. Exhale, releasing my fears and reservations."

"That's right. Just breathe, Maddie." She patted me on my arm and turned back toward the front desk.

I followed the instructions and walked outside to meet Nic at the car. My new car. Nic sat in the driver's seat of the 1966 Shelby Cobra s/c Roadster that I spent a lot of time working on here at the facility. My therapy car. It was supposed to be symbolic. I rebuilt the car like I rebuilt myself, and when I looked at it, I'd remember how far I'd come. Nic took it last week to get the paint job done. He told me that I didn't get to pick the color, that was going to be a surprise.

My breath was stolen as my eyes roamed over it. The candy-apple red was the perfect shade—not too flashy, but still stood out. The off-center racing stripe was quirky but still classy. My heartbeat picked up. It really was very much me. I loved that my friends knew me well enough to surprise me and nail the mark. Tears of joy welled in my eyes as my smile spread. Nic hopped out without opening the door. He grabbed a gift box from the passenger seat and walked toward me.

"Hey," I said, hugging him. "It's perfect."

"Isn't it?" He smiled, obviously proud of himself. He held out the box to me. "From the girls… all of them."

I opened the card first. It was from all of them, my daughters and my best friends. I opened the box and found a tube of lipstick, a black silk scarf, and a pair of those round Jackie O sunglasses. I laughed. Handing the box to Nic, I wrapped the scarf around my hair and put on the glasses.

"What do you think?" I asked, striking a pose complete with puckered lips.

He laughed. "You complement the car nicely." He shook his head, grabbed my bags, and walked back to the car toward the passenger side.

I followed but hopped in the driver's seat. I leaned over to use the side mirror to put on the lipstick. The shade was a perfect match for the car. I looked back to Nic and grinned. He smirked at me, somewhat amused. I get it, I'm a bit of a car nerd. So sue me.

My mood was light and happy. The day was a perfect spring day. And as I ran my hands over the steering wheel to really drive her for the first time, I couldn't be happier. But a shadow loomed in the distance because I knew before I made it home, I'd one last stop to make.

Now

I open my eyes and jerk to sitting. The dreams—or nightmares, really—are a frequent occurrence still. Even after the two months I've been home from the hospital.

Dex reaches for me, sitting up and smoothing my hair off my shoulder. His arms wrap around me. He's my rock, and every day, we grow more solid. His lips caress my shoulder, and my heart kicks up.

"Another nightmare?" he whispers.

I nod.

"You know—" He grasps my chin, turning my face to his. "I want to do your tattoo." His fingertips trail over my ribs, sparking tingles of electric sensations in their wake.

"What tattoo?" I ask, breathlessly.

He's scrambling my brain, which is his version of support; he distracts me from the terrors and holds me until I can get back to sleep.

"The one you came to me for when we first met."

Oh. That tattoo. The one I told him to fuck himself with. "I dunno…"

"What are you afraid of?" He snorts. "It's not like the pain is an issue for you."

"You," I state. "Hours of having your hands on me and not going anywhere with it... sounds like torture. Especially since we just got the green light from my doctor." I bounce my eyebrows at him.

His shoulders bounce with silent laughter. "I love you. Seriously, I do."

"I know..." I lean into him and try to steal a kiss, which he evades. "I love you, too." *Such a fucking tease.*

"I keep meaning to ask—why would you agree to the red calla lily?"

I sigh. I honestly expected him to ask a long time ago. "Because I was trying to take my power back. That shit— being stalked—makes you feel powerless and violated in the worst way. It was like he continually raped what was once a sweet gesture given to me by someone I loved. I decided that I needed to take it back. I needed to make it about Jared and stop him from having that piece of me."

"You..." His lips brush mine. "Are..." His hand curls around the base of my skull. "Amazing..." His teeth tug on my lower lip, and I open for him. His tongue dives in, and he kisses me until I feel drunk on him.

He breaks away. "But I gotta request."

"You do?" I'm not interested. I want to grab his cock and taste it. I want to put it in me. There are a thousand places my mind is at, but it's definitely not on tattoos.

"Yes." He holds me off as I try to climb into his lap.

He's got my attention now.

"I want to change it, but it will be a surprise."

"Okay," I say. "One condition."

"What's that?"

"Fuck me."

I'm on my back so fast, it takes my brain a second to catch up with it. We both sleep naked now, so it's quite convenient. I feel his hard length between my legs. The heat rolls off it. I want it.

His body slides down mine. "I gotta condition for you."

"Give it to me." I don't know if I'm asking for his mouth or his condition, but either will do. I'm addicted to this man. Mind, body, and soul.

"I get to blindfold you, we do it all at once since you can take it, and you have to be naked."

"That's three conditions. But you can make me come three times to make it up to me."

"Done."

Chapter Thirty

Then

Nic stayed in the car as I walked across the driveway and stepped onto the pristine green grass. My steps were slow. My feet felt heavy as I weaved between stones placed by countless loved ones.

My palms were sweating from nerves against the cool stems of the flowers in my grip. I found my destination. I decided to go with the easiest first. Though none of this was easy. The top of the wide headstone was inscribed:

> Our brief partings on Earth
> will appear one day as nothing
> beside the joy of eternity together.

God, they really loved each other. I guessed that was why she never moved on. It broke my heart that they didn't have more time with each other. And that I didn't have more time with them. I pulled out the first white calla lily and placed it on the left side. Directly underneath, I found the name of my father.

Alexander Josef Dobransky

Loving Husband, Father, and Hero.
Always in our thoughts...

"I'm sorry I forgot you. I don't think that says anything about you as a father. By all accounts, you loved me with all your heart. I'm told I was once a daddy's girl. I wish I knew what that looked like. I do love you. I hope you're taking care of Mom, wherever you guys are."

To the right, I placed the other white calla lily.

Catherine Rosita Dominguez Dobransky

Beloved Wife, Mother, and Friend
...Forever in our hearts.

Tears broke free and ran down my face. I used the end of the scarf to wipe them away from my chin.

"Mom—" My voice cracked. "I can't—you don't know how much I miss you. It's... I need you all the time, and you're not here. I'm trying really hard to be the best mom I can be to the girls. I fuck up more than I do good. I hope they see my breakdown as proof of my love for their father, and not just another in a long line of screwups when it comes to them. You'd have loved them fiercely. They're so beautiful. I named Cat after you, but really, Cora is just like you. She has that calm, quiet grace that I've only seen from you. She's also fierce like you. I know you're probably disappointed in the mess I made of my life. But I'm getting better. I'll make you proud, I promise."

I stood in silence for a bit longer before my feet found the will to move to the next spot. I weaved through several more rows before I found it. Grass had grown over the grave, but time hadn't fully flattened the earth that covered him. My hands trembled as I placed the final red calla lily on the gravestone in front of me. When I touched it, my knees gave out, and I fell to the ground. I stared at the name, letting the harsh reality sink in once more. The blood. The cold. I wouldn't ever forget.

"Jared," I choked out. "God, I loved you. I still do. You were my first love. And I'll probably still love you with my dying breath."

My fingertips traced over his name. Jared Ethan Wilson. Such a tragic end to such a beautiful soul. I knew all the angry words said, all the violence and temper, wasn't him. He was sick. So, I chose to remember the good in him. The guy who told me he'd love me forever. The one who would play me songs to tell me how he felt. The one who used music to guide his emotions, to connect with his soul, and taught me to do the same. I was forever changed by this man.

My fingers followed the veins of the white marble down to the inscription.

Though his song has ended, the melody lingers on.

His parents chose that, not me. I was rather catatonic in the days, weeks, months after his death. A weak, horrible fiancée. A shitty mother. I feared what my epitaph would say. Turning, I sat and leaned my back against the cold stone.

"I'm sorry... for everything. I think life boils down to those moments. The ones that are tough to handle. You show what you're really made of when pressed to act on instinct. You were right about me. I found out a couple of months later that I was pre—pregnant. I wasn't eating right, drinking enough fluids. My body was shutting down, so it did what it needed to do." I sighed. "I'm really starting to rack up the body count. You know the fucked-up part was that I won't ever know if it was his or yours. I'd like to think it was yours. That the girls had a little brother on the way. One that would look like you but have my hair and eyes. The physical polar opposite of the twins. He would've been so handsome. We would've loved him. That would've been a beautiful future."

I closed my eyes, and I could see his face. My doctor told me that it was important to visualize the good times, that focusing on the bad only feeds into the nightmares and flashbacks. And it made the panic attacks more frequent.

"I'm going to open a music school or someplace for children, in your name. I know you would like that as your legacy. You taught me to love music and saved me when I really needed saving. You need to continue to do that for other kids."

I reached into my pocket and pulled out a tissue to blow my nose when I could no longer breathe. I said goodbye and got up to leave. I'd said that today was a beautiful day and I was happy, but it was a lie. I was putting on a good front for everyone, but inside, I was dead. I was just living in a hell of my own making. This—all of it—was the punishment for my sins, and I'd suck it up and take what I deserve.

Now

The light switch flips with an audible click, followed by the hum of fluorescent lights as they warm up. I walk into the largest of the three rehearsal rooms we have at Mad Lane Records. Moving to pull off my leather jacket, I stop as the cool air kisses my skin and shrug it back into place.

My stomach is queasy with nerves. I won't throw up. I couldn't bring myself to eat anything this morning, so there's nothing to come up. I wring my hands and look around. It's the same empty room it's always been. There are a few couches against the wall where the door is. Scattered wires, microphones, and a few amps are lying around.

But all of that the eye easily skips over. What catches my eye and seizes my attention is the stained glass window. It casts a kaleidoscope of colorful shadows across the room.

The scene depicted in this one is Jesus cradling the head of a blind man, bestowing the gift of sight. The blind man is on his knees, begging for mercy. The whole window is in shades of blues, greens, and purples, but Jesus stands tall in blood-red robes. The artist who designed these many years ago was really good. You can feel the emotion from the way their limbs are placed. *Forgiveness.*

I'm not the religious type. I believe there's a higher power, but I don't think anyone on earth is truly capable of understanding what that is. I think we all grasp at straws and believe the most convenient lies. Lies that feel comfortable, whether it's ingrained from birth or, like a true rebel, you choose it on your own. It's like those scientists who theorize that there's another dimension, but we can't perceive it because our minds are too limited. We just aren't advanced enough to understand or comprehend the truth.

So, God, Buddha, Allah—whatever you want to call him or her—he's not a being. It's a force beyond comprehension. But there's one thing that I do believe: love is as close as we can humanly get to it.

The door clicks open behind me. I know who it is. No need to look. I only lied to one person and told him we were starting an hour before we were scheduled to be in here.

"Sorry I'm late," Asher says, his voice moving across the room behind me. "Where is everyone?"

"You're not late." My voice sounds hollow.

I look at the clock on my phone. He's only five minutes behind schedule. *Did he really think everyone gave up and left so quickly?* I don't really know. I'm too busy staring at Jesus.

"I know, Asher." I try to impart the full subtext behind those two words with my tone. "I know what happened that night."

The sound of his movement stops. I can feel his eyes on me like tiny laser beams burning through my back.

"But I suppose you've guessed that. You're the only one who would know that Detective Martinez wouldn't have confessed to murdering Jared."

The silence is my answer. The fact that we're standing in a soundproof room makes the stillness even louder. The kind of quiet that rings in your ears like the pounding blades of a helicopter as they whip through the air.

"I tried to stop him," he says, finally. "It was an accident."

I close my eyes. The tone of his voice sends shivers down my spine. Despair and pain.

"How?" My voice feels like it's detached from my body. "Tell me what happened."

"Do you really want to know?"

"Yes," I say with a nod, my eyes still glued to Jesus for support.

"Come sit," Asher coaxes.

I'm not sure that I can look at him just yet, so I stay frozen in place.

"I was here that night because I'd nothing better to do. I tried to go to the hospital, but they escorted me off the property. She wouldn't let me in, and I wouldn't take no for an answer. I couldn't go home. I couldn't sit alone in an apartment with my thoughts. I knew she was there, but no one would tell me why."

I cringe at the mention of Holly. That was a rough spot for all of us. We still don't know why she refused to tell Asher what happened. I know she still hasn't.

"Jared showed up here, his face was scratched and bruised. His shirt was torn, and there was blood on it. More blood than what could've possibly been from those scratches. He had a bottle of Jack in his hand, drinking straight from the bottle, a gun in the other hand. He was riled up, too. He kept repeating that it was over. That he fucked up. You gave up on him and it was all over."

I close my eyes. It doesn't matter how much time had passed, this'll probably always hurt.

"I was worried about you. I'd seen him come close to hitting you several times. And that was with an audience. I still have no clue what went on behind closed doors with you two, but I thought the worst."

Jared had only ever hit me once, before he lost himself to his madness. I don't think he would've ever done it again, but we never got the chance to test that theory.

"He had that gun. And my..." Asher's voice chokes on emotion.

I squeeze my eyes shut tighter as tears silently track down my face.

"My first thought was that he had finally snapped and killed you. I asked him what happened—where you were. He was mumbling things I couldn't understand half of. But I did catch the part where he said he hurt you and you broke up with him. I asked him for the gun because I was worried that he was going to use it on someone eventually. Especially the more that bottle disappeared... But he turned it on me. Started saying shit like I was after you, too. Slowly poisoning you against him."

"He was sick." My voice comes out crusty, and I clear my throat. "I wish I would've tried harder to get him help. But back then, I was so sure that it was me. That I needed to stop being me to please him. That if I were someone different he wouldn't look at me like I was a monster. He would look at me the way he used to."

"I wish I could've stopped him," Asher says, then pauses. "We wrestled for the gun. I tried to get it away, but at some point, he got it turned in his direction, and he pulled the trigger."

My legs give out, and I collapse to the floor.

"I'm sorry," Asher pleads, tears clogging his voice. "I'm so sorry, Maddie. I tried to stop him."

Asher's arms band around me. I turn into him, gripping his shirt in my fingers like a lifeline.

"The alarm went off and I ran. I panicked because—I don't know why. He wasn't dead when I left. And that's my biggest regret—that I didn't stay and try to keep him alive. I just freaked out, thinking the police were coming and if he didn't make it, they would call it murder. God, I'm so fucking sorry." A mournful wail wrenches out of him. He sobs for a bit until he continues. "I didn't want to bring you here that night. I didn't want you to see him like that, but I didn't know how to stop you. I tried telling you that we should wait, but you didn't listen, and I couldn't—" His body trembles violently as his eyes take on a lost, faraway look.

My heart breaks for him. To be holding this all inside for this long. To go through this alone. I know he loved Jared. He would've walked away instead of sticking it out with us. I can't imagine what I would've done in the same situation, but I don't blame Asher for his actions. It was time to let this go.

"I let them call it a murder and kept my mouth shut. I thought it was better for you if you didn't know. That it would be easier to not live with the guilt I felt."

I don't know why I do what I do next—a giggle bursts forth from my lips, and I can't stop it. But it's thin and reedy and holds a tinge of madness to it. Asher's red swollen eyes turn to me.

"It didn't work," I say. "I held on to that guilt, convinced that everyone was lying. Locked myself in my self-imposed prison. I knew he killed himself because I could see it in his eyes that night when I made him leave. He was done. But I also couldn't continue to be his victim. He took it too far when he attacked me."

Asher shifts next to me, his arms falling away. He wraps them around his knees. Our sides are touching, but we face opposite ways. He stares at the carpet, unmoving. We sit in silence so long, the tears dry up on their own.

"I was only hurting myself trying to save him. We both did it. But I've learned something, Ash. You can't blame yourself. Jared was one of the thousands who come home every year and do the same. Another body to add to the statistics. And maybe if we'd been a little smarter, we could've changed that. But you fought hard enough for the gun. Even Martinez tried to save him—he's the one who smashed the door and set off the alarm. And I was not the horrible monster that drove him to do it."

"Of course not," he says, and I know he's only answering

that last thought.

"I forgive you." I wait for a reaction, but none comes. I reach over and turn his face until he's looking at me. "I forgive you. And now you need to forgive yourself."

I look back up at Jesus and have the strangest sensation. Goose bumps prickle on my arms.

"Was it that easy for you?"

I snort. "Hell, no." I cut him the side eye. "It took over four years to fully forgive myself. And really, it wasn't until Dex knew the truth about me—everything—and still looked at me like I hung the moon that I realized that who I am was not to blame for Jared's downfall."

I lie back on the floor and stare at the carved wood molding on the ceiling.

"Everybody deserves to hang the moon in someone's eyes," I say to no one.

Asher snorts. "We don't all get a fairytale ending."

"You had it once," I say before my mouth catches up with my brain.

Shit. I didn't mean to dig that up.

"I remember believing that." His shoulder sag a little further.

"Ash, I promised both of you that I'd never get involved because I don't want to choose sides. But I feel like I need to offer you some advice. Call it a forgiveness freebie." I wink.

He gives a half-hearted laugh in return.

"When we put our running shoes on and fight tooth and nail to hide from someone, it's because that's the person who really matters. That's the one person you fear will see what's inside you and cringe. You'd rather live with the not-knowing than to give it a chance." I sigh, thinking about how much running I did from Dex. "I can guarantee you she has her running shoes on when it comes to you. That shit says something. Shouts it from the fucking rooftops. So, you can sit around and mope because she pushed you away, or you can fight for it."

Chapter Thirty-One

Now

"I call dibs!" Audra shouts, diving headfirst over the back of the couch.

Cora saunters up behind her. "That's fine, but you get to sit next to Mom and your dad."

"Never mind," she says and dives for the other end. "I call dibs here."

Cat sits just before she makes it, and Audra crashes into her.

"Nope. Mine." Cat grins.

I shake my head at them. I place the beer and sodas in the bucket and throw a few ice cubes in for good measure. Dex turns, setting a giant bowl of popcorn on the counter in front of me. His arms curve around me, pulling my body against him, and then he spins me. He starts dancing to the music the girls have on the TV. It's some new rap song I've never heard of. Ballroom dancing to rap music is a new one for me, but I follow his lead.

His fingers run up and down my side as we move, like he's mentally tracing the art he put on my body. That was an experience neither of us will ever forget. It involved strips of silk, binding me to the table and blindfolding me. His tattoo gun, a few key sex toys, and a bucket of ice—he's got a great imagination, and he keeps me on my toes.

The tattoo looks amazing. He played off the original designs, but the vines are no longer binding the flowers. They are falling away, so the music notes move freely. And behind the flowers, a firebird emerges. I'm so glad we waited because that perfectly matches where I'm at.

He has given me wings and helped me heal. The power of acceptance is a beautiful gift for the ones you truly love. He sees me and accepts who and what I am, but more than that, he loves me because of it—the dark and the light.

The song ends, and we move to the couch, taking the snacks to the coffee table. The girls have cued up the movie.

We're at Dex's place. I thought he had no TV, but it turns out that a massive screen rolls down from the ceiling in front of the windows with the push of a button, one that rivals a small movie theater.

"We should do this every night," Cat announces.

"Totally," Cora agrees. "Though maybe not with all the candy."

There's a buffet of movie theater candy in little boxes lined up in front of them.

Audra snorts. "Can't go getting all fat and letting Maggie steal Josh from you, Cor."

I watch them with a perma-grin stuck to my face. This makes me so happy.

"Mom," Cora says. "Pass me the popcorn."

Dex has the popcorn in his lap, but when my eyes latch on to it, I know she wasn't really asking for it. Because sitting in the middle of the popcorn bowl is a red velvet box. My breath halts in my chest. My body is frozen. I'm pretty sure that's what I think it is. I can't move, and I can't breathe. I'm going to pass out. We've only known each other for a little over six months. I wasn't expecting this.

His thumb brushes over my lower lip, and I meet his eyes.

"Breathe, Firebird."

I suck in a shaky breath.

"I agree with the girls. We should do this again. Every

night for the rest of our lives. I wanted to be a better man for Audra, but you make me a better man without effort. You accept me for everything that I am and never flinched, never backed down. You love unconditionally, with your whole heart. You're the most beautiful piece of art. All the colors, both light and dark. I love all of it. I love you. Madelaine Dobransky, will you do me the honor of being my wife?"

"And my mom?" Audra adds.

My eyes meet hers, watery with unshed tears and so round and hopeful. My heart feels fit to burst. Can you die of happiness? Because I feel like I'll keel over any second.

"Say yes," Cat urges.

Cora joins. "Do it."

I look back to Dex, but he's moved to his knee, holding out the ring from the box. I gasp, and the tears fall. I can't speak, so I nod my affirmation.

I struggle for breath. "Yes."

He slides the ring on my finger, and I get my first good look at it. It's a custom piece—it has to be—made of platinum or white gold, I wouldn't know the difference, and there's a center oval-cut diamond. Not too big and flashy, just right.

But the band—the band is a dragon and a phoenix, their bodies entwined, wings and tails outstretched to hold up the diamond. There are rubies set in their eyes. In fact, it matches the necklace he gave me.

My hand flutters to the necklace, and I meet his eyes again. He smirks, dimple showing like he knows that I realize that they were made at the same time. The only way he could've done that is if he had these made after our first night together at the Black Building. It takes weeks to make custom jewelry, right? Or maybe months, and he had decided sooner. *Holy shit.*

"A thousand times yes," I add.

Then his lips are on mine, warm and wet. Perfect. I shudder and press into him, hoping for more, until a box of candy hits my shoulder and I pull back.

Cat shouts. "Cut it out, you two!"

"Gross," Cora adds.

"I think it's sweet," Audra says, diving across the couch to hug me.

I already love this little girl. She's so full of life, yet I can see the shadows in her eyes. Her life hasn't been ideal. I want to fix that. I want to make sure she knows she's loved and cherished. I stroke her head and hug her back.

Dex wraps us both in his arms.

"Hey, I want in on the group hug," Cat says.

Cora comes around from the other side of Dex. "Me, too."

Dex adjusts his arms to let them in. I couldn't be happier. I meet his eyes, and I know. We don't have to speak. He feels the same. This is our family now.

"I love you," I say. But it's not just to him. It's for all of them.

He smiles, dimples and all. "I love you, too."

"I'm so happy for you, Mom," Cora says.

"I want to see the ring!" Audra says.

They grab my hand and dote over how much they love the design. Dex sits down at my side, and I curl into him.

"I'm not marrying a dude unless he makes me a custom ring, too." This from Cat.

I snort. "Hopefully, that won't be for a long while."

"Definitely," Cora agreed. "We're not getting married until like thirty."

"Okay, enough of the mushy talk," Audra announces.

"It's movie time," Cora shouts, walking on the couch back to her seat.

"You may have Dex, but I need me some Spider-Man," Cat says, following her the same way.

"I know, right? Tom Holland is so hawt."

"I can't—Dylan O'Brien has my heart. They need another Maze Runner movie, stat."

I look at Dex as the girls chatter away about hot teenage movie stars and smile. His lips are pressed into a firm line like he's biting back commentary, and I laugh.

We start the movie, and just as the climactic battle scene ensues, my phone rings. I scoot past Dex and bolt for it, so it doesn't ruin the movie for everyone else. I answer the phone, holding up my ring and watching it glitter in the flickering light of the TV screen.

"Hello?"

"Maddie?" Chloe's familiar voice comes through the line, and I drop my hand. She sounds upset. "It's Evan. He's—we—I'm at the hospital. He's in surgery. But I need ya—" Her voice breaks on a sob, and my heart falters.

Thuuuuuump... thuuuuuuump... I can hear the slow echoes of my pulse. It drowns out the noise of the movie. I gasp, drowning for air.

"Chloe," I choke out. "Where are you?"

"Mercy Medical in Mason City, Iowa." She expels the words like they've been trapped inside her. "I don't know—" She hiccups and doesn't continue the thought.

"We'll be there as soon as possible. Is this a number I can call you back on?"

"It's a courtesy phone in the waiting room. I'm not sure if it can take incoming calls."

"Well, I'll just call the hospital and have them page you if it doesn't work. But I need to go now. Make plans to get us there. Will you be okay?"

"Yes. It's all over."

I want to ask what that means, but I know I need to call Nic and get things in motion.

"Okay, Clo. I'll see you soon."

I hang up and try to dial Nic's number through welling tears. Hands pry the phone from mine. Dex dials the phone and holds it to my ear without comment.

"Neddie," Nic says.

"Nic, get Parker to set up the jet. Get us as close to Mason City, Iowa that we can get. Have him arrange a van or multiple cars. Get Dawn to call the girls. It's Evan and Chloe."

"On it." The line goes dead.

Now

Three hours later, I'm crammed in the back of an Uber with the twins and Audra. On the way to the airport, Dex chitchats with our Uber driver from the front seat. It's so normal. And I love him a little more because of things like that.

I know, deep down, he's a killer. A dark, murderous villain. But when he's not in killer mode, he's just so normal. I wasn't wrong when I called him a nice guy. He just is.

I direct the driver, and we pull up outside the hangar where Nic keeps his jet. I snort to myself as a familiar thought occurs to me. I can't help it. The guy built an empire with his dick. Not many men can pull that off. It's a rare talent. And one that makes me laugh every time I see the evidence.

The girls and I pile out as Dex pays the driver. The action tugs at me for a moment. I live modestly because I don't know how to live any other way, but my monetary value is beyond comprehension. That happens when you make millions and it sits in the hand of people that know how to make money grow and multiply. I know Dex isn't broke, but I also know there will never be a day that I'll want for anything.

"That's his plane?" Dex asks, looking over the shiny white jet.

I nod.

The girls each have a backpack, but Dex pries my duffel bag from my hands and leads the way. I don't make it two steps before another car pulls up. Holly and Bridget emerge, quietly laughing. Holly leans back in and pulls a sleeping Hope out of the car. The little girl looks around for a second before curling into her mother's shoulder with two fingers in her mouth. She's so precious.

My eyes move past her to the other car that has pulled up behind them as Sloane emerges. Then I see him. *Law.* I haven't seen him since the night they rescued me. Our eyes meet.

"What's with the jumbo jacket?" Holly asks.

I track her stare to Sloane, who is walking toward us in a puffy parka. I smile. God, I've missed having her around. Sloane notices us staring.

"What?" she asks, slowing her pace and gripping the edges of her coat.

"It's seventy-eight degrees, and you look like you're standing in a snowstorm," Bridget says.

Sloane halts, her mouth dropping open. "You *do* know we're going to Iowa in February?"

None of us say anything.

"You guys need to get out of Texas more if that's confusing you," Sloane says and walks past us to the jet.

Bridget looks to me, and I shrug. I brought my leather jacket, sure that it will be enough. But I'm no expert. Her gaze darts over my shoulder, and I know. I can feel him getting closer like my body is still finely tuned to his presence after all these years.

He grabs my left hand and spins me to face him. He looks at the ring before he meets my eyes.

"He put this on you?" Law asks.

I nod.

"It's not going to stop me. Not this time."

I open my mouth to tell him that it's a useless fight, but he turns away before I get the chance. He gets in his car. I can't take my eyes off him, and I watch his taillights disappear into the darkness before I turn back to the plane.

Bridget is still standing there with a smirk. She opens her mouth to say something.

"Don't." I hold up my hand to stave her commentary.

I really don't want to think—much less talk—about what he just said. We walk to the jet and climb the stairs in silence. Everyone is gathered in the main compartment, except for the kids.

"I sent the girls back with Hope to sleep in the bedroom." Holly answers my searching look.

I nod, pursing my lips. I want to be happy and hug everyone since it's been so long since we've all been in one place. But the reason we are all here hangs heavy in the air, like an oppressive cloud. I'm sitting next to Dex when it hits me that someone is missing.

"Where's Ruby?" I ask, looking at Dawn and Parker.

Their heads are bent together over a laptop that sits on Dawn's lap. They glance up, and Dawn's dark brow furrows under her green hair, tied up in a messy bun.

"On her way," she says. "She's coming on her bike since it can be parked in the hangar. I talked to her about two hours ago."

"I'll call her again and see where she's at," Sloane volunteers.

"And while we're waiting," Bridget says, setting her briefcase on the table between us.

She opens it and pulls out a sheaf of papers, then returns the case to the space beneath her seat. Laying the papers on the table, she turns them until they're facing different directions. I watch her with a morbid fascination like she's finally lost it, with all the pressure of keeping us out of trouble. There are about six sheets in all, lying haphazardly and overlapping each other, but they all meet with a corner in the middle, like a starburst.

"There," she says and motions with the palm of her hand for us to look at her odd masterpiece.

I lean forward, and my stomach drops. In the center of the papers, where all the corners align, is a hummingbird.

"What is that?" I ask.

"It's Roz's parole approval papers. They were sent to me yesterday. But look—it took me a while to get it because individually, it looks like just a smudge in the corner."

She lifts up the top page and hands it to me. She's right. It does look like a weird smudge. Like it got stuck in a printer.

"How did you figure it out?"

"By accident. I dropped a few of the pages, and when I was picking them up, I noticed that the two in my hand sort of fit."

Dawn frowns. "That's just like the one I found when I was tracing Chloe's WitSec hack."

"And the dead birds you had on your dining room table." Holly leans over the table to look more closely at the symbol.

"I need to tell you guys something," I confess, my voice shaky. "I didn't tell the police everything that Martinez told me. He said that the Hummingbird was the one who made him come back into my life. He was supposed to leave flowers and try and find or plant evidence to get me convicted of Jared's murder."

"Why didn't you tell us?" This from Dex, his voice deep and dark, his jaw clenched in anger.

My eyes bounce between everyone's gazes. They're all looking at me, and their faces are matching stamps of disapproval.

"I don't know." It's the only answer I really have.

It's the truth. I don't know why I kept it to myself. My best guess was that it was a feeble attempt to have it all be over. To move on to normal and leave behind the doom and gloom.

"Guys—" Sloane draws the attention from me, and I let out a relieved breath. "Guys, you have to hear this."

She waves her phone in the air, then pushes the screen and holds it out at arm's length.

"Go ahead, Martin, tell them what you told me."

Martin? Who the fuck is Martin?

A voice emanates from the phone. "The Raven got took."

Ruby's motorcycle is a custom chopper she built with her dad. It has raven's wings painted on the side of the tank. It's really a beautiful bike. And it's not the first time I've heard someone call her that. I raise a brow at Sloane.

"This guy has Ruby's phone," Sloane explains. "I was calling it, hoping that she would maybe pull over and answer.

Tell me where she is. But this guy answered. He's some homeless guy that sits in front of a gas station on 35. Tell them what you saw, Martin."

"The Raven stopped—she was pullin' out this handphone when all these guys on bikes come up around her. Looked like her friends until they stuffed her in a van. Then one of them even took her sweet-ass bike away. But she dropped her handphone. That's how I got it."

The room starts to spin. *Fuck.* Sloane thanks the guy and hangs up the phone. She looks over at the table and frowns.

"What is that?" She motions to the oddly arranged papers.

Bridget sighs. "It's Roz's parole paperwork."

"I've seen that before," Sloane says, and our heads all snap in her direction, almost in sync.

Dawn stands up, then moves closer to us. "Where would you have seen that?"

"It was on my papers for my severance package from work. I remember thinking it was odd because the company has never had a hummingbird in their logo."

I stand on shaky legs. I don't know what I'm going to do, but as I stand, the TV screen on the back wall of the cabin— behind Sloane—comes to life. The screen is white until the first bird drops. One hummingbird… two, three, four, five, six, seven.

It starts to click. My mind turning the puzzle, twisting pieces until they click into place.

He's not the Hummingbird.

"Martinez said that this guy had ways of finding out secrets and using them against you. That he could even turn people you know against you if they have something to lose. And the day that I got my tattoo, Dex found a hummingbird sketch on his chair when he got there that morning. I think it's a warning. That sketch was my warning, and he's the one who set all that trouble into motion after I received it."

I look at Sloane, standing in front of the screen—then Holly, Bridget, and Dawn. Ruby and Chloe, who aren't here because… And all the stuff that happened to me, but I survived. And I don't think I'm the only one this guy is after. I finally work up the courage to give voice to my thoughts.

"I think… we're the seven hummingbirds."

Ready for more? Because the story doesn't end here. No, there's lots more in store for these girls. Coming soon we'll kickoff the Seven Hummingbirds series with, Chloe's story, Penalty Kill.

Penalty Kill (Seven Hummingbirds, #1)

Three years ago I escaped. Three years of living a new life. Three years of living a lie.

But that's over now.

They know where I am and they're coming. I have to run.

Evan Langford was sent to make sure I returned, but he has no idea who he's protecting. I doubt that he'd still keep me safe if he found out... I'm not the girl he thinks I am.
I'm not Chloe Meade.

I'm the one he should be afraid of. They all should. Because I'm not a victim.

I'm a killer.

UNITED IN THE WAR AGAINST VETERAN SUICIDE

www.mission22.com

If you, or a loved one, are a veteran facing the challenges of PTSD and/or TBI, I encourage you to seek help. I've partnered with a worthy organization to make sure that the information is available. Also, I wanted to spread the message that it doesn't have to end in tragedy like Jared's story. Please check out their website and resources.

And if you don't know anyone personally, I encourage you to donate or get involved in helping veterans get the help they need.

Back of Book Shit

Welcome to the Back of Book Shit, aka the BoBS. This is the part of the book where I tell you some of the backstories to my books. Holy... fuck. I really never thought I'd make it this far. There were so many obstacles laid in my path to finish this book that I almost gave up.

You see my grandmother, who I called Mamaw, told me that if things are meant to be, then your path becomes easier—things work out effortlessly. If you keep running into obstacles, then someone or something is trying to tell you that you're on the wrong track. And in some ways, I think she was right, and that held true for these books. Well, most of the time I think that whole adage is pretty on point, but for this book, it was all about the timing.

When I finished this book, I had no clue how much I didn't know about publishing. You can listen to indie authors talk about it, you can read about it, and do thousands of hours of research, but there is no substitution for firsthand experience. And getting to this point has been a rollercoaster ride for sure. It wasn't until I found a fantastic support system through a group of authors on Facebook, that I started getting the answers I needed. And if life didn't throw up all those roadblocks, then I wouldn't have noticed them before I was ready to publish. Since finding that group, things have almost magically worked out for me, not that it didn't require effort, but it just started falling into place.

But I promised you the backstory to the duet so here goes...

I may have mentioned it once or twice, that I was once a

military wife. And during that time we were assigned to live in Korea, which was both an exciting adventure, and scary as fuck for someone who had only left her home state of Texas few enough times that she could still count them on one hand.

It turned out to be one of the greatest, most life-altering experiences of my life. I do believe in fate to an extent, and I think that me and the friends I made there were fated to meet each other and inspire each other. They have definitely inspired me.

The whole idea for these stories, The Falling Small Duet and the spin-off Seven Hummingbirds series, was inspired by meeting and being part of a close-knit group of friends from all different walks of life, with vastly different interests. The only thing we had that tied us together was an intense loyalty and love. And after finding that, I knew I had to write about it.

But more than that was watching more than one friend deal with a spouse who had PTSD or TBI. The effects of which are different for everyone, but the result is the same—it's painful and hard for the family to live with, to endure, and to love despite the endless pain, anger, and frustration.

Three of my closest friends from Korea, all dealt with this in very different ways, with very different outcomes. There was a part of me that felt every bit of their pain as I watched them endure what they did. So, I took elements from each of their stories and wrapped it into Jared's story, and that was where the ideas for Falling Small started.

In derby terms, falling small means to land in a way that you lessen the risk of tripping up other players and incurring a penalty. For me, that very much fit this story because Maddie's constant struggle was trying to take on Jared's fall and lessen the effects and the pain for everyone else around them. Which is a very typical reaction of anyone in that situation.

It was personal for me because while I didn't have to deal with someone suffering from PTSD, I did have my own struggles scattered among the pages. My own heart laid bare, and it was tough to put it all out there. I've spent fifteen years falling small for my kids, keeping them protected and loved while coping with mental illness and addiction in our family. It's not like you can walk away. If the person had cancer, you wouldn't abandon them, so mental health shouldn't be a deal breaker either, but it's hard—it takes its toll.

It's difficult to discern at the moment whether you're compromising yourself or doing the right thing. And for me, I had to let go of the guilt, let go of the misconception that I was the root of the problem, and to learn to love myself again. I read a poem back then called Dear Woman by Michael E. Reid, it inspired me to pick myself back up from the pieces I had become and find myself again through my writing and lots of deep soul-searching. It was a piece of wisdom that I tried to impart through Maddie's actions and her overall story arc.

I sometimes wish I had Maddie's support system. I do in some regards, but my friends are scattered across the globe now, and it's just my kids and me on our own, for now. But I have a good feeling that things might start looking up for us sometime soon.

One of my biggest goals with my books is to be realistic about the complexity of life in general. There are no good guys, and there are no bad guys. Well, we'll still have to wait and see what the Hummingbird is all about, but for this duet, there isn't a black-and-white storyline. Everything in life is shades of gray. There are always two sides to every story.

And if you got pissed at Maddie for finally giving in and sleeping with Law at the end, ask yourself: if you were in her shoes, neglected and abused, then faced with someone who came at you with complete adoration, you'd have a hard time saying no too. Because it's a fundamental need to want to be accepted and adored.

That need to be understood drives us all, it is the very heart of human nature.

The other part of this was inspired by a blog post I read

years ago on the three types of love. The article maintained that most people will fall in love three times. The first love is your ideal. What you believe that love and relationships should look like based on family values and societal norms. The problem with these relationships is often a lack of chemistry, and in the end, you lose interest over time, or the incompatibility begins to cause issues that lead to the relationship's demise.

The second type is generally instigated by the shortcomings of the first, and you go out looking for someone that fulfills that need for a chemical connection alone. These relationships are often intense and fiery, full of great sex, and lots of arguments. When that one goes up in flames, because they all do eventually, you'll be more self-aware and open to meeting the third and final type of love.

The third type is often called the soulmate. These are the ones who have one foot on both sides. They fit the ideals of what a relationship should look like, fit into your family values, and you have intense chemistry. This is your forever love and if you're lucky enough to find it—hold on tight and never let it go.

That article hit close to home for me, because I had been there, stuck in a repeating evolution of the first two, unwilling to learn from my mistakes, so in a way, this story was trying to impart some wisdom on that front.

Law took on a life of his own when writing him. He had more personality than he was ever meant to have and for that reason alone, I really don't know what the future holds for those three, but they'll have their final showdown by the end of the series. You will have an answer.

And I really can't wait to share the rest of the girls' stories with you. The inspiration for each comes from very different sources, but I think you're going to love them if you stuck with me this far.

Thank you so much for reading. I love you guys so much for sticking with me through this epic tale. You make every minute I spend writing worth it, you make every sacrifice my family had to endure to see these books published worth it, just by buying and reading my books. And as long as you stick with me and keep buying books, I will continue writing them. I have an endless well of inspiration to draw from.

Until then, be you. Stay original.

Rebel

Acknowledgements

Surprisingly there are a lot fewer people to thank when it comes to this book as opposed to False Start. Mostly because I had a hard time sharing this one. This is where the story got personal for me. I kept it close to the vest for a full year before I finally, finally relinquished it into the hands of my editor. And still, that was an excruciatingly difficult moment for me. I sat there with the email in compose mode for at least 12 hours before I walked away and made my soon-to-be-ex-husband push the button for me. And that's not a joke, I'm not divorcing him because he pushed the button.

So, I at least have to thank him for that. And for the sticking around and funding my first books, and for believing in my talent. But I said all that nice shit in the first book, and really, I'm kind of fucking sick of thanking him at this point. A lot of that comes from a well-earned place for me.

I really do need to thank my editor though, Sandra Depukat of One Love Editing is quite simply, my editing soulmate. She gets me in a way most others have failed. I'm not a delicate flower, you can straight up tell me when something's wrong, but you got to get the fact that I do have a point, I have a message and a moral to my tales. And when I'm failing to communicate that effectively, Sandra and I would have Q&A chats where she tried to help me pinpoint where I was going wrong.

I mean there were some profound philosophical questions thrown my way, but the fact that she knew that I had an answer for all of them pretty much attached me to her for life. She would laugh and say that she was venturing into

357

"book club territory," but it helped in the end. I think this book shines because of the extra care and attention to detail it got to make sure the story was told clearly.

Then there's Cassie Sharp, I really don't know what I'd do without this woman. She beta reads for me, but she does so much more than that. She's willing to give another pass to rewrites and additions to see if we cleared up misunderstandings and got the point across. She also puts up with my incessant questions over teasers and cover design, and what the fuck I'm writing in my BoBS and acknowledgments pages. I even ran my dedication page by her to make sure I didn't sound like a bitter, lonely bitch.

If Sandra is my right hand, then Cassie has quickly become my left. I couldn't do it without you two. Both of y'all are amazing, and I'm endlessly grateful for all your help, your belief in me and your support.

Also need to thank my other beta readers, Melissa Pascoe and Trisha Haberthur. Trisha, you did an excellent job as always in pointing out my story's weaknesses. And Melissa, your last minute confirmation that we had indeed fixed the story and suggestions for tiny tweaks were awesome. I can't thank you both enough for your time and work in helping me get my story told in the right way.

Jenn Wood of All About the Edits, I think you did a fantastic job of finding all the little errors. I don't think readers realize the potential amount of typos that can exist in a 104k+ word manuscript, combing through that for all the little bits and pieces is an extraordinary task. I think Jenn did an excellent job. But really time will tell because I still don't see the errors after living with this manuscript for more than a year.

And for the man who didn't get any credit for working on False Start because, well, I write all this before I give it to him. I really need to thank Erik Gevers. He helped me create not one, but two beautiful book interiors that really highlight the stories themselves. He's also the last line of defense in proofreading these books and making sure I'm delivering as clean of a book as possible to you. He made some absolutely good catches with False Start and I have no doubt he'll find a few in this book, too. And he put up with my picky long-listed feedback, patiently regarding my ridiculous demands for cool shit, and consoling my naiveté in thinking some things can be done that are just beyond current technology. He graciously made the changes that were possible and didn't even get a mention. Well, not this time, buddy. You're getting acknowledged and thanked for your hard work. I really do appreciate your skill, your knowledge, and your ability to put up with me.

Thank you again Regina Wamba for yet another amazing cover design. It took us more than a few tries to get this one right, but I couldn't be happier with the results. You truly do exceed my expectations every time. It's amazing to me how you nail the vision I had for each book with very limited instructions. Your work is truly astounding.

And a very special thanks to poet Michael E. Reid for the use of his poem *Dear Woman* as an Epigraph to this novel. I talked a bit about how it inspired me both personally and in the writing of this duet in the BoBS. It was so very kind of him to allow me to publish his work in my book. I hope his message reaches my readers who need to hear it, too, the way it did for me.

About the Author

Rebel Farris is a romantic suspense author. She's also the mom of three lunatics plus two perfect pups (Spike and Snakefinder) currently residing in Austin, TX. A native Texan and former military wife, she spent three years living in Seoul, South Korea (where part of her heart will always belong) and every corner of her home state before settling down. One day she hopes to live out the dreams of her nomadic soul, by traveling the world. All while pouring out the myriad of stories that fill her not-so-normal mind. She'll just have to wait until her brats graduate and leave the house first.

When she's not busy writing her newest project, she can probably be found curling up with a good book, hiding behind a lens of one of her many cameras, or going on adventures with her kids. Champion of the anti-hero, Rebel loves to write suspenseful and unpredictable stories while making people fall in love with the bad guy and the broken souls.

Standalones
Snapshot

Falling Small Duet
False Start
Pivot Line

Seven Hummingbirds Series
(Coming In 2019)
Penalty Kill
Whip
Transition
Substitution
Blocker
Turn Stop
Target Zone

Social Media

I have a reader group on Facebook. If you're into meeting likeminded readers or just want to shoot the shit with me, please join us at Rebel's Mad house.
facebook.com/groups/rebelsvillains

Stalk me on Social Media…
facebook.com/rebelfarris
twitter.com/Rebel_Farris
instagram.com/rebelfarris
www.pinterest.com/rebelfarris
www.goodreads.com/rebelfarris
youtube.com/AnimalLogicProd
Website: rebelfarris.com

If you prefer to skip the social media scene altogether and want to find out all the latest happenings and get in on exclusive shit, and have it all delivered straight to your inbox, then be sure to sign up for my monthly newsletter at subscribe.rebelfarris.com

Scene Inspiration Songs

Addicted to Love by Florence + The Machine
Be Mean by DNCE
Believer by Imagine Dragons
Hurt by Johnny Cash
I Don't Mine by Defeater
In Repair by Our Lady Peace
King Of The World by First Aid Kit
Let's Dance by M. Ward
Litost by X Ambassadors
On The Vista feat. Mos Def by Blakroc
Say Hello, Wave Goodbye by David Gray
Sign Of The Times by Harry Styles
Two Weeks by FKA twigs
Waiting Game by Banks
Whore by In This Moment

Blues

Awful Dreams by Lightnin' Hopkins
Baby Please Don't Leave Me by Buddy Guy
I Can't Quit You Baby by Otis Rush
I'll Take Care of You by Etta James
Love the Lonely Out of You by The Brothers Osborne
Never Gonna Give You Up by The Black Keys
Trust in Me by Etta James

Classic Rock

Going to California by Led Zepplin
House of the Rising Sun by The Animals
Laugh, I Nearly Died by The Rolling Stones

Punk

Beat My Guest by Adam & The Ants
Blank Generation by Richard Hell
Conform by Siege
Final Solution by Pere Ubu
Gloria: In Excelsis Deo by Patti Smith
I Cut Like A Buffalo by The Dead Weather
Institutionalized by Suicidal Tendencies
Orgasm Addict by Buzzcocks
Pink Turns To Blue by Hüsker Du
Promises by Fugazi
Snake Charmer by The Warmers

**You can find the whole playlist on
Spotify by searching for Rebel Farris.**

SNAPSHOT

by

rebel farris

PROLOGUE

I hear the crying from the next room over and try to ignore it. I'm not sure how I ended up in a place like this. I never imagined that this was what my life would look like.

Actually, I do know. Not only did it change my life permanently, but it's not the type of event that escapes one's memory.

You never forget the first time you see a dead body. If you're unfortunate enough to see one outside of a funeral, it's not a pleasant experience. There are things about the dead that they never cover in the movies. Smells, sounds, movements, the clearing of the bowels... all the disgusting stuff.

The crying gets louder, accompanied by the sharp rattle of wooden furniture. I know he'll take care of it, eventually, so I block it from my mind. *Where was I? Oh, yeah.*

My first time seeing death with my own eyes was on both the best and worst day of my life. When I think about it— even with years of distance—it's all shades of gray. A twisted mass of confused emotions and a racing heart.

Because it was the day I met *him*.

I remember being scared. At first, I thought he was the devil, come to claim me. Then I thought he was my savior. He was both and neither. But one thing was certain—he changed my life irrevocably.

The crying stops, and my shoulders release tension I didn't know I was carrying. But now—now, I can tell you my story.

CHAPTER ONE

Camera

Today was going to be a good day. I could feel it in the air as I walked out on my porch in the early-morning sun. The smell of morning dew and fresh-cut grass floated on the air.

Most people think that being alone is a horrible thing. I'd never really understood that. There was peace in solitude—a serenity in the quiet. In my experience, other people only served to bring about noise, distraction, drama… all things I could live without.

I released a contented sigh as I propped my boots on the railing of the porch. Leaning back in my lawn chair, book in one hand, coffee in the other, no sounds but the birds chirping from the nearby tree and the rustle of leaves on the wind, I could almost forget I had neighbors.

Almost.

It wasn't just that they were ten feet from my front door, within spittin' distance. I could tell the moment they woke up because their day always started with a crash. Then came the shouting: accusations of cheating, lying, being lazy, you name it. It was always the same. I wasn't even a paragraph in before they started. Living in a trailer park is not ideal for privacy. The walls are thin. Though, the way Billy and Joanne Watkins went at it, they could be inside an airtight vault with twelve-inch-thick concrete walls, and the world would still hear them.

I huffed, stuffing my bookmark into the book and

retreating back indoors.

Noise, distraction, drama... yep, definitely not missing out.

Looking around at my bare-bones furnishings, I settled on the twin-size mattress and box spring—what I called a couch—as my new cozy spot, nestling into the twenty or so pillows. Not that I'd much choice, since that and the wooden TV tray that sat next to it were the only furniture I owned, aside from my bed and a matching TV tray back in my bedroom. It wasn't much, but it was mine.

The bookmark dropped out onto my chest as I opened the book. *Hallelujah.* I was finally going to get to enjoy my day off. My first one in the last ten days. It had been that way since Tracey and Ronnie had quit last month, leaving the diner short-staffed. A grand total of three days in one month, and I was going to enjoy this one, Joanne and Billy be damned.

I'd finally gotten my hands on Dean Koontz's latest book, *Midnight*, and *The Queen of the Damned* by Anne Rice. And I was going to read these books before the month's end, come hell or high water.

It took me longer to get the newest *Vampire Chronicles* book because Jerry at the Book Shop didn't believe that female authors would sell if they weren't writing lusty romance novels. *Sexist pig.* But that's the price you paid for living in the country. You were subject to the whims of the local inhabitants. Unless you had the time and inclination to drive into the city—which I did on my last day off.

I'd just turned the last page on chapter one of the Anne Rice book when Billy and Joanne moved their incessant fighting outside. There was no escaping it. Now it was coming through *my* walls, loud and clear. Groaning loudly, I slammed the book shut, forgetting the bookmark. I frowned at it as I set it with the book on top of the TV tray. It was looking like reading would *not* be on the agenda today. But I didn't know what else to do.

I studied the bare walls as I ignored the screams and accusations happening outside. There wasn't much to look at, only one picture. One that had been given to me on my last birthday, by the girls at work. Actually, they were once my best friends, but things had been changing since we'd grown up. They had families of their own now and little time for me. So, we'd drifted apart. The picture was an Ansel Adams print, probably the most valuable possession in my home. And even if it was an incredibly nice gesture, part of it felt like a payoff for all the missing time together. It formerly hung in the window of the frame shop next to the diner. Every day, I'd stopped outside and stared at it. I'd always wanted to be a photographer. But it was just an out-of-reach dream, an expensive hobby outside my means to partake in.

Window-shopping was a specialty of mine. The other place I liked to stand outside and wistfully sigh was Big John's Pawn Shop. There was a brand-new Canon AE-1 35mm camera with a ton of accessories sitting there, calling my name. But I'd just finished saving up my emergency fund. It would be a good six months before I could afford it. If it was even still there when I was ready.

It might not be.

That was the moment I decided to throw caution to the wind. *Or maybe it's just my emergency fund burning a hole in my checkbook?* Spontaneity wasn't in my wheelhouse, but my mind was made up. I would get the camera, go to the drugstore for film, and find a pretty piece of countryside to take pictures. Just me and nature. I jumped up and tossed my purse on my shoulder and was out the door, narrowly dodging water flying in every direction. Joanne was standing in her front yard, threatening Billy with her water hose—again. I shook my head, not even understanding the point of being in a relationship where you obviously hated the other person. This happened every day like clockwork. And my own parents were a testament to the fact that love wasn't what they said it was in books and movies.

I dove into the front seat of my 1984 Pontiac Fiero, just as water sprayed across the windows. Somehow, I missed getting soaked, but a few drops still got in. Closing my eyes, I breathed deep to stop the impulse to say something. Bitch probably did it on purpose. She stuck her nose up in the air and turned her fire back on Billy, who looked unmoved by her antics.

Ten minutes later, I pulled into a parking space in front of the Big John's Pawn Shop. There it was, in all its black-and-silver glory. I walked in with confidence and looked Big John in the eyes as I told him I needed my camera. He smirked at me and went to get it from the window display. The rest of the time I was there, I avoided eye contact, carefully dodging his attempts at small talk. We'd gone to high school together. I knew he was an ass back then, and I was sure the same held true today. Taking over his family business probably didn't instill any more virtue in him.

Thirty minutes later, I was driving down the road with my new camera in my lap, four rolls of film in my passenger seat, and hope in my heart. Maybe this was it. Maybe today I would take the picture that would change my life.

CHAPTER TWO

Death

I drove for more than an hour down a farm-to-market road. There was nothing but trees, random cacti, and limestone boulders as far as the eye could see. Which didn't mean much, since I was in Hill Country, and the rolling hills impeded distant views. After not seeing another house for the last twenty minutes, I decided to pull over.

I loaded the camera with film and shoved all the extra lenses and filters into my purse, pulling out my Walkman. Eddie Thorpe—one of my regular customers—had made me a mixtape that I was thoroughly enjoying. He'd the best taste in music and the time to find songs outside of the incessant country music that permeated every radio station in the area.

I clipped it to my pocket and hit play. "Pictures of Matchstick Men" by Camper Van Beethoven rang in my ears as I pulled my long mahogany hair up into a ponytail. The manic violin hit my gut, springing goose bumps across my flesh. I bobbed my head to the steady beat and smiled.

My purse was a giant holdover from the hippie boom. I bought it from a garage sale a few years back. Made of brown leather, it had a slightly longer than normal strap and fringe on the bottom. Even after I pulled it over my head, so the strap crossed my torso, it still hung longer than my cutoff jean shorts.

The books poked into my hip, so I reached in and adjusted them. I briefly considered taking them out. I had water, food, camera accessories, the normal purse stuff, and those books, and it was quite heavy. I pulled *Midnight* out and looked longingly at the cover before depositing it on my front seat. No sense in carrying two of them. Even if I found a nice cozy quiet spot to read, I wouldn't finish one.

I looked down at the toe of my boots. The brown leather of the hand-me-down cowboy boots was already scuffed and faded, so I wasn't worried about messing them up on the hike. It just seemed like I should thank them for protecting my feet before I set out to abuse them more.

Shutting my car door, I turned to cross the ditch to the barbed wire fence. It was old and in need of repair, and it sagged enough that I easily swung myself through it. I squinted at the tree line and remembered my sunglasses on top of my head, pulling them down over my eyes. Not seeing a clear path, I walked forward, my camera thumping against my chest with each step.

I made it three steps beyond the trees before my heart started racing. Shit. I forgot about the compass. I dug around in my purse, pulling out the new compass I'd bought at the drugstore. I turned back to face the car. My heart calmed as I saw the glints of blue-painted metal through the trees. I held the compass up, waiting for the needle to settle. *West-northwest.* I was heading east-southeast. I turned back and marched off in that direction, keeping one eye on the ground for snakes and the other on the compass, occasionally looking around and snapping pictures of the landscape and wildlife.

This was rattlesnake country—you couldn't be too careful.

I walked through nearly two rounds of my mixtape. I knew the second side was coming to an end as "Blister in the Sun" by the Violent Femmes started playing. My feet couldn't help the hop they did in response to the infectious beats, and soon I was all-out dancing as I approached a cliff.

The view was stunning. A rocky creek bed lay below, and from my perch, I saw the hills rolling out before me. The sun was directly above me, but as I checked my compass, I knew. The cliff faced due east. The sunrise here would be amazing. I made a mental note to leave something to mark the fence where my car was parked so I could find my way back. *I will get that sunrise shot.*

I took a picture anyway, and the film gave on the rewind, releasing the wheel so it spun freely. I'd filled my first roll. I changed the film out for a fresh roll.

My stomach growled loudly at that moment, in protest of my continuous journey. I looked around and saw a nice shady spot next to a tree, not more than a few feet from the cliff's edge. I untied the flannel shirt around my hips and laid it out on the ground, dropping my purse next to it. Enjoying the view and the silence, I ate my peanut butter and jelly sandwich and dug into the bag of Bugles. I flicked a few curious ants off my flannel when they wandered near, but I'd never been more content.

When I finished eating, I cracked open the book. I don't know how long I sat there, but when the sun dipped toward the horizon and I was no longer sitting in the shade of the tree, I packed up my stuff.

I looked longingly over the cliff for a few moments. I wanted to find a way down there when I came back. The steady stream of water had glittered in the sunlight when I first saw it. There would be some good pictures down there too. After the sunrise. If I didn't have to go back to work, I would be there the next day and then the next.

Reluctantly, I turned and made my way back to the car. I didn't bring a flashlight, so it would be a race against the setting sun to get back before night fell. I pulled my earphones on and hit play. Devo's "Whip It" came on and I let loose, dance-walking my way back to the car, only pausing long enough to snap a couple of cool shots in the fading sunlight.

When "Heroes" by David Bowie came on, I was lost in the rhythm of my own feet. Confident I was heading the same direction I came from, I didn't bother looking at the compass. The setting sun was guiding enough. I sang out loud, no one but the critters and trees to hear me.

And that was when I tripped over a cactus.

I could feel the spines sticking into the flesh of my shins. I caught myself with my hands, but not soon enough. My chin bounced on the rocky ground. The pain shooting through my head was immediate. I reached up and brushed my fingers over it. There was a tiny smudge of blood, but it wasn't gushing.

My earphones had fallen off with the jarring impact, David Bowie's voice sounding far-off and tinny. But the sound that really captured my attention was the loud buzzing of flies. The second thing to hit me was the smell.

Once, when I was a kid, my foster mom was driving past a sewage plant. We had the windows down. She ordered me to roll mine up quickly, but it was too late. The wretched smell had invaded our car. Up until that moment, that smell had stood out in my memory as the worst smell on the planet.

This smell had that one beat, hands down.

It was like shit and piss and something else that was metallic, mixed with a sort of sickly sweet. I breathed out quickly and looked up. In front of me was blue fabric—a shirtsleeve, stained with rusty brown splotches. Dread swamped my gut. I shoved up to my feet, forgetting the pain of the cactus spines or the throbbing of my chin. I gasped at the sight before me and immediately regretted it. The horrible putrid smell invaded my nose. I swallowed hard and held my breath through several heaves of my stomach. Then I breathed in through my mouth, trying not to taste the smell on the air.

The body of a man lay there, twisted like a discarded rag doll, eyes just as vacant. Flies swarmed around his body. I was surprised that his face wasn't bloated. I imagined that a dead body smelling like this would've shown more signs of decomposition. Yet his eyes were a clear bottle green, hair a dusky brown with gray patches over his temple. The cause of death: a bullet to his forehead.

But that man had been tortured. His tormentor... and I say tormentor because someone had cut and flayed most of his body. Those wounds looked much older than the one between his eyes. Some had festered and leaked a green, oozing pus, all in varying stages of infection.

I found myself fascinated. I stumbled, the dark thought rocking me to the core. But I was intrigued. Who would be strong enough to take this man down? He wasn't small, easily a foot taller than me. He was well muscled, though, not quite fit.

I don't know what compelled me to do what I did next, but I lifted my camera to my face and pushed the shutter release. The snap of the shutter blades made my muscles tense like it was the sound of a guillotine's blade. Flashes of guilt and intrigue warred within me like I'd just witnessed my first beheading. I took a step closer and clicked again. Again.

I only stopped when the hand wrapped around my mouth, cutting off my ability to scream, and I was pulled against a hard body. It was then that I noticed the shovel and the half-dug hole next to the body. It was so stupid of me not to be more aware of my surroundings when finding a dead body in the woods. I pulled up my feet to kick at him. *Fight.* I was sure this was the killer and I'd just signed my own death warrant.

Curiosity being the cause of my downfall was not surprising in the least. Especially as he dragged me backward through the trees, away from the dead man.

CHAPTER THREE

Safety

"*Silencio*," a voice grated in my ear.

I didn't know Spanish, but I grew up in Texas. It's hard not to know some words. I knew he was telling me to be quiet. He wasn't the first person to make that mistake with me—to assume that I spoke the language of a Mexican based off my olive skin and my proximity to the country of my ancestor's origin.

"*Voy a dejarlo ir ahora. No grites o el asesino te escuche*," he whispered.

And though the meaning of his words were lost on me, the tickle of his breath on my ear and the tingle that followed its path rushed through me. The weight of his arm and the feel of his hard body pressed against my back calmed me a bit. It was like nothing I'd ever felt before, and the sensation stunned me.

His muscles relaxed. "*No voy a lastimarte. Estoy dejando ir ahora.*"

I shook my head, not sure if I was trying to tell him I still didn't understand him, or if I was trying to dislodge his hand. Both urges were forefront in my thoughts. The other urge that reigned was to hurt this fucker for having his hands on me in the first place. He was definitely going to kill me, but I wasn't going down without a fight. I'd been fighting my whole life to survive.

He released me and stepped back. I didn't scream. There

wasn't anyone to hear if I did, and it would be a waste of precious time. I barely registered the widening blue eyes because in a blink I spun, throwing my weight into it when I flung my giant purse at his head. It hit him with a heavy thud, and he stumbled back, trying to regain his balance. I stopped thinking and turned on my heel, running. His heavy footfalls chased me.

His arm came around me again like a vise. He pulled me back and halted our forward momentum. I grunted, and his hand was back over my mouth again. He grunted as my elbow flew back into his gut.

"You do not speak Spanish, do you?" he asked in a murmur.

My eyes bulged at his stilted European accent. It was obvious in the way his voice rolled over the *P* sounds almost like it had its own syllable, but the rest of his words came out in a staccato rhythm. It sounded like a cross between the Russian and German accents I'd heard in movies before.

I shook my head as much as I could in his grip.

His lips grazed my ear as he spoke quietly. "You do speak English?"

I whimpered as fear flooded my system, but gave a nod.

His arms tightened before they relaxed a bit. "I will not hurt you, but you need to keep quiet. There is a man out here. The one who killed that man. Can you be quiet before you get us both killed?"

I hesitated because I didn't believe him, but gave a nod anyway.

He spoke in hushed tones. "I think he heard you sing, but did not know where you came from because your voice echoes through the trees. He went that way."

He used the hand from my mouth to point. Using the distraction, I bucked hard and fell away from his grip. I stumbled and turned to face him. His sandy-brown hair was cropped close to his head, not the usual mullet or short waves or long stringy hair that I was used to seeing on most guys. And his eyes. His eyes were a clear blue, like sea glass. He wasn't much taller than me, only a few inches, but I could see the hint of defined muscles underneath his clothes.

The corner of his mouth tipped slightly like I'd spoken my assessment out loud. I frowned at him, but I didn't run. There was no use; he'd only catch me again. And he didn't seem interested in killing me at the moment, so I waited.

"I will not hurt you. You come with me? I will show you."

He walked past me, motioning with his hand to follow him. I stood still. My mind warred with the intelligence of following a possible killer through the woods. He realized I hadn't moved and turned back to face me. Our eyes locked across the distance. I could hear the whirring of my Walkman as it still played, but as I looked down at it, I realized that I'd lost the earphones in the struggle.

I sighed as I hit the Stop button and unclipped it from my pocket, stuffing it into my purse. When I looked up, he was gone. Fear raced through my veins like wildfire. My heart kicked into overdrive as I spun in a circle. Expecting an attack, I brought my hands up in front of me. But when I didn't see or hear him, I lowered them. I didn't call after him. That would just be stupid. If he was the killer and he left me, then good riddance. If he wasn't and a killer was out there as he'd suggested, calling him over would be even worse.

The sun had set, but still lit the sky in shades of pink, orange, and purple. I could still see, for now, but I couldn't follow it back to the car. Plus, I didn't know how far offtrack I was after that encounter. I ran in the first direction my feet would take me, without thought. I pulled my compass out and moved quickly in the direction the car should be. Even if I was offtrack, I should be able to find the road. And I should be able to see my car.

Should. Fuck this shit.

This day had started out amazing; now I was traipsing around with a killer and a crazy man. And perhaps they were one and the same.

As soon as the road came into view, I pocketed the compass. Just as I was about to breach the tree line, a hand landed on my arm. I gave a startled yelp, and the other hand clapped over my mouth. Then his face was in front of me, striking blue eyes imploring me. Releasing my arm, he raised a single finger to his lips. *Quiet*, his eyes said.

He grabbed my hand and started leading me down the road, just inside the trees. He stepped carefully, making no noise, so I tried to do the same. I still didn't believe his story, but what harm could come from going along that would be cured by running? He'd catch me; I knew that well enough.

We walked about fifty feet before he turned to me and pointed at his eyes with two fingers and then pointed toward the road with the same fingers. I followed the direction of his gaze, and my heart stopped. There was a man walking around my car. He wore a green camouflage sweatshirt and jeans, with a baseball cap pulled low over his brow. Despite the cap, I could see that he was bald underneath, and what I could see of his face were hard frown lines burrowed deep in his skin.

A cold shiver ran down my spine. He was right. There was another person out here. But I wasn't stupid enough to believe that one was the killer and the other was not. They could be working together. Though I didn't know what this man's motivations were for helping me.

The man next to me released my hand and made hand motions, indicating he and I should walk the way we'd come, down the road away from my car. Under raised brows, his eyes begged for me to follow.

Shit. I couldn't make my mind up. I bit my lip as my brows furrowed, and I wrung my hands. I ran the scenarios through my mind, and in every one, I came up dead. But maybe I could give him a chance. If he was telling the truth, then it was my only way out.

Reluctantly, I nodded. He grabbed my hand, and we were moving again, at a much quicker pace. Hearing the door to my car slam shut behind us had us full-on running.

It's a horrifying thing to put your life in the hands of a stranger. I don't know how long we ran, but as we approached a clearing where a small farmhouse sat, the sky was an inky purple bruise.

"We should go inside in case he followed us," he said.

I halted, the sound of his voice snapping me out of the blind panic that had fueled my run. I was breathing hard and gasping for air. I was not in any shape to run anywhere, much less run through the wood at dusk from certain death. Or toward it.

A sharp pain in my shin made me hiss, and I suddenly remembered the cactus. I bent down giving myself a moment to think this through, looking at my leg which much resembled Pinhead from the *Hellraiser* movie. My hands hovered over it as I sucked in a breath, trying to decide which to pull first. I wasn't one of those bimbos in the horror movies that stupidly trusted the stranger and walked into his house without thought.

Gentle, long, lean fingers wrapped around my wrist, stopping me. "I have a first aid kit in the house. Let me take care of you."

His voice did strange things to my stomach, causing it to somersault inside my body. My lips parted, and I nodded. He pulled me to standing by the wrist he held and we started walking toward the house. Well, I was more or less limping, now that the adrenaline and shock had worn off. But whether I was headed toward safety or certain torturous doom... I would find out soon enough.

To continue reading go to
rebelfarris.com/books/snapshot

57801281R00221

Made in the USA
Middletown, DE
02 August 2019